D0734389

The Claidi Journals

BOOKS BY TANITH LEE

TALES FROM THE FLAT EARTH

Night's Master

Death's Master

Delusion's Master

Delirium's Mistress

Night's Sorceries

THE SECRET BOOKS OF PARADYS

The Book of the Damned

The Book of the Beast

The Book of the Dead

The Book of the Mad

THE SECRET BOOKS OF VENUS

Faces Under Water

Saint Fire

A Bed of Earth

THE BLOOD OPERA SEQUENCE

Dark Dance

Personal Darkness

Darkness, I

THE UNICORN SEQUENCE

Black Unicorn

Gold Unicorn

Red Unicorn

Cyrion

Don't Bite the Sun

Drinking Sapphire Wine

Electric Forest

The Gorgon and Other Beastly Tales

Heart-Beast

A Heroine of the World

Kill the Dead

Red As Blood, or Tales From the Sisters Grimmer

Sabella, or The Blood Stone

The Silver Metal Lover

Sung in Shadow

White As Snow

The Claidi Journals

Wolf Tower
Wolf Star
Wolf Queen

Tanith Lee

Originally published in Great Britain by Hodder Children's Books, 1998
First published in the United States of America by Dutton Children's Books, 2000
Published in paperback by Puffin Books, 2001

Originally published in Great Britain by Hodder Children's Books, 2000
First published in the United States of America by Dutton Children's Books, 2001

Originally published in Great Britain by Hodder Children's Books, 2001
First published in the United States of America by Dutton Children's Books, 2002

First Science Fiction Book Club printing June 2002

This is a work of fiction. Names, characters, places, and incidents are either the product of the author's imagination or are used fictitiously, and any resemblance to actual persons, living or dead, business establishments, events, or locales is entirely coincidental. Some phrases and references have been changed for the convenience of American readers.

Published by arrangement with Dutton Children's Books,
a division of Penguin Putnam Books for Young Readers
145 Hudson Street
New York, New York 10014

visit the SFBC at www.sfbc.com
visit Dutton Children's Books at www.penguinputnam.com

ISBN 0-7394-2735-0

PRINTED IN THE UNITED STATES OF AMERICA

The Claidi Journals

AUTHOR'S NOTE

When I write, I go to live inside the book. By which I mean, mentally I can experience everything I'm writing about. I can see it, hear its sounds, feel its heat or rain. The characters become better known to me than the closest family or friends. This makes the writing-down part very simple most of the time. I only need to describe what's already there in front of me. That said, it won't be a surprise if I add that the imagined worlds quickly become entangled with the so-called reality of this one.

Since I write almost every day, and I think (and dream) constantly about my work, it occurs to me I must spend more time in all those other places than here.

TANITH LEE

Contents

Wolf Tower

BREAK THE RULES.

Traditional

CONTENTS

THIS BOOK

Yes.

I stole this. This book.

I don't know why. It looked . . . nice, I suppose, and nothing has been nice for years. Well, not often.

It was in her stationery chest, out of which she sometimes makes us—mostly me—get her a piece of silk paper or thick parchment. Then she doodles a few stupid lines of *awful* "poetry." Or a foul painting, like used washing-water in the Maids' Hall with something dropped in it—lime juice or jam. And then we all have to applaud. "Oh! How clever you are, Lady Jade Leaf. What bright-shining genius!" Because she's royal. And we are not. Oh no. We couldn't *ever* do anything wonderful like *that.*

Frankly, I think I could spit in a more interesting pattern. As for the poems . . .

Here is the latest example:

I drift like a petal all upon the air
And the roses bow.

Drift like a petal. . . . She's more like a hippopotamus in the river. I don't mean fat—Lady Iris is fat, but she's also glamorous and graceful. Jade Leaf is slim. But the way she moves . . .

If the roses bowed, they did it because they fainted with fright, screaming: "Don't let that great thing bash into me!"

(Having said this, I feel I should add that hippopotami are graceful, too, underwater. Besides, a hippopotamus has never picked up its little ornamental cane and cracked me across the palms of my hands so they bled. Which Jade Leaf has done so many times, I can't remember the number.)

If you found this, and are now reading it, need I ask you not to tell anyone? But hopefully you aren't. I'm just imagining you.

And there's someone banging for real on the door, which means I have to go and do something so much more important—that is, attend Jade Leaf.

I'll write my name here. After that, you'll know it's me.

Claidi.

Midnight. (I just heard the House clock.) Sky a sort of thick, stirred-up black, milky with stars.

Vile day. Daisy broke a vase, and Lady Jade slapped and slapped her till Daisy cowered on the floor. Then Lady JL kicked Daisy with her silk-slippered foot. Daisy has bruises and is also expected not to be given any dinner in the Maids' Hall for nine nights. Pattoo and I put some of our food in a napkin and gave it to Daisy when we went to bed. Pattoo and Daisy are sleeping now.

I'm so tired I have to stop, too.

Absolutely nothing to write. It's seven days since the last thing I wrote. But nothing ever happens here.

No, wrong. There was a dust storm yesterday that blew in from the Waste, and the slaves ran to work the fans and pull up the slatted roofs over the best parts of the Garden. In the House all the windows and doors were shut, and everybody was cooped up and bad-tempered.

LJL had a tantrum. She screamed and yelled and threw things. Then she was ill and had to lie down, and we put cloths soaked in cool scented water on her forehead. If it dripped in her eyes, she screamed again. We all had headaches, but no cool water-cloths for *us*.

I hate this place.

Nothing to write.

Except Pattoo and I were prevented by the Maids' steward from putting aside food for Daisy. She cried with frustration (and hunger), but now she's gone to sleep.

Perhaps I should say, we share this tiny room in the Maids' Hall and have three narrow mattresses and one mirror and one chest. These are not our possessions, you understand, but things *lent* to us, like our clothing, by Lady J and her mother, the Princess Shimra.

Sometimes we steal two or three flowers from the Garden and put them in a jar in the narrow window. But flowers don't last, do they?

Nothing to write.

NTW.

There seems no point, really, I sternly say to myself now, in having thieved this book, so craftily and unsensibly, if I'm not going to put anything in it.

Any news? Well, today was the Ritual of the Feeding of the Red Birds.

We went to the Red Aviary, a birdhouse full of feathers and trills and tweets. They fly about freely here, between the trees that grow up through the floor into the glass roof. They look, the birds, like flying flowers of crimson and scarlet, but the squeaks are sometimes piercingly loud, and also droppings fall on everyone, despite the parasols we dutifully hold over our ladies' heads.

The birds today are fed special grains and seeds, dyed to match or to coordinate with bird colors.

I like the birds a lot, but the smell is pretty overpowering.

Later there was an ordinary storm. Colossal bangs of thunder as if gigantic trays were being dropped in the sky. Lady JL is loudly afraid of the thunder and the lightning, but I ran off and watched from an upper window. Next, summoned back to *her,* she asked where I had been, told me where—she was wrong—then that I was a lazy slut, and predictably cracked me over the hand with her cane. Only one hand, though, the left one, so I can still write this.

Oh, and Daisy, who has been eating so much at dinner every night, making up for the nine missed ones, was violently sick all over the Maids' Hall floor, which had just been cleaned.

I ask myself, if you are reading this (and aren't bored with it all, as bored as I get with it all, and flung it on the rubbish dump or in a fire), I ask myself what you might find interesting to have me tell you.

Because perhaps you don't live in the House or the Garden but have somehow come from somewhere else. This seems unlikely, but then you aren't real, are you? Just some wonderful intriguing imaginary person I've made up. My fantasy.

So, I'll pretend you're keen to know. . . . Shall I?

Or not.

I'm sort of an orphan. My parents aren't dead—although I suppose they might be, in fact, by now. That's a grim thought. But I can't even really feel much about it, because I never knew them.

There are so many Rituals. The House and the Garden live by them. What else is there to do? But the Rituals are taken entirely and stonily seriously. They're immovable. And if you profane a Ritual—if you break one of the idiotic rules of this place—you're punished.

Sometimes they're only slight mistakes and the punishments aren't too bad. (Let's say you miss lighting every single candle in the Lighting of the Candles Ritual, or do it in the wrong order. Then you might only have to stand in the Black Marble Corridor for a few hours, something like that—though your lady would probably beat you, too.) But for profaning some of the most important Rituals and rules, the punishments are fierce. The worst punishment, of course, is to be exiled to the Waste.

It's a death sentence. At best, if you *do* survive, a living nightmare. Hell-on-earth.

The Waste is the worst thing in the world.

This is what they tell you.

It is always stressed how grateful we should be that we were born here, the House, the Garden, this earthly paradise, and not out there in the Waste. I can recall them drumming this into me when I was a child, a baby, and crying for my mother and father. To be an orphan, and the maid of a (cruel) lady in paradise, was better than existing in the Waste.

The weather there is unthinkable. White-hot heats, freezings, rains of *stones,* gales that tear up the dry starving landscape. There are terrible mountains of black rock, and the dust storms that sometimes pass over the Garden come from there. In the Waste you go hungry always, and thirsty. Water is poisoned. Nothing grows, or if it does, it's horrible to look at and disgusting to eat.

No wonder the people and *things* that survive out there are peculiar and dangerous. Madmen, murderers, and monsters roam.

From a couple of the highest towers of the House, if you're willing to climb hundreds and hundreds of stairs—I have—you can just glimpse something beyond the edges of the fortressed Garden walls. That must be the Waste. But you can't see much—only a sort of threatening, shimmering vagueness. A pale *shadow.*

Once a lion got into the Garden. A monster lion from the Waste. This was in the year before I was born. It was an ugly and lethal beast, foaming flame, they say, from the mouth. So they killed it.

But why have I gone on so about all that, the outside world, which I've never even seen?

Because my parents profaned one of the greatest Rituals. (I don't know which one.) They were promptly exiled to the Waste.

Now I can't sleep. There are clusters of huge, blistering blue-white stars.

Tomorrow is the Ritual of the Planting of the Two Thousandth Rose.

We have to be up extra early, before dawn.

I feel strangely guilty, since I think I'm going to stop writing in this book. Which makes me aware that I've mistreated it—the book, I mean—taking it and then spoiling it with my writing. And then worse, stopping.

But what is there to say? I'm sorry, if you've read this far. But then you haven't.

Something INCREDIBLE. Something unthought of and impossible has occurred.

I have to organize my mind, which feels as if it's whirling about, and my heart is bird-flying and flapping around inside me. I keep laughing out loud.

I'm not in our room. I've climbed up to another place. I'm sitting here, but inside me everything is jumping and spinning. How can I start to tell you?

Let me go back, back to the morning, and begin again.

EXCITEMENT BY AIR

The Garden stretches for many miles in all directions away from the House.

We walked slowly down the green, closely cut lawns, Pattoo, Daisy, and I. And then down lots of mossy steps, with mossy statues standing by them.

The Gardeners keep everything perfect, and the slaves attend to all the cunning mechanisms that keep the Garden watered and nourished. The Garden is even kept warm, when the weather turns cold, by a system of underground furnaces and hot-water pipes, quite like those used in the House.

Aside from maintenance, the Garden is also very artistic, to please the royalty. Here and there, areas may even look a little overgrown, or there might be a pavilion a bit ruined. But the overgrowings are always carefully clipped to just the right amount of wildness, and the ruin will be clean and gleaming, with ivy trained up on wires. Even decay is planned here, and controlled.

The House, which is the center of the Garden, showed from the steps every time we took a left turn. I'll describe it quickly. It's a terraced building with columns, white and pink, and with sloping roofs scaled in dark green and gold.

Above, through the leaves, the sky was that breathtaking blue that sings. The sort of sky that makes you feel something astonishing and marvelous is about to happen—only it never does.

"Oh, come on, come on," panted Pattoo. She's always nervous. She likes to please. Which is sensible really. She's seldom beaten.

But Daisy snapped, "I can't go any faster. I've already spilled some of this filthy stuff. Do you think they'll notice?" she added to me.

"Umm."

Perhaps they wouldn't. There are twenty or so Ritual oils that have to be brought to any special planting in the Garden, each of them highly scented and sticky.

Daisy's flagon of oil was noticeably low, and besides you could see the mark on her dress where most of it had gone.

(We were wearing melon green today, to coordinate with Jade Leaf's deeper green dress. And our hair was powdered *paler* green. The ladies generally insist their maids complement their own choice of colors. An order arrives before every function. The dresses weren't comfortable, either. For the past month or so, the fashion has been for stiff-bodiced, ankle-length silk tubes, which is all right in a way if you're not big, though Pattoo is rather. But when it comes to walking, you have to take mincing little tiny steps, or you [a] rip the dress, or [b] fall over flat.)

Pattoo and I scrubbed Daisy's dress-tube with our decorative gauze scarves. This made things worse.

"Stand behind us," I said. "She may not see."

But Jade Leaf almost certainly would.

We teetered on.

The sun was hot, but beautiful fragrances throbbed from the flowers. Sculpted woods and thickets poured down toward the river, which sparkled.

It's a lovely place, to be honest. I mean, it is to look at. And for royal people I'm sure it's lovely altogether.

At the bottom of the mossy steps, the lion house runs behind gilded bars. The lion house is large, complicated-looking, and their whole enclosure is enormous. But the lions are normally on view. They seem to put themselves where they can be admired. They play and sleep and sun themselves and are very peaceful. Sometimes they're even brought out on a jeweled lead, and royal ladies and gentlemen walk about with them and feed them sweets.

The lions seem contented, like the House hippopotami and all the other animals here. They never have to hunt or fight—everything's given to them. They're even groomed by slaves. But every year there are less. They can't even be bothered to have families.

I used to wonder, when I was a child, if these creatures *missed* something? Of course they do.

Another terrace went down in steps of marble, and there were fountains, and pools with golden fish, and lilies.

Then, the Rose Walk.

The smell is astounding; it makes you dizzy. Roses rise on every side, in arches and tiers and cushiony banks. They're every shade of red and purple, yellow and white.

Wicked thorns like claws scratched at us as we wended through, and Daisy almost spilled the rest of her oil.

In the center of the Rose Walk is a big oval of grass and a statue of a rose carved out of some shiny stone.

This is where the Two Thousandth Rose was to be viewed before planting.

It was apparently a very startling and special rose. One is always bred by the Gardeners for this Ritual, which takes place every three years.

You may wonder how there was ever room for a new rose in this dense chaos of roses. But obviously other roses die or are weeded out mercilessly when the princes and princesses get irritated with them.

Not that many of the royalty had come to the Ritual (a lesser one). It was a hot day, even though the sun had been up less than an hour.

We went and took our stations behind Lady J. No maids are allowed to arrive until this moment, and others were coming in from all sides of the Rose Walk, but Lady J seemed to think we were late.

"Why are you always dawdling?" she snapped. We bowed our heads, looking properly ashamed. Daisy edged in close behind me to hide the spill-stain. "You're moronic," decided LJL.

She has a pointy face, rouged all rosy, and now her hair was powdered a kind of cabbage color.

Her mouth sneered over her sharp little teeth.

"You deserve a slap," she said to me.

I lifted my head and looked at her. She doesn't like that. But then she hates me anyway, even if she would never admit to hating something as low as a maid.

"Don't you stare at me," she rasped. But I'd already bowed my head again. "I'm so tired of you, Claidi. I can't even beat any sense into you. I've asked Mummy, and she says she'll have you properly whipped if you won't pull yourself together."

Then her little eyes went over me and fixed on Daisy.

In all her green, Jade Leaf went the color of an exploding raspberry. "Why, you ghastly little *beast*," she shrieked. "That gown—you've ruined it—"

Heads turned.

Princess Shimra spoke coolly nearby, in the cluster of ladies. "Calmly, Jade Leaf. You'll give yourself another headache."

Several princesses murmured soothingly, slinking and swaying like one more bed of lushly tinted plants.

JL lowered her voice and leaned toward us like a snake.

"*Expect* something," she said. "And you too, Pattoo. You'll have done something, even if I can't see it."

I was already frightened. She'd never threatened me with a proper professional whipping from her mother's steward before. Now I went cold. Daisy was breathing fast, and Pattoo had crumpled. It was so unfair. *She'd* done nothing at all.

But now the Gardeners were pompously bringing the Two Thousandth Rose in a gilded basket, and the royal ones were bending over it and exclaiming.

It reached Lady J, and she too peered down.

What a nasty sight. This green and puce monster craning in over the new rose, which was itself extremely hideous.

It was exactly the color Daisy's vomit had been. And it was a funny squirty shape. And it had a perfume that, even through all the other perfumes, was so *sweet* it could make you gag.

"Ah, how lovely," swooned LJL, gentle and melting.

She undoubtedly thought it was.

Oh, I could have killed her. I truly would have liked to, right then and there.

We were all for it anyway. And why? I'd merely glanced up. Daisy had spilled the rotten oil because she had to wear a stupid fashion. Pattoo had simply been there.

My eyes burned. No one was more surprised than me to see a huge burning teardrop, heavy as a hard-boiled egg, thump from each of my eyes. They plunged into the lawn.

As I was gawking at this extraordinary thing, everyone else began to shout and howl, and a hot and frantic sensation filled the rose-thick walk.

Like a fool, I thought they were angry at me for spilling *tears*.

Then I looked up again, and it wasn't me at all.

You can't always see the moon. At night sometimes the clouds are thick as wool. And in the daylight, if the moon is there, it's transparent as a soap bubble.

Now I could see the moon clearly by day, and it was quite beautiful, and odd. It was a silver globe, shining bright, and slimly striped with soft red.

Something seemed to hang under it—an anchor, perhaps, to moor it to the ground when it set?

Which was fanciful and silly, because the moon wasn't like that at all. And this was decidedly *not* the moon.

Princess Flara yowled, "An invasion! An enemy! Help! Save us all!"

Panic.

I had seen this happen years ago, also in the Garden, when a swarm of bees suddenly erupted from a tree. Princes and princesses, ladies and gentlemen, and all their flounced and spangled kids, wailing and honking and running for their lives.

I'd been a kid myself, about six, and I just sat down on the grass and waited for the bees to go by. Usually, if you leave them alone, they don't sting you.

However, this was not a bee. What was it?

Someone supplied the answer, which also made no sense.

"A hot-air balloon—a *balloon!*"

They were off anyway, galloping up the lawn and on to the paths of the Rose Walk. I noted lots of tube dresses had already been split, some up to the waist! And lots of sticky oil was being spilled.

I looked at Daisy and Pattoo. A few of the other maids and a handful of slaves were lingering too, scared but undecided.

The "balloon" passed over the upper air and was hidden behind a stand of large trees.

Pattoo said, "We ought to follow Lady Jade."

"The bees can have her," I muttered, nostalgically.

Daisy blinked. "But if it's an *invasion* . . ."

Invasion, by the Waste. Where else could it come from?

Another of the maids, dressed in tasteful parchment silk, said uneasily, "Once a madman from the Waste flew over in a . . . *balloon* . . . and poured burning coals on the Garden!"

"When was that?" Daisy asked, wide-eyed.

"Oh . . . once."

The slaves were trotting off into the trees. A slave hasn't ever much time for him-or-herself, so even the moments before we were invaded or had burning coals slung at us were valuable.

Pattoo, though, turned resolutely and began to pad heavily up the path after LJL, who had promised us all "something" bad.

Daisy reluctantly said, "We'd better."

The others were also drifting off together, upset and dutiful.

If I stayed here, unless the invasion was total and nothing mattered anymore, then I'd be blamed, and I was in trouble already.

Just then we heard the alarm trumpets and bells sounding from the House.

We ran.

Earlier, I think I said I wondered what you might find interesting, but I didn't tell you much, did I? I apologize.

I didn't, for instance, tell you about the House Guards.

Didn't want to, probably.

As we came up on the higher lawns, with our ridiculous tube skirts clutched up to our knees (most unruly) to stop them tearing, the Guards were swarming through the Garden.

Sometimes you don't see them for days, unless your lady sends you on an errand into a part of the House where they are. LJ seldom did.

When I was little, I was horribly frightened of the Guards. I believe some really nice clever person had told me I'd better behave or the House Guards would "get me."

They're there to defend us: royalty first, naturally, but also the lowest of the low—like servants, maids, and slaves. They guard places in the House, too—the Debating Hall, for example, and the upper stories where the royalty sleep. But they are mostly in their own guard tower, which is one of the highest towers of the House, even taller than the ones I spoke of with hundreds of steps.

The Guards wear blackest black, crossed with belts of silver and slashed with epaulets of gold. They have high boots shiny as black mirror, with spikes sticking from the heel and the toe. They have knives in fancy scabbards, rifles decorated with silver, and embroidered pouches to carry shot. Medals cover them like armor.

Now they had on their copper helmets too which have visors and more spikes pointing up from the top.

They looked like deadly beetles.

We cowered back among a fringe of rhododendrons, but one of the Guards turned and bellowed at us in a sort of hating voice:

"Get inside, you damned rubbish!"

Daisy caught her breath, and I heard another maid start to cry. But everyone was scared already. And we bolted for the House up the terraces and steps.

The Guards were dragging black cannons on black gun-carriages.

I saw a maid—Flamingo, I think—accidentally get in their way, and one of the Guards thrust her aside so viciously that she sprawled.

In order to protect us properly, they were quite prepared to do us harm. In fact they seemed eager to hurt us, perhaps as a sort of practice.

I ducked under a buckled, black-clad arm. Pattoo was dragging. I caught her and hauled her with me.

And there was the House, sugary and cute in sunlight.

The *balloon* seemed to have vanished.

Had we all dreamed it?

No, for the Guards were angling every cannon one way. I could smell gunpowder.

I'd heard of events like this but had never seen—smelled—one.

Just then, over a crest of poplar trees, the balloon drifted back again into sight, like a charming toy.

The Guards roared. They appeared to have forgotten us.

It seemed crazy to be out in the open, but somehow we stood and gaped up at the silvery bubble I'd mistaken for the moon.

And in the crystal windows of the House, there was face upon face like piled vegetables, pink, tawny, black, all the royal ones, glaring up into the sky, having pushed such unimportant beings as *maids* out of the way.

I grabbed Pattoo again. "Look."

"I don't want to," she said, and she hid her eyes. Daisy was too scared to look away.

And I . . . I couldn't either.

Then there was a sizzling sound, and the cannons blasted—one, two, three, four of them. The noise—there were clouds of stinking smoke, and bits of fire splashed all around.

(Tinder has almost an almond smell, I absurdly thought, like marzipan for a cake. . . .)

The balloon turned over, a wonderful fruit disturbed up on the tree of the sky.

Even like that, it looked effective. But then there was another burst of flame, up where the balloon was. And it reeled sideways. And then it began to fall. It looked so soft, as if there was nothing to it—the stuff you blow off a dandelion.

But when it dropped behind the trees, there came a terrific thud. The ground shook. Smoke bloomed up there like a new plant.

It was only then the House Guards gave a raucous cheer. They were yelling, as if in a game, "A *hit!*" And "Well done, Jovis." And "Think we killed him?"

HIM

When we got into the House, everyone was going mad. People were running along the corridors, colliding when two or more were coming from different directions. They were running up and down the stairs, too, and sometimes tripping and falling. The row was almost as bad as the cannon.

Pattoo, Daisy, and I ran up the stairs toward the apartments of our evil mistress.

When we reached the double doors, they were open, and inside everyone also rushed about. JL sat in the middle of it all, screaming and pulling her own hair, thumping her fists on the sofa, and kicking her feet, off of which her green silk shoes had flown.

She seemed worse than usual. I thought it was fear of the "invasion," but surely she'd seen the balloon shot down?

Dengwi sidled up to me and hissed, "She says insects have gotten into her dress. Fleas or bees or something."

This nearly made me laugh. I'd wished bees on Jade Leaf, hadn't I?

I could see now the others were trying to get her dress undone so they could sort out the situation, but LJL was in such a state they could hardly get near her. Suddenly she sprang up and ripped the dress in two bits with her own hands. She's strong. (All those smacks and beatings she's given have undoubtedly built up her wrists.)

There she stood in her lace-trimmed petticoat, snarling and pulling at herself.

The other maids began wiping and dusting her off. A few poor little ants were being murdered for daring to get into her gown.

I rushed forward too and began, more carefully, dusting the ants off, then carried the rescued ones and tipped them out of the window.

Outside, smoke still billowed over the Garden. Some of the Guards were marching up the Cedar Walk, and there was someone, not a Guard, having to march in the middle of them.

"Is that—the *invader?*" whispered Daisy, letting go of more ants down the wall.

"Must be."

We tried to lean over and see more, but JL was screaming again even louder.

Daisy and I helped shake out JL's petticoat. Jade Leaf thrust us off, managing to poke Daisy in the eye.

"Oh you *filthyword* little sluts!" squawked JL.

Outside, they'd be marching right under the window now.

I leapt away, dashed back to the window, and looked down, calling as I did so, "Oh, madam, the Guards have a prisoner."

"Of course they have, you *extrafilthyword* little pest. Leave that and come here. I'm covered in these *filthyword-Claidi-doesn't-even-know* things!"

Under the window, the ghastly Guards swaggered, and this man sort of swaggered too. He wore a longish, grey, quite-military-looking coat, and the sun was gold, pure utter gold, all over his long, rough-cut hair. It didn't look possible, this hair. Powdered, perhaps? Didn't seem to be. It looked . . . *real,* in a way reality seldom manages.

Just then JL threw something at me—it was a paperweight, I saw later—and it caught me sharp and cold with pain in my back. My breath went in a silly *oof.* Below, the prisoner—the invader—turned up his head to see, in the midst of capture, what creature it was that made such idiotic noises.

"Come here, you filthy *filthyword!*" screeched dear Lady J.

I don't know what happened. I can't explain. Perhaps you can. Perhaps it, or something similar, may have happened to you sometime.

Spinning around, I pelted straight at Jade Leaf. And as I reached her, I slapped her a huge, stinging slap across half her disgusting, pointy pink face.

Although the House was bursting with noise, this one room became completely silent. As if we had all been turned to stone.

I gazed at Jade Leaf and had the thrilling joy of seeing the place I'd slapped turn from pink to boiling magenta.

Her mouth was wide open.

"You . . . hit me."

"Lady," I cried, very concerned, "I had to. There was this awful insect on your cheek—you hadn't noticed. It might have stung you."

But Jade Leaf only plumped down on the rug abruptly, like a child, and said, "Hit me."

"Yes," said Pattoo, surprising me by her invention, "look, madam." And Pattoo showed JL a piece of squished fruit she must have gotten hold of just that moment to help me. "It's horrible."

"A good thing," said Dengwi, "Claidi acted so quickly."

Jade Leaf's mouth opened more, and she screwed up her eyes. "Mummy!" she warbled. "I want Mummy!"

Magically on this cue, through the open doors stepped Princess Shimra in a cloud of attendants.

"Get up, Jade Leaf. What are you thinking of? The enemy balloonist has been taken to the Debating Hall. Change your clothes at once. Everyone will be there. Even Princess Jizania Tiger," added Shimra, with wondering scorn.

To go to the Debating Hall everyone has to wear blue. I don't know why. It's yet another rule of the House.

Changing that hurriedly wasn't easy, although JL was abnormally docile.

We powdered her hair on top of the green, and it looked fairly awful. Pattoo powdered the red slap-side of JL's face with white. Shimra hadn't even noticed.

We didn't have time for our own hair, so we had to tie it in hasty, untidy blue turbans.

My hands were shaking anyway.

The Debating Hall is huge—a high ceiling decorated with silver medallions, upheld by marble pillars, and below, a slippery polished floor. I know about the floor, because when I was nine or ten, I used to be one of the kids who polished it once every five days. And it took all day to do.

The ladies and princesses sat on their blue plush seats on the raised area, and the maids and servants and slaves gathered around to fan them and offer little tobacco pipes and calming drinks.

On the other side were the lords and princes, who, almost alone, make a decision at the end of every debate. However, at the head of the room was a long draped table and, behind that, seven gilded chairs under a canopy.

These are for the Old Ladies, the most ancient princesses. They too have an important vote.

Only three of the OL chairs were filled. There sat Princess Corris, who's eighty, and Princess Armingat, who's eighty-five. They attend every debate and argue wildly at the end, always disagreeing with each other.

Today a third chair had been filled.

Princess Jizania Tiger is said to be one hundred and thirty years old. She *does* look it, but she's absolutely beautiful. She seems made of the thinnest, finest pale paper. And her large hooded eyes are like pale amber pearls. She's bald, and today she wore a headdress that was a net of almost colorless silvery beads, set occasionally with a bud of emerald. (She alone hadn't bothered with blue. Her gown was ash-colored.)

I can't imagine ever being old, let alone old like this. But if I had to be, she would be my model.

She has a fine voice, too. Soft and smoky—musical. She sounds only about sixty.

As a rule, though, she never bothers with debates. Only the most unavoidable dinners and Rituals.

It must be nice to get out of so many boring and unimportant things.

Now she sat there, leaning her slender old face on her slender, crooked graceful hand, which had one colossal topaz burning on it in a ring.

The big space at the Hall's center was fenced on two sides by weapon-bristling Guards, standing three deep.

I'd looked for him—I mean the prisoner, the enemy-invader—the moment we'd arrived. But the Guards are often dramatic. Only now did they march him in.

He seemed quite good-humored and certainly not upset. I wondered if he'd been hurt when the balloon fell, and was bravely hiding it.

The Guards left him alone in the middle of the Hall, and we all now glared down at him, and some of the royalty held up magnifying glasses.

Under the lighted lamps, which are always lit in the hall, his hair looked like golden flames itself. The dark grey coat was swinging loose. He wore white under it, and boots that were a darker white. But mainly, he was young. Older than me (did I say I'm about halfway through sixteen?). Eighteen maybe, nineteen. In what some of them call my Age-Group.

Despite that, the thing that is making this so hard to describe is that he had a gleam to him, a polish to him. I used to polish this floor, but *life* had polished this man. *Being* alive. *Living.* And he glowed.

He came from the unknown outside places, the Hell known as the Waste.

And I'd never thought anything that came from there could look any good. Terrifying, yes; revolting, probably. But not glowing and handsome, packed with energy, and this kind of easy pridefulness. With hair like melted sun.

One of the princes—Shawb—had risen and now walked along the raised part of the hall, where the royalty were all sitting, until he came to the area just before the Old Ladies' chairs. Shawb turned swiftly and nodded to them. (Armingat cackled. Corris looked hungry for trouble. Jizania was unreadable.)

Then Shawb stared down long and hard at the prisoner.

"You speak, I understand, the language of the House."

The prisoner shrugged slightly. "Among others."

"That doesn't interest me."

"Nor me, really," replied the prisoner.

I liked his voice. It was clear and had a faint accent of something or other. I liked his cheek, too.

Shawb didn't.

"This isn't a joke. You're in a bad situation. Didn't you realize?"

"Well, after your men fired on me and brought my craft down, I had an idea or two about it."

The Guards growled. Shawb scowled.

"Your name?"

The prisoner half turned. He put a hand in a pocket of his coat, and at once a hundred knives and rifles were scraping up at menacing angles. But out of the pocket he took only a clean white handkerchief, very laundered.

"Nemian," he said. "That's my name." And then he walked straight across the space they'd stood him in, right up to the (unguarded) table and chairs of the Old Ladies. He laid the handkerchief in front of Jizania Tiger.

During this, Shawb was shouting and the lined-up Guards broke ranks, and I heard the rifles clicking and clacking, getting ready to fire. I'd dropped the fan I was supposed to wave and put both my fists over my mouth. What a hopeless gesture. But I didn't know I'd done it until afterward.

It was Jizania Tiger who held up her topazed hand.

"All right. What do you want, young man?" she asked in her excellent voice.

"To give you this, madam."

"What is it? The rag you wipe your nose on?"

Nemian laughed. I liked his laugh. So did she. A carved little smile moved her lips.

"Of course it isn't, madam. It's a flower from the Waste. You might care for it."

Shawb bawled, "Don't touch the muck—it may be poisonous."

But Jizania said, "Not everything in the Waste is bad."

I'd never heard anyone say *that* before. (It was then I noticed my fists clamped over my mouth and took them down.)

She'd unwrapped the handkerchief and lifted up the flower. It really was one. It was fresh and firm, with big juicy green leaves, and the color of the flower head was crimson.

"Oh, yes," said Jizania. As if she knew these flowers, although I'd swear there are none in the Garden, and so it *must* have come from the Waste.

And the Waste was hell-on-earth. So everyone had always said.

Nemian turned from Jizania with a bow. He looked around at all of us. He was smiling and unfussed even though I now saw there was a streak of blood across his forehead. His eyes looked tired. I felt sorry about his eyes. I liked their color, but I couldn't remember what it was—only the shape, and the shadow.

He said, "I'm on a search, a quest for something. I might have liked to visit your wonderful gardens, but alternatively I could have just gone elsewhere, if you'd preferred. In the end, I didn't have much choice, did I? You shot me down. I assume you're not used to visitors. Shame, really."

Then he *yawned.*

I never saw anyone sit down so elegantly on a floor. Even when he was lying full length, he lay in a stylish way. Presently he seemed asleep.

Maybe you're getting used to my odd type of thinking. But I thought just then: all those days and months I'd polished the floor and never knew one day he'd stretch out on it and lie there. There was a strange ache in my chest like the pressure of tears.

But the Guards milled forward now and surrounded Nemian so none of us could see him. It seemed they thought that by going to sleep, he'd performed another dangerous and life-threatening trick.

A few minutes after that, the Guards hustled almost all of us out of the Debating Hall. Only the most senior of the princes remained, Shawb among them. Even the Old Ladies were politely and firmly requested to go.

Jizania made no protest. The other two cackled and squeaked and struggled like nasty old children kicked out of a party.

In the outside chambers, the thrown-out royalty stood around chattering to each other. I thought Jade Leaf might be her usual self, but instead she went barging over to her mother, Princess Shimra.

"Mummy-mummy, may I stay with you?"

"I'm going to the library soon," replied Shimra, "to *read,*" looking uncomfortable as JL laid her head on Shimra's shoulder.

"Let me come too, Mummy. I *want* to, Mummy."

"But you don't like reading, dear."

Jade Leaf is about a head taller than Shimra, and now JL was acting like a little girl, making her voice all gooey. This didn't happen often, thank goodness, as it makes you sick. Shimra as well, from the look of it.

Soon after that, Jizania Tiger swept by, her two attendants proudly holding up her long brocade train. When she had passed, Shimra had somehow escaped her daughter, and JL came disconsolately back to us, her maids. Her one-side-reddened face was cooler, but she still seemed to be confused. Had *I* done that?

But I didn't concentrate. I kept thinking of *him.*

What would they do to him? I'd only heard tales of punishments delivered to trespassers. Remember the lion, the one they killed?

We couldn't hang about though, for JL went off upstairs to the Jewelry Chamber, and we all had to go too.

When I was a child I liked this room, which has all the most ancient jewels and ornaments of the House displayed behind glass. Now that room only made me annoyed. I don't know why.

Today I barely saw it. Daisy seemed to be in the same state, and a couple of the others. But not Dengwi and Pattoo.

I had an embarrassing idea that Daisy and I at least had got a *thing* about Nemian. Yes, I had, I was sure. My face had gone hot simply thinking of his name.

This was dismal, wasn't it? I'd fallen for an outcast from Hell, who anyway they were going to kill. Besides which, he would never have glanced my pathetic way.

JL mooned over the bracelets and earrings. But gradually I could see the vagueness leaving her—the little girlie business. She had that snakelike air again. Not that I've anything against snakes—only the human ones.

"Claidi," she said suddenly, very brisk and clear.

"Yes, lady?" I asked, my heart sinking even further. (Even with Nemian's arrival to distract me, I hadn't quite forgotten the professional beating.)

"Thank you so much for viciously slapping my face and destroying that dreadful insect. It was an insect, was it?" I attempted to seem bashful and pleased. "I never knew you were so loyal. I ought to reward you." She smiled brilliantly. "When I tell Mummy tonight, I'm sure she'll command her steward's whip-master to tie an extra-pretty ribbon on the whip. Do you know about the whip, by the way?" She bent closer. It didn't seem to be really happening. But a glass case pushed at my back and reminded me of where the paperweight she threw had bruised me. "It has spikes on it," said LJL, triumphant. Ah, the whip had spikes.

She turned in her clumsy bulking way and knocked a case, which shuddered. As I was shuddering.

The other girls looked glum. But some ladies had come tinkle-rustling in, loudly exclaiming that the enemy-invader had been imprisoned in the Black Marble Pavilion.

Daisy gasped. Then I did, because one of the ladies turned to me and snapped, "You, girl—Claidi-is-it?" "Yes, madam." "Her Oldness, Jizania Tiger, wants you."

Somehow I swallowed nothing the wrong way and choked. Pattoo thumped me on the back, luckily just clear of the bruise.

Dengwi guided me to the doorway. "Listen," she said, "I don't know what the Old Lady wants, but everyone says she's all right. Appeal to her mercy. You *mustn't* be *whipped.* You do know, don't you, Claidi? My sister was, and"—Dengwi's face was like smooth black steel—"she nearly died."

I didn't know what to say. (Had I ever heard that Dengwi had a sister?) There wasn't time anyway. A slave of the Old Lady's was standing there, looking haughty and patient—a slave of an Old Lady had more status than anyone's maid.

My head was already whirling inside. So much was happening in my life, where, as you know, for sixteen-ish years nothing had happened at all.

THE LION IN THE CAGE

I'm staring up at the moon, which, ironically, is visible tonight. Again ironically, I keep hearing a piece of LJL's terrible poetry: *O moon, of liquid floating lemon-green . . .*

In a way I feel sorry for her now. That's no doubt pretty stupid of me. But she's so hopeless. I mean, there really isn't a shred of hope for her. She'll always be like that, mean and spiteful and unjust and downright appalling. She isn't happy. If she were happy, she'd be different. Look at Lady Iris and Prince Eagle, and there are others. They're kind to their servants.

There's some lecture we were given, about the time I was polishing the floor where Nemian lay down so wonderfully and went to sleep. The lecturer told us hard work and suffering would refine our characters, make us *better.*

What a load of nonsense.

Anyway, here, at this very high window, staring at the moon, with something whirling in me and all of me trembling and yet somehow *serene*—I can't be angry at Jade Leaf.

But I feel weird about the other maids, especially Daisy and Pattoo. Because I won't be able to say good-bye.

To get back to my story:

Jizania Tiger's haughty slave took me along the glassy corridors (windows, burnished wood) and up marble stairs. We reached Her Apartment, and I found it was built up on a flat roof. There was a roof garden with trees in pots and a pool with a fountain and colored fish.

The Old Lady was sitting in a room open to this garden.

She'd taken off her jeweled headdress, and I admired her well-shaped bald head. She truly is magnificent looking. (But of course I have extra reasons to be impressed with her.)

"Sit down," she said to me. "Are you hungry? Thirsty?"

Startled, I mumbled I wasn't. Although my mouth was dry.

She seemed to know this—I suppose not too difficult. She had the slave pour me a glass of fruit juice, orange, I think, which we only ever had watered-down in the Maids' Hall.

"You have no notion," she said, "why you're here."

"No, lady."

"It's been a busy day so far," she said. She gave a short bark of laughter, like one of the Garden foxes. Then she said, "Jade Leaf is an unpleasant girl to serve, I should think. I intend to look into that. And no, I understand you can't agree. But your life, Claidi, won't have been much fun. Is that true?"

Amazing she knew my name. Amazing she'd singled me out.

I said, awkwardly, "Well, not really." I thought of Dengwi's words and blurted, not having meant to so soon, "I slapped Lady Jade Leaf's face today. And she says I'm to be properly whipped. The whip with . . . spikes."

Jizania Tiger slowly raised her exquisite eyebrows.

"A slap? A whip with spikes? I don't recall such a whip. I think there isn't one."

I was afraid for a moment. Dengwi knew there was.

Then Jizania added, "However, just in case, perhaps we had better think of an alternative to the whipping."

I blurted again, "Thank you, thank you." I knew well enough Jizania had power in the House. If she promised it, I'd be safe. At least for now, which always seems all you can ever hope for.

A crazy thought came to me. Perhaps Jizania Tiger would make me one of her own maids. They were of a rarer breed than us; they didn't even use the Maids' Hall but had their own rooms in the Old Lady's apartment.

Why such an extreme of good luck should come my way I couldn't imagine. This kept me cautious.

Then she said, without warning, "And what did you think of the enemy-invader, the young man called Nemian?"

Did I go red? Somehow not. I think I was too surprised.

"Er—well—he er—well he's—er—" cleverly said I.

"A very awful enemy, wasn't he?" asked Jizania. "I'm sure you were terrified."

It seemed daft to lie. Her eyes seemed to say she could read one's mind.

"He looked just like the princes here," I said. "Well, actually, better."

"Yes," she said, "very fit and bold. And that hair." She sounded younger than ever when she said this, only about fifty. I blushed after all. She took no apparent notice. "And the flower he brought from the Waste. That was a shock, wasn't it, Claidi? Did you ever guess things might grow there, beautiful healthy things?"

"No, madam. I thought the Waste was all poisoned."

"Some of it. Some."

There was a gap then. My eyes roamed uneasily. She had a spectacular indigo-feathered bird on a perch, which sat looking at me with wise old eyes like hers.

All at once, Jizania Tiger rose, with a stiff old grace.

"Come along," she said, as I scrambled up. Naturally I didn't impertinently ask where we were going.

Where we went, however, was through the room and a door, and down a back staircase—a winding cranky staircase with only the narrowest windows. Several floors must have gone by, and then she took a key from a bracelet and unlocked a narrow door.

Outside the door was a hanging. Brushing that aside, we were in the Black Marble Corridor.

It's not a lovely place. They send you there at night for lesser punishment. Strange, eerie sounds come through holes cunningly cut in the walls, and there are dimly lit, dismaying pictures of executions and people being cast out into the Waste, crying and pleading not to be. I'd sat here on the floor as a kid more than once and had nightmares afterward, as they know you will.

At the end of the long corridor is a courtyard and, in that, the Black Marble Pavilion.

Another key from the bracelet opened the door to the yard.

Huge paved slabs sloped away to the Pavilion. Its black columns hold up a black cupola. Between the columns run thick black bars.

Above, the sun was shining, but the Pavilion looked like total darkness. I couldn't see through the bars and columns to anything.

But Jizania Tiger, with only me to attend her, went sailing out on the paving.

Immediately two House Guards came striding around the Pavilion.

They saluted and stood to attention for the Old Lady, but as she got near, one shouted:

"Wait, please, madam. The enemy prisoner is here."

She just gave a nod.

"Why else am *I* here?"

"It's this, madam. The prisoner is an alien from the Waste. It would be better if you—"

"Tottered back to my easy chair?" Her voice sliced him in two. He lost his stern military stance. "Don't presume, my lad," said Princess Jizania Tiger, "to give orders to an Old Lady of the House."

Now there was creepy-crawl rather than salute. "Excuse me, madam." (The other Guard was grinning.)

She swept on, and I with her.

Nemian was around the other side in the Pavilion cage, where the Guards had been. Maybe they'd been insulting him, or just talking. Surely someone must be interested in the Waste just a teeny bit.

He stood there inside the bars. His coat hung over a bench. He looked . . . overpowering, so close. So I couldn't even squint at him.

"Oh," he said. "Hello, madam. A great lady, and a girl in a blue dress with green hair tangling from a blue scarf."

I could *feel* him staring at me, a long, long gaze. He, who would never have glanced my way.

"She is Claidi," said Jizania Tiger. And next she said, "Claidi for short, that is. Her full name is Claidissa Star."

My head shot up. I goggled at her. Most unbecoming I must have appeared. I had no words. I'd even forgotten the gorgeous Nemian.

Was that—*that*—my proper name?

My arm aches from writing so much, but I can't stop. There isn't time. The moon's moved. Can I squeeze the rest in before I have to go down?

For a minute, dazzled by the new name, I didn't take in what the princess and the prisoner were saying to each other. They were talking about something.

I sort of came back to hear him say, "It's kind of you to inquire, madam. I wasn't seriously injured, no. A handful of bruises, a scratch or two. The balloon brushed against some of your trees in falling, and I was able to swing out on a handy bough. Then the balloon veered again and crashed at quite a distance. I was damned lucky."

"Lucky but damned?" said she.

Nemian smiled, and I saw him color very slightly. My heart turned a somersault. I'd certainly remembered him again.

"Pardon my rough language, lady," he said. "I've been traveling some while and lost my good manners."

Then his eyes came back to me. For a moment they held mine, and I seemed to be sinking in them. (Still can't recall their shade—blue? grey?? Soon I'll know.) Then he smiled such a smile. And I thought, I really am not going to be so totally, tiresomely *soppy.* So I frowned at him in a grave and ugly way. And he laughed. And I turned my head. (Childish. I'd run out of ideas on coping.)

Nemian said to the princess, "She seems to have had enough, Lady Claidissa Star."

"I expect she wants her tea."

"Then please lose no further time in seeing she gets it."

I found that she was turning me with her slender claws, and we were going back over the paving, the Guards saluting. I was convinced I'd messed everything up—whatever everything was.

Back in her apartment a carved table had been laid with the most delightful "tea." (Really it was lunchtime.) I thought she meant for me to wait on her, but she said I was to sit down and eat with her.

In fact she only drank a glass of iced chocolate.

(It would be madness not to note down at least some of the "tea." There were sliced peaches and strawberries in painted dishes, and cakes still hot, and biscuits in the shapes of birds, and white butter shaped like a rabbit. There were hot and cold drinks of all types. How the cups and glasses sparkled!)

What a shame I couldn't eat anything. I tried. I'd never been offered such a feast. But you'll grasp why I couldn't.

And when Jizania Tiger saw I couldn't, she started to talk to me, and what she said made it impossible for me to eat and drink even the crumbs and drips I'd been trying to get down my throat.

"So much is said," she said, "about the House. Long ago, the House was a sanctuary. It was a pleasant enough place. But now it's like an over-wound clock. It goes in fits and starts and tells the wrong time."

Then she said, "They talk about the Waste, too, and terrorize little children with stories of it. But you saw the flower. The Waste isn't as bad as it's made out, just as the House isn't as good."

Then: "That young man, our handsome prisoner—they don't know what to do about him. He meant us no harm, but by now they're so used to distrusting and fearing anything from outside that they can only lock him away. They may keep him in that cage for years. Or, in some sudden unreasonable alarm, they may decide after all to murder him. Really, I think he should be allowed to escape, don't you? But then, someone needs to assist him. I have the means, but I'm old. I can't be bothered with such an adventure."

After this she looked into my eyes with her amber hawk's stare.

"Then there is you. You've had a deathly life here, Claidi, and what can you hope for or ever look forward to? Beatings, nastiness, endless uninteresting work. Perhaps a marriage with some suitably obedient servant, if even that's allowed. You too, my girl, ought to be let out of your cage."

I hadn't followed it all, not properly. My heart followed though, in rattling leaps.

Was she saying what my heart thought she was?

"You see, Claidi, you're reckless enough, and young enough, and *bothered* enough. If I gave you the means to let Nemian out of the Pavilion and spirit him away from the House and the Garden, and into the hellish Waste . . . which is the world . . . would you?"

Yes, heart, you hit the bull's-eye.

She said, "The Waste is more than we know. And you've said yourself Nemian is a lord. He comes from somewhere just as grand, grander, no doubt, than here. And he would take care of you."

Before I could think it through, I cried, "Why would he? I'm only—"

"Only what? Only a lady's maid?"

I withered at her words. The truth of them made them less swallowable even than the food. Maid—I was a *slave.*

Princess Jizania Tiger half turned and held out her wrist for the indigo bird to soar down to, weightless as muslin. As it perched there, she fed it peaches, which it tucked daintily into its beak.

"Claidi," said Jizania Tiger, "you recall that your parents were driven out in the first year of your life?"

"Y—yes."

"They profaned a Ritual. A most serious one."

"Yes."

"You don't know what it was? No one has told you?"

I shook my head. The bird scanned me and shook its head too, copying.

But then Jizania Tiger told me that the first profanation had been that my mother was a princess of the House, and my father her steward, and that the second profanation was *me*—the fact that I was born, because no one is allowed to be born here save when permission has been granted, and *never* of mixed rank.

"They saw fit not to exile an innocent baby," said Jizania Tiger. "Instead they condemned you to a life of harsh service to the House. And

Shimra, who was your mother's friend—a false one, evidently—gave you to her atrocious daughter, a human boil that someone should burst. These things I saw, but I've said how old and lazy I am, haven't I? Besides, until now there's been no way out. I must add: Nemian knows, since I've told him, that you are royal."

"Did he believe you?" I croaked.

"Do you?"

Do I? I don't know.

All I know is, she gave me every key I shall need to free him (she has, she said, a key to each lock of the House and Garden). And she's told me how to do everything, and where to go, and that it's my choice, all this. That I needn't. But then, the Waste has flowers in it, and Nemian's own house, whatever that is, is there, and also my parents, just possibly somewhere, if they survived. My courageous parents who fell in love and dared let their love make *me.*

It's all tumbling through me. Not just love—I feel I'm made of racing water and drums, and fired up by lightning.

And you'll have known all the time that I'll do it. I'll free him and go with him. Take the risk. Out *there.* Wouldn't you?

THE ESCAPE

By moonlight, the Garden looked heavenly—I mean like heaven, whatever that is; we never had it properly explained. But obviously, a lovely and special place. I felt a moment of terror. This was what I knew, good or bad.

She'd said I was reckless. I didn't feel it, just then. I wanted to creep back to the room in the Maids' Hall and say Jizania had only just sent me away. Dengwi and Pattoo had the night duty with Jade Leaf, so even *she* couldn't complain. She couldn't anyway. The Old Ladies were so powerful.

Jizania had told me she would say she had kept me in her apartment to serve tea—she only ever had "teas," never breakfasts or dinners. Then she'd dozed off—"Naturally, old women always doze off," said Jizania with a tiger's smile. I had then stolen all the keys and run away.

She would have to say that. They would think her careless and a fool, but clear of the crime of setting Nemian free.

She had added, though, that the next day, tomorrow, if there was no uproar—that is, if he hadn't escaped because I hadn't let him out—she would say nothing at all.

But I could picture what she'd think of me—Claidi the cowardly spineless creep.

Looking back on this now—I mean now it's too late, since I *did* do it and there's no going back—my nerves seem pointless.

Let me describe how the Garden looked though. I want to put it down, because I'll never see it again, will I? And the joke is: it *was* partly mine if what Jizania said about my mother was true.

The trees rested like soft, dark blue clouds and tapering, pale, dark towers, asleep. The lawns were like grey velvet. Black shadows tabled across. Here and there, a rim of silver, moon on water. One fountain I could see ceaselessly curving over and over, a stream of liquid spangles. . . .

Somewhere a bird sang a brief little silvery song. They often do on warm nights. And from the river a hippo grunted.

Then a lion roared. They didn't mean anything by it, roaring. Just exercising their lungs. But loud.

Above, all the stars. Would they be different over the Waste?

Perhaps it wasn't really fear I felt. Perhaps leaving this place that I hated—which had been so boring and vicious and frankly dangerous for me—I was sad, after all.

When I'd left Jizania, I'd hidden, as you know, and written in this book. I already had all the keys and the wine for the Guards at the Pavilion and some things Jizania had told me to get from the Maids' Hall. These included my strongest shoes, which I put on. I'd put everything else in a little bread sack from the kitchens. (Another theft. Several actually. I was even stealing Nemian from them, in a way.)

She'd said I should start at midnight. The clock high up on the House sang out its thin strokes, the only hour it sounds anymore.

I came down to the Garden and went along toward the Pavilion of Black Marble, approaching from the Upper Shrubberies.

(Jizania had said that it wouldn't do for me to go straight down from her rooms, the way we had earlier. I thought she was sensibly not involving herself any further. But now I wonder if she gave me a last chance to look around, to feel my nerves and my strange regret, to be *sure.*)

Then, as I was walking through the hibiscus shrubs, I met a lion.

We both stopped and gaped at each other. It seemed as surprised as I was.

I wasn't sure what to do. It was a *lion.* Of course, I'd seen them out before, but on leashes. Anyway, this one was perfectly friendly, or should I say indifferent. It shook its head and padded by, creamy in moonlight, and smelling of the white hibiscus flowers.

When I'd gone on a bit further, though, I looked over from a break in the bushes, and on the Vine Terraces that run down there, lamped by the moon, two other lions (lionesses) were playing together, rolling over and crushing the vines and the fat grapes, so the air reeked of juice.

On the night Nemian was to escape, the lions had also escaped. If necessary, this would make a splendid diversion.

A coincidence? No, I thought not. Jizania had sent someone else on another errand. . . . Hadn't she said she had keys to each lock in the House and Garden?—that would include the lions' enclosure.

Doubtless this feat would also be blamed on Claidi. It occurred to me that my name might live on in history here!

Then I could see the wall of the courtyard and the Pavilion cupola over the top.

Well, I felt sick. But somehow I kept walking and found I'd knocked on the door in the wall. So there was no time to throw up.

One of the Guards spoke harshly through the door.

"Yes? What do you want?"

"To bring you wine, respected Guard."

"Oh. Wine, eh."

Someone sounded pleased now. Then another one said, "Who sent it?"

"Her Oldness, Princess Jizania."

The door was opened, and I pattered through, looking suitably timid and modest.

There were five of them, sitting on benches under a lantern on a pole. They'd been playing cards. Behind them the Pavilion bulked, not a light showing.

I gave them the two large wine bottles and handed them the two kitchen cups, all I could carry. They didn't seem worried. One of them took a handy undoing-thing out of a pouch and uncorked the bottles.

They passed them around, taking huge sloshing gulps, which was glorious. Jizania had drugged both bottles, I'd seen her do it, inserting a long needle through the corks and letting in some herbal stuff, drip by patient drip.

It didn't work instantly, unfortunately.

"What's in that bundle?"

"Some things the princess sent for the prisoner."

"What things? What does he want with things? We'll be stringing him up tomorrow, hopefully."

"Or we'll behead him," added a particularly jolly one. "Off with that goldy head."

"Too right, Jovis."

"Too goldy," Jovis agreed with himself thoughtfully.

I remembered it was his cannon that had brought down the balloon.

"Here," said Jovis to me, "come and sit on my knee, girlie."

"No, thank you," I replied politely.

They all laughed, and one kindly explained, "No, he's not *asking* you, he's *telling* you."

This sort of thing had happened now and then. I looked coy and half smiled at Jovis the shooter and would-be beheader.

"I'd like to, respected Guard, but I have to get back to my lady. You know how it is."

"She won't miss you yet."

I fluttered sweetly, then said, "I'll just go over and give the horrible prisoner these things she sent him. Then, well, maybe . . . just for a minute. I mean, I've always admired the Guards."

"Yes," said Jovis, "all you girls like us Guards." Pathetic, really—he believed this.

But the wine was strong, and they were still gargling it down. They were getting *extra* stupid, having had a head start anyway.

They waved me off to the Pavilion, Jovis promising me how nice it would be when I got back to him.

As I reached the Pavilion, a lion roared—right outside the wall, it sounded like.

The Guards chortled. "Lions're noisy t'night." And one of them slumped forward and rolled off the bench. The other four looked at him, and it was good old Jovis who declared, "Carn'old s'wine."

I turned my back, more confident now, and called softly between the bars of Nemian's cage. I used his name. The first time I had.

At first, no answer. And behind me the Guards still toasting one another, not yet out cold.

Then Nemian spoke to me from the center of the dark.

"Claidissa?"

My heart jumped. My heart has no sense, really.

I coughed, recovered myself, and said, "Princess Jizania sent me."

"Claidissa," said Nemian again.

So I said fiercely, "Call me Claidi, please." Because I couldn't stand it. All this, and *him, and* this new name of mine.

There was a clatter and bumping sound. I glanced back. At *last.*

Nemian was suddenly right in front of me, up against the bars.

"God," said Nemian (another new name—some exclamation they use in the Waste?), "she did it, she drugged them. It's real then. You're going to get me out. She told me you would. Clever Claidi."

So I undid the lock, and the bars unfolded, and Nemian stepped out into the moonlit, lion-roaring night.

The Guards were in an unappealing heap. Jovis had his mouth wide open and was dribbling and snoring charmingly. Just what you'd expect of him.

"There are lions outside."

"Oh, good," said Nemian.

"They're very tame." I hoped.

It wasn't far, in any case. And we saw no more lions, only met a small lumbering badger.

(I have a sort of feeling the lions just trotted about for a while, messed the Garden up a bit, and then rambled back into the enclosure.)

I said before that under the Garden were systems of tunnels—where the heating mechanisms were located—tended by slaves. (I said, too, the slaves have a rotten time, worse than I'd ever had.)

Jizania had told me how to get down into these tunnels, and how it was simple to go through if you only took the right-hand turning every time. Traveling like that, from the entry we'd use, we would finally come out beyond the walls!

Thinking back again, I have to say I had no qualms about using these tunnels. Crazy. But it just seemed nothing could stop me—us.

Nemian didn't question me either. Jizania must have told him all the plan, before she put it to me. And he must have sat there in the Pavilion cage wondering and wondering if I'd have the courage to arrive.

The way in was at a carefully overgrown rocky hill, with trees leaning at the top. I found the door in the ivy, unlocked it (I suppose Jizania must have copies of all these keys), and went in. Then I lit the first kitchen candle from my bread sack and put the glass bulb over the top to keep it steady.

Nemian closed the door behind us.

"It's every right-hand turn," I said.

"I know," he said.

"And she said that if we pass any of the slaves, take no notice."

"Well would I," said Nemian, "of slaves."

Somehow that was disturbing, that he said this. I should have expected it. It meant, presumably, that princely Nemian's home-place also has slaves, servants, *maids*—and they don't count for much. Jizania had been very definite in giving him my "proper" name. "I've told him you are royal," she'd said.

But I couldn't think about that at such a moment, could I?

The tunnels were narrow, dark, and damp in spots, with water trickling down. Here and there they'd been shored up with planks. Here and there too, bricks had fallen out. Not organized picturesque decay, just age and neglect.

After a while we did pass a kind of room, where a vast black furnace stood like a nightmare beast. It wasn't going because the recent months have been warm.

Later there was another, and a few little holes in the tunnel sides, and once two slaves were there, but they were fast asleep.

In another area, a fox had gotten in and made a den. I saw her eyes glow as she glared at us in the candle's light. Bones, too.

After I'd lit the second candle, I began to feel exhausted. I was tired of being in the tunnels. And Nemian treading behind me—once or twice banging his golden head on low rafters or slabs of stone, and cursing—made me more edgy than excited now.

Then I heard the river. Jizania had said I would.

I looked down the passage for the last door the princess had given me a key to.

But when we reached it, the lock was rusty. When I tried to work the key, I couldn't, *couldn't.*

"Let me do it," he said. His voice was impatient. This managed to make me feel unintelligent and weak and exasperated altogether.

But he was flying for his life, after all. He'd been offhand about slaves probably for the same reason?

I stood aside, and Nemian, instead of undoing the door as I'd tried to, threw himself against it.

I was quite shocked when it gave way.

It was an old door, rusty and rotted, and outside was the world.

He walked straight out. I . . . followed him.

"But," I said stupidly, "the door—"

"No one comes here," he said.

"But something might get *in,*" I said, "from—out *there.*"

"*We,*" he said reasonably, "are out *there.*"

We were.

And in the dark, for the moon was gone, *there* looked no different from the Garden.

The river ran, wide and muscular and dully shining, with tall reeds like iron railings. Rocks piled around us, a lot of them about the door, hiding it quite well, which was lucky since he'd broken it open.

(They'll realize and go and mend the door. The Guards will keep a lookout until it's safe.)

I stared back, and away along the river. I saw the fortressed high walls of the Garden, black on blue-black sky.

Never before had I been this side of them.

My companion had sat down. He said, easily, lightly, "Did you bring anything to eat, Claidi?"

Flustered, I produced the snacks Jizania suggested I filch from the Maids' Hall kitchens and set them before Nemian. He didn't seem greatly impressed, but he ate them.

Then he lay back on the ground, and I realized he was going to sleep again.

All this time, I'd thought perhaps going to sleep in front of us all in the Debating Hall had been an act, a sort of ploy to seem harmless. But now I think he really can just go to sleep at will, and he does.

He's asleep now. I put out the candle because I was nervous about being spotted—from the walls . . . from the *Waste.* But it doesn't look like the Waste here.

I watched him a while, but that seemed rude. He *is* very handsome. And—a stranger.

In the end I lit the candle again, what was left of it, and wrote this. I'm bewildered, really. I don't know where I am. Literally. Also, he looks wonderful, but I don't know him at all. It's all unknown. And the future. Even myself, now.

HELL?

Next day, I saw the Waste. That was simple enough. The sun rose in front of me, red-orange, hitting my eyes and the rocks behind me. The river burned red. Some birds were calling, in a harsh *different* way. Nemian was still sleeping, like an enchanted prince in one of the library books of the House.

Stiff and chilled, I got up and walked toward the river, and in a little while I walked along beside it, until the land curved upward to the sun.

As I climbed this slope, I saw a shimmer on the air below the sun's disk. And when I got to the hill's top, I realized the shimmer to be other hills, far off. They were a parched whitish color. To my right the river coiled away through the hillside and vanished—was gone. Just a steaminess left behind.

Between this area and the far-off, pale, and dry-looking hills was a huge and terrible nothing. I mean, obviously something was there. But the something *was* nothing. A stretch of land—or sand—or dust—with vague shadows in it; and tilted bits the sun was still catching, but no actual *shapes.* Like a tree, a shrub, but certainly nothing like a building. Nothing I could recognize.

This seemed to go on for miles and miles, so much further than the Garden land about the House.

I looked back then, the way the exiles sometimes do in the paintings in the Black Marble Corridor.

Dawn bloomed honey and rose against the high walls I had left forever.

Birds were flying over them. It looked safe and gentle and beautiful. But it was a dream, and I'd woken up.

I looked out at the Waste again. I swallowed.

We ate the last of the snacks. There wasn't much. Nemian had had most of it the night before.

He said, uncaringly, "We should have gotten farther than this, but then, they won't be eager to pursue us. They won't bother, probably. Not out here." Then he added, "I'll miss the balloon, but they wrecked it. Then again, I'd have needed ballooneers to get the thing going."

"Oh, yes?" I said. I didn't understand a word about the balloon.

"I'm no engineer," said Nemian, seeming pleased he wasn't. "That's the trouble," he said, "always having everything done for you by your servants. We'll be a fine pair. I hope you'll be able to manage, Claidi."

"Oh, er—I'll try."

"It isn't going to be a bed of roses, on foot. And I suppose the only exercise you've ever had is dancing, or smacking your pet dog."

My mouth fell open. This seems to happen a lot now. There are lots of things for it to happen over.

"But I've worked all my life," I said flatly.

Nemian laughed. "At your poetry," he said, "at working out a riddle. Mmn."

"No," I yapped, "scrubbing floors, running errands, hand-washing linen, grinding face powder, making—"

He was laughing. Glamorously, of course. His hair in the sun—

"All right," he said at last. "Let's pretend you have."

We went down to the river to fill the flask I'd brought with clean if rather murky unfiltered water, doubtless with hippo droppings in it.

My mind was rolling about over what he'd said. Apparently Nemian thought I'd been a *real* princess in the House. I was royal, so I'd lived like royalty.

All this while, the walls of the House and the Garden were only about half a mile away, and I became more and more nervous that Guards would march out and arrest us. But no one came. Of course, they wouldn't. However near, we were in the Waste, hell-on-earth, lost and unreachable.

In the end we set out, up the hill again. At the top, Nemian gazed and sighed. He flicked a look at me.

"If you get tired, Claidi, I'm not going to carry you."

This was upsetting. Who precisely had rescued him? But I kept quiet now. I was used to keeping quiet before my betters.

On the downslope he spoke again and used that Waste word: "For God's sake, I never should have had to put up with *this*."

After that we marched in silence, Nemian a little ahead of me.

When we reached the plain—if that's what it was—the ground was like screwed-up parchment, sprinkled with powder.

Dust rose from our footfalls as we walked. We coughed, and then the dust seemed to settle in our throats. We got used to it.

The sun was higher. Far off, the blistered ghosts of the hills. The House walls had disappeared. I'll never see them again.

It was hot. Already.

I have become so used to holding anger at unfairness inside.

And then, well, I've told you, I'm in love with him.

And also, here we were, and he seemed to know the way. (Did he?) I knew nothing.

But that first day, it was murder.

In my sack, now tied to my shoulders—the way wrongdoers carry their crimes in the House pictures—bounced this book. I hadn't the heart to write in it and anyway had no chance, and then was too worn out.

He'd been right. I might be tougher than he reckoned, but I'd *never* had to do anything like this.

The ground was so hard. That sounds stupid. But it was as if, every time you took a step, the ground whacked your feet, and the jolt shot right up your back. The sun thumped down on your head from the other direction.

The landscape was featureless, as it had seemed to be from the hill. There were a few nasty-looking rocks. (They did look nasty, like bad things changed into rocks that might suddenly turn back.)

I saw a lizard. It was pink with a black wiggle on its spine. Nemian never noticed, or he was just used to such sights.

There were some birds in the sky, too, big black ragged things. They seemed interested in us but then veered away.

We had a rest by a particularly bad-tempered-looking rock at noon. We drank some water, and Nemian went to sleep.

I don't often cry. It doesn't do much good. But I felt rather like it. And then I thought of my parents having to make just this appalling trek. I hoped and hoped they'd succeeded and gotten to somewhere, because presumably there *was* somewhere to get to. . . .

If I hoped they'd done it, I must, too. I wished, childishly, Nemian had been nicer to me. I wished that instead of saying he wouldn't carry me (as if I'd have asked), he had said, "Claidi, you've saved my life. We'll see this through. I'll help you."

But I gazed at his face, and once he had a dream or something, and he stirred and frowned and shook his head on the pillow of his rolled-up coat. I leaned over him and whispered, as I used to with Daisy when she had worrying dreams, "It's all right. Yes, it'll be fine."

I hope Daisy *is.* And Pattoo, and the others. I'll never know, will I?

That day truly was awful. The land never seemed to alter. The far hills got no nearer.

The sun went over and behind us. At last a glimmering, gold-stitched sunset, with birds arrowing like the stitching needles, hundreds of them it seemed.

Then thankful coolness with the dusk, which quickly turned chilly.

We'd reached a weird place by then. Distance had hidden it that morning, or the slope of the land. There was a small pool in rocks, with a waterfall, quite elegant, the sort of thing they *make* in the Garden. But this pool was a dull ancient green, and the waterfall was the same color.

"How foul," said Nemian. "Whatever you do, don't touch that water. It's undrinkable. Lethal."

I was thirsty and starving hungry. Sometimes I'd been made to miss meals (like Daisy) but never all of them for a whole day.

We sat down near the pool. The fall made a soothing noise that somehow stopped being soothing when I thought of the poison. This was just the sort of filthy thing they'd always told me was in the Waste.

However, Nemian took a narrow enameled box out of a pocket. Undoing the box, he offered it to me. There were little sugary tablets in the box.

"Take one," he said. "It has all the nourishment you'd get from a roast chicken with vegetables. Or so they always say." I did take one, cautiously. He did too. He ate it quickly and leaned back on the rock. "Not as interesting, definitely, as roast chicken. Or do you think it is?"

I crunched the little pill. It tasted spicy and sweet, like one of Jade Leaf's candies. But once it was down, I stopped feeling hungry. And I wasn't tired in quite the same dragging way.

We shared the last water.

"I'm sorry, Claidi," Nemian said as the blackening sky filled with whitening stars. "I'm not, right now, marvelous company. I'm angry at what's happened—but then, I'm also glad, because I've met you. That was something . . . almost miraculous. You're—" He faltered and so did my pulse. "You're a wonder, Claidi. Please forgive me for being such a dupp."

I blinked. What was a *dupp?* Never mind. I was warmer. How bright the stars. He didn't loathe or regret me.

I fell asleep listening to the poison pool and dreamed I fell in, but Nemian rescued me. The sort of dream it's lovely to have and embarrassing to tell. You know.

Next day, everything changed.

STORMY WEATHER

I must have half awakened sometime. The stars were bright red. I sensibly thought I was dreaming, but I wasn't.

When I woke again, it was daylight.

Only, not really.

Nemian was shaking me. One should never wake anyone like that, unless it's a matter of life and death. But I suppose this was, in fact.

Dust storms had come over the House but mostly by then had blown out, repelled also by the changed atmosphere, the different climate-in-miniature of the Garden. They'd never been anything like this.

Slabs of air were tumbling on me like walls. They were marigold-color or blood-red, and in between a shifting, spinning greyishness.

Spirals whirled. The light flashed off and on, then was gone, smothered in redness, then broke again like lightning.

You couldn't breathe, or it felt as if you couldn't. I'd put on an out-of-fashion dress for the escape, with a normal skirt. It had a sash, too, which now I found Nemian had pulled off and was tying over my nose and mouth. He had done something similar for himself.

But our eyes—how the dust and sand particles stung. And there were spiteful bits of grit.

We crawled among the rocks, trying to find some sort of shelter, but the water was also splashing out from the fall and the pool as the winds stirred them, and Nemian bellowed that we mustn't let this poisonous fluid even touch us. Then somehow we were outside the rocks and couldn't, in the chaos, find them again.

The noise of the dust winds was fearsome. It sounded like something truly terrible, without pity or thought—which it was.

I'd grabbed my little sack—a reflex.

We staggered about, and Nemian grasped my other hand. I find it reassuring to report that, in this situation, I wasn't thrilled when he did that.

He bawled at me that we mustn't become separated.

Heads bowed, we tried to push forward. The dust winds slapped and punched us. Apparently, so I gathered from his yells, there had been another rocky place further on, which he had spotted as the wind started to build up. This might provide more shelter.

But it was useless. In the end, we crouched down and covered our heads with our arms. Actually, in his case, only one arm, as he had put the other around me.

At another time, bliss, I suppose. But I was terrified—not of what the storm could do, exactly, although he said after they can kill, and I believe him. Just of the sheer ferocity of it.

Then, with no warning, the winds—there seemed about six of them—dropped. They fell around us like dry hot washing, and the grit and tiny stones rattled along the ground.

We raised our faces and saw the strangest—to me—sight.

In House books I'd stolen glances at, I had seen pictures of ancient cities that once had existed in the world before the Waste claimed everything. And this thing I saw now was surely such a city, or its remains.

The land had dropped gradually, and there was a sort of basin, and in this were some tall towers with windows, or spaces where windows had been, and ornamented roofs with domes and pedestals. There were pillars too, a whole long line of them that might have stretched for a mile. Mostly there were walls, and carvings, or the bits that were left of them. There was one huge vase with stone flowers still rising from it.

My eyes streamed, and everything wavered.

I said, "I never saw that from the higher ground."

Nemian said, sounding irritated, "You probably couldn't. The winds uncover things, just as they bury them."

I'd thought the storm was over, but no. A second or so more, having shown me the city ruins as if to educate me, and the whole thing started up again.

How long it lasted this time I can only make a guess. It felt like hours. Finally I was lying on the ground. I cringe to say it, but I think I was whimpering. Well, maybe I wasn't. Just grunting. Anyway, Nemian was utterly still. And once everything stopped, I was afraid he'd smothered completely.

But he sat up, and shook himself, and combed handfuls of white and yellow dust out of his hair with both hands.

I have this ridiculous idea, only it couldn't be, could it? He'd *gone to sleep again.* Didn't dare ask.

I stood up and shook out my skirt and my own hair, and then gave up. (I must, I thought, look like Nemian, as if I'd been dampened and dipped in flour.)

When I looked around, the city ruin was gone again. The dip in the plain had become a mound.

Presently, about an hour later, when we walked up it, I stumbled on one stone blossom still sticking up from the buried vase.

Nemian made no mention of having taken my hand or seeming to try to protect me. He scowled at the Waste, then his face simply became smooth and beautiful again. (His hair had lost its glory, though.)

He said, "Well done for bringing the water flask." (It was in the sack.) And then, "Reliable Claidi."

But I'd grabbed the sack because it had this book in it. The flask, after all, was empty.

There were so many questions I should have asked, weren't there? I bet you would have. You would have asked, for instance, *Where exactly are we going?* And *What will happen to me when we get there?* And you might have insisted he knew that, though Claidi was perhaps half royal, she'd lived first as a drudge and floor polisher, and next as Jade Leaf's maid-slave.

I didn't ask or say anything much. I'm not completely making an excuse. For one thing, I was so *tired.* Compared to this tiredness, my other tired times in the House seemed nothing.

Someone else would have been upheld by a sense of excitement and optimism. But I felt exasperated a lot—with the Waste mainly. And with Nemian. And with me.

The sun got higher and hotter and more unbearable, and I was desperate to have a drink of water. One doesn't realize how awful thirst is until something like this happens—worse than hunger.

After the buried city was behind us, the land was very bumpy and yet totally the same. Crash went the ground, hitting my feet.

Far, far off, still no nearer, were the pale parched hills which looked, anyway, most uninviting.

We reached a rock, one rock, but it threw a shadow. So we sat down in the shadow.

Nemian stretched out his long legs. His clothing had been perfect but wasn't now.

"You've been very strong," he said to me, "not drinking any water."

"There isn't any."

I'd thought he knew.

"Oh," he said. He frowned. "Didn't you bring any?"

"Yes. You—we drank it."

"Well, yes. But I thought there was more. I thought you understood that this might be a long journey. Didn't the princess tell you?"

Had she? I didn't think she had. I suppose it was common sense, and I was just a twit. Then again, I couldn't have carried much more. He would have carried it, maybe.

Nemian took the enameled box out of his pocket. He offered me another of the sugary tablets.

The pill was difficult to chew with such a dry mouth and scorched dusty throat.

But it did help. Even the thirst became more uncomfortable than sharply painful.

"You see," said Nemian, "there is a town over there somewhere." He waved idly at the hills. "I saw it from the balloon. We can get transport there, perhaps—unless they're very unfriendly, which they may be."

I'd thought everyone and everything was unfriendly in the Waste. But Nemian had come from the Waste.

He closed his eyes. I heard myself say in a faint panic: "Don't—"

"Don't? What?"

I wanted to say, Don't go to sleep. Talk to me, please. But what right did I have to demand that?

When I didn't add anything, he shrugged and . . . slept.

Glumly I sat there.

I tried to be brave. I tried to think he was wise to sleep, and I should try to as well. But the sugary pill seemed to have made me wide awake in addition to staying tired.

So I sat and stared uneasily out over the plain.

Little spirals of dust still spun there, huge hollow clouds above. A large black bird hung motionless on the air, as if from an invisible rope.

He'd only held my hand and put his arm around me to keep us together. He had felt responsible, like a kind prince for his servant. And I'd let him down—hadn't brought enough water.

I thought if anyone in the House had been the way he was, it would have annoyed me. Because it was Nemian, I felt in the wrong. Was this a very bad sign?

A huge new blond cloud was streaming along the plain, getting bigger.

I watched it, then properly saw it. Before I considered, I jumped up with a howl.

Nemian woke.

"Are you a girl or some species of jumping deer?"

"The storm—it's started again!"

He looked with those cool eyes.

"No, it isn't the storm. Riders, and vehicles."

And he sprang to his feet and ran, all in one coordinated bound, across the plain away from me, toward the dust cloud.

Had I been abandoned? Was I expected to follow? I'd better follow, hadn't I?

I floundered into a panting gallop.

The cloud (riders and vehicles) was going from right to left across the near horizon, slightly looping in toward us as it went. Because the ground was fairly flat now, I didn't see at first they were on a sort of makeshift road that the storm had obviously uncovered.

How far was it to reach them? Miles. Probably not. Toward the end I had to keep stopping, gasping for breath, but by then some of them had slowed down and then halted.

When I eventually staggered up, Nemian was in conversation with seven brown men in the two halted vehicles. The others had gone rolling on.

There was a *mad* noise. This was because the two chariots (I recognized them from the riding vehicles the princes sometimes used in the Garden) were each drawn by a team of six very large, curl-horned sheep. Some of the sheep were bleating in deep voices. And then I grasped the chariot riders were also bleating. And Nemian was bleating too.

For a minute I thought I'd lost my mind. Or they all had.

Then Nemian turned and saw me standing there with my hair raining down and my mouth, as usual, wide open.

He smiled and raised one eyebrow.

"Hello, Claidi. You needn't have rushed. These are Sheepers. I know their language."

One of the brown men—who wore their hair in plaits, braided, like the wool of the sheep teams, with beads and sheep-bells—said loudly, "B'naaa?"

Nemian turned back and bleated in return.

A few moments more, and one of the riders in the second chariot got out and jumped into the first chariot. Helping hands drew Nemian and me into the second chariot.

Everything smelled very oily and wooly. But—oh wonderful—a leather bottle was being offered to us. Nemian politely let me drink first. It wasn't water but warmish sheep milk, and I wasn't terribly delighted. But it did soothe my throat.

"We're going to the Sheeper town," Nemian informed me.

A whip cracked high, well clear of wooly backs, and we were off.

CHARIOT TOWN

There was quite a welcome.

Under a square gateway in a thick wall, but only just high enough so we could drive through, and into the brown town of the Sheepers. And everyone had come out, in the dusk, with lamps. Women laughing and holding up babies, and children screaming and bouncing, and old men leaning on wooden staffs, and grannies (they call them that), old women, and almost all of them were banging drums and blowing whistles, and some even threw flowers—a particularly *hard* sort of white poppy.

I gathered, but not right then, the chariot-riding Sheepers had been off somewhere, trading. With some other settlement of Sheepers? Anyway, it was a success. Best of all, the road had reappeared after the storm, which made the journey quicker. Although in fact we'd ridden with them until after sunset.

As the sky flamed, the hills had abruptly seemed to come nearer. Then the sheep chariots bundled around a swerve in the road, and we saw the town lying in the curve of two really near, rounded low hills, as if in the paws of a lion.

They call it—not for the sheep, as they do practically everything else, but for their chariots—Chariot Town.

Nemian says the walls may belong to something older and lost. The Sheepers patched them up and built inside.

The houses are made of wood and skins. (*Not* sheep. They *never* kill sheep.) Each has a strange little open garden, a stretch of neat close-cut fawn turf.

In the middle of the town is a bigger garden, green in parts, with some trees. Water wells up from the ground into a string of pools. The water's clean (except for what the sheep do in it, of course).

When not employed, the sheep simply wander about the town. Everyone pats them, or gets out of their way, and even if they eat the washing, they're allowed to. They also stroll in and out of everyone's houses and sometimes leave sheep pats, but these are used for kindling on the fires (so are useful).

People groom their sheep carefully and plait ribbons and beads in their wool. Sometimes they paint their horns.

The sheep are shod. Otherwise they provide wool, milk, and cheese. (It's quite good, once you get used to it. I *think* I have.)

The Chariot Towners can talk to the sheep (?), and apparently the sheep can talk to them (?) (all baaing). They do seem to understand each other with no trouble.

The guesthouse, where we've been staying, is hung with sheep-bells. And at night they light candles in the skulls of famous old sheep that died peaceful natural deaths. All the houses own such skulls. They're heirlooms.

The sheep graze the lawns; that's why they're so neat—the lawns, not the sheep.

The lord here is called the Shepherd.

Look, I've gone on and on about sheep.

You catch that here.

I've written everything up now to date.

We've been in the town five days.

Nemian *talked* to me today. I don't always see him, except at breakfast and/or supper. (Mounds of cheeses, milk-soups, salads, gritty bread. Beer—which gives me hiccups, to add to the bad impression I make.) Then he chats in baaas to the locals.

He said, when speaking to me, that I was being "astonishingly patient." Some choice.

Nemian is out all day with the Sheepers. He mentioned that other travelers come and go here, and soon we should be able to hitch a ride to somewhere else, perhaps where there are balloons and ballooneers. So *home* (to wherever his home is). The Sheepers like him, of course.

Desolate.

That sounds yukky. Just like some swooning princess of the House. *Ooh, I'm sooo desolate. . . .*

But I am.

I wander about and try to talk to some of the women milking sheep or making sheep-cheese or grooming sheep, or their kids. But we can't understand each other. I find I must simply amble past and give a quick cheery bleat, which they seem to take as a well-mannered and pleasant hello.

Nemian looks amazing again. We're able to wash our hair and have baths here, though the water is rather cold (one heated bucket to three not). He's dazzled them.

He did say the sheep are fierce and can fight lions. (Do they kick them with their shoes?)

Yes, we too have talked about the sheep.

Depressing.

Have now been here eight days, also depressing.

Depressed.

I'm fed up with me. How can I be depressed? I'm OUT IN THE WASTE. With NEMIAN. Almost.

Depressed.

My God—I know what that means, sort of—and shouldn't perhaps use it like that (?).

Daisy and Dengwi used to accuse me of being prissy because I wouldn't swear.

But the royalty at the house used to swear, and I hated them, so I didn't want to do anything they did that I could avoid doing.

(If Nemian swears, it doesn't seem so awful, I have to confess.)

And God is a kind of supreme supernatural figure—*not* human. I don't really understand. But I've caught the phrase from him, as I've caught this habit of talking about the sheep. . . .

Anyway. Nemian took me aside this evening, and it was sensational. We actually had a conversation, and for hours.

It began with supper. The rough wood tables are outside on a trip-you-up terrace of piled stones. The air was clear and fresh, and the sky got dark very slowly.

Everyone baa'd away. I sat there resignedly, only nodding with a quick smiling bleat when anyone greeted me: "Claaa-di-baa!"

When it got to the serious beer-drinking stage, Nemian rose and said to me, "Shall we go for a walk, Claidi? It's a fine night."

One or two of the Sheepers grinned and looked away. And I felt myself blush, which was infuriating. So I said, blankly, "Oh, I'm a bit tired. I think I'll just go in—" wishing I'd shut up.

"Let me persuade you," said Nemian, very gracious. "We can go up to the water pools. It's cool there. We have to talk, don't we?"

"All right," I charmingly snapped, got up, and stalked away up the terrace toward the big garden further along the track. Let Nemian catch up with *me,* for a change.

He didn't bother, of course. So then I had to pretend I'd gotten a stone in my shoe. It could have been true; my shoes are wearing out fast.

He sauntered up and asked me, all concern, "A stone?"

"Oh, I've shaken it out now."

"Look," said Nemian, "there's the moon."

We looked. And there it was. Since the storm it hadn't been properly visible. Now it looked clean and white, a half-round, like half a china clock-face but without hands or numbers.

"Poor Claidi," said Nemian. "Are you very angry with me? I've been selfish, haven't I?"

I had to remind myself here that although he is a prince, he thinks I'm a princess, at least a lady.

"Everyone's selfish," I said. "We have to be. How else can you get by?"

"My God, that's a judgment," said Nemian. "But you could be right. Can you forgive me, then, since you never expected anything much from me in the first place?"

I stole a look at him. Wonderful.

"Oh, yes," I said, as firmly as I could.

We walked into the garden.

The trees grouped around the pools, and the moon shone in each scoop of water as we went by.

He found a smooth stone where the white poppies grew, giving off a ghostly musk in the moon-watered dark.

"You see," he said, "I never expected the balloon to be shot down. Most of the places I passed over were so primitive they didn't have the means. I thought anywhere that was sophisticated would also have balloons itself. Perhaps be used to travelers. But then all those guns went off, and I thought I was going to be killed." He looked across the garden, bleakly. "It shook me up. And then—quite a reception your people gave me."

"You didn't seem . . . ," I hesitated, "upset at all."

"Oh come on, Claidi. That was an act. All noble and dashing. I was at my wits' end."

"So you lay down on the floor in front of everyone and went to sleep."

He frowned and cast me one slanting look.

"Actually, I passed out. I'd had a thump on the head getting into the tree. Rather than just fall over flat, I did it that way, noble and dashing again, and *very* careless. An act, as I said."

I was amazed. I felt strange. I can't describe it. I'm not sure I'd want to. I admired him, too. And . . . I felt guilty. Those times on the journey when he'd simply gone to sleep—had he been feeling ill? And he hadn't trusted me or was too proud to show it?

"Anyway," he now said, "I owe you my life." (The words I'd wanted before.) "I won't forget that, Claidi. I have an important position in my own city. You're going to have wonderful experiences there. You'll live in a luxury beyond anything in that House. And you'll be respected and honored."

All this sounded so bizarre, I couldn't take it in. Me? I didn't really care anyway. Just wanted him to go on talking.

So then he told me things about his city. I was impressed. Apparently it far outshines the ruin we'd glimpsed. A mighty river runs through, a mile or more wide, so in places you can't see across from one bank to the other. The water is pure as glass. The buildings rise to vast heights and are so tall they have sort of clockwork cages in them, they call lifters, which carry people from the ground floor to the top story.

He said they'd let off fireworks in celebration to welcome him home and to greet me. I've heard of fireworks but have never seen them. He said they're the colors of a rainbow, shot with gold and silver stars.

He said the city is governed from four great towers. The most powerful tower is the Tower of the Wolf. And he was born in this tower.

Then I remembered something he'd said in the Debating Hall, about being on a search or quest.

I asked him what that was. Nemian laughed. "Oh, I was just making it sound grand. I was only traveling."

I asked him where the red flowers grew, like the one he'd given to Jizania Tiger.

"In my city," he said. "We call them Immortals. After you pick them, they can live for months, even without water. You see, Claidi, even here the Waste isn't all a desert. And there are places where everything's . . . like your Garden. Only far better. Cooped up in that House, you must have found it very dull. You must have been very bored."

"It was all rules and senseless Rituals," I muttered.

"I can guess. Rules should *never* be boring," he oddly replied.

Then he leaned over and kissed me lightly on the lips.

I was so stunned, it meant almost nothing as it happened. So I have to keep recalling it, reliving it, that kiss. Trying to feel its staggering importance.

In a funny way it makes me think of when I scalded myself once as a child. For some moments I didn't feel a thing.

I'm still waiting to feel this. I know when I do, it will be colossal, sweeping through me like the pain of the scald, only not pain at all.

After he'd kissed me, we went on talking as if nothing at all had happened.

He knows so *much.* But then, I know *nothing.*

My head's bursting now with sketches of other places in the Waste—towns, cities, places where they use hot-air balloons for flight.

A couple of times, people had passed, more or less unnoticed by me. But then some sheep came wandering by, and after them some couples, saying to us shyly, "Brur'naa-baa," which apparently (for Nemian) means something like "Are we disturbing you?" And since they seemed awkward, and it's their garden, we got up and walked back to the guesthouse.

When I'd climbed up the ladder (no lifters here) to my narrow bed, piled with woolen blankets and scented by sheep, I was frozen.

Since I couldn't sleep at all, I've sat and written this down, and now I think that may be dawn, that light low in the window—or is it?

After I went down the ladder again, I peered over the sort of gallery there, where a famous sheepskull called *Praaa* burns a big candle all night.

Coming into the guesthouse was a crowd of men, mostly young. They were dressed in a rather fantastic way—skin trousers, tunics, boots, jackets with gilded buttons and tassels, and whirling cloaks. They had a lot of weapons, knives, and bows, and a couple of rifles.

The Sheepers were baaing and bowing.

Candlelight pranced on wild tanned faces.

I wondered if Nemian knew about this, and if it was going to be useful.

But really, they looked—the newcomers—like accounts I'd heard mumbled in tales in the House. Wandering bands of bandits from the Waste, criminals who'd stab you as soon as say hello.

I crept back up the ladder and huddled into bed.

Of course, the House told lies about the Waste. The Waste isn't like anything I was told—or not all of it. Or not all of what I've seen so far.

* * *

Finally I did go to sleep, because I was woken by a riotous row downstairs.

Was it the bandits? What were they doing? Murdering everyone and about to set fire to the guesthouse?

I scrambled up and got dressed, but just then one of the Sheeper women came in, bleated, and handed me some milk and a piece of bread.

You can imagine I wanted to ask her what was going on, but I couldn't speak the baa-language, and pointing anxiously at the floor and straining my eyebrows up and down only seemed to make her think *I* thought there were mice in the room. She hurried about looking under the wool rugs, found nothing, and bleating reassuringly, went out all smiles.

Presumably, as she'd brought the breakfast and was smiling, nothing too awful was taking place.

I ate. Then I washed my hair in what was left of last night's washing-water. I did it for something to do, really. The day was already hot, and I was soon almost dry. Someone knocked.

It was one of the Shepherd's men. He put a small chunk of wood into my hand. I bleat-thanked him and stood there stupidly. Then he pointed at the wood, and I saw something had been scratched on it. The Sheepers didn't have paper. Their writing seemed to have something to do with the patterns they make with the beads and things on the sheep. . . .

Anyway, the scratches read: "Go with him. Bring everything you want. We're leaving at once."

I gulped. "From Nemian?" I asked.

"N'baa miaan'baa," said the man. Or something like that. But nodding.

There wasn't much now to pack in the sack. This book, of course; the ink pencil I write with; the flask, even though I hadn't had a chance to refill it. A few bits and pieces.

I was scared. I had to face it now—the Waste still frightens me. Although apparently full of towns and tribes and settlements and even "sophisticated" cities, there were all those deserts and poisonous areas in between.

No time for qualms. I climbed down the ladder after the Sheeper.

In the main indoor room, where usually we'd eaten breakfast, the loud noise was going full tilt. Men were roaring and laughing, and someone was singing, and plates were smashing or just being used very roughly. Through a doorless doorway I caught a rush of tan cloak, flaming with gold fringes.

We went along the gallery, through a side door, and down an outside wooden stair.

In the dirt-floored side yard, a chariot had been hitched up with a team of four sheep with painted horns.

Nemian stood in the chariot with the driver. He made a brisk, princely movement with one arm, hurrying me to come over and get in.

"Nemian, I didn't fill—"

"Shut up, Claidi."

Nice.

Oh well. This was obviously not the time for a chat. If he wasn't the gentlemanly joy he'd been last night, we were probably in danger right now.

We left the yard slowly, not making much sound. I don't think the rowdy bandits would have heard us anyway.

I could hear *them.*

Bash went something, and *slam* went something else, and gales of happy laughter, and someone crying more or less in the language Nemian and I spoke, "You kill it properly, Blurn. Don't try to eat it alive."

Oh . . . *God,* I thought.

Outside the yard, the whip cracked, and the sheep—thank Whoever—kicked up their shod hooves. We went at quite a lick down the main track and not long after were let swiftly out by the gate of Chariot Town, at the feet of the pale hills.

TROUBLE ALWAYS FOLLOWS

Pattoo used to say, solemnly, "If you run away from trouble, it always follows."

Rather my impression, too. Though that never stopped me trying.

It's certainly what happened that morning.

After the first bolt up the rattling hill slope, the going got very steep. We had to slow down.

But looking back from quite a high spot, you could see some of the town and the gate, and nothing was going on there.

Nemian and the chariot driver had baa'd a bit. Now Nemian said to me, "You realize why we left?"

"They were dangerous, the men who arrived."

"According to the Sheepers, that's putting it mildly," said Nemian. "They're all mad, those wandering people. Theirs is a hell of a life." He smiled. "Tempting, really. To live by skill and courage. One long adventure. But pretty foul too. No comforts. And they can't afford any politenesses."

Neither had he, I thought. Which summed it up: In constant danger lay constant rudeness. What an extremely petty thought.

It's just . . . Well, I've had enough of people treating me like rubbish. I'd innocently thought that would change. And last night . . .

Last night was apparently last night.

The sheep trotted for a while where the ground leveled, then clambered, the chariot lurching, on the steeper parts.

I couldn't be bothered to explain now how I'd had no chance to fill the water flask. I suppose I could have used the hair-wash-water, all soapy, with hairs in it. Hmm.

"Don't sulk, Claidi," said Nemian. "Did you like it there so much? How silky your hair looks today."

"Where are we going to now?" I asked with thin dignity.

"The Sheeper will see us on to a hill village up here. We'll have to find our own way from there. There may be a cart or something we can barter for."

I knew about barter, the exchanging of one thing for another, although in the House it never happened. *Buying* things didn't either, but I'd heard of that too, and Nemian had mentioned (last night) that his city on the wide river used coins, money.

The Sheepers hadn't seemed to want any returns. They just seemed friendly. I hoped that would keep them safe with the bandit band.

The hills were opening out all around us now and weren't as ugly as I'd anticipated. Very little grew on them, however—an occasional bush with whitish fluff, a type of short pale grass. In the closer distance, they looked soft, like pillows.

We pulled up after about an hour, and the sheep chomped the grass. Nemian and the Sheeper shared some beer, but I didn't fancy it.

I was looking back down the hills when I heard—we all heard—a beating *clocking* sound, ringing from the hills' backs.

Suddenly, over a slope to the left, precisely where we didn't expect them, five men appeared, less than a quarter of a mile off.

I managed an especially unsuitable idiot question.

"What are *those*?"

"Horses," said Nemian. "And the others, *on* the horses, are the mad knife-men from the town."

I noted no one was trying to start the sheep and chariot. Then I realized we'd never get away, for the bandits had seen us. I saw their white grins flash, as all the buckles and bangles and buttons and *knives* were doing. They smacked the horses' sides lightly, and these new beasts came racing at us, like a wind or a fire.

(I'd never seen a horse before that. In the House the chariots were drawn by—you guessed it—slaves. The horses are rather beautiful, aren't they? If you know horses. The long heads and the hair flowing back, just as the bandits' long hair flowed back.)

In about ten seconds, so it seemed, there they were on the hillside with us, all reds and tans, and metal-and-tooth flash.

"Couldn't let you go," said one, "without saying hi."

They laughed. They had an accent—intense, guttural, and somehow extra-threatening.

Their politeness was unsettling not because it wasn't real, but because, as Nemian had said, they couldn't afford politeness.

Nemian, now, said nothing.

The Sheeper didn't seem talkative either.

The horses were polished as any floor.

One of the bandits swung off his horse. He walked over on long legs.

"Not from these parts?"

Nemian said, "No."

"South? Peshamba?"

Nemian said, "Yes, we're heading for Peshamba."

The bandit leaned on the side of our chariot, companionable. From inside his shirt, he drew a small glassy thing—some sort of charm? He gazed down at it in silence, as if all alone. How odd. Another bandit, still mounted, craned over as if to see. This other one gave a sudden whoop (which made me jump). He drew out his (ghastly) knife and flipped it in the air, catching it gently in his *teeth.*

The bandit leaning on the chariot took no notice. He closed the charm in his fist and put it away. Then he looked straight into my eyes.

His were dark, like his long hair, which hung to his waist. He was the color of strong tea with a dash of milk. A color that matched the horse he'd ridden. I'd thought he would be older. I never saw anyone so—I don't know what to say—*terrible.*

I shrank.

To my surprise, he at once looked away and right at Nemian.

"Any money on you?"

"Money," said Nemian.

"They use it in Peshamba, or whatever big place you're headed for," helpfully explained the bandit.

"You want some money," guessed Nemian. From one of his host of pockets he took a flat leather case and offered it to the bandit.

The bandit accepted it, opened it.

The bandit and I both stared with curiosity at the weird turquoise-green leaves of paper that were revealed.

Then the dark *eyes* glanced at me sidelong. I felt sick and sidled back.

"Right," said the bandit. "Well, I can't use this." (He sounded as if he was saying it wasn't good enough!) "Any coins?"

"Sorry," said Nemian. He didn't seem worried. Just well-mannered and willing to talk, as though the mad bandit killers were perfectly normal people met in a garden.

One of the other bandits (not the one with the knife) called, "Tell the tronker to shake out his coat. And what's that bird got hidden?"

Tronker? Bird?

The chariot-leaning bandit gave him a casual look.

"I don't think they're good for much," he said pityingly. Oh, we'd let him down properly.

"Come off it, Argul," said the other bandit. "*She's* all right, that bird, eh?" (Ah. The "bird" was me.)

All the old tales of the Waste raced through my bubbling mind—horrible stories, with death at the end of them.

But I glared up at the talking bandit on the horse. I felt so terrified I thought I was going to be sick or cry, but instead I screamed at him, *"You touch me and I'll bite your nose off!"*

There was a shocked silence.

Then all at once they all burst out laughing.

This included the chariot-leaning bandit, the other four bandits, and Nemian. *Nemian!*

Even the Sheeper was smiling—perhaps thinking we'd all now be best friends.

And I was appalled. What had I said . . . done?

Nevertheless my fingers had curled. My nails felt strong and sharp. How revolting it would be to bite that bandit—but my teeth were snapping.

I'd slapped Jade Leaf; I'd escaped the House. I wouldn't be stopped, not anymore.

The bandit called Argul shifted away from the chariot. "Better watch out," he told the other bandits, "she means what she says." He handed the leather container with money back to Nemian. "I can see," said Argul to Nemian, "you've got enough on your hands with that bird you've got there. She scares *me* all right."

"Yes, yes," warbled the other bandits, "he's got real problems there."

Then the bandit leader spun around, ran at his horse so I thought he meant to knock it right over, and leaped—*leaped*—up the side of it, as if it were only a little still rock.

Next second he was astride the horse. And unruffled, the horse looked down at me from a dark smooth eye.

"So long. Have a lovely day!" the bandits cheerfully called as they galloped away back down the hill.

We didn't get to the hill village until late in the afternoon.

Nemian said nothing about the bandits. He had said all he wanted, earlier, when he told me they were mad.

Somehow I kept thinking they'd appear again, mad minds changed, to rob, terrify, shame, and slaughter us. They didn't.

We had some sheep cheese and lettuce and some beer. I got hiccups.

I was fed up—in a mood, as Daisy used to say.

The sky turned deep gold, and we rumbled over yet one more hilltop, and there was the village. It wasn't a thrilling sight. Huddles of lopsided huts all over the place, a huge rambling rubbish heap you could smell from far off. Dogs wandered, snarling. A few sullen human faces were raised to glare at us.

It was as unlike the friendly Sheepers' town as seemed possible, as if specially formed to be off-putting.

Well, I think it was. I'm writing this last section at night, in a sort of barn place, which stinks and is full of enormous rats. Actually the rats are rather handsome, better than the hill-villagers. Quite easy, that.

They behaved foully as soon as we got there. Some stared at us in the sheep-chariot, and some just went in. They'd have banged their doors if they could, but such doors as they have would have fallen off.

Presently a fat gobbling sort of man arrived and baa'd at the Sheeper. Nemian said to me he baa'd so badly the Sheeper obviously could hardly understand, and Nemian not at all.

Even so, the Sheeper told Nemian, baaing properly, that we'd "be all right here." And yes, they'd let us have a cart with a mule—what is that?—either tomorrow or the day after.

They are called Feather Tribe. They like birds?

Naturally they wanted paying? No, said the Sheeper, apparently. I saw he looked embarrassed. He had to leave us here (to go back to his own so-much-pleasanter place). Nemian didn't comment. I couldn't.

We got out, and the Sheeper went into a hut with the awful fat gobbly person. (Later the Sheeper reappeared loaded with sacks of something, got in his chariot, and went off, not even waving good-bye.) Nemian and I were sort of shoveled, by a couple of revolting women, into one of the barns. This one.

I thought Nemian would throw up at once. His face went white and his eyes went white and his nostrils *curled.*

"Oh, Claidi. What can I say? What will you think?"

"It's not your fault," I said. Grudgingly, I have to admit. I didn't think it *was* his fault. But in a way it was. I mean, he'd gone "traveling" and then involved us both in all this. I really mean I was angry with him. Love is like this, so the songs of the House used to say. You adore them one minute, then want to throttle them.

Anyway, he didn't hang about. He left me sitting on the smelly straw and went to find someone to do something. He didn't come back.

At first I wasn't worried. Then I was worried. Going to the barn door, I saw Nemian in conversation with the Gobbly Fat One. (Nemian must speak this language too.) They were both drinking something and yowling away with amusement. Typical.

I sat on the stony ground outside the barn.

Soon a dog wandered up and bared yellow fangs at me for no reason. Stupidly, I snapped, "Oh stop it, you fool." Then I thought it'd leap for my throat. But it whined and ran off with its tail on the ground.

Nemian and the GFO—their leader?—went striding off on what looked like a tour of the village. (This dung-heap goes back to my grandmother's day. This hole in the roof was made by my great grandfather's pet pigeon, which ate too much and so fell through.)

A woman came up near evening and plunked a bowl down beside me.

"Er, excuse me. What is it?" I asked fearfully.

"Germonder pop," said she. Or so it seemed.

I tried the germonder pop. And it was OBSCENE. So no dinner for Claidi.

There are no lamps in the barn, though the huts lit up later. The moon is very bright, and I've written this by the light of it.

The village Feather Tribe are making dreadful sounds. Are they eating, or talking, or what? It's sickening.

(I saw Nemian again, about an hour ago. He wandered by with the GFO and saluted me. He seemed happy, enchanted by these Featherers, some of whom were now trailing him in a merry group. Was he drunk, or just being tactful? Or is he . . . is he useless? When the bandits were there, I never felt for one moment Nemian could save me, as in the old stories the hero always does the heroine, but am I even a heroine? Some chance.)

* * *

Retreated back into the barn. I might as well go to sleep. Deadly day. Yes, of course I should be glad and pleased I'm on this big adventure. But I have to assure you, the smell in here is enough to make the boldest flinch.

Outside, it seems to be getting brighter and noisier. The moon? Is the moon noisy? Who knows?

I keep thinking of that glass charm the bandit had, the one who leaned on the chariot.

I think they were the end, being so insulting about me (bird! problems!) when I was only desperate to defend myself, which nobody else would.

FLIGHT

The roof goes up so high, it's hard to believe it's a wagon. The bumping helps, though, to remind me.

It's difficult to write here. I'll leave this, I think, until we stop.

Have to note the colors in the roof—deepest crimson, and purple with wild greens. The pictures are of horses and dogs, mostly. And a sun done in raw gold, dull with time.

They've had these wagons forever.

Bump.

I'll wait.

When I'd been asleep in the Feather Tribe's barn just long enough to be confused if woken, and not long enough to have had a rest, thumps and yodels started and someone was shaking me. (I believe I said before, that's a terrible way to wake anyone.)

I shot up, and there were all these Feather Tribe people, looking entirely changed. That is, they were beaming and nodding at me, and one of them was flapping a feathery thing about in front of me, like an enormous wing.

Not amazingly, I sat staring.

Then Nemian appeared through the crowd.

"It's all right, Claidi. It's a gift."

"What? What is?"

"That dress."

"Is it a dress?"

"It's made out of feathers sewn on wool. It'll be rather hot. I'm sorry. But they seem to want you to have it. There's some sort of festival tonight."

"Oh."

"They want us to go with them to some shrine in the hills."

"What's a *shrine?*"

"Don't worry now. The women will dress you, and then we'll go with them. We need their help, don't we? So we have to join in, be gracious."

I was only more bewildered by this explanation.

Anyway, he and the men had gone, and there were only these four or five large women intent on putting me into the feather-dress. I'd been clothed by force quite often in childhood. I knew it was safer not to resist.

My God (Am I using that right? Think so—seems to be a sort of exclamation used in alarm or irritation), that dress. I think I looked like a gigantic white chicken. Also, it *was* hot, and it itched.

Having clad me, the women were leading me to the door, but I snatched up my bag when I saw one of them fumbling with it.

Supposing they could read? And read *this?* (Which was far-fetched. They barely seemed able to talk.)

Outside, the whole village had assembled with torches.

They were clapping their hands and now started to sing. I think it was singing.

Frankly I wasn't sure if I preferred this jolly, festive side to them. I preferred the scowling, standoffish way they'd been earlier. Now they kept touching my arms and hair, or my back, and I hated it.

I shouted at Nemian, but he only waved. He was with the GFO at the procession's front. I say "procession," since this is what it became.

We walked quite briskly out of the village and up a stony track into the hills.

A few dogs ran after, and the festive villagers threw stones at them until they turned back. Sweet people. No wonder the dogs were so dodgy and cowed.

These hills are strange. The whole of the Waste is strange, of course, to me. But all the parts are bizarre in different ways. They all have a different character.

The hills . . . are like a place where something intense, perhaps heavy, had been, which now was blown away. They had a weird beauty in the moon-and-torchlight. Where the grass is thick, the hillsides seem covered with velvet, and then bare pieces strike through, harsh and hard. Also there are bits that are worn thin, translucent, and you seem to see through them, down into darkness.

It was all uphill.

The Gobbly Fat One, who was lord, had to keep having a breather, so then we all got one. They passed around a putrid drink. Luckily, when I shook my head, no one forced me to try it.

Inappropriately I recalled climbing all the stairs of the high tower at the House. Perhaps when we got to wherever we were going, the view would be worth the climb.

And it was.

Suddenly we were up on a broad, flat table of land.

They all gave a glad bellow and stamped and clapped and "sang" again, and more drink went around, and I thought if they kept pushing it past and breathing it over me, I'd probably puke all over them and serve them right.

But then they drew off, and I looked up.

A colossal sky was overhead, the biggest sky I'd ever seen. It was quite *blue,* with mottled wisps of cloud, but mostly encrusted with masses of diamond stars. In the midst of it, the moon was at its highest point—so white it burned—and was held in a smoky, aquamarine ring.

Dizzy, I looked down. The hills had drawn back, and in front there was nothing but the moon-bleached flat of land, which seemed to stop in midair.

I thought, I bet it drops off there, into a chasm.

This was correct.

Over to one side there were some caves, and the Feather Tribe villagers were scrambling into them with raucous yells.

You can guess that I wasn't keen to follow, and no one insisted.

To take my mind off the itchy feather dress, I gazed up again at the stars.

I felt I could float right out of myself and up to them, and in among the drifts of night there would be adventures beyond anything ever found below.

When I looked back this time, Nemian was there, gazing at me. "You have such a graceful neck," he said to me.

All the starry adventures faded. I was happy to be in this one.

"Thank you."

"The stars are wonderful, aren't they?" he said. And then, "But I'd think your favorite time would be dusk." He hesitated and said, "Because of your mother."

A lot of noise was coming from the caves, and down the slopes behind us, I could hear some (big?) animal scuffling, and who knew what sort of animal, out here. But all that was instantly rinsed off my mind.

"My mother?"

"Because," he said, "of her name. Twilight."

I stood there. "I didn't . . . know."

He said, "But . . . didn't you? I understand you lost her when you were young, but even so . . ."

I must pretend something. I was a princess of the House. Of course I knew my mother's name. Or, why pretend?

I said, "No one told me. Who told *you?*"

"The Princess Jizania told me."

And not me? Had she forgotten to?

I said humbly, feeling numb with *feeling,* "It's a good name."

(Nemian was frowning, about to ask something. I braced myself.)

At that moment the Featherers began to erupt out of the caves. The torches jounced and splashed the dark with light.

Peculiar contraptions were being trundled along. I saw wheels and . . . wings. As the crowd swarmed around us, Nemian said, "Claidi, I really need to ask you about—" But then we were being swarmed on along the flat table of stone.

"Ask away," I shouted.

"It's all right," he shouted back. "It'll have to wait. There's this thing they do here. The chief told me. They fly."

"Oh, I see."

Of course I didn't. And besides, all this seemed irrelevant after the sky and my mother's dusk-sky name.

When everyone bundled to a sort of halt, I idly watched about six of the Featherers being strapped into the wheeled and winged structures.

There was a kind of seat, and pedals to move the wheels. Their arms were fitted into the wings, which were made of wood, I thought, and covered with feathers, like my gown. It all looked absurd.

The crowd was calling out a single phrase over and over again, everyone dead drunk and grinning from ear to ear, and the men on the winged things raised and lowered the wings with a dry, creaking sound.

"What are they calling?" I said to Nemian, not really caring.

"Well, Claidi, you see, they pedal over the cliff here, and then they flap their wings."

"Oh. Sounds daft to me."

"In a way. It's a festival to honor their god."

"You mean God?"

"Not quite."

"If they go . . . over the cliff? . . . then isn't that dangerous?"

"Exceedingly. The flying action somewhat lessens the fall. But they usually break an arm or a leg. That's what they're shouting: *Break a leg!* It means 'Good luck.' "

My mouth, trained to it by now, fell open on a reflex.

The pedalers were off anyway, thundering forward along the flat, arms and wings already vigorously waving.

And each one came to the edge, the edge of white cliff and diamond-dazzled night—space—and *rolled off.*

Everyone else, also Nemian and I, ran to the edge and peered after them.

There they went, down and down. In the air, they flailed, flapping and spinning, grotesque and funny, and frightful.

And one by one, they hit the ground far below, each with a crash and a scream. Clouds of what looked like steam came foaming up.

The Featherers were cheering. I was so frightened to see, I couldn't look away.

But one by one all the men crawled from the shambles of their flying machines, which were all in bits now.

"Only two broken arms, apparently," said Nemian, turning from the GFO, who was burping and guffawing next to us. "They take all year to build their craft and one minute to smash them. You can see, though, Claidi, it's a dust-pit down there. Like the wings, that helps cushion the fall."

I was going to reply with something witty, or just pathetic, when I found all the villagers were touching me again. Some had hold of my arms. They were tugging and hoisting, lifting me off my feet.

At last I lashed out. It wasn't any good.

"Nemian, make them *stop*!"

Nemian looked startled. He said something in their awful language and then turned and said it to the GFO.

But the GFO just gobbled and slapped Nemian on the back, and offered him the jar of drink again.

From Nemian's face I finally realized what was meant to happen now.

Whether they thought it wouldn't hurt, that I'd only *break a leg,* I didn't know. Or whether I was the best sacrifice at hand, a strayed traveler there exactly on the right night of the festival, I didn't know either.

Whatever it was, wingless in my feather dress, I was about to be slung over the cliff.

I screamed and kicked. I think I managed to ram my feet into someone's stomach. But it wasn't much of an achievement really. It wouldn't help.

And Nemian had been grabbed now and was on the ground. I couldn't see him through their great stomping unbroken-unfortunately legs.

My bag—with this book—dropped back on the ground. I lost sight of it.

I was screeching and wailing. (You'll understand.)

And then, through all the din, the blur of panic and fear, a kind of dark explosion tore. All at once I was flying, not off the cliff but through the air, until I hit the ground, which was only the flat hilltop. Then someone hauled me up, and I landed on something both harder and softer. . . .

Inexplicable. I kicked again and the something caught my foot.

"Here, you morbof, don't kick my okking eye out."

Like surfacing from a depth of water, I rose and snarled into an unknown face. And yet, not the face of a Featherer. He was black as ebony, and he laughed even as he prevented me from clawing at his left eye.

"Watch it, chura. I'm here to *save* you."

His hair was long, in tight braids, about ninety of them. How magnificent. But I didn't care. I tried to rip them out. Then he got my hands. He said, and he was running now, carrying me with him somehow, "Look, chura, you're all right. We're going downhill, not off the cliff."

It was true.

"My name isn't Chura."

He looked vague but unconcerned.

"No," he said, "the Sheepers said you were Claadibaa."

"*Claidi.*"

He laughed again. "Fine. Claidi. You don't know, do you? *Chura* only means 'darling.' "

We arrived where? It was a hillside.

Up there, torch flash, howls, cries, the rasp of metal clashing, and a sharp bang—the noise of shot, a gun.

"Nemian!" I cried. "My *book*—"

"Book's here, Claidi," said this fantastic being whom I'd tried to disfigure. "Nemian? *That* him? He's all right."

He handed me this book. Not the sack—that was gone. Didn't matter. I clasped the book and sobbed. Sorry, but I did. Only once or twice.

My rescuer kindly patted me. "Everything's all right."

Apparently everything was all right.

"They were going to throw me over," I unnecessarily reminisced.

He said, "Drink this." I pushed it away, but it was pushed back, and it was only absolutely delicious water. As I gulped, he said, "We had to wait, you see. Be sure. Make certain we hadn't gotten the wrong end of the stick. So we followed you up, hung around the Feather village. Argul said, let them—the Tribe, that is—get drunk, make it easier, seeing we were a bit outnumbered. He ran straight in to get you just then, only he was sort of detained—a couple of blokes with knives. So I had the lucky pleasure of getting you away. I'm Blurn."

You'll think I'm dotty. I instantly remembered the shouts at the Sheeper guesthouse: *Kill it properly, Blurn. Don't eat it alive.*

Somehow I kept quiet. He'd saved me. There are limits.

Men were streaming down the hill. All bandits. Oh well.

Argul stood by the spot where they'd planted one torch left over from the Throwing-Claidi-off-the-Cliff Festival.

He stared at me, his dark eyes much darker than night. And not so friendly. (Blurn had told me Argul's name. I think I already knew, and that he was their leader.)

"Thanks," I said to Argul. But that was mean. I added, "I owe you my life." Just what I'd thought Nemian ought to say.

But Nemian was over in a wagon, lying down, rather the worse for wear.

Argul nodded coldly.

"Don't mention it. We went out of our way. But I'm sure you two can pay us back for our efforts."

With what? I glared at him. "Do you only help people in order to get a reward?"

Some of them laughed—I realized at once, only at my cheek.

Argul glanced around anyway, and they stopped.

He looked back at me.

"No, Miss Nuisance, I don't. I wouldn't normally bother."

I'd been scared of him, but honestly, nearly being thrown to my death had made me a little braver. For the moment.

"I'm so glad," I said sarcastically.

"See if it lasts," said Argul.

He was the Grand Leader of the Mighty Bandits(!). He'd leaned on the Sheeper chariot, and gazed at that glass charm, and mocked us for not being worth robbing. And all the time waiting to see if I was, as the Sheepers must have let slip, the chosen Feather sacrifice. Making sure it was true, following, watching, seeing if he'd really have to bother to rescue me.

I felt angry and silly in that feather-itch dress. I felt alone. But one always is, I suppose.

THE BANDIT CAMP ON THE MOVE

Until morning, we waited in the hills. They'd made a camp there, the five bandits. They'd come on ahead, and all the rest had to catch up.

All night they came riding in, on horses, with wagons and dogs—these very well trained, alert and glossy and quiet.

In the increasingly enormous camp, there was one big central fire. They sat around it. Unlike the dogs, they made a lot of noise, just as I remembered.

The Featherers had fled. Probably not all of them, judging from the sounds of knives and rifles I'd heard.

Blurn had told me, matter-of-factly, that the Sheepers had sold us—me—to the Featherers. I was *barter.* Worse, the Sheepers had actually been out raiding to catch a girl sacrifice for the Featherers. No wonder they didn't mind taking Nemian and me to their town. (I recall the welcome, the drums, whistles, and poppies.)

I feel awful about this. I'd rather liked the Sheepers. They seemed innocent . . . and kind.

The bandits, of course, seemed horrifying, and they were the ones who rescued me.

Obviously they too have a (probably sinister) reason for this. I must be on my guard. I've learned the hard way not to trust anyone out here. One always learns the hard way. Is there any other?

During the night I went to see Nemian. There are bandit women, too, and one had given me bandit girl's clothes—trousers, tunic, even some bracelets with *gold coins* hanging from them, and coin earrings! I was touched, but I think all the women look like that here, and it was as automatic on her part to give me ornaments to provide me with covering.

Nemian was sitting on some rugs in one of the bandit wagons. He didn't recognize me, just glanced up and said, "I'd appreciate some more beer, if you can spare it."

"*More* beer? You'll burst," I said, annoyed.

He flicked me his *look* then. Smiled.

"Claidi. I always know it's you by your gentle manner."

Someone had apparently kicked him in the ribs though. And there was a purple bruise on his cheek. (Is he accident prone? No, that's unfair. He'd been trying to stop them from throwing me off the cliff. He hadn't been able to, but that wasn't his fault.)

A girl came in with the beer anyway, without being asked. He was so lovely to her, I was jealous and left the wagon. (He seemed to have forgotten he'd wanted to question me about not knowing the name of my mother.)

Apparently I'm bad-tempered and jealous. A pretty awful person. I never knew this before. But then, I was never in love before. Am I? In love? I don't know what I am. Or who.

Argul, the leader, had gone into a tent and was soon joined by his second-in-command, who is Blurn.

I saw the bandit who'd whooped and caught the knife in his teeth. He's called Mehmed. Every time he sees *me,* he *laughs.*

I'm not sure I'm so pleased to be here, really.

Finally I went to the wagon that another woman said I could sleep in, and when I woke up, we were traveling. The wagon was still empty apart from me. I'd thought I'd have to share it.

I put my head out, and we were coming down from the hills into yet another dusty desert. It looked so dreary. I tried to write a bit of this but gave up because of the bumpy ride.

After that, I admired the paintings on the high leather roof and thought how Blurn had told me the wagons are old but in good repair since they're always cared for. He said each family had one and passed it on. The horses and dogs are mostly the same, these descendants of others from centuries ago. Blurn said that the word *Hulta,* which is *a camp,* also means *Family* to the bandits. To be part of the bandit camp is to be part of the bandit family. But it's a family always on the move.

I feel insulted, as if I've been made a fool of, but I'm not sure why. I found out, you see, the wagon I've been traveling in is Argul's own.

There were, of course, chests in it and pieces of wagon furniture, rugs and stools and jars. There were even some books I found—yes, I was nosing about, but not much. I recognized the language in only two of them. I'd also noticed knives and scabbards and shirts and boots and things lying around in corners. This morning, so as to make conversation with the bandit woman who came by with some food, I asked, "Where are the others who live in this wagon?" And she said, "It's Argul's wagon."

She did add that he rides a horse by day and prefers the tent at night, and only uses the wagon now and then, but I felt immensely uncomfortable, as if he'd played a joke on me. Also in some way labeled me as a possession. I can't think why he would want me. Does he imagine I'm valuable? That must be it. Nemian has said something. I'm a princess from a House. So it's threatening as well.

Naturally I got out instantly.

Nemian was elegantly riding a horse by now, talking to the bandits as if they're old friends. He does seem to love being with new people. Is this a nice quality or rather shallow of him? And does it mean he has totally lost interest in me because I'm not *new* anymore? Doubtless.

Then Blurn appeared and said that there was a mule for me to ride.

Only after I'd managed to get onto the mule—nearly fell off both sides twice—did I think to demand, "Is this mule *Argul's?*"

"Nope," said Blurn, "my aunt's."

"Then doesn't your aunt—"

"She's got plenty more," said Blurn, as if we were discussing pairs of slippers.

The mule is a pain.

It has an adorable face and wonderful eyelashes, but it kicks out at things and *wriggles*. Nemian says a mule doesn't wriggle. It does, it does. I've tried to feed it and groom it to show it I'm worthwhile and it ought to like me. But it takes no notice, just tries to kick me as I turn my back, and then wriggles as I try to swing gracefully into its saddle.

Needless to say, passing bandits, men and women both, find this exquisite fun.

"There goes Claidi-baa again," they say as I plummet off in the dust. And that's another thing. They keep calling me by a Sheeper version of my name. After what the Sheepers did, I find that extra aggravating.

Tonight there was a Hulta council.

We all gathered about the huge central fire, from which the cook-pots had been removed, though some vegetables and loaves went on baking in the hot ashes.

Argul strode out of his tent. He looked . . . astonishing.

I mean, he did look the way a leader should. A young king. Polished black hair and eyes, tall and lean and tawny. He was covered in gold fringes and coins, and silver rings and things. Barbaric, I'm sure the House would have said. A "barbarian." Nemian was smiling a little. But then, one of the prettiest bandit girls was sitting next to Nemian, as she always seems to be now.

The council was because we were all going to Peshamba. The bandits hadn't been there before, or not for generations, although they knew of the city. (At first I'd been confused and thought Peshamba was Nemian's city, but it isn't. I'd thought *all* cities had crumbled or been blown over. Wrong, obviously. The House told so many lies to us. Or else the House was extremely ignorant. Both?)

Anyway, the route to Peshamba is long and passes through this dust desert, or there's another way, across something called the Rain Gardens. The council was to decide, by vote, which way we would go.

I'm impressed, but skeptical. If Argul is leader, doesn't he ever lead? What's the point of having a leader if everyone has a hand in every decision?

(Blurn said they'd voted on rescuing me. I assumed they all must have been in favor, but apparently only half had. Now when I talk to them, I wonder which ones didn't think I was worth the trouble. I don't blame them. But yuk. In the end only five bandits went after the Featherers.)

I didn't have the nerve to ask Blurn, Why *did* Argul bother? Afraid of what the answer will be. Oh, we're going to sell you as a mule acrobat in Peshamba or something.

They talked about the Rain Gardens. It was vague. None of them are sure quite what happens there, although travelers tend to avoid the place. It does rain.

Personally, anything rather than this dust bowl.

But I didn't get a vote, nor Nemian.

He didn't seem put out. Princes are above such things? I'm only a pretend princess, aren't I? Or was it less interesting than the bandit girl combing his hair? Hmm.

The vote was for the Gardens.

Afterward, the bandits sat on, drinking. Some of them talked and played with their dogs. Several had stolen female dogs from the Featherer village. I was really glad, because already these dogs are being cared for and looking healthier and more calm.

This in mind, I went to see my mule. Also so as not to have to look at Nemian as the girl plaited blue beads into his golden lion's mane. Come on, Nemian. That's what the Sheepers did with the sheep.

The mule, of course, wasn't pleased to see me.

I stood over it, rubbing its nose—it does have a nice nose—and offering it some mule food.

"It's Claidi," I said firmly. "Dear Claidi that you know and love. Giving you a delicious snack you don't deserve."

"You expect too much of it," said someone. "With a horse, you'd have a better chance."

It wasn't Blurn, whom I halfway trust—must remember I mustn't—so I turned.

There stood Argul the Bandit Leader, gleaming from the distant fire and lamps at his back, as if rimmed in gold.

What should I do? Grovel because I owe him my life? Or be rude because I know I'm being used?

You'll have guessed.

"Well, since I don't have a horse, that's such a help, isn't it?"

"I'm surprised you haven't taken one," said Argul. "Just bite someone's nose off and steal his mount. Why not?"

"You're the practiced bandits, not me."

"You could learn."

I thought, I'm Princess Claidissa Star. My mother was called Twilight Star. I raised my head.

"Why did you save my life?"

"Why did I?"

Inside my raised head I thought, *Yes, and I spent my days as a slave.*

I looked down.

Argul said, "You can have a horse instead of a mule. Starting to ride will be uncomfortable at your age, but it'll be worth it. Want to try?"

Seeing me slipping and rolling off the mule wasn't fun enough. Off a horse might really be a laugh.

"No, thank you."

"Tronking hell," said Argul.

He turned his back and strode away. His hair swung like a wave. The cloak swung, and gold disks chimed on it. Musical.

I wish I'd said yes. And what did he mean, my *age,* as if I were thirty or something.

A long time has gone by since I wrote that. A lot's been happening, in all kinds of ways.

Something needs to be said about the bandits and the Hulta.

It's awkward.

The House depended on life being carved in stone, and the rules of life were iron. You couldn't make changes. You couldn't change your mind about anything important.

But I think life isn't about that. It's *about* changing. If you grow, you change—don't you? A kid becomes an adult. A puppy becomes a dog. You can't stay still, and you can't stay always thinking one thing only, especially when you see it wasn't right. It was a mistake.

But you know all this. I bet you do.

It's just . . . I didn't. Or did I?

First of all, I have to describe a morning, still in the floury desert, and me coming along to the fire, and there's Blurn, stuffing himself with the nut porridge the bandits often have. And Mehmed the knife-thrower yells, "Kill it, Blurn!" And another man, Ro, shouts, "Make sure it's dead!"

And Claidi stands there, seeing for the first time that what she heard through a window wasn't something horrible, but just a *joke.*

They were joking about Blurn's method of eating. And then Blurn turned and made other appalling comments on Mehmed's and Ro's methods of eating (which, admittedly, are worse).

So, you don't always learn the hard way. You can learn a silly, funny way.

Which, too, is another lesson.

I'm getting tangled up.

For example. Since leaving A's wagon, I've slept each night in the open on a pillow with a blanket, supplied to me by the woman who'd come by with the food.

She must have seen I was nervous.

She said, "There aren't many insects here." Then, noting I was still unnerved, "No lions. But if they come around, the lookout will know." *Then,* seeing me *still* worried, she added, "If you don't want a man friend, no one will disturb you." "*Oh,*" I said. She looked me up and down and said, "Where you come from must have been a bad place. People don't creep up on people here. We're not leopards. If you like someone, tell him. If not, you can be private."

Did I believe her? No.

I was panicky and couldn't sleep.

I *had* a man friend. I had Nemian.

Correction. I didn't have a man friend. Or a friend?

In the House, people had fallen for each other (never me). But you had to be so careful. (My parents, for instance—exiled for being in love and having a child.)

One heard such stories about the Waste. And *bandits* . . .

They're all right. No one intrudes.

Probably they just don't notice me. I'm so bad-tempered, boring, jealous, tacky.

I saw Nemian one evening, one *twilight,* talking to the bandit girl. They were gazing into each other's eyes. I felt a sort of pain, sharp and cold-hot. I slunk off.

Next day, a horse arrived. Blurn brought it.

Can't help this. I like Blurn. It isn't just that he rescued me, he's just . . . I just *like* him. And he's with Argul a lot. So . . . I don't know. Somehow it helps. (Blurn, by the way, has a girlfriend. She's terrific. Anyway I don't mean I like Blurn *that* way.)

The horse. Let me tell you about the horse. It was blue-black, like the sky that night. And it had thinking black eyes. It stood there, thoughtful and beautiful, its silk tail swishing faintly, and Blurn said, "He says, for you."

"Who says?" As if I didn't know.

"Him. Argul. This is a female horse, a mare. She's bred down from"—couldn't follow—"something of something-something line. She can run like the wind, but she's gentle as honey."

Naturally I was about to refuse, but the horse, the mare, made a soft noise down her nose. I went up to her and stroked her face.

"Not scared, are you?" approved Blurn.

"She's wonderful."

"Hey, Claidi," said Blurn. He gave me his huge white smile. I felt happy. I'd done something right, at last.

And the horse—she's called Sirree—is a dream.

She's so patient with me. You can tell she knows I'm learning, finding out. But when I feed her or talk to her, she *listens.* Absolute agony, though. I might as well be thirty. The bandit woman—she also has a name, Teil—explained that it will be awful for a while. Your body has to get used to getting into, and holding, this position. It isn't too bad during the day. But when I totter off, and in the morning—Ow! Ow! Ow!

Don't care.

That mule gave me a look. Blurn said mules always do. They have Mule Ideas. But horses understand people, as dogs and wolves do, and often cats and birds.

Then we came across some travelers in the desert.

In a valley, about five low-slung carts, and some *thing* under lots of sacks, being pulled by dogs.

When Argul's outriders spotted this, and we (me) heard and rode along the line of wagons to see, I thought, Oh, now A's bandits will tear down and rob and murder everyone.

However, the bandits just went down and helped put a wheel back on one of the carts.

The dog teams were in fine tail-wagging condition. The bandits laughed and mucked about among the other travelers. Sounds of this jollity drifted up the valley.

They came to supper.

Speech was a problem. Hardly anyone spoke their language. Argul did a bit.

Among the sacks they had a big stone statue. They were taking it somewhere, for some reason.

No one was robbed.

Argul *gave* them supplies: bread and dried oranges, rice and beer.

The Hulta do rob people. They came after Nemian and me and the Sheeper, and wanted money. (Although A said he couldn't use it and gave it back. And they were following us to see if I was going to be sacrificed. . . .) They *do* kill people. Unless they just frightened the Featherers off.

Dawn broke, and the travelers went away with their statue, which was of a huge bear. (Blurn said it was a bear.)

Under the pink sky, we all saw a wash of land sweeping up and up, and beyond something was giving off fumes, pushing redness into the pink.

"Gardens," said Mehmed. (Did I say, Mehmed's really all right too?)

I've lost touch with Nemian. He hasn't been anywhere near where I am.

"The Rain Gardens?" I inquired.

"Yup."

We stared at red melting in pink.

It's unknown, to me, to Nemian, and to the Hulta.

Just like life. No one knows what's around the next bend, over the next hill. It could be heaven-on-earth or death. We can only go on and find out.

Nemian appeared at this moment. He rode up on his smart horse, and the bandit girl was on a horse beside him.

He shot me a loving smile.

I glared.

"Ah, Claidi . . . how are you?"

"I haven't thought about it. How do I seem?"

"Fantastic," enthused my absent-now-present "friend." "We must talk," said Nemian.

"Oh, talk."

"Save it," said Mehmed. "We have to get through *there* first."

Just then soft rain began to fall. It was pale, yet it smelled sooty, like old fires.

Nemian's hair was flattened. Dark gold. Something hurt in me, and worse when the bandit girl, whose name I don't even know, handed him her scarf to wipe his face.

As they rode off, he sent back a stare that seemed full of yearning, as if it was me he wanted to be with. As I say, as he rode off.

I can't trust Nemian either, and I never could.

So on over the next hill, around the next bend.

I decided to go back to the wagon to write this. All right, Argul's wagon—but he'd be out there in the rain, planning, and if he turned up here I'd be off like a shot. And I'd only borrowed Sirree. A borrowed friend's better than none. I could feel my face getting very long.

When I was outside again, Mehmed said vaguely, "Still wondering which half of us didn't want to rescue you?"

My head jerked up. He grinned at my defiance.

"You're a bit slow, Claidibaari."

"*Thank* you."

"It was a *joke,* Claidi."

I wanted to hit his dark face. Was too sensible to do so.

Mehmed said, "I *told* Blurn you'd believe it, take it to heart, get all miserable. We didn't *vote,* Claidibaabaa. There wasn't time, anyway. When Argul found out, he just picked four of us who weren't doing anything, and we rode after you. He is *leader*, you duppy girl."

NIGHTMARES BY DAY

Once you're really soaked, it probably doesn't matter being in the rain.

So that's all right.

Everyone looks half drowned.

Even inside the wagons it doesn't stay dry, because crawling in and out of them, the rain rubs off.

The rain is red.

That is, it looks red and stains reddish.

Teil brought me a piece of treated leather to wrap this book in, to protect the pages. She said, wasn't this a long letter. She thinks it's a letter. Is it? Maybe. She also told me the bandits have a store of ink pencils, so if this one runs out, that will be handy.

I'm not in A's wagon now. In this weather, I assume he's using it. I share one with some of the girls. I may be beginning to follow some of the bandits' language, too. They have two languages, really—the one I speak and this other one mixed in it.

At night, as the red rain drives on the roof, we suck sticks of treacle candy, and they tell stories. I told one, as well. I made it up as I went along but sort of pinched bits from my memory of House books. They seemed to like it, but theirs are better. I think theirs are true.

No one likes this place at all.

There are rocks and stones, some of them hundreds of *man-heights* high, as the bandits say. Either they've been shaped by the weather or people carved them long ago. There are arches, walls, columns, towers with openings, and peculiar stairways, partly steps and partly slopes. It could almost be another ruin of some great city, not fallen but *melted,* like old candles.

On the horizon, on either side to which the stone shapes stretch, about a mile or so away, are craters, out of which sifts smoke and sometimes bubbles of crimson fire.

From some of these smoke holes, pillars of smolder rise into the sky, which is always cloudy and tinged like a blush.

The smoke, the cindery heat, and sudden flares of fire seem to set the rain off overhead.

When it comes down, which it's always doing, it's like *wet* fire.

Why do they call this place the Rain *Gardens*???

Last night one of the bandit girls, who's only a kid really, about seven—but she's just like a woman, striding about with a knife in her belt, and fierce as anything—told us a story of the Rain Gardens. She said the earth burst open, and fire rushed out and over, and smothered everything here. She said the ground we're riding and walking over is made of powdered and then cemented human bones.

Word goes it'll take seven or ten days to get through. We've been in for five so far. It's a bad dream, this.

Eleventh day and no sign of the end. Argul rode around again, chatting to everyone. He was very cool. Blurn sat on his horse, looking proud to have Argul for a leader. Even the older men listen to what Argul says. His father was the Hulta leader before him, and his mother was also very powerful. She was an herbalist and, they say, even skilled with chemicals. A magician.

"Did you see that charm he wears around his neck?" asked Teil. "His mother gave him that."

I thought he was lucky to have known his mother. If that seems selfish, it is. I wish, how I wish, I'd known mine.

Then Teil said, "She died when he was a child." As if she'd read my mind and was putting me right.

Today, from a rise, we could see where this ends, still some miles off. But the new region doesn't look very promising.

Peshamba is this way. Somewhere south.

What's first is apparently covered with some sort of vegetation. It looks thick and murky.

From books, I know lava and sulfur will nourish the soil once they've settled, and this vegetable area must be the result.

Everything *tastes* of soot and frequently smells of eggs that have gone bad.

Sirree is damp and streaked with red, no matter how I rub and groom her.

In the middle of last night we heard a weird sound.

It was a sort of booming *scream.*

The bandit girls and I pelted out of the wagon with our hair on end. Everyone else was doing the same. All the usually quiet dogs were barking and yapping, and the horses trampling at their pickets.

It went on and on—then stopped.

We were all asking, What is it? What is it? And children were crying with fear. It was like a nightmare that had woken up with us all.

About two miles off to the left, a particularly vivid volcanic crater then started puffing up wine-red streams.

People began to say to each other that the noise had come from a lava vent. The gases build up there and can make strange sounds before the lava bursts out.

We hung around in the rain for ages, afraid the dire noise would start again. But it didn't.

Thought I would never sleep. But I did.

By the way, I haven't seen Nemian for days and nights. If I still suspected the bandits as much as I did, and perhaps still should, I'd think they had, as they say in the Hulta, *put out his light.*

One of the girls, though, told me he keeps to a wagon, with the family of the girl he's taken up with.

He wouldn't like the wet, I suppose. And I'm sure they fuss over him. "Ooh, can we get you another cushion, Nemian? Another slice of cake?"

Sometimes, when I think of it, I feel white-hot anger. And bitter, too. Oddly, I *don't* think of him all that much. Am I the shallow one?

The land was like cracked paving, huge slabs. Behind us lay the wet, red smoke, and before us lay a shadow.

Nemian rode through the last rain until his horse, blond and sleek, was walking by Sirree through the damp, hot weirdness.

"Hello, Claidi."

"Hi."

"You look and sound like a true bandit lady."

I didn't reply.

Nemian said, "What must you think of me?"

"Would you like a written answer? But it might cover several pages."

"Perhaps not. It's admirable the way you've adjusted here. A princess among thieves."

"I'm not a princess," I said.

Now he didn't speak.

Down and up the line of horses, wagons, mules, and so on, rolled a rumble of wheels, calls, curses, and clatter, this now-familiar music.

"On the Princess Claidi thing, Jizania lied," I said. Though I wasn't sure I believed it.

"She would never do that," said he.

"Wouldn't she? She was going to have to. Otherwise they'd know she let you escape."

"I see. That's observant. Clever. You are, aren't you, Claidi? Claidi, you're a jewel."

"Yum," I said.

I wouldn't look at him.

If I looked, I'd see. I'd lose my lofty tone. I'd start thinking he was really something all over again.

"Claidi, you've adjusted, and so have I, here. I'm also good at that. It's the way to get by, to survive. Don't judge me, Claidi. When we get to the next city, we *must* talk. I need to tell you things."

"Fine."

Ahead, someone called out. We were coming to the vegetation. The shadow.

"Claidi," said Nemian, low and strong, his voice magically throbbing, "I *need* you. Please, remember that."

He was gone.

And we'd reached the—

The—?

Thinking later, I wondered if it's called Rain *Gardens* for this part. It is a kind of . . . garden. A wood, an orchard, of a sort.

Meadows of a sort came first. They had dark moss and clumps of things that were "flowerin"'—whippy dark leaves, pods like grey-pinkish bells. And mushrooms, striped black and yellow—they looked as poisonous as wasps.

In the "meadows" there were "trees." The "trees" became thicker and drew together, and we rode into the garden-orchard-wood.

Well, the trees had trunks, veined and gnarled, and roped over with ivies and creeper. But you could see through these trunks—they were semi-transparent, like enormous stems. And in the branches, where the creepers and ivies weren't, were bladelike leaves, a pale luminous green. And fruits.

Actually, the fruits were the oddest of all. The House Garden grew all kinds of fruits and vegetables in special plots and glass-houses. I'd never seen anything like this.

They were most like carrots, but carrots that had gone mad, twisting and turning, some of them curled up almost in a circle.

In those stories I'd now and then read in the library at the House (hiding behind book-stacks, generally found and beaten), any travelers who find unusually strange fruit always eat it and get ill. None of the bandits touched the fruit. Even the children didn't.

They must have known not to.

So neither did I. Nor can I offer an educational insight into what the fruits tasted like, or their effect.

The other bad side to all this is, of course, that this is exactly the kind of bad place the Waste is supposed to be filled with, according to the House. They'd been right.

And the trees dripped. Another sort of rain—some sticky juice or resin. It didn't seem dangerous, didn't burn or sting, but it was soon all over everything, including clothes and hair. I felt as if I'd fallen into jam.

The tree-things rose up and up. Some were as tall as towers, tall as the trees in the Garden. It was dark, the overcast smoky sky mostly shut out.

The Hulta wagons seemed to move more quietly. The vegetation muffled sound, but also very little noise was being made. No calls or swearing. No kids running about. When the horses shook their bridles, which have bells and coins on them, the tinkling sounded flat, but also I saw riders putting out their hands to stop the bells jingling.

I said, Nemian had ridden off. I clucked to Sirree, and we went up the line of wagons, and Ro and Mehmed were there, riding along.

"It goes on for miles," said Ro.

I hadn't asked. Everyone was probably asking everyone: How long does this bit last?

"Like it?" Mehmed asked me.

"Not a lot."

"Gives me the creeps," said Ro. "Like that forest over north, remember, Mehm?"

"The one with panthers?" inquired Mehmed.

"Yeah, and those trees that lean over and grab you and wind you up in stuff so you can't move, and then slowly digest you over months."

"Oh," said Mehmed.

They looked greenish. But we all probably did from the green-black shadows.

A carrot fruit fell off a tree and landed on the ground, where it burst in a repulsive way.

We were looking at this, when another shower of carrots came down, all bursting. And then the vegetable wood was *shaking.*

Long dull thuds seemed to come up from the ground, out of the air.

"An earthquake," Ro decided.

The branches overhead also shook furiously. Creepers snapped and uncoiled, falling like ropes. The air was full of wiry stems and leaves and horrible bursting fruit.

There was already shouting, but now there were yells, shrieks.

Through the depths of the wood came a terrifying crackling *rush.* It was like a wind blowing, but a wind that was solid.

"Something's coming!" yelled Mehmed.

It was. People were calling in panic, "Where is it?" And "Over there! It's there!" or "No, that way—" And then one voice cried out in a ragged howl, "No—up there! It's *above!*"

And so we all looked up, and from high up in the trees, the face of a *demon* looked back at us.

My heart stopped, or it felt like it.

That face—

It was yellowish, a mask, with large black eyes and pointed tusks. It had a mane of darkness that somehow flashed with golden fires—

And from the mouth there burst an impossible ear-shattering thunder that was a *scream.*

The horses reared. Sirree reared. I don't know why I didn't fall off. Ro did. Dogs howled. Then somehow, silence.

Dogs flattened on their bellies. Horses shivered. The rest of us turned to stone. Staring, beyond terror almost. (And a glimpse of Argul, I only recalled after, somehow up at the front, confronting the menace, between all of us and it.)

While the thing in the trees stared *down* at *us.*

It was like the bear statue, only not. It had long arms, incredibly long, hanging now loosely over the limb of the tree where it squatted. Its claws were the length of my arm, or so they looked. I think it was altogether about twice the height of a man.

It was covered in fur, black fur, streaked with what looked like rust. But also the fur was full of creepers and ivy, like the trees, and with other growths—savage flowers, funguses. And there were smaller things living in the fur and the growths—mice, maybe, snakes—all weaving in and out, so tiny eyes sparkled and were gone, and sinuous little bodies moved like fish in a pool.

Around its head, its insane face, whirled this golden crown that spun. For the crown was several enormous flies, golden and green, constant companions to the demon bear-thing, must be, for it took no notice of them, as it took no notice of all the creatures living on it.

It was a *world.*

That awful face stared down. You know, it was a wise face, too, but not wise in any way I'd ever understand or want to.

The jaws stretched, and again out came that appalling ear-splitting roar-scream.

None of us now made a sound.

The beast hung over us, still, yet also in endless total motion from the movement of its companion life.

But then it grew bored with us. It raised one long, long arm, dripping with hair and leaves and mice; and the great gold flies, each the size, I'd say, of one of Ro's huge feet, whirled in a joyful dance. And smoke poured from its fur—dust, I think, from the lava pits.

The beast plucked a handful of the fruits and put them in its mouth.

Then flinging up both arms now, in clouds of leaves and smoke, it sprang high, high across the boughs, caught some distant tree limb, and swung away into the shadow of the wood.

No one moved or spoke for about an hour.

"An ape," said Ro.

"Bear," Mehmed.

"Ape, stupid. Bears don't swing through the trees."

I began to hear whispering and then some loud joking all around. Argul was talking to some men and women, glancing our way a lot, no doubt to see what M and R were doing.

We were alive. Shakily I stroked Sirree.

The House had been right again. There are monsters in the Waste. This one, luckily, was a vegetarian.

PESHAMBA

After all that, Peshamba was a relief.

Also a shock.

Peshamba is beautiful.

In fact, getting through the rest of the monster wood, wondering off and on if there'd be any more of the bear-apes, these more hungry and less fussy ones, or worse things than bear-apes (?!!) only took the rest of the day.

We came out of the wood before the sun set. This in itself was a relief, and I heard some "prayers" spoken, sort of chants to do with thanks. (I'm still puzzled about this God-gods thing. I must ask somebody sensible. There were no gods, prayers, or shrines in the House. No idea like this at all. Or none I ever heard.)

Beyond the wood there was a grassy plain. It started as dry, burnt-looking grass but then unrolled into greenness, and then *rainbows.*

As the sun went down I stood up on a rise, and the distance was emerald with films of mauve and blue and rose.

"Wildflowers," said the seven-year-old with the knife (she's *called* Dagger).

"Oh," I said.

Now what should I think? The House said monsters and deserts and criminals. They were right. But the House said too that only the House and the Garden had greenness and flowers.

Jizania hadn't, though. But I don't somehow trust Jizania now.

"You've been here before?" I asked Dagger.

"No. We don't normally travel in this direction. Best trade is north and east."

She must mean the best places to rob.

Politely I didn't say this.

"You've seen lots of wildflowers?" I asked.

"Seen about everything," boasted Dagger.

Could be true for all I know.

That night, grasshoppers sang on the plain.

In the morning the Hulta rambled on. We rode across the green grass with the flowers. They were something, all right. Wild hyacinths, wild roses, drifts of convolvulus and lilies. Wonderful scent. Looking back, the shadow wood just slid away.

Then the city started to be visible ahead.

I didn't believe my eyes. It was like jewelry.

But as it got nearer and nearer, it got better and better.

The pale walls cascading up were topped with gold. (It isn't quite. It's thin gold leaf, but even so.) Windows glittered like sweets because they had colors in them. And there were domes: white and lucent as lamps with a faint candle inside. And ruby, and turquoise blue, with gold patterns all over.

The bandits were also impressed, but they had heard of Peshamba.

I wondered what Nemian thought. According to the little he'd said, his own city was tremendous, better than anywhere. Could it be better than here?

When you come close, the walls appear higher than five houses, piled one on another, and inside, other, higher walls go up.

At the front, like a blue shining apron, is a lake. Peshamba seems to be standing in it, and partly is. The reflection of the city floats in the water, and Peshamba floats above, between water and sky.

"Is the water drinkable?" I asked Dagger. She shrugged. She does this when she doesn't know something, as if to say, "If I don't, it can't be important."

Anyway, when we reached the water, half the bandit men flung off their shirts, cloaks, jackets, and decorations, and plunged in to swim. The women found a quieter part among some willows.

Was anyone watching from the walls? Did they think an invasion had arrived?

But later, when we went over the stone bridge that I forgot to mention stretched across the lake, a gate in the wall stood wide open.

Beyond was a narrow way paved with marble. And on it stood a giant, half the height of a man again.

He was encased in a uniform made of metal, and in his hand there was a huge axe. His helmet was gold with a white plume. His face was entirely masked in gold.

I'd moved up near the front of the Hulta horde, and I could see Argul sitting on his horse, gravely looking in at the giant.

Thinking of books again, I said to Mehmed, "Does someone have to fight the giant?"

"Wouldn't fancy it much. He's one big tronker."

Just then, the giant spoke.

"*Name yourselves.*"

The strangest voice. Perhaps the mask made it sound so peculiar.

Argul called out, "The Hulta."

"*Your business.*"

"Travelers," said Argul. And lightly, "Sightseers."

The giant lowered his axe.

"*Do no harm in Peshamba, and Peshamba does no harm to you.*"

The Hulta consists of a mass of people. We squashed through, wagons and animals, the lot, and the giant stood aside in a kind of alcove in the marble wall.

Ro was there. "Wouldn't fancy taking *him* on."

Teil pushed up, carrying one of the little girls astride her horse. (The Hulta children can ride at four or five. Hence Argul's comment on my great age.)

"I've heard of this," said Teil, waving at the giant. "It's clockwork."

Ro snorted. He went up to the giant. "Here, mate. You a *doll?*"

The gold mask creaked down to Ro. It wasn't a mask. It was a gold-painted face made of metal, which gave no answer.

Ro backed off.

We went on and, where the narrow way ended, passed through another, wider gate.

Here were two long lines of guards, standing bolt upright. They had axes over their shoulders, wore scarlet, and were covered in braid, epaulets, spurs, spikes, metal plates. They weren't giants, however. Really not much taller than I am.

As we went by, they presented arms, bringing their axe-hafts down on the ground with a bang.

"Are they crazy here?" I said.

Teil said, "No. If someone attacks, these things go wild. And they can't be hurt, either, or stopped."

I asked how she knew. "Oh," said Teil, "word gets around."

There were several more passages and gates, all with the clockwork doll-guards. Some even had rifles with silver set in the stocks. They certainly were better looking than the House Guards.

Eventually we all muddled into a huge garden—they call it here a *park.*

Blue cedars and olive-green palms stretched across the sky. Cypress trees carefully shaped to dark, waxed tassels. Fountains. A procession of snow-white ducks idled across a lawn.

Argul was riding down the line.

"If you don't know, be careful here." He saw Ro peering greedily after the ducks. "Watch it, Ro." Argul pointed. High on a slim tower as pink as marshmallow, a glass thing was turning slowly around and around, flashing in the sun. "They keep an eye on everything. See that? It's looking at us."

"What, *that?*"

"That."

The message went down the line of people and wagons.

Across the park, we could now see wonderfully dressed figures moving about and girls in glimmering silks playing ball.

Blurn appeared.

"Watch it, Ro."

"All right, all right."

In the park was a large building with courtyards clustered around and inside it. It was burstingly full. It's named the Travelers' Rest.

I saw some new (to me) animals that someone told me are "zebras," not horses. They have black and white stripes that make you dizzy. And there were three teams of "oxen" the color of walnuts.

Tents had been pitched, carts and wagons stood about, courtyards streamed with drying colored washing. There were wells and pools and ornamental fountains, all crowded.

Impossible racket. Sounded to me like a thousand different languages.

Going up some stairs carrying bundles, I saw, over a wall, more of the city lying below. There were the jewelry domes, and there a slim green tower with a golden bell in it, and squares, and roads, and buildings as decorated as cakes, and all pale glowing colors with sun on them. And gardens—everywhere gardens. (There was another of those turning, flashing crystals I could see, as well.)

Over the smells of Hulta and people and animals generally, scents of spice and cooking and tobacco, of vines and flowers, and the smell of *brickwork* in the sun that I'd half forgotten.

* * *

We girls and women on our own got quite a big room to ourselves. Like all the other women in the Rest, we immediately began washing clothes and underthings and sheets, hanging them out of the windows and even from the rafters.

The queue for the bathrooms was long but worth it.

I'd forgotten too the delight of cool-skin-temperature water scented with a few stolen herbs and perfumes. Here you can *buy* them. Or I couldn't, but Teil did and gave some to me. And soap and other things to keep one smelling nice.

I washed my hair. The last time was in the red rain. (I'd gone to groom Sirree, but it had already been done. The Rest has its own grooms, and Argul had *paid* to have all the horses and dogs tended. Even a couple of Hulta pet monkeys were being brushed and scented with banana essence.)

At first, the people of the city were hard for me to sort out from all the other people packed in here.

They seem a mixture, like everyone. But their clothes are always the most amazing silky stuff, and fabulous colors. So that's how I identify Peshambans now. Oh, and sometimes they wear masks—not over the whole face, just the eyes. It's a fashion—to make them more like the dolls this city's supposed to be full of?

Excitement in the room we share. There's a festival tonight. (I thought of the Featherers and felt uneasy, but it's nothing like that.) Large chests from the wagons had been opened and astonishing garments taken out. Fit to rival Peshamban clothes.

One of the girls insisted on giving me—it was a "present"—a deep blue dress sewn with embroidery and silver disks. Everyone clapped when I'd put it on. I felt shy, touched, and also rather resentful. A funny combination, but I think they feel sorry for me about Nemian. (Who, I may add, someone told me has already gone off swanning in the city.)

I did like myself in the dress when I glanced in the mirror.

We made each other up: black around the eyes, and powder, and scented sticks of color for the mouth.

"Pretty Claidibaabaa!" they cried, prancing around me. I really *was* the center of attention.

Someone else then gave me silver earrings with sapphires in them. Real true sapphires.

"*Hultai chura!*" they squealed.

I concluded that must mean "darling of the Hulta." (!!!) (But why?)

We had lunch in the main hall, where food can be *bought*—pancakes and vegetables. Then later, in the room, they were teaching me steps to wild Hulta dances, gallops and stampings and tossing the head (like a horse).

I haven't laughed like this for so long. We laughed ourselves daft.

I feel a bit guilty now, thinking how Daisy and Pattoo and I found ways to giggle and mess around despite the filthy rules and cruelty of the House.

But the afternoon is turning over to sunfall, and soon it'll be the time that is my mother's lovely name.

I can't help it. I want to have fun tonight.

Nemian . . . well. Grulps, as the ruder Hulta say. Yes, *grulps.*

Someone will like me, dance with me, hold my hand. I'm not going to worry about if or who. Someone *will.* It's that sort of night.

And I never was a princess. That was a lie. Wasn't it?

There's a song . . . It said: Moon in a cloud . . .

How to make sense of this.

I'll try, but please, please, my unknown, invented friend, be patient, it's not easy.

A huge square in the last daylight, with tall gracious buildings around, views of parks, and cloudy dark-green trees, and down here orange trees with orange-gold fruits. At the east end of the square, some steps go up to a pavement of apricot marble. On this stands another high white tower. At the tower's top, a clock. Actually, a CLOCK.

It must be—if it had been down on the square and anyone could've measured it—about the size of the Alabaster Fish Pool in the Garden of the House. Vast.

The CLOCK is in a frame of gold and silver, and up there, in front of it, stood three carved figures, very lifelike, except for being so big, painted, and gilded. One was a girl and one a man, and in the middle was a white horse up on its hind legs. Out of the horse's forehead ran a crystal horn. And later I noticed it also had silvery folded wings.

As we arrived, people were leaning out of small windows at the tower top and lighting hanging lamps.

The square was full, and a cheer went up from the Peshambans and from everyone else. Even we cheered. I wasn't sure why, but it seemed polite.

Blurn appeared, very smart and over-the-top in dark red, patterned boots, and earrings.

"Hi, Claidi. Like the CLOCK?"

"It's good."

"They worship it," said Blurn.

"Sorry?"

"The Peshambans. They worship that clock."

The CLOCK was a . . . god?

But Blurn had strode on. And as the soft lights spangled over the CLOCK, other lamps were lighting all around.

The sky got bluer, deeper. Twilight. Stars came out.

There were long tables laid with such pretty food, wonderful colors and designs, and fruits I'd never seen before. And there were glass jugs in ice of wine or juice or mixtures of both, shining like rubies and topaz and jade.

Dagger slipped through the crowd. She wore green and a Peshamban mask shaped like a dragonfly.

"It's all free," she breathed. " 'Cause of the festival."

She grabbed a plate and piled it with food, far more than I've ever seen her eat, and darted off.

But by then the center of the square was clearing. There was to be dancing. Apparently all this tonight was done in the square to honor the CLOCK.

One of the bandit girls, Toy, pulled me.

"Come on, Claidi."

"But I can't dance."

"Haven't we spent *hours* teaching you, Claidibaa?"

"But those were Hulta dances—" I feebly protested.

"There'll *be* Hulta dances. They play all dances for all the visitors. And we showed you three Peshamban dances too."

"But—"

"Hulta have come here before, in the past, remember?"

I was sure now I *wouldn't* remember a step, would make a fool of myself.

But somewhere a band was tuning up, and I recognized for a second a phrase from a tune the girls had sung that afternoon in the Travelers' Rest.

I found myself in the square's center in a line of laughing girls and women, between Teil and Toy.

A glance along the line made me feel happy, because everyone was shining and glittering and laughing. Peshamban girls with glass or real jewels sewn all over their clothes, and masks of cats and butterflies. Bandit girls clinking with coins. Women from all sorts of places I didn't know, hadn't ever known *existed.* At least I had Nemian to thank for *this.* For this freedom, this finding out. (Incidentally where was . . . ?)

You've guessed, haven't you? I was avoiding looking at the line of men opposite. It wasn't going to matter too much this time. You changed partners three times in this particular dance.

Even so.

The band was over there under that fringed awning. Stringed instruments and flutes, what looked like a cello, and two drums. And two silver sheets that were suddenly clashed together, and the dance had begun.

I looked up into the amused and rather (already) drunk face of Ro.

A surge of relief and disappointment.

Too late to think of anything else.

We were off.

Ro and I swept around each other, joined hands, and galloped sideways, just as everyone else did.

Then we swung in a circle with hands still joined.

Whoops and shouts.

We parted, stamped, and hands on hips, raised our heads like proud horses.

Now all the women joined hands, and we did light tapping steps on the spot, while the men looked on haughtily.

Then we stood back and clapped to the rhythm of the dance, and the men pretend-fought in pairs.

On Ro's right was Badger, who now accidentally hit Ro on the nose. (This is *not* meant to happen.)

Ro dropped back, spluttering, and crashed into the man on his left—Mehmed—and Mehmed's pretend foe.

"Hey, you tronker—"

Stumbling, Mehmed trod on another man's foot. This man wasn't bandit or Peshamban. His head was shaved except where hair, tied in a horse's tail, flared from the back. And he gave a roar and smacked his fist, painted blue, into Mehmed's face.

Next second, three or four men were rolling on the ground, swearing and kicking, with two bandit women—and a girl, also shaven and horsetailed—trying to separate and/or hit them with a nasty-looking metal-studded sash.

The Hulta girls, used to brawls, started laughing. But some of the Peshambans down the line looked upset. The dance had come all undone, though the band was still playing.

Next moment, a space opened in the crowd, just the way the wind had blown on the plain through all the flowers.

I'd seen more of the watching crystals that turned, up on buildings.

They did watch, for now through the parting of people and orange trees came marching six of the clockwork doll-guards from the gates.

"Oops," said Teil.

Toy said gloomily, "Now we're in for it."

To my horror I noted two of the doll-guards had *rifles* pointed right at us all.

Then another voice shouted loudly as a trumpet. I didn't recognize it; it sounded made of brass.

But instantly somehow Ro and Mehmed scrambled up out of the muddle, leaving the horsetail man and another one flailing on the ground.

The doll-guards had reached us.

From out of a clockwork chest, a harsh unhuman voice, different from the one that had shouted, ordered:

"*Cease fighting.*"

"I have," said Ro, annoyed.

"Shut *up,*" muttered Mehmed, who had a blue smear on his cheek from the horsetail man's fist.

However, the horsetail man and the other one rolled apart and sprang to their feet. They stared in alarm at the guards.

A silence settled as the band gave up.

The deadly doll now demanded something—the same something, I think, over and over in what seemed many different languages. It sounded very frightening. Finally the deadly doll demanded, "*Are you at peace now?*"

"Sure, yes, completely. Love everybody, eh Mehm?"

"Love 'em, yeah."

The horsetail man and the other one had already mumbled something at other points in the language performance, doubtless also saying how they loved everyone.

Then a man in scarlet and gold moved in between us and the rifles. He was breathing fast from running down the line of dancers, and from shouting.

"A misunderstanding," he said to the dolls with rifles and axes. "I sincerely apologize. It won't happen again."

I hadn't recognized his voice in the battle-bellow that had stopped Ro and Mehmed as nothing else could. Now it was different again—like poured cream.

And the rifles were being lowered.

"*Do no harm in Peshamba,*" said the doll. "*Peshamba does no harm to you.*"

The weirdest thing. Some of the oranges on the orange trees flew open, and little colored clockwork birds flew out of them and up into the lamplight to circle around and around. Just a coincidence, possibly.

I was taken aback anyway. But the guards had turned around and were marching neatly away again.

The horsetail girl fetched the horsetail man a ringing smack across his face. He cowered. What she was hissing at him I couldn't understand, thank goodness.

Ro and Mehmed laughed.

The music started once more, and the crowd was closing over like a repaired split seam. And the dance began again, again taking me by surprise.

It was apparently time to change partners as well.

The magnificent man in red grasped my hands and whirled me away down the avenue of dancers before I had time to wonder if now I'd *really* forgotten the steps.

CHANGING PARTNERS

I didn't cause it."

"I'd take a bet you did. You're trouble, girl."

We paused to swing around hand in hand.

The lines of men and women clapped in time to the music.

He was smiling.

Argul.

I'd never seen him look so sensational. His hair was like black Peshamban silk. The color red suited him. All that gold—

And now he took me by the waist and lifted me high in the dance—steps I truly didn't know—I couldn't do a thing, just stare down at his smiling, marvelous face. His teeth, in that tawny face, are so white. . . .

He looks happy tonight. He looks *alive.*

I couldn't help laughing. I put my head back and laughed at the spinning starry sky.

When he set me on my feet, he steadied me, helped me get my balance again, but all the time we were still dancing. . . .

The dance had changed, in fact.

It was a Peshamban dance the girls had shown me. You move quite slowly, holding hands and taking easy, simple steps. Looking into each other's faces.

This was the dance I'd been afraid no one would want to choose me for.

"I don't mean to be trouble," I said.

"Oh Claidi," he said. "You can't help it. Don't try. It's what a bird like you's good at." I frowned. But I didn't care. Although he was insulting me, they didn't feel like insults. He said, "Don't change. You're wonderful."

The music of the dance had a song. It was something about the moon in a cloud and getting lost in the cloud of the moon.

Sky so dark now, and the stars behind his head. The lamps, and the little mechanical birds flying.

Everyone enjoying themselves, yet far away. The mood of the night like rosy curtains in the background.

I thought, I *know* this person. I know him as well as I know myself. But I didn't know him. I don't know myself.

We danced every dance.

Sometimes there were dances where we were separated. But we always met up again. Then he caught hold of me strongly. I felt I couldn't go wrong then.

I've never felt like that before.

Maybe I never will again.

At midnight, and midnight came so quickly, the CLOCK does something magical.

Not much warning. The band stopped playing. And everyone in the square, following the lead of the local Peshambans, raised their heads to look at the CLOCK.

Suddenly there was a strange noise, like a gigantic key turning in a lock. And then tinkly music began to drift down from the tall white tower.

The three figures on the CLOCK started to move.

The girl twirled, dancing as I had. The man bowed and stretched out his hand to stroke the horse with the crystal horn, which, at that moment opened its wings.

And then they glided away behind the CLOCK, and other figures emerged from the other side. There was an old man leaning on a stick, and an Old Lady in a high headdress, and a monstrous beast. It had the body of a lion, a tail like three snakes knotted together, and the head of a bird.

The old man regally raised his stick in greeting, and the Old Lady raised her slender hands. And the beast opened its mouth and *fire* came out, cascades of yellow sparks.

In the crowd below lots of people cried out in surprise. But the Peshambans only sighed with joy, looking up with loving eyes at the CLOCK that was their god.

I whispered to Argul, "It's amazing. But do they really worship it?"

"Yes," he said.

"Why?"

"Because they say it's beautiful, and God is beautiful."

Somehow this wasn't, at that moment, confusing.

"I see," I said. I thought I did.

"And," said Argul, "they say the CLOCK needs only a little attention to keep it working, and that's all religion needs too."

"Religion . . ."

"Their worship of it, belief in it. Only a little work to keep perfection perfect."

The music faded, and the three new figures became still. They're the figures that face the city from midnight to sunrise. Then they change again, but silently.

When the CLOCK had finished its display, and the Peshambans who were praying had stopped, Argul brought me a goblet of green wine. (Prayer isn't only for rage or dismay. It seems to be just happiness, sometimes.)

Suddenly I could see why that first time I'd thought him so terrible, terrifying—he's so strong, so powerful. So *there.*

After that we walked up through the city, beyond the square and the CLOCK. I don't think we discussed why.

The streets were hung with trees, and were cool, and smelled of flowers and scented dust and darkness.

There was another park. Peach-tinted lamps drooped from boughs.

We sat on a marble bench shaped like a bush under a large bush that had been cut and combed into the shape of a chair.

"Oh, *look,*" I said, "another mechanical doll!"

It was a fantastic bird, gleaming blue in the park lamplight. It had all at once lifted its drifting tail and opened it like a fan of green and turquoise, purple and gold.

"No, Claidi. It's a peacock."

"It's real?"

"Yes. As real as you."

"I don't feel real tonight. I never knew cities existed anymore."

"When I was a child," he said, "my mother told me about Peshamba."

"Did she?"

"There's something written on the face of the CLOCK. You can only see it from the top of the tower. It says: *There's time enough for everything.*"

"Is there?"

"I hope so," he said.

Testingly, I said, "I haven't met your mother, have I?"

"No. She died eight years ago, when I was ten."

I felt tremendously sorry. It was true. And now it reminded me of Twilight, my own lost mother.

"That's so sad."

"Sad for the ones she left behind. She knew such a lot. Herbs, and chemicals. Some of them, now, call her the Witch. But she wasn't that. She understood science, though she did have second sight."

"What's that?"

"She could see things the others couldn't. Sometimes the future. She gave me—" He made a gesture toward his collar, then stopped. "A charm, or so we call it now. But it's scientific. It can tell you things."

"I remember it," I said. "It's made of glass."

"No. It just seems to be."

"You were looking at it . . ." I hesitated, "that time . . . when I thought you were going to rob us."

"We're not bandits, Claidi," he said. "We get called that. I won't say we've never thieved, but only to protect our own people, and never from people who hadn't enough themselves. And we've fought and killed for the same reason. But not from choice. Do you believe me?"

"Yes."

He looked at me for some time. The moon had risen late; it was in the sky. His dark eyes seemed more intense. Or the moon . . . was in a cloud, perhaps.

"I saw you first," he said, "in that dry old park in Chariot Town. You were with him, your posh lordly friend."

"Nemian."

"That one, yes."

"I didn't see you—"

"No. It was just me and Blurn, out for a stroll. We trade with Sheepers, but we don't always trust them. We were just making sure of the town before any of the others came in later. We looked . . . a bit different."

"And you *saw* me?"

"Yes."

He didn't add anything, so I said, "You didn't realize I was going to be bartered to the Feather Tribe."

"You'd left by the time I did. Then we came after you."

"Why?" I said.

"Why do you think?"

I said, humbly, "Because you help people."

I wanted him to say, of course, "I did it because you're so incredible, Claidi."

He wouldn't. He stared down his nose at me, his eyes burning and the moon pale in the trees behind his head.

What he did say was this: "Why don't you stay with us? You're a pleasure to watch with Sirree, a natural rider. And you look your best in Hulta clothes. We live well. We look after our own, and others, when we can. You don't have to be afraid of anything with us—not be hungry or thirsty, or in danger. We travel. We go everywhere there is. Did you know there are enormous seas, Claidi? You do? Miles of just water and sky. And animals so odd you'd scream. Join our Family, Claidi. Stay."

Thud, thud, my heart in my throat.

Couldn't speak.

I thought of Nemian, and the House. Of the ones I'd trusted and shouldn't have trusted.

"I—" I said.

The moon turned blue and winked away like a closing eye. Distracted, I stared at it, and then a wash of icy cold sank over me, over the world.

Something like wet silver spat into my face.

Argul stood up. He pulled me up too.

"What is it?"

"*Snow.* Damned *weather.*"

"What's—"

"Tell you later. Now we run."

The park was full of flying figures, shrieking and yelps. Wild laughter, too. So many couples thinking only of each other, and then this—

White hurtled from the sky.

Soon we were running through a blanket. It was like feathers—that awful sacrificial dress, plucked and flung in my face.

On the square, when we reached it—rushing figures everywhere—people were carrying the orange trees indoors out of the cold.

I wanted to carry the night indoors in the same way.

But the night was flying off from us. This was a new dance. It was too fast.

We ran together as far as the Traveler's Rest—hand in hand. I think there were streets.

In the Rest, windows blazed. Shouts and thunders. Everything was in turmoil.

"Claidi, I'll meet you here tomorrow—one hour after sun-up, by that tree. Yes?"

"Yes . . . yes—"

Into the dance of the snow, Argul vanished.

* * *

In the morning, that tree—which he'd said we would meet by and which had been shaped like a candle flame of green—was *white,* a round white ball, from the snow.

That's how things can change. Overnight.

Anyway, they changed before I saw the tree in the morning.

After I got upstairs that night, to the women's bedroom, I found it was empty.

I wished Argul hadn't had to go, but he would be seeing to things, making sure of the horses. Blurn would have gone too. I expected Blurn's girlfriend felt as I did. Did that mean Argul and I . . . ?

Really, I couldn't work it out.

So I stood at the window, watching the snow falling on Peshamba, settling in white heaps everywhere, changing things. And quietness came. I never heard such quiet.

Snow had never fallen in the Garden. Perhaps it doesn't happen in that area, or the Garden was kept too warm.

To be honest I felt happy. And scared. I wondered if I'd imagined things had happened that hadn't. The way he looked at me. He hadn't said anything about my being with him. He'd simply suggested I stay with the Hulta.

And I wanted to. Did I? Yes. But, you see, I'd rushed off with Nemian from the only life I knew. And I'd loved Nemian. And now I was ready to rush off again in another direction, and was that any more sensible than the first time? And was all my life going to be like this—rushing from one place, one person, to another? Exciting, maybe. Also exhausting, and fruitless.

The snow fell, and my thoughts swam around and around, and then someone knocked on the door.

When they didn't come in, I went and opened it.

I jumped back in—well, sort of horror, really. It was Nemian.

He'd bought or found new clothes—black and gold. He looked striking and painfully handsome. He was very pale.

"Claidi, can I come in? Or will you come out for a minute?"

"There's no one else here," I said unwisely.

I let him walk into the room.

He glanced around. Bandit—no, Hulta—women's stuff everywhere.

Nemian looked back at me.

"Did you have a nice evening?" I asked acidly.

"Not really. I was looking for you."

"I wasn't so far off."

"Perhaps not." He paused. He said, "I wasn't playing about today,

Claidi. I was trying to find ballooneers. Peshamba used to have balloons for travel. Not anymore."

I nodded. I tried to look polite and vague, but a flaming fierceness, chilly and desperate, seemed all over Nemian, sizzling in the air.

"Claidi, I know what you think of me."

"Do you?"

"You think I'm a skunk."

"What's a skunk?"

"Claidi, don't start that." (I felt and must have looked annoyed. I didn't know what a skunk *was.*) "Claidi, that girl—"

"Mm? Which girl?"

"You know which girl. I'm sorry. It just . . . happened."

"Well, lovely," I said. I smiled my best congratulatory smile.

Then he really astonished me.

He dropped on one knee in front of me and seized both my hands.

"Claidi, don't play with me. I know I deserve it. But, all this has been so strange for me. I've been confused. I didn't think it through, and now . . . Claidi, tell me I haven't lost you."

He really is beautiful. The snowlight burned on his hair. I trembled, without quite knowing why.

"Lost me?" I asked casually. "How do you mean?"

"You *will* go on with me, to my city on Wide River? I have to know you will. Oh, Claidi . . . Claidi, I'll lose everything if I lose you. Please forgive my hopeless, mindless stupidity. Stay with me. Come with me."

I swallowed. I couldn't think what to say. Can you just say *No* in a case like this?

He was sweating. His eyes . . . had *tears* in them.

He wrung my hands like washing and only loosened his grip when I squeaked "*Ow!*"

"There *is* a method of transport," he said, "not a balloon. Precarious, rather. But I'll look after you. I promise I will, Claidi."

"Er. But—" I faltered. Well, you know, I never claimed to be intelligent.

"Claidi, in my city, my grandmother is very, very old. Like Jizania. And I have to get back to her, and to my duties there. I'm a prince. My life isn't entirely my own. You'll know." (He'd forgotten again, I thought, about whether I truly am royal.) "And this life of mine, Claidi, frankly isn't worth anything if I can't take you with me. I *need* you. If only I can make you understand."

And then he stood up and dropped my hands with absolute snow-cold dignity.

"It's your choice, of course. And I don't deserve anything from you. I've been an absolute fool. Shall I go now?"

In the silence then, in the corridor outside, we heard the soft laughter and footfalls of the Hulta women coming back to the room.

At the agreed time, I stood in the snow by the white ball that had been a tree.

Kids were out, throwing snow at each other. The horsetail men and women were charging their zebras up and down. Chimneys I'd never noticed puffed up blue, and there was a smell of hot bread, and bells rang sweetly.

Argul came toward me over the white. It was miraculous, just watching him. I let myself pretend, just for a minute.

And as he reached me and saw my face, and his altered, darkened, closed in, I said, "I'm sorry, Argul, but I can't stay." He stood there then. Silent. "I thought I could, and I wanted to, but now—the situation seems very serious. I have to go on."

"With him," said Argul. A storm went through the back of his eyes. He shook his head. The storm was gone.

"As you know," I said primly, "we've traveled together this far, Nemian and I."

Argul said, "He's an okk."

I blinked.

"You don't like him."

"Oh, I love him." Argul's eyes on mine. I had to look down. He said, "No, excuse me. You're the one who does that."

Then he turned and walked away, striding off across the snow, and as he did, something dropped from his hand.

It wasn't until one of the kids ran over and picked it up, and it sparkled, that I saw it was a ring with a brilliant stone. Had it been for me? Surely . . . not.

The children ran away with it, after him. They were Peshamban and very honest, and I think it was a diamond.

MARSHES OF THE MOON

Some time has gone by before I came back to this book to write any more. We're at a place called River Jaws and have to wait a day or something, for something or other. I forget why or what.

The ink pencil ran out, too (I've written enough to use up a whole one). And I'd forgotten to ask Teil for more, so I had nothing to write with.

He gave me a sort of pen-thing, his, I suppose, only it doesn't write quite the same. Which somehow makes writing not so easy.

Or am I only making excuses?

Yes, Claidi—I hear you say—you are.

When he said, I mean Nemian, "So you're still writing in your book," I was afraid he'd want to read it. But he doesn't seem interested. I think he just thinks I like doing it. He called it my *Diary*. He said lots of "ladies" keep diaries in his city. So it's fashionable, so it's all right. Perhaps helps convince him I'm royal.

He's been attentive. But also he looks . . . nervous? If he wants me, then maybe that's all it is. But he doesn't touch me now.

I feel sorry for Nemian. I try to be friendly and cheerful, to show him I'm all right and I like him, and I do *try* to like him.

I don't *dis*like him.

But I can't feel the way I did. I wish I could.

Why else did I leave Argul and the Hulta? It's hard to explain. I wanted to stay with the ban—the Family. But it was about what I'd felt before. That I'd kept changing my mind.

You can see, I hope, how I felt. Disloyal. I *don't* want to rush from person to person, never knowing who I'm going to want next. Like some spoiled horrible little child.

The people in the House were always doing that. Now they were friends with X, then with Y, then with Z. And then they had an argument with Z and went back to X. Revolting.

I'm not like that. I hope I'm not. Nemian was the one I chose to be with. All right, he behaved badly, but then, I'm just Claidi. He got distracted from me. Not too difficult, I expect.

I have to be loyal to him. I chose him first. If I can't trust my own feelings, my own self . . .

That was what I wanted, to be loyal. To prove to myself I'm not a shallow, silly, worthless little idiot.

So I did what I did.

The Hulta acted oddly to me. Not nasty, just fed up and a bit short. Only Teil said good-bye. Dagger came up and *confronted* me. She looked terribly fierce. "Why are you going with *him?*" she demanded.

Tried to explain. The loyalty thing. Nemian. She snorted like a horse. She said, "You're mad." And some other words I shouldn't have been surprised she knew.

It doesn't make sense, yet it does. Doesn't it? Of course it does. Yes, I'll be glad later, when we get to the city.

He was so definite, how much he needs me.

Argul doesn't. (That ring, it wasn't for me.) He has all the Hulta, loving him and loyal to him. He even knew his mother.

Nemian and I—I'll do the best I can. Please, God, even if you're a CLOCK, help me to do the best I can.

The first part of the journey from Peshamba was fairly ordinary, except for the snow.

All the plains about the city were white, like book paper with nothing written there. I wondered if the flowers would survive. Probably somehow they do, for obviously snows have happened before. (In fact, the lake had gone solid, frozen, and they were sliding on it and "skating.")

Nemian gave me a big fur cloak. He said it didn't come from an animal but that the Peshambans can make these garments, like pelts. It was warm.

We rode in a chariot again, one of three, but drawn by donkeys. They had red blankets and little bells.

Jingle jingle.

When I looked back, a blue haze floated over the city on the pale grey luminous sky, from all the smoke.

There was hot tea and mulled wine in flasks. But it got cold quickly and wasn't so nice.

For several days we were in the plains.

Once we saw some large white things, like clouds, blowing slowly along. Nemian told me they were elephants. They grow thick wooly coats like sheep, in the cold, and have noses like tails. That sounds crazy, and maybe he made it up to amuse me. We weren't near enough to see for sure.

At night there were tents put up. I had one to myself. There were burning coals in iron baskets for heat.

I sat and reread this book, or bits of it.

I don't seem quite the same person now as when I started it. Does that make sense? Who am I?

Finally, although it can't have been that long, the weather started to alter, and so did the landscape. I could see enormous hills, mountains, appearing far to the left. It felt warmer almost at once.

The sky began to break open in cracks of blue. Then it was all blue with cracks of white.

There were grasses again, but very tall, higher in parts than the chariots. (The donkeys tended to eat their way through, chewing as they trotted.) There was a trackway, and then we reached a large village or small town.

Normally I'd have been interested, but I wasn't very. I'm useless—on this extraordinary adventure and wasting it all.

Let's see. There were round-sided houses and fields where they kept having to hack the grass back from the grain. Weird trees with boughs hung right down to the ground, like tents, and huge black and pink birds rumbled about in them making quacking noises.

They had a stream, which rushed and was white with foam.

Everyone else stopped in the village-town, and only Nemian and I got a boat with a boat driver (apparently you don't call them that, but what?), and we set off down the stream. Although we'd stayed a couple of nights in the village-town, Nemian didn't go rushing off with everyone, although, again, he could speak their language. (They also take money for things, and he paid them.)

He'd started to tell me where we were going. Through marshes, he said. The people there are odd but would provide the means to take us to the River.

I had this awful feeling, which had begun on the plains and now was getting stronger and stronger. It was a sort of fear, and a sort of ache. Later on, Nemian, who had also begun talking to me regularly, said he'd felt "homesick" for his city. And I realized then that I'm homesick, but not for any place.

I used to see him every day. Argul. You could always expect to see him. Riding along the wagons, checking stores, at the fire by night. (I didn't often speak to him. Didn't think he noticed me.) Or I'd seen him wrestling with his men, or playing cards—he could do very clever card tricks, magic tricks too. Once, on the flower plains, he produced a sparrow out of Teil's ear. Couldn't work out how he did it—a real sparrow, which flew away. Or when they took turns singing, he'd sing. Not that well, actually. You always could see him, doing something. Or just there.

Just there.

(I've been trying to work out how long the journey has taken so far, from the House to this house overlooking the River. I've gotten muddled though. It seems to have gone on forever.)

It was sunset when we reached the marshes. The stream, which had gotten wider and slower, with islands of the tall grass, eventually became choked with reeds.

The boat driver (I never did learn his proper title) poled us carefully between. The low sun glinted red and copper on the water, all striped with reed shadows.

Out of this somehow mournful picture, a building rose, not very cheery either. Black stone, with pillars and a strange up-pointing roof.

Nemian told me it was a shrine. Ah. I knew about shrines. (?) This one was in honor of the marsh god.

But when we landed at the water-steps and climbed up them cautiously—they were slippery and very old—there was an image of the god on a black slab. I thought at first it was another clock, but it wasn't. They worship the moon, to which, they say there, the marshes belong.

"Why?" I said. I've never stopped asking questions. If that stops, frankly I think I'm done for.

"The Wide River lies over beyond the marshes. It's tidal, and so are they."

"Tidal. Like seas?"

Apparently so. They drain and fill, affected by the pull of the moon. So, the moon's a god in the marshes.

Later, when we were in the hall of the shrine—a gloomy old place and no mistake—eating some gloomy bread and bitter, crumbly (gloomy) cheese, I spoke to Nemian about this thing of God and gods.

"God is everything," he said. "Gods, individual gods, I mean, are expressions of God. As we are."

"We're *part* of God?" I goggled. I'd begun to have great respect for this (unknown) and superastonishing Being.

"God gave us life," said Nemian simply.

He looked so special, and so quiet and sad, and what he said, the way he'd explained or tried to (God may be inexplicable, I somehow guess), I could see Argul in Nemian. Just for a second. So different, like the voice, the accent. But . . .

I put my hand on his. I hadn't been very nice to him—not affectionate or flattered, after he'd gone down on his knees. (Well, one knee anyway.)

He glanced at me, and he smiled. He seemed suddenly very pleased, delighted, excited.

And I was flattered after all.

Perhaps it might be all right?

"Claidi, may I ask you a favor?"

Cautious, as on the stairs, I nodded.

"I'd like to get back to calling you by your full name."

"Oh."

"When we reach my City, they'll expect it. In public. You'll be treated as you should be, as someone important, vital. And *Claidi* is a bit . . . not quite dignified enough, is it?"

"Really."

"Don't be angry, Claidi—Claidissa, may I?"

"All right. But I'll have to get used to it."

It isn't me. So, more confusion. Who's this Claidissa woman?

We were at the shrine of the moon until moonrise, when one of the shadowy people there told us the Riders had come.

Out we went, and there below the water-steps I saw this:

Over the dark marshes, the dark sky and the moon. And in the water between the reeds, enormous lizards, colored the dark red of a Garden-bred rose. Some just lay there, wallowing, as the hippos had done in the Garden river. But others had openwork cages strapped on their backs, and men were sitting in these.

What I'd expected I can't say. I wouldn't have gotten it right, whatever it was.

"What are—?"

"They're alligators, Claidissa. And those things on their backs are riding-jadaja."

"Ja-daja. I see."

The alligators, some of them, flickered their tails. All their red scales skittered moonlight. They were very beautiful, but their eyes were cold and shone a moonish green.

The moon did have a green tinge too. A sort of vapor was wisping up the sky, wrapping over it. The moon in a cloud—lost in the cloud of the moon. Or just lost in the marshes of the moon.

"What fun," I depressedly said.

But then the Riders were slipping off, all agile, onto the steps. They carried things to offer the moon god. Things they'd shot with arrows mostly, in the marsh.

People have to eat. I suppose they have to make offerings, too. But it looked pretty dismal.

Nemian, to my amazement, couldn't speak the language of the Alligator Riders. Someone from the shrine had to help. At last, something was agreed, and then an alligator was guided by its Rider up to the steps, and somehow we stepped on it, and got into the quite-big cage, and sat down on its padded floor.

I wondered if these people used money. Decided they might not. Their hair was unevenly cut short, and they wore reed-woven garments. (Nemian told me after; at the time I could only see they looked rough and ready.) Their jewelry consisted of polished pebbles, alligator claws, and teeth.

The cage jadaja thing was also made from reeds.

Our Rider didn't seem to mind not calling in at the shrine. Perhaps they consider it part of their worship of the moon to assist travelers who meet them by moonlight.

As he guided his beast away, by gentle kicks and pats on its sides, the Rider began to sing, raising his eyes to the moon.

The moon was green in its veil. Mists rose from the marshes. The water glimmered like old glass.

His miserable-sounding song, with its no-doubt-miserable unknown words, made me want to howl like one of the Hulta's dogs, only they seldom had.

We were in the marshes a few days and nights. We stopped off at tiny villages of reed houses, where people sat fishing or mending nets, and the women wove cloth from reeds, at reed-built looms.

A silent people. They didn't say much to each other. Nemian communicated by signals. They gave us fish and edible leaves and unpleasant-tasting water that must have been all right.

The mouth of an alligator is one man-length long. Or a little longer. They have about three million teeth, or so it looked. But I saw Rider children swimming around with them, diving under the water with them. Even toddlers.

Alligators smell fishy. Or these did.

We did, soon.

One sunset—I must describe it. Some salts in the marsh sometimes cause weird colors. But the sky went lavender, and the sun was ginger. And these hues mixed in the water. Lightning fluttered, dry, without rain or wind or thunder. And the lightning was rainbow-colored and in shapes—like branching trees, bridges, rolling wheels.

He said, "It's pretty. I've never seen this, although I've heard of it. Marsh lightning. It's nothing, of course, to City fireworks."

We got here, to River Jaws, yesterday. The marsh ends here, and from the upper story of the guesthouse, if it is, you can see over the lines and ranks of reeds to an endless sheet of water. Wide River.

It does sink down and rise up—tidal, as he said.

There seem to be servants here. They speak the language I do, and some other language. Nemian can speak both of these.

The reason we're waiting: Nemian sent someone from here to arrange another boat.

No sooner did I write that than Nemian came by, just now, and enthusiastically told me we'll leave tomorrow.

In three days, he enthused, we'll be there—in his City with the fireworks and the Wolf Tower. His home. Mine.

HIS CITY

Wide River's wide. One seems to drift in the middle of space or the sky, because the sky reflects in the River, and they become one. And there's only the boat—no land on either side.

A huge curved sail, filling slowly with steady, *breathing* wind. Like a lung.

They *were* slaves—I mean, the people who waited on us. I'd never been waited on—the opposite, of course. I wasn't keen on it. And they were slaves, not servants. Two men and a woman, who sat in the boat's back—its *stern*—cross-legged, heads down, ready for Nemian to call or snap his fingers.

Also, there were two sailors to drive the boat. (Or, it was a ship, I think.) Very respectful. No, they groveled.

Feeling so uncomfortable with this, I spent a lot of time sitting by the side, staring out.

Sunset the first night was glorious.

"Look at all the gold," I said to Nemian. Every so often I tried to speak to him.

"If you like that, I think I can really please you," said Nemian.

Baffled, I let him take me to the cabin room where I was to sleep. The slave woman was there, and she bowed almost to her knees.

"The Princess Claidissa," said Nemian, "will be shown the dress now."

So then the poor old slave undid a chest and brought out this dress.

Even in the House, I admit, I never saw a dress quite so magnificent.

In the wild light reflecting off sky and River, the golden tissue of the dress seemed made of fire.

"That's what you'll wear," announced Nemian, "when we sail into my City."

I was meant to be thrilled, and thank him, and tweet with delight.

Well, I did thank him.

"It's a very grand dress."

"Oh, I know you prefer simple clothes," said Nemian kindly. "Jizania told me about that. I even do believe you used to polish the odd table or whatever it was. You're a funny little thing. But in public you'll need to dress up."

Obviously, not to let him down. That was fair. He was bringing me back, showing me off. I had to be acceptable to them. It was worrying, all this. If I was to be with him—I mean *be* with him as a companion, perhaps a wife (I'd never been sure)—I'd have to be responsible. Take pains.

Princess Claidissa.

Oh.

"Oh," I said, quite humbly.

We had dinner on the deck, waited on hand and foot, arm and leg, as it were. Wine and fruit and dishes under silver covers.

Rather like the House.

What had I expected?

Maybe, at the start, I'd even wanted it—to be served, have things done for *me.* What other system had I ever been shown? It was either lord it or live as a slave.

Since then . . .

I chatted brightly. Oh, see, there were birds flying over. Oh, look, there was an island with a tree.

Dusk went to night. I went in to sleep. Couldn't.

It was almost four days, in the end. The wind was often slow; the tides made it take longer, or something. They said these things to him, apologizing, acting bothered in case he got angry. But Nemian, thank God, was just offhand and idle with them, only slightly impatient once or twice. Never rude or vicious or violent.

On the last day, the land began to appear regularly on either side. But the weather had changed. It got chilly. The skies and the water were two silk sheets of grey.

Then clouds came, and rain fell in tired little sprinkles.

Just after lunch, a tall, tall, smooth, slim, grey stone appeared, standing on the nearer bank—we could now see both of them. There wasn't much else—a few trees, trailing down into the water, and a flattish plain, with thin mountain shapes on the left that must be months in the distance. (Altogether rather a bare sort of place, it seemed.)

"Ah!" cried Nemian, though, and jumped up.

He saluted the pillar, or whatever it was, standing very straight, just as *it* was. And all the slaves and boat-slaves bowed over double.

Nemian turned to me. His face was alight with energy.

"Only an hour or so more, Claidissa. Then we'll be there."

I felt immediately sick. This seemed ridiculous. I should be interested, at least.

"I'm so glad," I said.

"Go and get ready now, Claidissa."

"Oh, but—"

"It's all right. I'll change on deck in that tent thing. Just concentrate on yourself."

In fact I'd been going to say I wouldn't need "an hour or so" to get ready. But it wouldn't matter, really, so I did what he said, and the woman slave followed me into the cabin.

How wrong I was. It did take all of two hours.

First washing, and hair-washing, and drying, and then perfumes and things. All fine, only I felt peculiar, so it wasn't.

Then the slave dressed me in lace undies and slid me into the golden dress.

After that stockings and shoes, bracelets, earrings. (Even a gold bag for this book.) My hair was still damp, but the slave began to arrange it. Parts were plaited, and bits were put up with pins, and some hung down in curls that were made with two heated iron sticks—tongs, she said—and there was a nasty smell of scorched hair—mine.

She made up my face. She put on powder, and dark around the eyes, and blush for the mouth and cheeks.

She even colored my fingernails with gold, and I had to sit there like an insane sort of tree, holding out my hands, fingers stretched apart to let the stuff dry.

When I got back on the deck, Nemian was standing there in his black and gold, looking regal. He gave me a nod—which seemed mean after the two-hour preparation. He could have said, I thought, How nice you look, or something. Even if only for the slave's benefit—she'd worked so hard.

The slaves served us yellow wine in tall glasses.

And the City appeared.

I'd been thinking, uneasily, how dreary it all looked, all this flattish greyishness, with higher greyish things—I didn't know what—starting to poke up. There was a vague rain-mist. Everything looked ghostly.

And then this enormous *heap* swelled up and closed in all around.

Out of the mist reared a gigantic black statue. It was slick with rain, gleaming. What was it? It seemed to be a frowning man, his head raised high into the mist.

I was still puzzling over it, but other shapes, all completely huge, were now pushing in behind, and the ship-boat floated as if helpless in among them.

High stone banks rose from the river. Up from these, piled terraces of dark buildings, stone on stone. And towers loomed in the sky, softened only by the mist. From one or two windows, a faint light seeped. They glistened, though, in the wet, like dark snakes.

And everywhere, the gigantic statues, in pale marble or black basalt. Rearing beasts (lions, bears?). A grim stone woman leaned down toward the River, so I thought for a moment (terrified) this statue was tumbling and would fall right on the boat. In her upstretched stone hand, a real (vast) mirror, which reflected our upturned faces, small as the faces of mice.

Roofs, layered on the sky, vanished in mist and cloud. Everything was so big. So smooth and burnished. So clean and cold and dim and dark.

"Yes," he breathed. "I've missed this place. Home. My home. Yours. And look there, over there, can you see?"

I gazed where he pointed and saw a tower that somehow managed to be even bigger than all the rest, and even smoother and dimmer and etc. On the top, a furious black stone thing crouched, snarling, one taloned paw upraised, and a flag in it, dark and limp in the rain.

So I didn't need him to say to me, in his emotional and exalting voice: "*The Wolf Tower.*"

Perhaps not unreasonably, since Nemian was important, and after all he'd said about a welcome, I'd expected crowds.

There weren't any. Or only one.

The ship was guided in to the bank, and there, in a long stone porch that stretched from the Wolf Tower, with its demon wolf, were some people richly dressed and a group of others, obviously more slaves.

These other slaves lay down on the pavement, in the puddles.

"Our" slaves on the ship lay down on the deck, even the one tying us up to the bank, once he'd finished.

The royalty approached the steps and looked down at us. They wore fantastic clothes, thick with gold and silver, more like *armor.*

But they were smiling and waving soft hands.

"Nemian . . . Nemian," they cried, "darling . . ."

They all looked alike to me, in a funny way. A lot of them had golden hair just like his.

Nemian got ashore and walked up the steps. Then he turned and gestured back toward me, showing me to them. And they clapped and gave little shrill cries.

I didn't know what I was supposed to do, so I just stood there like a twerp.

One of the men said, "Your messenger was here before you, Nemian, in good time. The Old Lady will come out." Nemian colored with pleasure. (His grandmother, must be.)

"I don't deserve it. I nearly failed you."

"No, no, Nemian. We heard how things went wrong. And still you took success."

They beamed at me. Should I smile too? Or stay ever so dignified? Before I could decide, a horn wailed from somewhere in the tower. *They* all fell deadly smileless and silent. Their heads all turned toward the door that opened on the porch. It was a high oblong door, of two steely halves.

Two slaves emerged first, holding out their arms, as if to shoo everyone aside. They looked haughty. Then she came out.

Instantly I knew her. Instantly again I didn't. I wished I hadn't drunk the wine.

She was tall, thin, *smoothed* like the buildings. She had their colors or noncolors.

No mistaking her eyes—black in her dry, elderly white face. They were glaring straight at me, as if to strip me to the bones.

The two haughty slaves yapped in chorus:

"Princess Ironel Novendot."

And suddenly I knew who she reminded me of, for all her utter unlikeness: Jizania Tiger of the House I'd left behind.

THE LAW: FINDING

Looking around, for the thousandth time, I wonder if there's any way I can use that window, or that one, or even the door. Or is there anything I can do? I think about the million and one times at the House I got into hot water and usually got myself out of it again. Maybe with a slapped face or bleeding beaten hands, but nothing too final. However, this is difficult. No, it's impossible. Argul told me I was trouble, or made trouble, and he was absolutely right. I just wish he was here to say, *I told you so.* Although I don't, really, wish he was here. I wouldn't wish many people *here.*

Sorry, I'll start again. You won't know yet what I'm going on about.

When did I first start to panic? Well, that was long before *this.* Really almost as soon as I saw the Princess Ironel.

She came walking along the stone porch with her black licorice cane tapping on the ground. Her hands were white claws.

She wasn't beautiful like Jizania, and Ironel had all her hair—partly black still, or iron-colored—pulled back off her masklike face into a towering topknot stuck with silver pins.

As she approached, Nemian and all the others kneeled down—not one knee either, both knees.

And the slaves were flat, all but her slaves, who presently kneeled and bowed their heads.

But I stood upright, there on the boat-ship. Why? In a way, I was frightened of tearing the dress if I kneeled. (It seemed very flimsy material.)

Or getting it dirty. I mean, it couldn't be mine. *They'd* provided it, this lot. (Just as maids had been dressed by the House.)

I did bow my head. But that was shame more than anything else.

And why was I ashamed? Second sight, maybe, like Argul's mother.

Sort of cricking my neck, I saw Ironel Novendot raise Nemian and embrace him. It was a stiff and a cold embrace. It was as if one of the towers did it. But he seemed awfully happy. He kissed her claws.

"You found her," she said.

"Madam, I did."

"What is her name?" I heard the old voice rasp. (Me?)

"Claidissa Star." (Me.)

"Yes," said Ironel Novendot. "That is correct."

The hairs rose on my scalp under all the curls and coilings. *What did she mean?* He'd *found* me? She *knew* me?

Then the appalling slaves on the boat were help-thrusting me up the stairs onto the bank and into the porch, and I was right in front of her.

"You are welcome to the City," said the old woman. She spoke—as he had—as if only this City existed, capital C. Like the capital H of the House. All lies, as now I knew. "We are very glad you've come," she added. "I, certainly."

She. She didn't look it. Her *eyes,* jet black with grey rings around the black. Awful eyes. But she *did* look like Jizania, in a way. Was it just her age? No—and anyway, how old was she?

"We will go in now," she told us.

An order.

Everyone got up, simpering.

She turned back to me, sudden as something springing, and caught my face in a bunch of claws.

"Do you speak?"

"Yes, madam."

"Good." She smiled. Ah. Her teeth were false. They were wonderful. Pearls set in silver. She must save that smile for very special moments. (She does.)

First of all, the slaves let us into a hollow in the wall and closed a gilded gate. Then they worked a handle inside and the whole thing—hollow, gate, us—went rocking upward. Walls shut us in on all sides. I didn't like it. But I recalled Nemian telling me about clockwork "lifters" that could carry people to the top stories of his City.

Just as I thought I'd go mad and scream, we reached another open hollow. To my horror, we went right up past it.

There were some more of these. When I'd given up hope, we came to a hollow and stopped. More slaves outside opened the gate.

Outside was a colossal hall. It seemed to go on forever on every side, and the ceiling too was high as a sky, or looked like it. It was painted like a sky too, only the paint had faded. Unless they did it that way in the first place, grey, with grape-dark clouds. (Probably they did.)

On the deep grey marble expanse of floor were spindly tables with things to eat and drink, tobacco, and open boxes of strange stalks and tablets. These were like the things Nemian had given me instead of food in the dust desert. I couldn't see why they would be necessary here.

Nemian, though, took a handful of them and ate them. Then he took some wine from a slave. So did I, the wine, although I didn't want it.

The old woman took only a glass of something that looked like muddy pond water, sucked it, and pulled a face like a kid who'd been given burnt spinach when she wanted an ice cream.

But she clasped Nemian's arm. As they walked along the long, long floor away from the crowd—who all watched admiringly and went on simpering—she called, "You, too, Claidissa."

So I, too, went with them.

There were vast windows stretching floor to ceiling. They had glass in them, and eventually we stood at one, looking out over the City. (There was also something nasty bulging over the window top, twice my height again, over my head. Took me a while to realize it was one black *paw* of the evil wolf statue on the roof, curled down over the window. What a place!)

The City looked vile too. How could he be proud of it? Homesick for it?

Rain boiled among the stupid, too-high buildings. The depressing statues lurched and craned. Everything black or grey or like sour milk. Absolute rubbish.

I'd been vaguely wondering if there were any outer walls to guard it. (I've since learned there aren't. Instead they have lookouts and other things, like Peshamba but more "serious.") But right then I thought just one look at this place would make anyone, friend or foe, turn around and trudge off in another direction. Any direction.

Nemian and his gran had been murmuring things to each other. Not exactly loving, but sort of secretive and sneaky, somehow. They both had a sly, smug look. It didn't suit either of them. He didn't look so handsome. His face seemed to have changed. And glancing at me, abruptly he laughed. It was a cruel laugh. One couldn't miss it. It was a laugh of heartless triumph.

I didn't want to make a judgment. I'd done a lot of that and been proved wrong. I just stood there meekly.

Ironel Novendot said to me, also glancing sidelong, "And how is Jizania these days?"

That was so much what had been on my mind, and I said at once, "Blooming."

"Blast the creature," said Ironel, snapping her pearls spitefully. "Wouldn't she just!"

"I'm afraid," I said sadly, "she forgot to send you her regards." (Forgot a lot of things, I mentally added. Like the fact she and you seem to know each other.)

But Ironel only sucked her drink again.

"One day," she said to me, "you too will have to live on muck like this. Has he told you my age?"

She waited. Old People often like you to be astounded by their ages. I said, "No, madam."

"One hundred and seventy," she informed me.

Well, I didn't believe her. She wasn't more than ninety-nine, I'd have said. But I widened my eyes and exclaimed, "A great age, lady."

"You too," she said, "will reach a great age here in our City. And you too will end as I am, drinking slops." And she smiled again, pleased at the idea.

A curse?

No, it seemed to be simply a fact.

I went colder, far colder, than if she *had* cursed me.

Nemian said, "She doesn't know yet, Grandmother."

"Doesn't she? Nice surprise for her then. How did you get her here?"

Nemian shot me a little-boyish, rueful look. He seemed to be saying, I just know you'll forgive me, Claidi. He actually said, "Well, madam, I lied to her a lot."

"And with your pretty face," said Ironel, happier by the second, "the poor little fish was hooked."

My mouth *didn't* fall open. And I *didn't* throw up on their shoes. I remain proud of both these things. I was so afraid, I felt as if I were floating in the air inside a ball of ice. Struck dumb, I couldn't question them. So I stayed mercifully silent.

Nemian said, "When Jizania's people shot the balloon down—*not* in my plan—I thought I'd had it, I confess. But luck was on my side. And Jizania stuck to her vow, once I'd shown her the flower. It's just possible she might have forgotten if I hadn't. Her mind isn't as sharp as *yours,* Grandmother."

They smirked at each other.

Then Ironel said, "I must show Claidissa the garden of Immortal flowers."

I couldn't work out any of it. Sometime one of these monsters was going to have to explain it all to me. Not only had I been made a fool of, I was a fool to start with.

Strangely, I had then a sudden image of Argul. He'd never have been tricked by such people. He'd have known what was going on. But in such a situation, he would have been terrific, I just knew. This is hard to describe, but all at once, I seemed to myself to *become* Argul. I wasn't Claidi anymore, but him, tall and strong, confident and clever. And brave.

I looked at them with Argul's eyes, and I said, "This wine's rather bad, isn't it? Perhaps you're just used to it. But really." And I upended the glassful and poured it on their horrible floor.

They both *gaped* at me. What a sight.

At that moment, a bell rang.

Everyone looked—even they did. Through a gauzy curtain came two new slaves, bowing. And then this girl.

She was—I don't know where to begin. I'll try. If you took one newborn primrose and mixed its color in the purest cream, that was her skin, the exact shade and as smooth. She had black-blue eyes, slanting upward at the outer corners. She had *blue*—must have been black—hair that hung straight as sheet metal to the backs of her knees. She wore white, and the rain must have drenched her and then turned to opals.

"Ah, now," said the old witch, Ironel. "Here's Moon Silk."

This girl, Moon Silk, came along the floor, gliding on perfect moon-pale feet.

And Nemian gave a sort of strangled cry. And down his cheeks ran more rain, only this was tears.

He left me, he left his fearful granny, and he strode to the exquisite girl and raised her into his arms. He kissed her. It was . . . a *kiss.*

Despite everything, it startles me to have to report, I felt as if I'd been hit in the stomach.

And Ironel said, not needing to, as Nemian hadn't needed to name this awful Tower, "How touching. Lovers re-meeting. Nemian and his young bride. They were only married, Claidissa, a month before he had to leave us on his quest for *you.*"

She told me. (Ironel.) She must have loved it. I tried to be Argul, still, but he'd never have gotten in this mess. In the end I just had to be Claidi and listen and cope as best I could.

It's soon told, though she went on and on, embroidering bits lovingly. Lingering. Watching me to see if I'd cry or jump about.

Before, she took me with her, alone, along the top story of the Wolf Tower. From various windows she pointed out ugly important buildings. The other three Towers, for example, in the three other quarters of the City. They are the Pig Tower, the Vulture Tower, and the Tiger Tower. You'll probably see at once, the Tiger Tower used to be Jizania Tiger's—where Jizania was *born.*

Ironel also showed me a courtyard in which, in four grey stone vases, grew the brilliant red flowers with juicy leaves. One of which Nemian handed Jizania in the House Debating Hall.

Meanwhile, downstairs, in the Wolf Tower, Nemian would be blissfully alone with his wife. Moon Silk. Ironel kept going back to that.

But she slipped up there. In the end, I got used to it.

Let's face it, too, he was a rotten husband. Married one month, and the moment he had the chance, off with a Hulta girl. He'd led me on because he had to. But there was no excuse for *that.*

We were by then seated in Ironel's apartment in the Tower, in another far-too-large room that echoed. Outside was a view of where the River grew hugely wide again, and the opposite bank wasn't to be seen.

The Wolf Tower isn't very warm. They don't have the heating system the House had. Just fireplaces and baskets of coals (braziers), both of which smoke.

Anyway, I must now write down what Ironel Novendot told me. This book is the story of my life, and she—or the Law of the Tower—made it all happen.

Yes, the *Law.*

But I think I'll have to explain about that separately. It's a story in itself, the Wolf Tower Law. I've only become a tiny desperate bit of it.

The Law (and as I say, I'll go back to the Law) decreed that Nemian had to find a girl to take over a particular duty in the City. Probably the most necessary duty. And that was because Ironel, who until now had seen to this duty, was at last too old for it—or she said she was.

And here Law is LAW. Is Absolute. No one goes against it.

So Nemian, just married and all, set off in the hot-air balloon, of which the City has a fleet, although they seldom use them.

Some things then went wrong with the balloon, and there was a chance he wouldn't make it. Then he did make it, only to be shot down by the guns of the very place—the House—he'd been traveling to. He told them he was on a quest, and he was. *I* was the quest. He was on a quest to find me. This makes me sound of great importance, and I was. I am.

Because, you see, Jizania Tiger, in her youth, over a hundred years ago, had also left this City and had gone to live in the House. (No one says why. Honestly, I should just think she'd have preferred to.) I don't know how the House is related to this City, but obviously it was then.

When she left, she promised—made a vow by the Law—to present to the Wolf Tower, when required, a girl of royal blood from the House. A girl suitable to take on Ironel's duty when Ironel gave it up.

If Jizania eventually forgot this vow, I don't know. Very likely. It was a damn silly, nasty thing to have to remember.

But Nemian gave her the red flower, the Immortal, which was the token by which she'd know the time had come.

I suppose, as in certain stories I've read, maybe it was meant to be her own daughter, or granddaughter, she'd have to supply.

Did Jizania perhaps even tell Nemian that I was . . . that I *was* her granddaughter, her daughter's child?

You see, Jizania lied to Nemian, and she lied to me. And she knew and doubtless told him, he'd better lie to me too. Even when he started to have doubts I was the princess-girl Jizania had assured him I was. By then I was all he could get. I *did* come from the House. I have the House accent—which Ironel would recognize. Perhaps I'd do. And I was daft enough to believe him, to stay with him.

He did nearly lose me, that once, in Peshamba. But when he knew he might, he rushed to me and pleaded to try to get me back. He really was desperate and afraid that night. When he said his life wouldn't be worth anything without me, that *wasn't* a lie at all.

I said, the Law is the LAW. If he'd come back empty-handed, he'd have lost his title, his money, his wife. They'd have flung him in some cellar and left him there.

That's what the Law is like. You don't ever go against it.

Maybe he could just have run off in the wild, never come back. But he wanted to, was "homesick." Or . . . well, he probably wanted Moon Silk.

That I'd be reluctant to come with him was obvious. That is, if I'd known what they wanted me for. He wasn't surprised Jizania hadn't warned me or told me everything. Or that he had to pretend.

That's all bad enough. But there's this other thing. Jizania was determined to send me off with Nemian, to keep her vow. So did she lie to me as well about my mother being royal? She couldn't say both my parents were royalty—I'd have seen the House wouldn't exile a prince and a princess. But the story of a princess falling in love with her servant rang true.

Of course, Ironel knew my name, or the full name Jizania told me was mine. Claidissa Star. Jizania must also have promised the Law she'd give this name to the chosen child. But then, you see, she could just have made sure some child of around the right age, any old child, *did* get this name. And that just happened to be me. So my name doesn't prove a thing.

And she'd seen I was nuts on Nemian. So I'd go on with the lie in any case, making him believe I was a princess and *worthy* of him.

I mean, do I strike you as princess material?

Heaven knows who I really am, or who I really was. . . .

Because now, I belong here, to the Tower. To the Law. To this place of stones, where their statues make even animals ugly.

And for this I gave up Argul. I made him think I didn't care. And that ring he dropped—oh, it was for me. Of course it was. He was for me, and I was for him. And anyway, even if he was just being kind, I could have been out there, in the world, in the Waste-that-isn't. Free. I could cry or laugh until I was sick. But instead, I'll go on writing. There's more to say. If you can stand it.

THE LAW: KEEPING

In the evening, I dined with Ironel.

Her apartment is sprawling. The size of the Travelers' Rest. Maybe not quite.

The Wolf Tower, as Nemian told me in nonlying mode, is the most powerful of the four Towers that rule the City on Wide River.

But the food wasn't up to much.

She only drinks her mud drink. I think it's because she doesn't have teeth and doesn't dare chip the fabulous pearl ones.

Candles burned on an iron candelabra that was standing on the table and was taller than I am.

Why am I talking about candles?

By then, she'd shown me the holy part of the Tower. Holy used to mean to do with God, but now, despite Nemian's poetic spoutings that I liked so much, the Law the Wolf Tower makes is "holy," and more holy than anything else.

The Law.

I don't know how to start to tell you. It's—it's—I'd better calm down. Again, I'll start again.

Once, all four Towers had a say in making the Law. Then there was a fight, or something, which the Wolf Tower won. So now the Wolf Tower does it, and everyone else obeys.

There are no servants, no maids. Only slaves. But the royal people who fill the City, and whom the slaves serve, they too are slaves. Slaves to the Law of the Wolf Tower. And so am I. I have been since I let Nemian escape from the House. Or even since I first thought I loved him.

It *stinks*.

The holy area, in which I now "live," clusters around the main room, which they call the Room.

It isn't—amazingly—very big, this Room.

But it's black as dead burnt wood.

Huge lamps, too large for the Room, burn with pale, feverish fires.

Along the walls are shelves, and stacked there, like the books in the House library, are black boxes. And in the boxes, carefully filed and preserved by slaves of the Room, who suffer if they get it wrong, are cards with the names of every man, woman, child, and infant in the City. There are even names of ones who've died—or, I hope, maybe run away. But they keep them anyway, with a red mark on the little card.

They enter new ones too. I saw this, the first night. *She* did it. Ironel.

The slaves brought a box, and another slave, from a house in the City that had had a baby, brought a card with the baby's name. Ironel took the card, read it, *smiled,* and put it on top of the box. That was all. The slave has to number and file it correctly. And, as I said, if he or she doesn't . . .

Bizarre enough.

But what actually catches one's attention in the Room at once, are the Dice.

Ironel said they were dice.

I asked (you see, my light's not put out yet, though I don't know why not), "What are Dice, madam?"

She told me, and told me their use in the Law. Do you know about dice? I'm still a bit blank really. The Dice have eight sides. Every side is painted with a number, from one to eight, inclusive.

How to show you. Well, let me draw it.

They are this shape:

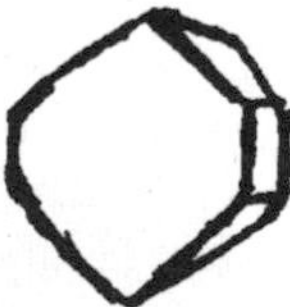

Like some cut diamonds, almost. There are only two of them.

They're held up in silver-gilded sort of things. They remind me of egg cups, only with pieces cut out, so most of the shape of the Dice is visible.

And the Dice can move. They have to. They spin and turn over in many directions. This happens four times a day—at dawn, noon, sunset, and midnight.

What makes them spin like this I don't understand. Some mechanism. But Ironel has to be there. And—once I've learned—*I* have to be there. Instead of Ironel.

They call her the Wolf's Paw.

That's what I'll be called.

Wolf's Paw.

She *reads* the Dice when they come to rest, from the way in which all the numbered sides fall and face. And from that, looking in three books of ancient mathematics, which lie handy on a marble table in the Room, she can tell what the Law is saying must be done. And who must do it.

Although the Dice must often fall the same way—only two of them, you see, and only eight sides each—apparently the day and time of day always make a difference, or something to do with the math—or what phase of the moon we're in. Can you follow this? I can't.

So, I don't understand the books, or the Dice.

Or the way she can tell who must do what.

But apparently one *can* work it out in numbers. Every spin of the Dice shows something someone has to do. You then tie up the message the Dice give with sixteen City people (for the two lots of eight different sides). And that happens four times a day.

So that's . . . I can't even work *that* out.

I'm hopeless with numbers—four times sixteen, that's sixty-four people every day and night. (I worked it out on a different bit of paper.)

And whatever the Wolf's Paw tells them, the Law says they must do, these sixty-four, they MUST. Each day.

Ironel gave me examples.

Nemian married Moon Silk because a fall of the Dice told him he should. (How about her?)

And Nemian came after me and found me and brought me back here because another fall of the Dice said he had to. (And how about *me*?)

The point is, if you're picked and you don't obey, or you blow it, they imprison you under the City, in dank darkness, where the River seeps through. (She liked telling me about that, as well.)

Apart from mere horror, I can barely add it up. Science is a mystery to me. How in the world's name am I going to master these awful Dice, these dreadful books of numbers and moon phases?

I didn't admit this. Just stood there, all cool.

Ironel let me see her make her judgment that sunset. It looked easy when she did it. But then she's done it for over fifty years. The Dice whirl and end up sideways or upright. She goes over and looks at them. Then she walks to the books. She makes a big thing about the books—keeps telling me there are only these three in the City, and how precious they are. (She showed me, in them, the hundreds of columns of numbers and my head went around like the Dice.)

She ran her finger down the columns, flipped pages, clicked her tongue on her pearls.

Then she spoke the Law, and the slaves wrote down each order. After this, messengers (slaves) of the Wolf Tower carry the orders to the lucky persons concerned.

The messages of the Law were frightful, though.

Some man (number 903, I think) had to leave his house and go and live on the street as "best he could." (Incredible.) And number 5,334, a little girl, was to be made to wear the disguise of a snail, complete with shell.

I forget the others. They weren't so bad. No, one was. I don't even want to write it.

But I will write it. I don't remember the number, or who. But they had to dive into the River and swim up and down. They might rest on islands, or the banks, for a few minutes when "exhausted." Their relatives might bring them food and "comforts."

There was no indication when this punishment would end, if it ever would. It wasn't called a punishment.

And this—*this*—is the *Law.*

They live here, and some people can go their whole lives without the Dice ever summoning up their numbers and names, so they need never do anything but enjoy themselves. Or they might be told to do something rather stupid, but not unnice, like going and buying a new shirt.

Or they might be told they must have a baby before a year has passed.

Or that they must stand naked on a wall. Or go into the desert and fight a lion.

And I'm going to have to find this out from the Dice. And then I'm going to have to tell them. I'm going to be Wolf's Paw, to be *her.*

She said that I'd grow old here.

If I don't learn, God knows what they'll do to me. And I won't be able to.

But I don't *want* to be able to. I don't want to hurt people, make fools of them, blight their lives like this, and smiling as I do it, as *she* does.

My rooms are large. There's a bathroom, a bedroom, and a living room. Brocades and furs and fireplaces and lamps.

One wall with dresses thick with gold and jewels. I hate them.

Five slaves to wait on me.

When I take her place, I'll have more. I'll have everything I "want."

Except I must always be available for when the Dice mechanically turn, to read the books and interpret the Law. And give it.

That night, after the midnight Dice, I made believe I'd gone to sleep in the luxurious white satin bed.

I got up in blind darkness and tried to go out.

But the slaves were there, leaping up to "serve" me.

And their eyes are like the eyes of the moon alligators in the marsh: cold and blind, without a mind or heart.

Sometimes the Wolf's Paw goes out in a procession, she'd told me. Next day I asked to go walking.

No obstacle, except the five slaves who walked with me and that man in a white uniform, with the rifle.

Very few people passed us. Most were carried in chairs by slaves.

None of the slaves have faces. Well they do, but they might as well be made of paper. They don't seem human.

The buildings soar into the never-changing rainy gloom.

I prowl these rooms. The windows have cute lattices of gilded iron and, anyway, are ten man-heights from the ground, or more. I'm a prisoner.

Well, I have considered various tricks—the sort you read of in books. Giving slaves the slip, running very fast, pretending to be ill in case they then relax their watchfulness, assuming they are watchful . . . which they are, aren't they? But somehow, I don't think this will work, any of it. I mean, they are always there. And the City itself does watch. Not crystals like in Peshamba but, rather, black poking things—like guns—turning to follow you on the streets.

Everyone's name is in those boxes, even mine now, and hers.

I'm so afraid that I don't even feel loss. And when she lectures me on the mathematics in the precious books, she seems to think I understand—and I *don't,* of course I don't. I was never educated. Two and two make three.

She asks questions and I attempt to answer, I bluff or I say nothing, and she doesn't fault me. She nods. Is she mad? Or just so old?

I haven't seen anyone else for some time. Only the slaves and the guard in white. And occasionally people passing far below on the paved streets of this doomy City. And her.

The Law is a game. I mean, they play a *game* and call it a law, and failure to obey it is death.

And Ironel is keeper of the Law until I learn the rules, and then I'm the keeper. (And to think, the Rituals of the House used to annoy me.)

Nemian seems like someone I made up. Argul does too. And you—well, I *did* make you up. But oh, you, you, help me—tell me what to do—help, help me, you're the only one I can turn to. And obviously, you can't answer.

How curious. It was as if I heard you, calling. All sorts of words and voices. And it did help me.

Thank you . . .

Thank you.

WOLVES

She's ill.

She did the dawn Law today—I don't have to be there for those—then went back to bed.

A slave told me, and I had to go and visit her. Another slave handed me one of those red flowers to give her. Apparently that's a polite way to show her I think she'll get better soon.

(Would have liked to chuck it out of a window. Didn't.)

Ironel sat up in her bed, which is like a boat for size, with curtains of golden chains.

She looked all right to me.

When she'd sent everyone out, she said to me, "I've never told you the reason for the Law, have I? I must, since you're learning so fast and so very well."

I gulped. She's dotty.

But she said, "Random blows and insane adventures. The Law copies life."

That was all. I didn't understand but just nodded, coolly, and gazed into space as if deeply thinking.

Then she made me really jump. She *laughed.* It was an awful old cackle, you can imagine, and those pearl teeth bouncing about in it.

"Claidissa, dear," she said when she could, "you may have to take over the Law very soon. I'm ill. It's too much for me. So be ready. Get fit. Go out for a walk, Claidissa. Walk around our spectacular City. Look at the darling River. Have some exercise. *Think* about what I've told you. You will be a Wolf of the Tower. And those powerful Dice, those delicious rare books, those important boxes, by which we live."

I was shaking. I said, "Yes, madam."

Her word is Law, isn't it? I'd have to take over. And I'd have to have a walk! (And go down the Tower again in one of those lifters.)

So I'll do that. I'll walk. I can do that. I *can't* read the books or do the Law thing. I might as well jump in the River.

I don't think I said, I had to wear the proper clothes now always. People were supposed to know who I was—the next Wolf's Paw. No wonder no one spoke to me or looked.

These dresses are so heavy. I feel like a beetle or a lizard, all wrapped up in scales and bits of carapace. My hair, too, wound up on a golden comb and pulling. I don't know myself in mirrors anymore, which matched how I felt, pretty much.

This time, though, down in the City, I studied things with more care. I'm not sure why. Guilt maybe, because I wasn't going to jump in the River.

The people who passed—carried in ornate chairs, or sometimes walking, with slaves pattering behind—all looked the same. They looked like me: overdressed, starched, and so unhappy.

Well, I didn't need to be a genius to realize why, did I? They lived here because they felt they had to, or surely they'd have gone. And while they did, even if the Law so far had *never* fallen on them or anyone they cared about, four times every day they knew it still *could,* and probably would.

I wandered down below the Wolf Tower and along the banks, quays they say here, where tall grim ships are tied by chains. Then the River gets wide again, and you can't see the far bank, which is just how Nemian described it.

Rain plished miserably.

And I noticed someone swimming in that icy grey water.

I knew who it was, who it had to be: the one whose number I don't remember.

Tears flooded down my face. I clenched my fists.

This was all crazy. It was a nightmare.

One of the slaves came over and offered me a hanky to mop up. The one with the umbrella that I'd sent off crept close again.

I turned on them.

"I want to be left alone." Their faces were flat and told me nothing.

"All right. Stand there. I'm just going across into that square. I'm going . . . to buy something. Don't follow. I don't need you yet."

To my amazement, as I started to walk, they didn't. Even the guard with the rifle.

Was it so simple?

I'd never thought of this—that they'd just do what I said. Could I dodge away and make a run for it?

Where though? Beyond the City, I'd seen, was only that grey, bare deserty land. And anyway, would they let me go, that is, the City itself? The House hadn't bothered to pursue me. I knew now why. Jizania had made sure Nemian and I got away. But here it would be different, although for the same reason.

I crossed the street and went into the square. Perhaps I should still try to make some plan. . . .

There was a group of people over at the end of the square. That surprised me. I hadn't often seen any big group here before.

They do use money in the City. I'd been given a chest full of those blue-green notes Nemian had had. Although everyone seemed to be royal, some of the people here made things, although they weren't very good. They sold them to each other. (Clothes and food and urgent stuff the slaves saw to, without of course being paid.)

Was someone here selling something? The crowd seemed very interested, which wasn't usual either.

There seemed to be someone sitting on the ground, and two others lounging against a pillar. The ground here wasn't made for sitting on, and the pillars weren't for lounging against. It also looked as if these three odd people were slaves, too, because they weren't sparkling.

As I got nearer and nearer, I saw there were children as well, standing staring in their awful, tight jewelry-beetle clothes. But suddenly they all squealed, and there was a brilliant flash, yellow, blue, and up into the air shot all these burning stars.

Fireworks! I knew at once from what Nemian had said. The City had fireworks, but I'd never seen any before.

There were slaves standing around the back of the crowd, also watching the man sitting on the ground.

Then there was a little *crack,* and the children went *Ooooh!* like *real* children. And into the air rose a bird of fire. It was emerald and purple, and slowly, beautifully, it spread a fan-tail of gold—

A peacock. A firework peacock.

I'd reached the edge of the crowd. No, the three men—now I could really see them—didn't belong in this City. They were old and *filthy,* their long old hair and long, scraggly old beards full of bits of mud and twig, like badly made nests. Their faces looked like crumpled dirty rags. Their clothes *were* rags—layers of rags and gruesome old fur jackets.

The seated old man moved his hands, in dirty darned gloves, and out of the thin air between them bloomed a ball of colors. And birds flew out of it, white, like pigeons. They flew up, and I thought *Oh God, what will happen to them here?* Because I hadn't seen a single bird or animal in the City that wasn't stone. Not even a fly. And never trees or any flowers—only those red things called Immortals.

However, the birds dissolved in light. They hadn't been real.

And of course, then I thought of how Argul had taken the living sparrow out of Teil's ear.

But I wasn't going to cry anymore.

The children were laughing and pointing. Little rabbits made of light were jumping around their ankles. (Had they ever seen rabbits?) And there were some smiles from the adults, too. Even—my God—one of the slaves was smiling. Hey!

The darker old man leaning on the pillar was giving me a funny look. The other one abruptly shouted three very strong words.

The crowd didn't take much notice. They didn't know that these words weren't polite, as I hadn't when I first heard them.

"Tronking okk grulps!"

Oddly, the second darker old man turned and thumped, with surprising force, the other old man on the chest.

And the other old man roared in a hurt voice: "Watch it, Mehm. She's h—"

"Then don't make a scene, man."

I wasn't standing on the street anymore. I was floating up and up—like the magical chemical lights Argul's scientist-magician mother must have taught him how to make.

The doddering, seated old man was getting to his feet now. Of the three, he could have won a prize for the disgustingness of his beard. He took some time, too, so stiff and ungainly.

The children were clamoring for more tricks. Instead, he was handing each of them an apple baked in toffee, from Peshamba probably. And to each adult—and slave—a Peshamban chocolate sweet in colored paper.

Then he came grunting and hobbling over, snuffling, leering, his ghastly mucky beard flapping, until he stood in front of me, and I had to look up to reach his eyes.

Behind him, Mehmed and Ro slapped each other (clouds of filth rose) and guffawed. The children were prancing and tearing chunks out of the toffee apples. The adults were wonderingly unwrapping their sweets. It broke your heart. You could see they too had never been given anything very nice, and *never* for free.

"Hello, Claidi-sheepy-baa," said Argul, through his brilliant disguise, the cakes of makeup and mud and horsehair stuck on his face. "Got yourself in a mess again, I gather."

"Yes, Argul."

"Don't cry. I never saw you cry."

"It's the rain."

"Oh yeah. Of course."

In the porch of a building, out of the rain, we spoke so quickly to each other, as if there was no time. But as the Peshamban CLOCK said, There's time enough for everything.

(Through the rain, I could see my slaves and guard, still unmoving at the edge of the square, waiting, presumably noticing me talking to this wild old man and not knowing what went on.)

"Why did you follow me? You were so angry—"

"That changed. And I didn't trust *him.* So. It took a while to get here. He'd talked a lot about his perfect City and glorious Wolf Tower. Can't miss it, can you? What an eyesore. Wolves aren't like that."

"No . . . What are they like?"

He laughed. "Still Claidi. They're brave and loyal. They fight when they have to, or they don't fight. They like each other and stick together. Hulta. That's wolves."

"Argul—"

"I saw you ditched your guard. If we just walk slowly, maybe—"

"No, I've thought about all that. They won't let me go. If I got away, they'd come after. It's their rotten Law."

"We have to take the chance. I've brought Sirree. Yes, she's well. She missed you."

"I missed her. Oh, Sirree . . ."

I stood gazing at this dirty wreck who was HIM.

In the holes and tatters of his shirt, I saw the glass charm winking.

"I can't, Argul. It's too dangerous."

"Chicken."

"I am. And for you, too. I don't want you to get hurt."

He put his hand up over the charm. "See this?" he asked.

"Yes, I remember."

"Remember I looked at it when you were in the Sheeper chariot?"

"Yes."

"It tells me things. My mother—she said if ever I saw . . . if I saw a woman who meant something to me—" He stopped.

He was embarrassed. Here, in the middle of all this. I looked down, to give him a chance. And he said, "The stuff in the bulb, that you think looks like glass, is a chemical. It reacts if *I* do. I mean, if the feeling is real. And it does react, Claidi." He slipped the charm-that-wasn't off and held it in his hand, and I saw the glass-that-wasn't turn cloudy, and then a kind of movement happened inside. That was all. But it was love I was looking at.

I thought how Mehmed had whooped when he leaned over and saw it too and threw a knife and caught it in his teeth.

"Argul, I daren't go with you. I mean, I *do* want to—"

"You've said this before. Look what happened."

"Do you *know,*" I asked him, "about the *Law?*"

"Yes. We're foreigners, they can gripe to us. I know all of it and it's—" He said a word I hadn't ever heard before.

"Well," I faltered, "then you see—"

"Claidi," said Argul. "Do you really believe two Dice rolling about and some old books of rubbish can tell a whole city to live like this, in terror? You saw those kids over there. And the rest of them. Dice aren't wicked. Books aren't. People can be. *People* caused this."

Something clicked in my mind. I can't describe it any other way. I stood speechless.

"Claidi—"

"Wait . . . just a moment—oh—"

And he did wait. He likes me, too. He thinks I have a right to scrabble around, trying to think for myself.

Then I spoke to him *very* fast. He listened.

When I'd finished, he said, "Claidi, I wish you were a fool. It'd be easier."

The kids were playing games on the grey square despite the rain—running about and screaming with joy. The adults, mouths full of chocolate, didn't stop them.

Oh, I can see now why Nemian went mad and played about so much when he got out of this place.

I feel sorry for Nemian, and his exquisite moon-wife.

Mehmed and Ro were standing near in the rain, wet and nosy.

"All right," Argul said to me. "Try. But if not—"

I shook my head.

Then he caught me and kissed me. Through that *beard.* And even so . . .

(They jeered, whistled, called out "Hultai chura!" Which means Leader's sweetheart. That was far away. They fell silent, tired.)

I'm writing this now in such a hurry. I saw love in the "glass charm." You could miss it so easily. Yet it's so vast. It's miraculous. Just like how I found him, walking into that square, as if I had to.

And even if I fail tonight, if I die, I'll have that kiss to keep.

It isn't like being scalded. It's like having wings.

FIREWORKS

When I met Ironel in the Room, at midday, she looked me over and immediately said, "I don't remember that ring."

"My mother, Twilight Star, left it for me. Princess Jizania passed it on."

"Is it a diamond? What a barbaric setting. But, I like it. It's like . . . a star. How fitting."

"Thank you."

"She must have loved you," said Ironel regretfully.

I don't know if she did, or even if she was called Twilight. Argul gave me the ring, which the Peshambans returned to him. And he *does* love me. And I know. (And the ring belonged to *his* mother, so it's almost not a lie.)

I watched very carefully as Ironel did the noon reading and spoke more awful Law I'm not even going to put down.

Leaving for that walk, I'd been praying Ironel would continue doing this for a long time. Now, as the business ended, I said, "Madam, you should go back to bed. You look so ill."

She didn't. She looked repulsively healthy in her iron-old way.

And she narrowed her eyes at me.

"Do I, Claidissa? Indeed."

"As you say, madam, you've trained me for this. It's my job now. I'll take over."

Remember how I described the alligators? Those great long mouths of teeth? Well, that was how she smiled. Her mouth seemed to undo her face in two pieces. And her poisonous eyes were bright.

"Ah, Claidissa. That would be kind. Two or three days in my bed—that should set me up again. And yes, you're so wise now in the reading of the Law. After all. Perhaps I needn't return."

I hadn't been sure. I mean, it was only about an hour ago I'd really thought of it. And even if I was right, this might still be some plan of hers to hurt me. It was a chance I was going to take.

The same as when I shouted at the "bandits" that I'd bite off a nose before I'd give in. I *won't* be stopped. Not anymore.

I bowed low to her.

"I think, lady, I'll just stay here in the holy Room. Make myself more familiar with the wonderful books and things."

"Do, Claidissa." Then she did up her face again. She said, her voice suddenly hollow and ancient, "I've waited so many years for this hour."

And she turned and stalked out, her cane rapping like shots on the floor.

One huge wave of panic.

I ignored it. Sometimes it's all you can do.

"This Room is freezing," I yakked to the nearest slave. The Room wasn't. If anything, it got too hot from the lamps. "Fetch me two or three lighted braziers."

After I had the braziers in, burning away roastingly, I sent the slaves out. I had about seven hours until sunset. And if I was truly successful about this, some extra hours until midnight.

Would she suddenly come back, "Oh I'm so much better!"? Somehow I really didn't think so. She'd had enough of this, after fifty years. And that means she must have had enough of herself too.

Because if I was right . . . *If* I was . . .

She'd kept telling me I'd mastered the Law. Well, now I *would.*

At the House, I'd been used to hard work. And this was. Climbing up the movable stepladder, getting down all the top boxes, then the lower ones, kneeling to get the lowest. Making sure I put them all back exactly as I'd found them. Well, not quite.

Once or twice I went out into the room outside the Room, mostly to cool down. There was a window, and I was faintly surprised, because the grey day changed. The clouds went blowing off slowly down the River. The sky turned palest blue.

That was good. I could check on sunset better.

No slaves loitered. Outside, the corridor leading to Ironel's apartment was empty—almost. I could just see my white guard's rifle propped up there as he waited with my slaves.

The Room was scorching. It was like being in an oven. But I went on with my work.

When I walked into the outer room later—and the western window was starting to flush, and the sun was actually there, gleaming low onto the River—I had the sense to stop.

I just stood in the Room then, haughty and poised, and waited for the slaves of the Law to appear.

They did, dead on time. They couldn't ever risk being late.

I could already hear noises in the egg-cup things that held the Dice. They were warming up to spin.

Partly, I'd had a last fear she might come back simply to watch me. She hadn't. If she had, that might have meant I'd been wrong. Or maybe not. I'll never know about Ironel, or Jizania, come to that. Maybe they felt they couldn't change but knew that, in choosing me, they'd selected someone who wouldn't put up with it, and that I'd do what I have.

I hope they thought that, for their sakes.

The slaves filed in, and we all stood religiously in proper awe.

And the Dice chugged and spun. And stopped.

Now was the moment.

I walked over and examined the Dice with care. Then I hesitated in thought. Then I went to the three old books. I rustled about in them, peering, shaking my head. I frowned. Pompously I spoke.

The slaves wrote everything down.

There was one difference. *I* gave them the numbers *and* the names, so they didn't have to look them up in the boxes. I'd chosen these numbers and names earlier. The slaves didn't argue.

Now I can't even recall all the things I said. Or can I? Claidi's Law . . .

One man had to go and buy all the badly made pots some woman had been making and tell her they were fantastic. And another man had to go and light all the candles in his house and then ask all his friends to dinner. And then they had to ask him back.

I told a woman that she must fall in love, I remember that. And six separate families I told to dress their children in loose clothes and then play with them.

I told two men to leave the City and buy plants, and some animals, and bring them back and let people see and look after them. And another couple to organize a way of making gardens and orchards.

Two or three were ordered to find something really funny and laugh at it.

Not that brilliant, I admit. But the Law that sunset was no more stupid than it had been before, and it might not do so much harm.

No one challenged me. The slaves went sloping off with the orders, and when they were gone, I shut the door of the Room again and finished my work.

Seems to me, I'll often dream about it: Carrying all those black boxes to the braziers and tipping in all the cards with names and numbers, and watching them burn so brightly and then vanish forever.

Or maybe I'll dream more about all the pages I tore, every single one, from the precious books, the only ones in the City—as Ironel had kept on telling me. Page after page of tough parchment, which sometimes burned with a weird brown flame.

Sparks flew up to the ceiling, like Argul's magic, or the Peshambans' CLOCK.

My arms and back ached. My throat was sore and my eyes were smarting from smoke.

I was hungry too, although not very.

Finally, it was finished. And then I did the very last thing.

I took a burning wick in its holder out of one of the lamps and carried it over to the Dice. And carefully and thoroughly, I burned off every number painted on them, until each of the sixteen sides was just a smudge. They could spin all they liked. It wouldn't mean a thing.

Then I burned a message in the black wall, burned it so it went white and was easy to see and hard to get rid of.

It said:

This is the Law of the Wolf Tower: There is to be no MORE Law.

Under which I wrote my name: *Claidissa Star.*

Then I thought, WHAT HAVE I DONE???

But it was too late. So I picked up my gold bag with this book in it, and ten ink pencils and pen-things I'd stolen from the Tower, left the Room and the other room and walked down the corridor. My slaves were at the end as always, and the guard in white with the rifle. I had the feeling they'd all been asleep.

It was full night. The windows were black, but I could see stars over the City.

I knew the way to the nearest lifter. The slaves and guard padded with me. Actually, there were seven slaves now. Increased, no doubt, because I'd read the Dice.

"I think I'll take a quick walk before the midnight Law," I chattily told them. So we all piled in the lifter and down we jumbled to the ground floor.

When we got to the quite small door by which I usually went out, some odd sounds were ringing over the City.

The slaves didn't do anything, but the guard took firm hold of his rifle.

"It's all right," I said to him. "It's only music, and someone singing."

Had I told someone to sing? Probably.

Elsewhere, barking—dogs? I'd never known there were dogs here. And then laughter, quite a lot of it.

Many windows seemed alight. Or brighter, warmer. Something.

I said loudly to the seven slaves, "You stay there, please. Sit down. You should relax." And they sat in a row on a bench by the door. Then I said to the guard, "I've always so admired that rifle. May I look at it?" And the fool gawked at me and then handed the rifle to me. I was Wolf's Paw, wasn't I? I could have what I wanted.

The rifle wasn't with me for long, though. I turned and gave it to Argul, who was now standing there just beyond the doorway, as arranged.

"You took your time, Claidibaabaa."

"I warned you. It took ages."

"You're ready now?"

"Yes."

Argul's disguise was gone. He looked . . . there wasn't time to look.

Argul pushed the guard quite gently back into the Wolf Tower. The guard seemed convinced he'd wake up in a minute.

Until Argul shut the door on him.

Ro and Mehmed were already dragging me onto a horse—difficult in the armored City dress—but I made it. (And the dress split.) "Sirree?" I whispered, "Sirree, you *are* Sirreee. . . ." And Sirree blew down her velvet nose at me.

Then Argul was also up on his horse, and we were riding so fast, like the night itself, all made of black horses, racing.

I looked back once. The Tower door was still shut. Nothing seemed to be happening there.

And as we galloped, I glimpsed those gun-things that watched, swiveling after us—and I cowered each time—but nothing happened there either.

The City people had forgotten how to think. They'd have to remember. I hoped the slaves would remember, too.

I tried to call to Argul as we raced neck and neck through echoing caverns of stone, the hooves of the horses sounding like hammers.

"There's still a chance . . . if I misjudged her—Ironel—a chance she might just go on as she did before—"

"Can't hear you, Claidi," Argul shouted back.

So I had to answer myself. Yes, there was a chance Ironel might do that. If I'd guessed correctly, she hadn't used the books or read the Dice for years. She'd said any old number she thought of, and as for the Law, she'd just been making it up. And what she'd made up was pretty evil. (Except for Nemian and herself—letting him marry someone he must really have wanted, and sending him on a quest to fetch what Ironel wanted—me.)

She was old and mad. But then again, she knew—I'd swear she did—what I was going to do. She left me no choice. Scaring me, making me angry. Leaving me on my own in the Room. I mean, she practically told me how to do it.

Even so, I longed for some sign I'd done the right thing.

We got out of the City much more quickly than I'd have thought possible. Perhaps it's not so huge as I believed. It had only seemed too big for me.

The starlit land rolled away, away to other places. Away to the Hulta camp, and Blurn and Teil and Dagger, where they were, far along the River, which was only a river. Away to somewhere where I could keep still and breathe and be. And where I can stop bothering you, my invented friend, who's stuck by me and helped so much.

The starlit land. The Waste that isn't.

We paused in some thin trees on a rise to give the horses a rest. (Sirree was terrific.)

I kept asking myself, Did I do the right thing? (I keep asking that, still. What do you think?) But you see, I couldn't stay if I had a chance of escape. And I couldn't leave them as they were. *I'm trouble,* as Argul said (and as Nemian never knew). And by then, on that rise, it was well past midnight, the time of the Law.

Argul took my hand and shook it up and down. His armlets jangled, and for some reason we both grinned.

"Ring not too painful?" he asked.

I said, truthfully, "It feels like it's part of my hand."

And just then, dull thunder, a roar. I nearly screamed.

"Oh God. Argul—*Argul*—the city—it's exploded—it's on fire!"

We stared. And above, the night changed color: silver, scarlet, amber, violet, gold, and white.

It was Mehmed who said, explaining, pleased, "No, Claidi. It must be a celebration. They're letting off about two thousand fireworks."

Wolf Star

IT RUNS LIKE CLOCKWORK.

Traditional

CONTENTS

THIS BOOK, AGAIN . . .

Are you still there?

No, of course you're not. How could you be? You were never there in the first place. I made you up, selfishly, to help me feel less alone. Someone to confide in, the most trustworthy friend I ever had.

Of course, then, too, there was a chance someone might read it, this book. But surely, no one ever will *here.* Or if they do, what I write will be some sort of weird curiosity, something to sneer at, amazedly. So it would be best to destroy this book, wouldn't it, instead of picking it up to write in again . . . after I thought I'd *never* write in it again.

Only I remember, when I left the Tower in the City, I took these extra ink pencils and pens. As if I knew I'd go on writing. But that was a reflex.

Naturally, once Argul and I (and Mehmed and Ro) got back with the Hulta, and we'd moved far enough away from the City, and there was some time—then I did write up the last bit. I remember it was a sunny afternoon on a hill, and Argul and some others had gone hunting, so I stayed where I was and finished the story.

I explained about how I destroyed the name-cards and the volumes of numbers, and all that evil stupid junk that made up the Law in the Wolf Tower. Burnt them. And burnt my message in the wall: NO MORE LAW. About how Argul got me away, and about how we then saw the City let off all those fantastic fireworks, celebrating its freedom. And I thought after that there'd be nothing much to write, because though I could cover page after page saying *Argul, Argul, Argul,* how wonderful he is, how happy *I* am—I could *live* that, didn't need to write it.

I did think I might put down an account of our wedding day so I could look at it years later: my dress, Argul's clothes, our vows, what we ate, what everyone said, and the games and dances—that kind of thing. A keepsake.

Well, I can't even do that, can I? The marriage never happened. And Argul—

I suppose, if you did exist and were still patiently reading, you'd prefer me to tell you all this in the right order.

But . . . maybe I won't do it just yet. . . .

THE UN-WEDDING DAY

That morning, the weather was beautiful. Teil had said it would be, the night before, because of the sunset.

"Red sky at set,

Sheepers not wet."

"Excuse me?"

"Oh, Claidi. Don't you know that old rhyme?"

"I only know about the Sheepers being very dodgy. And anyway, their language is all baa-baa-baa!"

"Well, yes. But it's an ancient *translated* saying of theirs. A red sunset means it won't rain tomorrow. Which is perfect for your wedding day."

Then Dagger strode into the tent. She'd just turned eight years old two days before and looked fiercely motherly.

"Claidi, I want you to have this."

"Oh, but Dagger—it's your dagger."

"Yes. You can peel oranges with it really well, too."

I put it in a place of honor with the other things—how I wish I'd kept it by me. I don't expect it would have made much difference.

People had been bringing me gifts for the past six days. It's the Hulta custom, so the bride can build up her store of useful things for her wagon. But really, Argul's wagon had tons of everything—pots, plates, knives, clothes (some of which had been his late mother's, when she was young, and fit me). There were even books—I mean printed ones.

Still, the gifts touched me. I was an outsider, but no one ever made me feel like one. Once Argul wanted me, and they'd seen a bit of who I was, they made me part of the Hulta family.

Wonderful to be *liked.* As opposed to having some special horrible power over people, as in the City, when I'd been Wolf's Paw for that short, foul while.

Anyway, Argul arrived then, and we went to supper at the camp's central fire.

I remember—won't ever forget—the firelight glowing on faces, the last scarlet at the sky's edge, jokes, stars, eyes gleaming in bushes and Ro wanting to throw a stone because they were "leopards," only they weren't, they were fireflies.

And alone with Argul, and how he said, "Are you happy? You look happy, Claidi. Cleverly disguising your misery, no doubt."

"Yes, I've been just crying my eyes out at the thought of marrying you."

"Mmm. Me, too."

"Shall we call it off?"

"Can't disappoint the rest of them," he gloomily said.

We held our faces in grim expressions. I burst out laughing first.

"I never thought I'd keep you," he said. "You're such a maddening, mad little bird."

"Mad, I'll accept. Maddening. I'm not so little."

"I could put you in a nutshell and carry you about in one hand," he said, "oh, Claidi-baa-baa!"

I remember my wedding dress. Well, I suppose I can say about that. After all, like Argul's ring, it's even here with me. I came away in it.

It's white, with embroidered patterns of green leaves. White for luck and green for spring, the Hulta bride's wedding colors. And Argul was to wear sun-yellow, for summer, the groom's colors. (Spring and summer were seasons. We don't really have them now.)

With his tea-colored skin and black hair, he would have looked incredibly splendid.

Only I never saw that.

No.

Anyway, the night was cool and still, and in the morning the sun came up and the sky was golden clear, and it was warm, as Teil had promised.

We'd been traveling about fifty, sixty days, since leaving Nemian's City.

First there'd been the flat grey plain by the River, and the thin mountains in the distance. Then we'd crossed the River, which was probably only *r*iver by then, by an old bridge I hadn't noticed when Nemian and I came down that way—or else it was higher up, beyond the marsh. (I didn't notice quite a bit of the journey.) Next we turned more south, and then our wagons were in another of those desert areas, which went on and on (only this time, with Argul, I didn't care).

The weather gradually got nicer, though. Lots of sunny days. Then there were grasslands, not as pretty or lush as at Peshamba, but still lovely. There were stretches of woods and orchards in blossom, and streamlets gloogling merrily by, and deer feeding and other dappled things with long necks, whose names I can't recall. We held races. (Siree, my black mare, went so fast I actually won *twice.*)

There were villages, too, made of painted wood, with grass-thatched roofs. Smiling people came out waving, and we bartered with them. And once there was a big stone circle on a hill, where no one could go in, only stand outside and look, because a wind god lived there, they said.

Then the land just sort of flowed, with the breezy grass running around islands of hills and trees in sunlight. Argul said we were now only twenty miles from the sea, and I'd never seen a sea. We'd go there, said Argul. But first we'd have our wedding, and we'd use the grassy plain as our dancing floor, because the Hulta marriage dances stir up flowers and make trees grow—or so the Hulta boastfully say.

Oh.

You may as well know, a tear nearly thumped on the page. Damn.

(I never used to swear. I wouldn't, because the nasty royalty in the House, where I was a slave-maid, were always swearing, and I didn't want to be like them.)

Anyway, if I'm going to cry and swear, I'll stop writing. So that's that.

(I think I do have to write this down. I don't know why. Like a spell or something. But I'm not so daft that I think it will *help* in any way.)

On the wedding morning, it's thought bad luck if a Hulta groom and bride see each other. But—well, we did. But we only laughed and separated quickly for custom's sake. Didn't even really kiss each other good-bye—had no reason to, of course. (Every reason to, if we'd known.)

I went first to groom Siree. Ashti and I plaited Siree's mane and tail with green and silver ribbons. I'd ride her to my wedding. A Hulta bride always rides.

After that *I* had to be groomed.

There was this terrific private pool Dagger had found in the woods, and Teil and Toy and Dagger and Ashti and I went there to bathe and wash our hair. We took our wedding clothes, and the jewels and makeup and everything, plus some hot bread and fruit juice and sweets. I'd brought this book, too, and an ink pencil, to jot stuff down—although I didn't really think I'd have time.

The trees grew in close around the pool, but above there was a scoop of cloudless sky. Flower-bells in the water.

Brides are supposed to be nervous. I wasn't, just happy. But our game was that I was really upset and scared, and somehow we got into a story, splashing around in the pool, about how Argul was a dreadful bully, about sixty years old, who'd unhitch the horses and make me pull the wagon with his other *six* wives.

In the middle of this, I looked up and saw it go over. Then the other two.

I just stood there in the water, and I went—not cold, kind of *stony.*

"She's just properly realized it's that hideous hundred-year-old Argul she's got to marry!" screamed Ashti.

Dagger said, "Shut up—what was it, Claidi?"

But they'd gone.

"I must have—imagined—I don't know."

Teil looked stern. "You do. What?"

"Balloons."

They went blank. Then realization dawned.

"You mean like from the grey City?"

"Well—not really. I mean I only ever saw one from there, and these weren't the same."

That was true. Nemian's balloon had been silvery, round. These were more sort of mushroom-shaped, a dull coppery color.

Had I imagined it? Had they been some odd, big, new kind of insect that looked larger but farther up?

In any case, many places had fleets of hot-air balloons, Nemian had always been going on about that. Peshamba had had them . . . or hadn't they?

Though the sky was still cloud-clear, a sort of shadow had fallen. We got out, not really dry, and shoved on our best clothes. I even put my wedding dress on fast, without much care. (Without thinking, I thrust this book in my pocket.) Shaking out our wet hair, we went up through the trees, leaving most of our picnic, and everything else.

The main camp wasn't much more than a quarter of a mile away. Not that far. (Only, down a slope, through all the trees.) It hadn't seemed to matter earlier.

Argul knew all about what had happened in the Wolf Tower and the City, and what I'd done. Mehmed and Ro had some idea but weren't really that bothered. I'd never discussed it with anyone else, nor had they pestered to know. They seemed to accept that it was something I'd prefer to forget.

Only now Teil said, quietly, "Claidi, is it possible they might have sent someone after you?"

"Me?" But it was no good being modest. I'd wrecked the Wolf Tower Law. The fireworks had seemed to prove that most of the City was glad about that. But I had some doubts. The Old Lady, for one, Ironel, what about her? I'd never been sure, there. "It's—possible."

We began to walk quickly, not running, in the direction we'd come, back toward the camp.

And then, the strangest sound, behind us.

I thought afterward that it was only startled birds, lots of them, flying up and away. Then it sounded as if the wood had sprouted wings and was trying to escape. The light and shade were all disturbed with fluttering and flickering, and then there was a thud behind us.

Something had come down—landed.

None of us said anything or yelled. We all just broke into a run.

Instantly every single tree root and bush and creeper in the wood seemed to come jumping up to trip and sprawl us.

But over the chorus of panting and crashes and yelps, and Dagger's always impressive bagful of rude words—another *thud.* This one was quite close.

The light had altered. Something was blotting it up . . . a brownish-reddishness, and on the ground a huge shadow, cruising . . . and I looked up, having tripped again, and a balloon hung there, right over the trees.

It looked *enormous.* Like a dirty, bloated, fallen sun. No, like a copper thundercloud.

And then—I don't know really what happened. I've tried to piece it together, can't, as if somehow I've *forgotten* those completely crucial moments.

But it was as if the wood changed again. This time all the trees became *men.*

They were in uniform, white or black, with plates of metal, and *guns,* and I ridiculously thought, *The House Guards!*

They must have grabbed hold of me. I was in a sort of metal web, and I couldn't see where Teil and Dagger and the others were. As I kicked and tried to bite, I hoped they'd gotten away. And I thought, *They'll get help,* and then *Anyway, someone will have seen.* But the camp had been so busy getting ready for the wedding. And these woods were uphill. And the trees . . .

Then one of the armored men said to me, "Stop struggling, or you'll wish you had."

They weren't House Guards. But I knew that tone, those words. He meant what he said. (It was useless anyway.) I became quite still.

Another one said, "Is this the one?"

"It's *her,*" said the first one, who must have been the one who had hold of me in the web. "I saw her almost every day in the City."

"He'd never forget," said the other, "would you, Chospa? Not after she made such a blazing great fool of you."

"Chospa" growled and shook me angrily, and the chain-web rattled. Who was he? Just one of several enemies from my past—

Then there were shouts of "Haul away!"

And to my disbelieving horror, *I* was being hauled upward—up through the slapping branches of the trees, so that I had to protect my eyes—up into the air. Up to the disgusting balloon.

I kept thinking, someone will come in a moment. Argul and the Hulta had rescued me before—once, twice—Argul will rush in, gorgeously bellowing, and Mehmed and Ro and Blurn and everyone.

I kept thinking this even after I was pulled over into the basket under the balloon. Kept thinking it even as the balloon lifted, with a terrifying hiss of hot gas over my head. As the ground fell away. As the trees became like a clump of watercress, as I saw the Hulta camp—like a child's colorful, tiny toy, spread out, peaceful, far away—too far even to see if they'd noticed.

Then suddenly, as I lay there on the balloon basket's floor, I knew it was now too late. And then it was as if some mistake had been made and it was my fault, my mistake. Only what had I done wrong?

BALLOON RIDE

Some girls would give their front teeth to ride in a balloon like this," said one of my captors haughtily, about an hour later.

So I was ungrateful, presumably?

Chospa, who was in the white uniform, glared at me under his steel helmet crested with a stiff white plume.

"Chospa's still very angry with you," said the one in black.

I thought *I* was quite angry with *Chospa.* Or would be if I weren't so frightened, so *numbed* by what had happened.

"Look, she doesn't remember you, even, Chospa."

"No. She never looked at me once, until that last time."

"Tell us again, Chospa. It's always good for a laugh."

Chospa swore.

He said, "She was going to be *Wolf's Paw.* I *respected* her."

"You trusted her," said the one in black.

"We all did. Who didn't? She was absolutely correct in everything. Couldn't fault her."

The one who'd remarked I might want to give my front teeth for this exciting ride (I found out later his name was Hrald) said, "But listen, boys, she'd destroyed everything, even the holy books, and then she prances down with our Chospa here, to the street. Says she wants a walk. Then she says (here Hrald mimicked a female—*my*—voice, high and stupid and squeaky, how he thinks females sound, I suppose), 'Dooo let me see that delicious darling rifle, dearest Chospa. Ee've always admeered it sooo.' And what does the dupp do, but give it to her."

"I didn't know she'd destroyed the Law—or that she had savage barbarians waiting by the Tower door," snarled Chospa.

I knew him now, of course.

He'd been my guard/bodyguard in the City. Meant to protect me and/or keep me prisoner.

It's true, I'd never really glanced at him. Most of the people there looked like mechanical dolls, clockwork, without minds or hearts.

I'd just been glad that night it was all being so simple, getting away.

Argul had taken the rifle from me and shut Chospa in the Tower, and I hadn't really thought about it again. Not even when I wrote down what happened.

Chospa now said, "I couldn't open the Tower door. You can't from inside, unless it recognizes your rank—like it did hers. I had to sit there. Later I was called in to the Old Lady. I was in there, explaining, two hours."

No one laughed at this.

Two hours with Ironel Novendot. Ironel either furiously angry or else making believe she was. Her black eyes, snapping real-pearl teeth and poison tongue, her dry white claws. I didn't envy him. His face now, just remembering, was pale and sick-looking. (The way mine felt.)

"Lost his house in the City," said Hrald. The one in black—his name is Yazkool (I haven't forgotten their names, once heard. Never will, I expect)—said, "Just barely kept his place in the City Guards. Allowed to come with us on our joyous quest—weren't you, Chospa?—to identify Miss, here. Ironel's orders."

(I hadn't realized he *couldn't* open the door. Thought they'd just sat there and not come after us because they were insane.) (The Tower door could *recognize* me? That was new. But so what—)

Drearily I huddled on the floor of the balloon basket. Were they going to throw me out when we got high enough? We were high up now. No, they were going to take me back to the City, to the Tower. To *her*. And then—well.

Would Argul realize? Of course. He'd come after me, like before. Rescue me, somehow.

A spark of hope lit up bright inside me. I was careful not to let the three Guards see.

But I did sit up a bit. The web-chain had fallen off. I tried to glimpse over the basket's high rim. Couldn't see much.

Rolls of landscape, soft with distance, but down—and down—below.

And the vast moving sky, with clouds like cauliflower blowing up over there, where the plain looked oddly flat and *shiny*—

It was choppy, riding in the balloon. I hadn't noticed that either, except as part of the general awfulness.

Above roared the fire-gas thing that powered the balloon. There was one more man in the basket, shifting some contraption about (like a boat-driver) to guide the balloon, probably. I didn't understand it.

Even though I'd brightened a bit, I was hardly lighthearted or very observant. But I now noted that one of the other mushroom balloons looked miles away. We must be going quite fast?

I felt rather queasy, but it wasn't airsickness, just more shock.

"I must say," Hrald must-said, "I was surprised you took all that, Chospa. I mean, the way the old bag ranted on at you."

Even *I* was astonished. Chospa gaped. *Old bag*—Ironel!!!

"She's the Keeper of the Law," gasped Chospa.

"Yeah, well. But she went too far. Disgraced you. What happened was her fault, too."

"Definitely not fair," agreed the other one, Yazkool.

Chospa shrugged, turned away. He now looked blank and mechanical again.

I saw Hrald and Yazkool exchange a glance. Hrald shook his head, seeming to say, *Let's not upset him any more.*

The balloon driver—ballooneer, I think they call them—had looked around, too. He was a short, bearded man, and he gave an ugly grin. That was all.

I didn't think much about this, or anything. I was glad that I had stopped feeling sick. Also, I concentrated on seeming resigned and meek, in case there'd be any unlikely chance later to get away.

Sometimes it felt hot in the balloon, and then chilly. We were in a chilly phase when Chospa suddenly barked out, "Tell that fool to watch what he's doing!"

"Oh, he's all right."

"Are you blind? We're going over too far east—" and Chospa shouted at the ballooneer, "Pull her around, you moron. The City's *that* way!"

"Calm down, Chos," said Hrald, in a chummy voice. "Trust me, it's fine."

"What is this?" shouted Chospa.

"Oh, we're just," said Hrald, idling across the bumpy balloon basket, "going to do something, er, first—" and then he reached Chospa and punched him *whack* on the jaw. Chospa tumbled over and the basket plunged, and the ballooneer cursed us all.

As we bucketed about the sky, the land dipping, clouds dipping, sun turning over, I saw we were also much lower, and that shining flat plain was gleaming everywhere to one side. It must be the sea?

Chospa rolled against me, and I stared in alarm at his poor unconscious face, with the bruise already coming up like a ripe plum.

Yazkool laughed, seeing me worrying.

Hrald only said, "Bring us down over there, that stand of pines."

"They always want miracles," muttered the ballooneer.

And then the air-gas-fire was making ghastly dragon-belches, and we seemed to be dropping like a stone.

All around, the sky was empty of anything—but sky. The other two balloons were completely out of sight.

The ground came rushing up, and I thought we'd all just be killed, and was too frightened even to be sick after all, and then we landed with a bump that rattled everything, including my bones and poor old Chospa.

Well, we were fairly near the pines. . . .

Next thing I knew, they were dragging me out of the basket. Yazkool was, unfortunately, securely tying my wrists together.

"There's the sea," pointed out Hrald, still apparently determined for me not to miss any of the travel or sight-seeing opportunities.

Beyond the hill slope we'd crash-landed on, and between the black poles of the ragged pines, a silver mass gushed and crawled. Chunks of it constantly hit together and burst in white fringes.

Argul would have shown me that. Helped me make sense of it.

It was now cold, or I felt cold. The clouds were swarming in the sky, bigger and darker and bigger.

The mushroom-pod of the balloon seemed to be deflating. No one did anything about Chospa—just let him lie there on his back.

"Then where are they?" demanded the ballooneer.

"Don't bother your pretty little head about it," said Hrald. "We've made good time."

The ballooneer scowled but said nothing else. Yazkool produced a pair of nail scissors and began neatly to trim his nails.

The wind blew, hard and spiky from the sea. I wanted to get out of the wind, so sat down, with hand-tied awkwardness, against one of the pines.

I didn't realize even then that the harsh, silver-salt wind was going to be my constant companion for quite some time to come.

About half an hour later, some wild men came trudging up the hill.

They'd called the Hulta "barbarians," as I'd have expected City people would. These really *did* look barbaric. Their clothes were all colors, all patched, mismatched, too bright or faded, and all filthy. They had rings through their ears, noses, eyebrows, lips, and *teeth,* and had beads plaited in their hair, mustaches, and beards. Several had one shoe or boot different from the other. There were a lot of knives, clubs, and nasty-looking catapult things.

They spoke another language, too, which only Hrald seemed to have any idea of. One of them, who was dark but with very yellow hair, spoke a bit of the language the City speaks, that language I suppose is also mine.

No one mentioned me.

I had the strangest feeling that I had nothing to do with any of this. I tried to merge into the tree, but of course that was silly. Yazkool presently came and pulled me up, and I was marched down with the others toward the silver waves.

They're going to drown me, I decided. *It's some new quaint ritual.*

I'm sacrifice material, obviously. I mean, the Sheepers saw that at once and gave me to the Feather Tribe, who meant to sling me off a cliff. As for Jizania and Nemian, I was the best sacrifice of all to them. My life was *barter* for their royal lives, in the House and the City.

But we skirted the sea—which was very *wet,* very icy, with colors like tea and lime juice in it now, seen so near. We went along a strip of sand and over slippery pebbles and black stones. Around a curve of headland, I saw a ship on the water. Ah, we were going to the ship.

I didn't cry. It was as if I'd known somehow this would happen.

It had to be too simple just to kidnap me and carry me off to be killed in the City, where just possibly I might escape or Argul rescue me.

No, no, I had to be *re*kidnapped *again,* put on this rotten ship with its mucky, old stained sail, and taken off somewhere with this ship's crew, who all looked completely dangerously *mad.*

We rowed out in a leaky boat.

They pushed me up a ladder—not easy to climb, hands tied, shaking, the sea going *glump-whump,* everything rocking.

("Enormous seas, Claidi," said Argul, in my mind. "Miles of water and sky.")

Something, some bird, flew over, shrieking. A gull. I didn't know it was. I didn't ask, or care. They bundled me into a dark cabin and slammed the door, and there I was.

YET MORE TRAVEL OPPORTUNITIES

When I think about it now, I think I should have just jumped into the sea. That's what a proper heroine in one of the House books would have done. (Although, naturally, a handy passing boat or giant fish would then have rescued her immediately.) I'm not a heroine, anyway. I'm just Claidi.

Anyway, I didn't, did I.

How long did it last, that thing they called a *voyage?* Months, years.

Oh, about twenty-five or -six days, maybe. I kept count the way the (in-a-book) captive is meant to, by scratching on the cabin wall by the wooden chest. I did it promptly every morning, without fail. And then, obviously, being me, being Claidi, I *forgot* the number the moment we got off the ship.

But, about twenty-five, thirty days. Perhaps.

Oddly, I sometimes thought about Chospa. It seemed so unfair, because, through no fault of his own, he'd be in trouble all over again. I could cheerfully have punched him on the nose myself, but at least he'd been honorably doing what he thought he should.

Instead of Chospa, there were Yazkool and Hrald. (The ballooneer hadn't joined the ship. I don't know what his plans were, but I hope so much they went wrong.)

I hated them, Y and H. Was *allergic* to them. Not just because they'd made my escape-chances totally hopeless, either. They were so smug and—*royal*—always cleaning their nails, their teeth, brushing their hair, complaining about the way they had to "make do" on the ship. And at the same time so *smilingly-mysterious* about what they were up to. That is, what they meant to do with me. Of course, I *had* asked.

I asked them the moment they opened the cabin and said I could come out now, since there was nowhere to go (obviously having *never* read any of those jump-overboard books *I* had).

"Where are you taking me, and why?"

"Why not let it be a wonderful surprise?" suggested leering Yazkool.

"Tell me *now!*" I cried. I meant to sound like the Wolf's Paw, or apprentice Wolf's Paw, I'd been. I didn't manage it. The ship was also pitching about, and although I found I was (thank heavens) a good sailor (that is, I didn't want to throw up), I could hardly keep on my feet—even now that they'd untied my hands.

Hrald looked bored. "I'm off below," he said.

Yazkool beamingly said, "Lady Claidissa, why not think of this as an adventure for you?"

Hrald, who hadn't yet gone, added, "And much nicer than being imprisoned for life in the City cellars, wouldn't you say?"

"How did you know where I was? How did you find me?" I gabbled. They were already staggering, sea legs almost as hopeless as mine, down the deck.

One of the wild sailor-people undid a hatch, and they stepped-fell through and were gone.

I made the mistake of looking around then. I didn't throw up, but I nearly screamed.

Everything was galloping and tilting this way, that way. The vast mast, with its dirty sail, seemed about to crash right over on us all. Waves a hundred feet high (they can't have been, but looked it) kept exploding up in the sky and hurling spray into the ship and all over us.

No one seemed upset. Cheery sailors strode bowleggedly up and down, or scrambled across rope arrangements on the mast, calling merry, other-language insults, and singing.

Water sloshed down the deck, ran into the cabin, and then, as we nose-dived the other way, ran out again.

In fact, it wasn't quite as bad as it looked that first time. But it took me hours to get used to it, and by then the wind had settled down a little (temporarily), and the sea was flatter. Then this happened to me, too. My brief anger went out. I felt flat and utterly lost.

Obviously, the "voyage" was disgusting. It would have been, even if I'd wanted to do it.

I've read or heard these stories of glorious days aboard ships.

Blue waters, amazingly shaped clouds, dolphins (?) and other fish or sea-animal-things, leaping, the comradeship of sailors. This wasn't my experience.

The sailors fought a lot.

I think it was boredom. They never seemed to do anything useful, but they were always either rushing acrobatically about or sitting playing dice or card games, or even peculiar guessing games (I'd picked up some of their language by then).

Yazkool told me (he and Hrald kept coming and talking patronizingly to me, as if I should be flattered by their attention) that the sailors have 907 words for *Sea*. Perhaps it was a lie. They certainly had about a thousand filthy words for Go Away, or Idiot! (Dagger would have loved it, memorizing them for future use.) (I mustn't think too much about Dagger. Or Siree. Or anyone. Not now. I refuse—I REFUSE—to think I won't see them again. But . . . it won't be for a long while.)

Anyway, the sailors were rowdy. H and Y strolled about, discussing how shirts were cut and trimmed in the City that year, or how this water was too salty to shave properly. Some days the sea was blue—but never for long. Storms came regularly. Hrald (another lecture) told me that it was the Stormy Season.

Once or twice, when they cornered me, I confronted them.

"Did you both *enjoy* life in the Wolf Tower City?" I demanded.

"What other life is there?" drawled Yazkool.

"At any moment," I yapped, "the Tower Law could have picked you out for some terrible fate."

"Oh, it did once. I had to marry some girl."

What could I say to that? *I'd* seen the Law force a child to wear, day and night, the costume of a snail, with the *shell.* Or send a man swimming up and down the River, allowed only to rest briefly, when "exhausted," *forever.*

"It's probably nicer there now," I acidly remarked, "since I stopped the Law."

"It's much the same," said Yazkool. What an okk.

Hrald said, "Anyhow, the Law may be reinvented."

That shut me up. I hadn't thought of that.

Surely it would be *impossible?* All those names to gather again—besides, there had only been single copies of the Books of Law—and I'd destroyed them. Or had Ironel lied to me? Were there other copies? I nearly burst into tears, this idea was so depressing. I wouldn't let *them* see, of course. I looked out to sea, as if indifferent, and said, "Well, if your City is stupid enough to do that, it serves you all right."

Which was, and is, true. I'd given them a chance, more than they'd had since the Law began. A chance is just about all you ever get.

The cabin (I'd seen a cabin before, on the river-ship that first carried me to the City) was quite large. I had it to myself. From that I decided, wherever they were taking me, they were supposed to take care of me. Not damage me or insult me beyond a certain point. (As if being abducted wasn't the worst thing they could have done, short of killing me.)

There was a (lumpy) bed and a wooden chest, with things in it that had fairly obviously been put there for my "comfort."

In the wall (the ship's side) was a round window, glass crisscrossed with iron, through which I could admire the endless, jumping dolphinless sea.

I didn't stay in the cabin very much.

When I did, I could be private. (H and Y brought me meals, and I didn't have much to do with the sailors, or wasn't allowed to.) But when alone, I sometimes started to cry. Well.

So I tended to go out on deck, where people could see me, and I had to *not* cry.

I did glance at this book a couple of times. Wondered if I ought to write in it, couldn't bring myself to.

Argul knew about this book. (Nemian had called it my "Diary." He would. It wasn't. Isn't. I don't know what it is. My long letter to you, perhaps, if you ever read it.)

Argul just accepted I'd written things down in a book. He didn't ask about it or want to read it. Yet he wasn't dismissive either. But that was . . . well, Argul.

Argul.

I had taken my book with me to the wood pool because I was going to write down a few things about my wedding day, some as they happened.

And when we left the pool, I stuffed it in the pocket of my Wedding Dress, which by three days into the voyage was spoiled, dirty, sea-stained, and torn.

The horrible idea I keep getting is that I brought this book with me to the pool and then put it in my pocket—not out of old habit, but because I somehow knew *this* would happen.

Y and H were having lunch on deck, in an odd hour of sunshine.

Blue sky and sea. Gentle lilts from the ship. Even the sailors were mostly below at a meal and quiet.

I went and sat with my captors. They instantly made room for me. Y even passed me a glass of wine. They'd actually *expected* me to come over to them sometime—the extra glass, their unsurprise. I mean, they'd ruined my life, but they were so *wonderful,* how could I go on ignoring them?

"You see, it's a nice day today, Claidissa."

(They always call me that, my full name, which I'd only learned months before and had never gotten used to—or was ever sure I liked.)

"Is it?"

"She's never satisfied," said Yazkool, who, as I approached, had been going on and on (again) about the salty shaving water.

"How strange, isn't it," I said, "that I'm not satisfied. Everything's so lovely, isn't it? I'm kidnapped and trapped on a stormy ship and going I don't know where or why or to what. Funny me. Wow."

Then I wished I hadn't spoken. They'd think I was trying to have a conversation with them, flirting even. (They both think they're gorgeous. They aren't. Oh well, to be fair, they might have been all right, under other circumstances.)

Hrald said, however, "No, we've been childish, haven't we? You must be miserable." Then he grinned, naturally.

Yazkool said, "You see, Claidissa, the City was all rejoicing and fireworks, but the people at the Top"—it had a capital T as he said it—"they weren't happy. You have to have rules, Claidissa. Or where would we all be, I ask you?"

The people at the Top? Who? Ironel—I thought she was at the Top. Nemian—no. Though a prince, he was just as much a slave, in a way, as I was, to the Law.

Did it matter anyway?

Only the result mattered. This.

Hrald finished picking at his food, pushed plates aside. He took out one of those City dainties, a tablet from a little gold box. Once he'd eaten the tablet, he lit one of the long black stems of packed tobacco they smoked in the City, a thing they called a *beetle.* (I *don't* know why. The first time I heard Nemian say, on the river-ship, that he was just going to light a *beetle,* I'd gone rigid.)

"In a few more days," said Hrald, "we'll reach land."

"Unless another really bad storm crops up," optimistically added Yazkool.

"Then, we go inland," said H.

"More exciting travel. How blissful."

"Yes, an interesting trip," said H.

It occurs to me that perhaps H and Y are less sarcastic and cruel than plain stupid.

"Why?" I said again.

"You'll soon find out. Don't be so concerned. You see the trouble we've gone to. You're valuable, therefore valued. No one's even stolen that gaudy diamond ring of yours."

"Then what do you get out of this?" I inquired. "I mean, *you've* annoyed the Wolf Tower now, haven't you? They had me captured, and you recaptured me. What about these Top People?"

"Mmm," said H. He blew a smoke ring. Typical.

Just then Y slipped an arm about me, and I turned and slapped him really hard across his still-beautifully-shaven, rotten face.

Some sailors had come up from below and now went into great gouts of glee. The dark one with yellow hair called out something, which I think meant, "Hey, she *bites!*"

Which brought memories, and I got up and went to the cabin and shut myself in.

Ages after, when the sea was getting rough, again, and the sky and the window purplish, I thought, *But* why *am I valuable?*

No answer to that.

I started wondering again if Teil and Dagger, Ashti and Toy had gotten away from the other balloons and their riders. Then again I had that nagging unease.

How did the balloons know where to find me? Well, yes, they could have spotted the big Hulta camp from the air just by careful searching. But to come to the *pool,* where I was almost alone? Dagger had found the pool. Teil suggested we go there. Betrayal? Not Dagger. Not Teil. Not Toy or Ashti either. Ashti is Blurn's girlfriend, and Blurn was my friend—Argul's second-in-command and—

How can I be sure?

About anything.

Toward the end, the "voyage" just seemed as if it would never end. Then there was a really frightening storm. The sky went green as spinach. The sea was black.

Yazkool got seasick. It was one of my few moments of pleasure. Then I even felt a bit sorry for him. (There's something wrong with me.)

The sailors were scared. They took in the sail and tied themselves to the mast or the helm. They weren't swearing! Gigantic waves broke on the deck, and the men were baling water out in buckets, and then H came and pushed me back in the cabin and locked the door from the outside. I thought I'd probably drown.

Finally all the noise died down, and the sailors started swearing again.

When I was let out, the deck was still awash. The sea was now green, but the waves were more playful than murderous. The sky was pure gold, thinking itself into an after-storm sunset.

And there across all this vista was a shadowy gilded hem on the sky's lowest edge, which I thought was a cloud. Until I made out the sailors' word (they apparently have one) for *land.*

Y was still heaving dedicatedly over the side.

H strolled up.

"*There* you are, you see," he announced proudly, as if he'd done just what I'd begged him to.

We came ashore in our old chum, the leaky boat. Actually, it almost sank just before we got to the beach.

I'd anticipated something else. In books, I'd come across seaside docks and ports with towns or villages attached. I'd thought the ship would go somewhere like that. It hadn't. Also, we left the ship at dusk, and only the dark sailor with blond hair, who H and Y called Bat-Nose (!), and one other one, rowed us.

The land had faded from the light and grown black, with the sun vanishing behind it to the left. The sky was deep red, magenta, then quickly darkening. Stars sparkled out.

Above the sandy beach, which ran back and back, more than twenty man-heights-lying-down, was a forest. A wall of trees where strange (bird?) calls sounded and then went quiet. I didn't see much of all this, the light went so fast, or seemed to. But the forest didn't look like any forest I'd seen, not in the Garden, or at Peshamba. More than luxuriant, it was—*fat.*

Bat-Nose and the other one (I think he was called, in his own language, Charming) lit a fire. We sat down around it, all except Y, who was still sick and had fallen in a heap, refusing to talk.

On the sea, the ship twinkled a lamp at us, like a fallen star.

I looked at it dubiously.

Not that I was fond of the ship. But I'd gotten used to it. Physically, too, the beach felt a bit roll-y. And where to now?

I slept apart, rolled up in two blankets, though the night wasn't cold, but I didn't want to share the fire with *them.*

During the night I woke up once. Something absolutely terrifying. A shadow-*something* was prowling along the beach. It looked rather like a lion, but paler, and with a sort of snakeskin-like patterning on its pelt that a young moon had risen to show me.

It went to the margin of the sea and sniffed at the waves—or drank them or something, only they were salty. . . . Then it glided back and threaded through the sprawl of sleepers around the dying fire.

They'd been too lazy to set anyone to watch. Too smug. Too smug even to wake up and yell.

I wondered if the ghostly cat would attack them, but it didn't. To me it paid no attention at all.

In the end it trotted back up the beach and vanished in the forest. Took me ages to doze again.

Next morning they were all in a flap, because there were pad-marks in the sand inches away.

Bat-Nose and Charming cast me unliking looks.

Y, now mostly recovered, announced this to me: the sailors thought *I* had changed into a "white tigapard" in the night.

I pointed out that if that had been the case, I'd hardly have hung around.

It's called a Jungle. A jungle-forest, this forest.

I'd never seen anything like it, not seen a picture like it, or even a description.

The trees are about two hundred feet high, or higher. Miles high, perhaps.

And at the top, mostly, they close together, so there's a ceiling of foliage.

The light is almost wet-green, but often most like a soupy green dusk. Sometimes there is a break in the leaf canopy, and the sky is there, but looking almost colorless, luminous yet somehow *unlit.*

Lower down, apart from boughs and leaves (plump, juicy leaves, or long whippy leaves, or dense fans of leaves), there are creepers and vines, many thicker than a man's arm. Some have flowers, trumpet-shaped, or petal-plates. They're pale generally, because of the lack of proper light. Higher up, you glimpse brighter ones, where thin trails of light pierce through, flashes of crimson, turquoise, or tangerine.

But the flowers could be birds, too, because the jungle-forest is full of birds, some very small and some very big, and all of them in all colors. There are also monkeys and other tree-swingers. Silent as shadows or else shriekingly, jumpmakingly noisy.

On the ground grow great clumps of black-green fern, often taller than I am, or bamboos, which I'd seen at the House, but not like these—these were taller than tall Yazkool.

Perhaps most important, all the vegetation constantly knits itself together. The vines are using the bamboos to curl around and so climb from tree trunk to trunk. The trees take root in each other. Other creepers come unwound high up and loop down and get caught by ferns. Ferns grab high boughs and sprout forty feet up.

Through these attachments weave other things—ivies and grasses and funguses and blue-white orchids—all trying to climb *up* each other and reach the light. Any traveler has to hack his way much of the time with broad-bladed knives.

Once you're in the middle of all this, if you can ever see far through any occasional gap, the jungle weaves on and around into the distance.

It goes on forever in all directions. Or seems to. Sometimes a huge rocky hill may go staggering up out of everything, with trees leaning out sideways from it. But although a hill, it's also smothered by jungle, and its summit won't break through the canopy, only make part of the canopy from all its particularly high trees.

Once there was a shower of rain. We heard it pattering above. Not a single drop fell through.

Just after the business about the tigapard on the beach, three men appeared out of the trees.

I've thought since, how did they know to meet Y and H just there? The storm had surely blown the ship away from any course she (they're called "she"!) might have had. And the shore where we'd landed was quite a distance from the jungle-road that we eventually reached.

None of that occurred to me then. It just seemed horribly inevitable.

Two of the newcomers were slaves, the kind I'd seen at the House, and in the City, though these were dressed in absolute rags. It was so warm and humid, even by night, maybe their master didn't think that mattered so much.

This other man, presumably the master, wore extravagant clothes, all colors (like the parrots in the trees) and with fringes, tassels, bells, buttons, holes cut out and embroidered. He jingled as he moved, but he had a hard face, like a brown nut no one could crack.

"Hello there, Zand," greeted Yazkool and Hrald. Then everyone started speaking mostly in yet another language.

Presently we went into the jungle. (Bat-Nose and Charming didn't go with us.)

There was an instant clearing, with two more slaves (in rags) and a round, hooped openwork little carriage. It was drawn by two stripy deer with horns. There were other, bigger deer, with antlers, in reins and saddles.

Hrald said, "Man, do we ride *those?*" looking haughty.

The antlered deer snorted and looked even haughtier.

They put me in the carriage. I didn't try to tell them I could probably have ridden as well. The deer seemed less reasonable than my lovely mare, Siree. Well, they were *deer*.

I didn't even laugh at Hrald, slipping about all over his deer, which at once bucked and cantered about, taking extra pains to cause him trouble. Like a mule, really.

One of the slaves drove my carriage. His rags were a bit nicer, and he was black, like Blurn, but without any of Blurn's quick wit or good looks. Of course, they all looked ugly and hateful to me. Maybe they weren't.

At first the other three slaves went in front, hacking a way through the undergrowth and creepers. Sometimes it got so bad that my driver, and then Zand, Hrald, and Yazkool, had to join in the hackery.

Should I have slipped out of the carriage then and run away into the forest?

I vaguely considered it once or twice. But the jungle just looked—was—impassable. And where could I go? I was totally lost.

I should wait until I knew more, had learned more. Did I say that to myself? I think I just sat there.

Of course, the jungle was (is) fascinating.

Sometimes I'd feel a dart of real interest—those monkeys with velvet-black faces, yet white on their hand-paws and lower arms, like long white gloves. That huge snake twined around and around a fig tree; there seemed more snake than tree. For a split glimmer of a second I'd almost be *happy*. Forgetting. Only for a split second.

Soon we reached the road.

Zand seemed proud of the road, as if he had personally designed it and then built it himself. Which I doubt.

It wasn't much, anyway, not anymore. Stone paving about three lying-down-man-heights across . . . eighteen feet, maybe. But the jungle-forest was busily seeding all over it. Trees and shrubs grew out of it, closed over it above. And in places it had been entirely swallowed.

So then hack-hack, curse-curse, moan-whinge-whine.

Yazkool was the worst.

"I didn't *know* this would be so *primitive!*"

Or was Hrald worst? "I could have been at home, you know, in my tower, civilized. Playing the mandolin."

(The idea that Hrald plays the mandolin is incredibly infuriating. I can just see him, in that stone City of Law and miseries, smilingly plinking away.)

This part of the journey took, not years, but a whole century.

Perhaps only a month.

Sometimes we saw more big catlike animals, which made an impact on the deer (so they were even more difficult) and on Yazkool, who seemed to want to kill them, not to protect us, or to eat, but just for their spectacular skins.

Then, once or twice through those choked gaps in the trees, there were ruins of buildings.

At first I thought they were only pieces of other overgrown rock-hills. But some had carved roofs and columns. And once there was a huge stone statue of a robed woman, about twenty feet high—I'm not exaggerating or guessing; Zand told us all its height, showing off again, as if *he* had carved it. But it was older than Zand. Older than even Ironel had said she was, which was 170. That statue was hundreds, thousands of years old.

But I wasn't in the mood for rare plants, animals, and educational ancient ruins. Or for any of this guided tour which had been forced on me.

The worst part is that it's still going on, in a way, because it's still right there now—jungle, stones, beasts, right outside this high window.

For anyway, at long last, my captors brought me *here.*

HERE

By the morning we arrived, I'd given up the notion of ever arriving anywhere. It was very silly, but I just thought we'd go rambling on and on until everyone died of boredom or anxiety or both.

Then we were bumbling along the road, which was more overgrown than ever. The deer were frisky and Hrald was grumbling. Hack-hack went the knives. Then a greenish glow came through the tunnel over the road, the last creepers gave way, and the last bamboo collapsed.

The world yawned wide.

After all the closed-in-ness, this abyss of space and sunlight was almost unbearable.

Colossal openness. Above, the shell of a white-blue sky, ringing with sun.

Everything hazed in sun, and *spray*—although at first I didn't see why. There was too *much* to see.

"Behold!" announced Zand, in his own language.

He'd invented and built this, too, of course.

Out of the jungles rose and rose, soaring upward, a cliff of yellowish stone, bulging, pocked and cracked, and clambered by huge trees that looked small as grass blades.

It did seem the widest, tallest thing I'd ever looked at. Higher and mightier than any city. And much more magnificent.

There was a rushing roar, which I'd heard faintly for so long, getting ever louder, but by tiny degrees, so I'd never really heard it, or understood that I had.

It was a waterfall.

The House had had them. A fountain made to tip from a height, cascading over and down. The best one was above Hyacinth Lawn. It was about two stories high.

This waterfall, here, began way up on the towering cliff. It burst out of the rocks, which were lost in a blue fog. Then it fell, tons of liquid, straight and *solid* as a pillar, yet it smoked and steamed from bounced-back water—and the spray filled the ravines and valleys below as if something were on fire.

Rainbows hung across the gulf of air, bridges we couldn't cross.

Everyone had gone quiet. Even Y and H were impressed. It turned out they hadn't seen the cliff before, or the waterfall.

Hrald didn't even give me one of his guided-tour remarks.

I expect anyone else would have been thrilled, despite themselves, at seeing this amazing sight.

I felt as if the waterfall had crashed over me, crushing me. It was the last straw somehow. To see something like this, alone, and with *them.*

The place here is tucked in under the overhang, below the road, where the land goes jaggedly down toward the ravines at the bottom of the cliff.

It was quite difficult, descending all those overgrown terraces. (They left the carriage and deer in a sort of shelter with the slaves, at the top.) Everything was slippery from blown spray.

Dragonflies drizzled through the spray-rain.

Then, we got here.

The building is built of the yellow stone, like the cliff, and again to start with I thought it was a natural rock, then I saw windows with glass, glinting.

It's just a low, square house, like something you'd find in Peshamba, maybe, but not so pretty.

In the courtyard H and Y started to act very picky and *Now we must do this the right way.*

No one seemed to be there, and then this woman came along the veranda above the steps. She looked like a servant, but she didn't bow or anything, just came up to us and stood there. I thought perhaps she wasn't used to visitors, out here, and hoped H and Y wouldn't get nasty with her.

"Is it one of those *things?*" asked Yazkool.

"Looks like it," said Hrald.

Zand spoke in his language. Something about, "Are the rooms ready for her?"

The servant nodded.

Her hair was odd. It didn't look like hair, more like tangled string.

When she spoke finally, in Zand's tongue, I realized.

"Click-click. Follow-click-me," said she.

She's a mechanical doll, clockwork, like the Guards and things at Peshamba. Rather rusty, as they weren't. Perhaps it's the damp.

All three servants here are the same.

The Peshamban dolls had seemed very efficient, and they'd looked good, but I never really got used to them in the short time I was there.

These ones made—*make*—me uncomfortable. I suppose because I'm usually dealing personally with them.

Y told me to follow the first one. (Nobody bothered to keep tabs on me, or warn me—where could I go?) It—well, she—led me to a suite of rooms, really one big chamber divided by bamboo or paper screens, or thin curtains. There was a bath, and she ran water into it. Hot and cold, from taps, just like the House and the City have. She also showed me a closet, and there were clothes in it. She said, "Clickety-clok: Shall I bathe and dress you, clack?"

"Er—no thanks. That's great. I'll manage."

"Shall I clunk clokkk?"

"Excuse me?"

"Clok: Bring refreshments?"

"Oh—that would be nice. Can I have some fresh drinking water?"

The food was basic on our journey, and the water had run out the last few days. You can get very tired of strong, sweet sticky wine.

"Clum-clucky," said the doll, and sailed out. (She walks in an odd way, a type of gliding *limp*.) (I still can't get over the urge to brush and comb her hair. Madness. Anyway, it might all come out and then the poor thing would be bald.) (Her face isn't so bad, but it's expressionless. The eyes sometimes blink, startling me every time. Her lips part when she speaks, but sometimes only these clucks or cloks emerge.)

When she came back anyway, I'd had a fast nervous bath, not enjoying it as I'd have done normally. I'd put on a long loose dress from the row of long loose dresses, white or pale grey, in the closet. There were also some ankle boots of soft leather.

I rolled up my WD with this book still safe inside the pocket. (A Hulta

Wedding Dress always has a pocket. The bride is given so many small gifts all through her wedding day, she has to have somewhere to put them.) I'd thought of that, too, got very down.

Then I shook myself. Just in time, for there was Dolly again.

On the tray she'd brought was a wonderful blush-and-cream fruit, some thin slices of a sort of crunchy bread, and a decanter and glass of green crystal. Cool water, as I'd asked.

"Thank you!" I cried.

She just went out.

Do you thank them? Does it matter?

Well, I do anyway. It feels wrong if I just snatch without a word, the way the other three do.

I didn't see *them* again until the evening. By then I'd slept a couple of hours on the low couch, a really deep, seemingly dreamless sleep. I felt better and stronger.

Dolly came into the room, clucked something about dinner on a terrace.

The view from my room's three high windows looks straight down into the jungle ravines, or up into leaf-fringed sky. Either way, mostly an impression of distance and things growing. A wild fig tree wraps the third window up almost entirely. So when Dolly led me up a short flight of stairs and I came out on a roof-terrace, the view made me dizzy again. All that largeness and space I'd seen earlier, but now we were perched right up inside it.

The sun was going down behind the house and jungle. Across from us, over the ravines, the cliff face was burning hot gold, and the waterfall like golden silver. And the sky was a spicy color. Overpowering.

Not taking any notice, Y, H, and Z were sprawled about, smoking beetles.

Then we had dinner served by all three dolls: Dolly and two male dolls I've since called Bow and Whirr. Not very clever, I admit. Bow talks, but keeps bowing, and Whirr—just *whirrs.*

Dinner was all right, quite tasty, lots of fresh vegetables, fruit, and salads, and some hot rice and pastry. No meat or cheese, or anything like that.

Hrald complained. "Can't they get fish, even? There's a river down there, isn't there? Under that waterfall? Bad management. All this way, and not even milk for the tea."

I didn't take much notice of them. They ignored me.

The sky was a smoked rose, then suddenly ash-blue. Stars starred it.

Then something *strange*—stars—gems—in the wrong place—at first I thought I was seeing things. Blinked, saw I wasn't.

I couldn't keep quiet.

"Over there—*what's that?*"

"What? Oh, *that.* Hmm. What do you think?"

I scowled at Yazkool. "If I thought I knew, I wouldn't ask."

"Oh, Claidissa, you're so loud and argumentative, so unfeminine—"

It was Zand who broke in. Gravely he told me, in my own language, "The palace is there, madam."

"Palace—that's a palace?"

The top of the huge cliff—I'd noticed in the last of the sun how it was all different shapes, especially along the top. I'd thought that was just how it had weathered. I've seen mountains, hills, shaped like towers or clumps of roofs. And this was all in the same stone. . . . But now in the sudden dusk, spangles had fired up everywhere, up and down the entire cliff. They were gold and white, delicate lettuce-green and ruby, amethyst. . . .

Windows.

"It's called the Rise," said Hrald. "Didn't we say?"

Those beasts, of course they hadn't.

So the cliff is called the Rise. It runs for miles, up and down and along. And it's not a cliff, or not only a cliff. Not a palace either—it must be a city. And it's occupied, because all those windows were gleaming and blazing now in the dark, from lighted lamps. Like they do over there every night I've been here.

I sat feeling completely astonished. I was frightened, too. Everything was too large. Nothing was properly explained. Perhaps it couldn't be.

But I wouldn't say anything else.

In the deep hollow of evening, far off yet weirdly clear, something growled, above the thunder of the fall.

"Tigapard, out hunting," said glib Yazkool, knowingly.

"Or tiger," added Hrald.

Zand shook his head. He said, still in my language, "There are other things, on the Rise."

And then—and then, to cap it all, as if too much hadn't already happened, this STAR rose over the cliff.

"My," said Yazkool. Even he looked awed, for a moment.

Hrald just gawped.

Zand got up, jingling, and bowed even lower than Bow, to the Star.

Argul told me something about stars, the way some of them are suns of distant worlds, and some are nearer and are planets, worlds like ours, that wander through the skies by night. I've never quite understood, although I loved to hear him talk about it.

Is this a star, then? A planet? What? I don't know. Only that it's enormous. I mean I actually sort of measured it later. Holding up my hand, the Star up there, by then even higher, neatly vanished behind my thumbnail—but for its *glow.*

It's blue-white. It *gushes* light, dazzles. Stark shadows fall away from it over the ground, as if from a nearly full moon.

Zand named it, in his own tongue. But I know what it's called now. I asked Dolly its name.

It's called the Wolf Star.

Well, that's all.

I mean, I've finished writing down the story of my kidnapping. Nothing else has happened.

We've been here three days and two nights. I've marked them on the top of a page in this book.

I stay in my room as much as I can. Some monkeys sometimes come and play in the fig tree, and I can watch them. They're noisy and funny. They throw fruit at each other, but sometimes they get violent, screaming and beating their chests.

Every night, if I look (I do look), the lights are lit in that cliff-palace over there, or whatever it is. And the great Star rises, gets higher, circles around somehow, is gone, comes *back,* and sinks. Did I ever see a star behave quite like that?

The Wolf Star.

The name isn't lost on me. No coincidence—it can't be. I don't know the link, though, between Wolf Star and Wolf Tower.

Y and H are getting impatient, I can tell. Little things like the way they curse and stamp about and throw fruit all the time. (Though no screams or chest-beating.)

Everything has something to do with over *There,* probably.

Zand left the day after we arrived. I didn't see him go. Why was he so polite that time he spoke to me?

I'm a prisoner.

Yes, I suppose I know something else will happen, to do with the cliff, the "Rise." But why should I think about it? I'm here, it's there. I can't see any way to cross, unless they or we fly.

Did think about running away again. Getting food from Dolly and saving it up, sneaking out at night. Surely cranky Whirr and Bow couldn't stop me? And if there are tigers and tigapards growling and roaring in the jungle and . . . "other things," well, so what?

Maybe I will.

Tonight, maybe.

But anyway, I've done what I said I'd do, put all this down. I've written all I'm going to.

I have nothing else to say.

THERE

Today, I was sent over there. *There* is where I am now.

That other window was high. This one is HIGH.

The morning started with a bang. Literally. A monkey jumped in through the fig-tree window, which I'd unluckily left open.

It landed on the tiled floor, day-edged and furry-looking, but its eyes were like angry red coins.

Then its mouth pursed up and it kept going *Hwoup-hwoup* at me.

Obviously, I hadn't left in the night. I'd felt too tired, not ready—I was confused. (Cowardly.) Now I stood by the bed and the monkey stood about ten feet away, going *hwoup* at me and showing its teeth in between, which I recalled Hrald had said, and even the Hulta had said, meant a monkey wasn't in a relaxed mood.

"Lovely monkey," I gooed, creeping toward the door. "Look, tasty mango in dishy. Have delishy mango-yum—"

But the monkey made a sudden leap and bounded up one of the curtains. As I said, they were thin; the material tore, and the monkey fell out of it, hit one of the paper screens, and screen and monkey went rolling about and now it was going *AargruffOOR!* at the top of its voice.

I ran out of the door and slammed it and rushed up the steps to the terrace.

Dawn had happened about an hour ago behind the Rise. The sky was tall and full of birds.

Something was wrong with the terrace.

The table had been laid for breakfast, which looked started on, and Yazkool and Hrald's usual chairs were pulled out. But another chair lay on its side with a broken back. And there were three broken plates and one of Yazkool's enamel beetle boxes—just lying there, too, on the ground, open, with beetles and tobacco spilling out.

Monkeys were yammering from all the trees by the house.

Something had happened.

I yelled, "Dolly! Bow!"

Odd, really. H and Y were hardly my best friends, but I felt panicky.

For ages no one came. I heard the monkeys bashing about and thought they might come up on the terrace and perhaps I should go back into the house. Then Dolly appeared and limped across to me.

"What's happened? Where are they? I mean Hrald, Yaz—"

"Clickups, clankit."

"Oh *Dolly*—"

"Gone," said Dolly.

"Yes, Dolly, but where—why?"

"Cluck: Duty done. Now you go to *Glack!*"

I nearly howled—and now here was Bow lurching up bowing and saying, "More juice, more toast!" And Whirr going "Whirr," and I could hear the monkey in my room breaking more screens.

Then I saw the bridge.

I said we'd have to fly to reach the Rise. It wasn't necessary after all.

It was like a long white tongue that had licked out, a frog's or lizard's, from a little black mouth in the distant cliff-side. It had slid across the drop, through the spray of the fall, slid on and on until it touched and somehow attached itself into the rock on this side, and stiffened to stillness. By craning over the terrace, I could see the bridge's end, just by the courtyard wall.

"Someone came from over there," I brilliantly guessed. "By the bridge. And Yazkool and Hrald—"

"Away," said Bow, bowing over his tray of excess toast.

"Do you mean *killed?*"

"Whirr," said Whirr, thoughtfully.

This was useless. It would have been simple, presumably, for someone, or their guards or slaves, to hurl H and Y straight off this roof and away to the ravines below, to the jungle trees and the fish-river Hrald was always grumbling about.

Dolly was saying, "Yack come over. You to go over cluck click."

Me to go—

The bridge was for me to go—over—

Whirr was pushing at me. Was he trying to herd me to the bridge? Or worse—? I tried to fight, and into my punching hands he thrust a piece of paper, folded once and sealed with black wax.

I stared at it. For a minute the seal was all I could see. The wax had been stamped with the shape of—a wolf.

The dolls had all moved back, and now the monkeys were making less of a row. And like a fool, I recalled, last thing last night, hearing Yazkool cursing away from the house stairs about dropping his second-best beetle-box. So that had happened *then,* not because of some attack. As for the monkeys, the bridge would have scared them. Everything explained.

I broke the wax seal (it was a wolf with some sort of bird flying over it?) and undid the paper.

The writing was in blackest ink, in the language of the House and Nemian's City, though some of the words were spelled another way; this didn't look like mistakes. It said: "Greetings from the Rise. The men who brought you here have been paid and you may release them." (Fine chance, they hadn't waited.) "The bridge is for your convenience. Cross at your pleasure. The slave will escort you. Until we meet—*V.*"

That was all.

"What slave?" I nervously asked. The least important question.

Then anyway I saw him, standing waiting in the courtyard below. A man with thick green hair.

At the House, there were fashions and even rituals that involved differently colored hair or wigs. At first I thought the escort-slave was wearing a wig.

Before I left, I ate a mouthful of toast, swallowed a few sips of the green milkless tea. I had a bath and put on another dress. I brushed my hair. All this to waste time, to put off going. Also to see if it would be allowed.

Apparently it was. No one came to hurry me.

When I came out in the yard, the slave was still waiting, still just standing there, as if he hadn't moved an inch.

He wasn't mechanical. I kept wondering if he was. He was . . . odd.

I carried my WD and this book and pen, and a few things—under-clothes, comb, etc.—in a bag I'd handily found in the closet. Put there to be handy for me?

Dolly, Bow, and Whirr stood in the veranda, as if sending me off. So I waved. They didn't wave back. Why would they?

It'd been no use asking any questions either.

As we walked down the uneven slope between the fig trees and palms, toward the white bridge, I tried questioning the slave.

"What's your name, please?"

Instant reply. "Grembilard," he said.

"I'm Claidi," I said. At the House, or in the City, one didn't speak to slaves like this, but what the hell.

"Lady," said the slave promptly, however.

"No, *not* lady. Call me Claidi. Try it."

"Lady Claidi."

That sounded ridiculous. But I let it go. Wanted to move on. "Who sent you for me?"

Then the slave said something I thought meant he *was* a doll, and his mechanism had gone funny, like Dolly's and Whirr's.

"Could you repeat that?"

He did. I realized he'd put *Prince* on the front, too, both times.

Was it a name? I tried it out hesitantly:

"Prince Venarion-yellow Kasmel—"

Obligingly, Grembilard helped me.

"Prince Venaryonillarkaslemidorus."

"Oh."

Then we came around a giant stand of blue blooms like lupine (eight feet tall) and there was the bridge.

I'd felt nervous. Now I felt Nervous.

"Who is he?" I demanded, stopping.

The slave stopped. "Prince Venaryonillarkaslemidorus."

"Yes, I know, but—" Grembilard took my bag. I looked at it in his hands. Everything had been taken out of my hands.

The bridge was terrifying.

How it had anchored itself into the ground on this side I couldn't make out, but the earth was all displaced. The bridge looked solid. Immovable. It was straight as a ruler, as it spanned the tremendous gulf. It was white as icing on a cake, with a lace-delicate rail that would come, once I stepped on the bridge, to just above the height of my waist—not very high. And it was *narrow.* Only wide enough for us to go single file. The distance from here to *there* was about a mile.

He walked in front. I was just supposed to follow. I followed.

At first I was afraid to look anywhere but at Grembilard's back and peculiar leafy hair. My legs shook. I could *feel* the distance rushing below, down and down.

But the bridge was if anything *horribly* solid. It didn't even vibrate from our footsteps or the roar of the fall, which got louder as we went on.

And everything was slick with moisture, and then in places dry where somehow the fine spray didn't come.

(The noise of the fall is always there, and I seem always to be hearing it suddenly for the first time, as if I've only just noticed it, or it's only just started, like a vast faucet turned on in the cliff. But that's *because* it's constant; you just forget to hear it most of the time, hear other things above, below, around it.)

I think we were about halfway across when I thought I *would* look down.

The thing *anyone*—you, for example—would have said *don't do.* But I kind of had to.

So I stopped and put my hands firmly on the little handrail. I looked straight out, then over.

For some moments I was simply so astonished I didn't feel anything but—astonishment.

If the way across is a mile, it must be three miles, four miles, down.

There *is* a river at the bottom—a tiny, shiny dark blue worm, coming and going through veils of spray. The fall reaches it, growing slender as a pencil, and *detonates.* And the sides of the Rise, and of the other cliffs, cascade toward the river, green bunched curtains caught with flowers and pineapples and tree-limbs, where parakeets flash red. Then, above is a sky so large that I could just float free and up to one of those bubbles of cloud.

And that was when my head seemed to fall off *upward,* and I sat down bump on the bridge.

"I can't move," I said. "I *won't* move."

Giddy and mindless, I thought fearfully of what Argul would do—scold me, pick me up, drag me, or just sit and hold my hand until I felt better.

How I wished he was there. I started to talk to him.

"I'll be all right in a minute, Argul."

The slave stood over me, indifferent.

"His hair," I said to the imagined Argul, "*isn't* hair. It has leaves in it."

My head cleared. I said to the slave quite sharply, "Why are there leaves in your hair, Grembilard?"

"They grow in it," he said.

I felt sensible, nodded, and stood up. I was all right after that. I kept asking questions about his hair.

He answered them all, but we—I—got nowhere.

He says his hair is partly hair and partly leaves. Has to be washed and then watered, or something. It looks *real.* Couldn't be.

But I was all right.

I started to notice the cliff, the Rise, when we were about an eighth of a mile away from it.

It truly is enormous, and it does look natural, most of it, but every so often there is a part that, close up, you can see is carved out—a balcony or a bulging upper story, long ranks of windows, with glass or lattices. Steps, too, appearing and angling around, and towers, these with roofs of tiles but they're almost all faded, just a wink of indigo or lime here and there.

Masses of vines grow up the face of the rock walls, and trees thrust out of them, as I'd seen from the other side.

Where the waterfall water*fell,* all I could see was spray like smoke, with a glitter of sun like dancing coins. But the fall itself was about three miles away along the cliff to my left.

Where the bridge had come out wasn't a hole, but a huge gatemouth.

We got nearer and I began to dread the gatemouth more than I'd dreaded the bridge.

But I couldn't really stop to admire the view again, so I went on.

Some pink parrots flew over as we got there. Then we were simply off the bridge and standing on another terrace. Cut stairs led up into the dim cavern or hall or whatever.

If I go in, will I ever get out?

And then I thought, *Oh, come on. I've gotten out of everything else!*

So I marched behind leafy Grembilard, up these old sloping stairs, and into the Mouth of the Rise.

WHERE?

What I said to him, to Argul, all that time—only a month or so—ago, about how the ring he gave me felt like a part of my hand. It does, so much so that I forget I have it on half the time, and in the beginning I sometimes knocked it on things.

The stone (diamond) is part cut and part polished. It's like a great tear.

I mention this now because it's all I have left of Argul. And because of what the slave said, Grembilard, as we walked into the cavern.

"Lady Claidi, I must ask, is that your mother's ring?"

My *mother.* I hadn't thought of her for a while. I mean, I'd never been sure that what I was told about her was true—that she was called Twilight Star, was a princess, and so on. The story of my mother was one of the things that made me escape from the House with Nemian and go to the City of the Wolf Tower. So it was told me, no doubt, to help make me do just that. On the other hand, *I* told Ironel Novendot the ring was my mother's, so I could wear it openly in the Tower. Ironel was the *only* one I told.

"Who told you that?" I asked Grembilard.

But all I got was "The Prince—" (and that *name* again) "may like to know if that is the ring of Twilight Star."

"Then he can have fun guessing, can't he?"

But did all this really mean that Ironel had sent word here, to this prince with a name of—what was it?—*eleven* syllables. Then that also meant she'd known I would be brought *here?!*

I looked around briskly. The cavern-hall was several stories high, the ceiling rock carved with flowerlets and wiggles. The floor was old stone, polished with wear in places, and damp and going mossy.

Anyway, *why* did they want to know about the ring?

"Why does he want to know about the ring?"

"It has properties."

"Like what?"

But only slavey silence now, and I was (slavishly) following him up another staircase, which had carved marble animals on either side—tigers with beards, and things like bears.

Didn't matter, did it, anyway. It *wasn't* Twilight's ring. If I was even her daughter.

A door opened to one side, straight off the stairs. It opened, I suppose, by clockwork, since we didn't touch it and no one else was there.

He went in. I went in. The door shut.

There were lots of corridors after that, some quite narrow and others wide. Carvings, tiles, and here and there water dripping down the wall.

All the corridors had windows, some very high up so only sky was visible. In one wide corridor was a line of ten windows, floor to ceiling, about two man-heights high. They were of rich stained glass in complicated patterns. I must have seen them when I was across the gulf, once they were lit up at night. From this side you couldn't see through.

Sometimes there were closed doors, or other passages, arches, stairways.

I kept expecting to meet other people. There must be hundreds, thousands, in this palace-city inside the cliff.

We met no one.

That seemed—not right.

Once there was a very odd noise, a kind of grating rumble.

I said, "What's that noise?"

Grembilard said, "Just the palace."

"Is it unsafe?"

He didn't answer. After that I kept thinking I'd see and feel galleries shaking or wobbly stones or plaster falling off the walls. But mostly the whole place seems in goodish repair. Even the water spills have only grown some attractive indoor mosses and ferns.

Anyhow, the sound died away.

We must have walked for about twenty minutes. Then he opened a door.

He handed me my bag. "Here are rooms where you can stay," said Grembilard. "For now," he added. (Ominously?)

These rooms are high, and pale banana-yellow. There are three—no, four.

I sit in them or pace around.

Again, few furnishings. Low couches, a table or two, some fruit, water and wine, a sunken bathtub—hot and cold water—a jar of some essence on the side, towels laid ready.

No *doors* in these rooms. Only curtains to screen the doorways.

And nobody about. Grembilard, having bowed me in, had bowed out, and I'd said anxiously, "Where are you going? Now what happens?"

And he shrugged with a long face. "Who can say?"

"What do you mean? When will I meet this Prince Venaridory-whatever?"

"Perhaps, soon. Or later. Whatever else, madam, please don't leave the rooms."

"Well, I thought you'd no doubt lock me in."

"No. Unless you'd prefer it?"

"No I *wouldn't!* I might like another stroll."

"Lady Claidi," said Grembilard, "there are . . . certain dangers in the palace—for this reason you shouldn't go outside the door."

"Oh. I won't, then," I airily replied.

When he'd gone and I'd wandered around a bit, I did go and try to open the outer door to the corridors. And it did open.

What dangers? Do tigers and panthers run wild through the passageways?

Nothing out there—but then I heard that odd rumbling again. What was it? This time there was a definite vibration through the wall.

So I came back in.

I eventually noticed some of the fruit in the onyx dish had gone rotten.

Most of the windows in here have panes of milky non-see-through glass. They could face out onto anything—even other rooms.

Then I found *this* window, behind a gauzy curtain I'd thought was just a drapery.

Clear glass. You can look straight down and down to the blue slow-worm of river.

Sitting by this window, I've written everything up.

What can I say? The most—well, it's—

Did I go to sleep and dream it?

No, because *she's* still there, the girl slave, sitting all innocent and cross-legged on the floor.

And the cat's here, too, somewhere.

Sorry—that's confusing. What happened was this:

I got bored sitting. I had a bright idea. Since I'd found the window behind a curtain, there might be other things behind other gauzes hanging decoratively down the walls.

Not much to start. A mirror was behind one, and I saw myself and frowned hard at me. I looked changed and not myself. Behind another curtain was a door, an actual door made of wood and painted like the walls. I tried it but couldn't make it open. Left it, feeling irritated.

In the fourth room there was a cupboard behind a gauze with gold threads. In the cupboard I found piles of books, all in other languages and without pictures. Some did have maps, which made no sense to me. I wouldn't expect them to, never having been educated at the House.

The last gauze was also in the fourth room, and when I dragged it aside I found another door. Another cupboard, I thought, as I easily pulled it wide. It wasn't.

Outside was a vast hall of echoing stone. Granite pillars soared up, smooth as glass, and there was a great marble stair. Light streamed in at a round ceiling-window, a skylight. It was high above, and through it I could see faint chalkings of cloud.

On the stair was this girl with short black hair, sitting crying her eyes out.

I said, idiotically, "Are you all right?"

And I took a step out of the doorway—

What happened?

It's hard to describe it, really.

It was like being on that ship again, and like getting off the ship for the first hour or so, when the ground seemed to be moving as the deck had.

Everything *lurched.* I nearly fell flat, and then I did, but the other way, backward, because the girl came hurtling off the stair and jumped at me. We tumbled into the room and got wrapped up in the curtain, which tore right off the wall.

The floor hit me in the back and the girl had landed on my stomach. Luckily she wasn't very heavy. As I lay there, gasping, saying things I usually try not to, I saw this:

Midway up, the stair separated.

The top part then flew slowly up into the ceiling, and when it was almost at the skylight, a large area of wall glided away, and the stair slid through. Then, from somewhere else—the other wall, only I hadn't seen it start—came what looked like half of a room, with a fountain in a stone bowl, trickling away. And this wheeled past and filled in the space between the door and the now-in-half stair.

Then everything stopped.

I couldn't see the pillars or the stairway anymore. I couldn't see the skylight. This other room, which now looked like a whole room, had latched on to *my* rooms.

The girl had rolled away, and I sat up and stared. Then I, too, got up. And I was just going to go out into this sudden new room with a fountain, had one foot over the threshold, when the girl jumped at me again and grabbed both of my arms.

I tried to push her off.

She shook her head so violently I thought it might come loose. She'd stopped crying. She had been streaming tears, but her eyes weren't even red. After we'd struggled for a while, I snapped, "All right. You don't want me to go in there. I won't."

She let me go at once.

What was in this new room? Just the fountain. It was shaped like a big fish, quite elegant.

Then something moved in the stone bowl. It sprang off and came bounding over and through my doorway.

A stone-grey cat. The oddest-looking cat—flame-green eyes and this *different* forehead—but it shot past and rushed into my rooms, and I don't know where it's hidden itself.

The girl just went over there, and sat on the floor, inside my doorway.

No tears. *Had* she been crying?

She doesn't speak, or can't, or won't. I don't know which.

Apparently I'm not allowed to go away from in here. Deliberately I walked to the outer door, and when I got there she came tearing after me. So I came back, and at once she sat down again.

Wait. I'll try asking—

I did. I said, "Can you speak?" and she shook her head.

I said, "Is it dangerous for me to go outside?"

Vigorous nods. Her neck must be really supple from all that urgent nodding.

I said, "The stair—part of it moved—didn't it?"

To that, almost a *lazy* nod.

Then, this totally absurd thing.

She opened her eyes wide as wide, and streams, rivers of tears rushed from them. She had no expression. She didn't look upset.

When about two pailsful of water had poured on the floor, the tears ended. She got up and stood in the wet. Then she hopped and jumped about the room, like a kid playing, making wet footprints (wet from her own *tears*), looking at them—and silently giggling.

She did this for a quarter of an hour.

Now she's sat down again.

As for the cat, I just saw it. It's in the fruit dish in room two. It's eaten every grape, orange, and peach, and even the rotted mango. Now it's just sitting in the dish, washing itself nice and sticky. (Its head is shaped like—well, it's—?)

Claidi, you need to make a plan.

Any plan.

No, I haven't, didn't.

Instead, this room—

Moved.

No, I didn't imagine it. Very loud rumbling started, and the floor jumped and shook for about two minutes. Next, when I looked out of the door to the passages, everything was different. There's a courtyard out there now, with roses and vines growing from pots. At the other door, which I'd left open, the room with the fountain is still there. It obviously came with us.

Probably the Tear Girl would have stopped me if I'd tried, but I didn't try, to go out by either way.

Something else has happened. The rooms became dark after we'd moved. I think the windows, though I can't see through, don't look outside anymore. Certainly the clear glass window doesn't. It now looks at a tall side of the cliff, where there are windows, too, but also a looming cedar tree hangs over. (I noticed the Tear Girl did now appear rather worried.)

After it had been gloomy and dark for about five minutes, and I was wondering if there were any candles or lamps, *lights came on.*

That's the only way I can put it. Think of about fifty candles lit and burning up at once. Only steady, not flickery. And no one *lit* them.

The source of the light seems to be some of the carvings at the tops of the four rooms.

I mean, this light is perfect, soft but clear. But how—what is it?

I've heard them—the House, the Hulta—talk about magic. Is this magic?

Before, I was scared, but I had gotten used to being scared. It wasn't too bad. Now I'm frightened. It isn't even that. I'm—really lost. *Where* on earth have I come to?

These rooms haven't moved again. But I keep thinking they will. The lights burn steadily. Nothing's happened for about three hours, except that the cat's gone to sleep in the fruit dish. Oh this is awful.

Obviously, at last I decided I *was* going to leave the rooms. I couldn't stand this anymore. I said to the girl, "I'm just going to have a quick look outside. . . ." I meant to make a dash for it. Though a dash to where or what I hadn't a clue.

I put my bag casually over my shoulder by its carrying strap, walked about, walked to the door, yawned and stretched.

She didn't seem agitated. . . . I'd fooled her?

Really, it was quite an attractive yard. The roses were scented and twined around pillars. There was a grapevine heavy with fruit.

Tall, windowless walls enclosed the court above. At the top was sky. It seemed very dense and blue—afternoon? I'd probably been here longer than I thought.

Was there another way out?

I'd delayed too long by being casual. Here was Tearful at my side. The cat had woken up and come, too, smelling strongly of peaches. What it was with its head was that the area between the ears was too thick and high—its ears looked tiny, but weren't. Its eyes were enormous, though.

"Isn't that a strange cat?" I said to Tearful.

Then I broke into a sprint.

Oh, they both shot after me, Tearful with her thin arms out to clutch, and just missing me, and the cat with its little ears laid flat on its big domed forehead.

Luckily there was an archway behind the vines. I belted straight through (with the bag thumping me on the back as if to hurry me up), and as I did so, I heard something start creakily to *move* behind me and felt the ground *sway.* But I just pelted on. (Once I also felt Tearful's clawlike fingers catch my hair, but I managed to rip it free.)

I don't think I ran *that* far.

There were more corridors and courts and hallways, and now and then more stairs. We were deep inside the cliff, I thought, for at no point did I recognize the outer wall of it, and although there were colored windows in places, they seemed to look into rooms, not out at the gulf. Towers piled above.

In darker corners, and behind some windows, there was this light burning, often from a source I didn't even see. Twice I ran under a great lit hanging lamp—the glow in both of them was as steady as if the light had gone *hard.*

Of course, I didn't know where I was going, and anyway I got tired. I was emptily hungry, too, painfully dry—and scared, fed up.

Suddenly in front of me reared an arch with a gate of curly wrought iron.

Unable to stop, I ran right into it and it swung gently open.

I burst through on to a broad path laid with bleached gravel.

And then I couldn't run anymore. I was bent almost double, crowing for breath. I had a stitch, too.

The pumping of blood in my head made everything zoom in and out. When that stopped, I saw I'd come into what looked like a formal, exotic park.

Behind and to either side was the cliff-palace. And far over there, through a cloud of trees, some other tall rocks-or-buildings, going up, one with a golden globe on its top, blinding back the afternoon sun. The rest was sloping lawns, blooming shrubs, twenty-foot bamboos.

On the path behind me, by the gate, stood Tearful, also panting for breath. The cat had kept up, too. (I think it had found cat shortcuts and jumped over things we'd had to run along.) Another cat, a brown one, now came to join it, also with a curious domed forehead. But they were soon having a completely ordinary catfight, yowling and kicking and bashing through a rhododendron.

Then Grembilard walked out of some tulip trees.

"You're here, then, madam," he said. I still couldn't speak. I scowled at him instead. "If you'd stayed in the rooms, it would have been easier," he had the unbelievable sauce to say.

"For whom?" I had to croak.

"Everyone," he patiently moaned.

"They *move,*" I accused. "The rooms. The stairs—"

No reply. He was taking my bag again. I let go. We walked down the path, Grembilard in front, then me, Tearful, and next the cats, falling in behind.

IN THE AIR-HARP GARDENS

There are fireflies in the gardens. Also nightingales. And the harp-things sometimes sing, too.

None of that is important. I'm sorry, maybe it is.

Maybe I'd better tell you about Venn.

I really must try to start at the beginning. All right:

Grembilard led me (us) across this park, which I've since been told is called the Air-Harp Gardens. I did notice jungly colossal trees, and pavilions (like at the House, but different). There was a *little* waterfall that splashed down three or four terraces to a pool. The thunder of the big fall was softer, away around the side of the Rise.

We reached a lawn with a statue of some sort of spread-winged heron. Here on a table was food, some of it under covers, and another slave—only he turned out to be another *doll*—waving insects and tiny little birds away from the plates and bottles.

"I thought you'd *never* get here," he fussed, flapping around us. Though he was mechanical, all the parts of his face moved. He had *expressions.* "Please, *do* sit down," and he seated me and Tearful, treating us both like royalty.

The lemonade had gotten warm and the boiled eggs were cold, but it wasn't bad.

It was a Tea. (Like the Teas Jizania had, at the House, for every meal.)

The doll—Grembilard calls him Jotto—fussed around all the time.

He leapt to serve us all. He even let the cats on the table and put out plates for them, and he spooned on eggs and toast and biscuits and butter, and chopped them all up to make them easier for the cats' teeth to get to. When he wasn't running up and down doing that, he was running up and down waving off the bees and dragonflies and hummingbirds with a feather fan.

I felt tired when I'd eaten but still very Nervous. Also, the sun was westering behind the rock-buildings. The sky was that spicy color it goes just before and just after sunset. Where had today gone?

"Oh, I do hope he'll be here soon," fussed Jotto. He was nice, really, kind and wanting to help so much that you wanted to slap him. But, I mean, he's clockwork! No doll I've ever come across (although I suppose my experience with them is limited) ever had a *personality!*

"He?" I demanded. "Who?"

"Prince Venarionillarkasl—"

"Oh, him."

"You see," fussed Jotto, opening a jar of fruit and offering it to the grey cat, "he knew it would take ages to find you, probably. But now he's probably having to do it *twice,* since you unfortunately left the first set of rooms."

"I see," I lied.

"Poor prince," said Jotto rather cheekily—or not? They wouldn't have stood for that at the House. "This place can be *such* a trial."

I was surprised he thought so, too. Surprised he *thought* anything.

"I don't understand about the rooms moving," I announced flatly.

Jotto opened his mouth, then hesitated. "I get a bit muddled."

Grembilard said, "Prince Ven-etc.-etc. will explain."

"Oh, yippee."

The sun set. Grembilard scratched at his leafy hair, and Tearful got up and went and cried on it, gallons. Grembilard rubbed the water into his scalp. "Thank you, Treacle. That feels much better." (He's not really like a slave, Grembilard. And she's called Treacle.)

Then, in the quick red afterglow, Jotto pointed excitedly.

"Look, there's his light!"

We looked. A tall yellow window had lit up under the golden globe, in the rocks.

"Lights here just light anyway, don't they?" I said.

"Oh yes, lady dear," said Jotto kindly. "Only *his* is a special *oil* lamp. He does so like to be different."

Oil lamps, like candles, are what I'm used to. I realize by now, it may not be the same for you.

But well, anyway, we got up and trooped off into the darkening trees, through the fireflies that were also lighting up, and after about ten minutes we were under the rock-building, looking up about seventy feet at *his* window.

"Helloo! Helloo, prince!" yelled Jotto.

Grembilard made a kind of loud whooping noise. Treacle and the cats danced about.

I stood there like a total twit.

In the end, after an age, part of the lighted window opened.

A dark figure leaned out its head and shoulders.

"Yes? Is that you, Grem?"

Something about his voice—I didn't know what, at first—made all the fine hair on my scalp and neck stand up.

A City voice. A Wolf Tower voice.

Like *Nemian's.*

Pale moths flickered between us and him, attracted to his light.

"Shall we come up, prince?" cried Jotto.

"No." That was definite. "Wait. I'll come down."

As the window shut, Jotto whispered to Grembilard, "You don't think he was—*up* there all the time? I mean, I thought he was still *looking* for her."

Grembilard said nothing.

I wanted to move back into the deepest shadows, but I stayed where I was. It *wasn't* Nemian, even if he'd sounded so like him.

No, he wasn't Nemian.

A stair curved down the rock-tower, and he came down that. He was carrying another lamp, which lit him up in a peculiar way, from one side and below.

He just looked like what he was, a stranger.

Then, when he was only about ten steps up, he paused and looked over at us all, angling the lamp.

I thought, *He's nearsighted or something.*

He was peering at us.

And then, the way the light fell, suddenly it filled in his face properly, as if it hadn't been completely there before.

He's pale-skinned and his hair, which is thick, falls to his shoulders and is light brown and loosely curling. His eyes are black. That's the same. I mean, that's the same as the one he looks like. He looks like—

(I swallowed air the wrong way.

Jotto hit me on the back.

Treacle wriggled in a giggle without sound.)

Argul.

He looks like Argul.

No, he can't, he *can't*.

He does.

There was an eerie whining noise. I thought it was just something *I* was hearing. But Jotto waved up at this oval hoop with strings in a tree. A night breeze was passing and made the strings "sing," apparently. (It's very unmusical.) Then a monkey screamed somewhere. Stopped. "The air-harps," Jotto said, smirking. "Clever, aren't they?"

Then a nightingale started.

I burst out madly laughing. Jotto looked startled: Should he thump me on the back again?

He just stood ten steps up. And now the angle of the lamp was different, and he didn't look like Argul, or not so much.

And the awful, horrible thing is—I wanted him to. Such a lot.

"That's late tonight," he said, as the huge Star rose.

We were sitting, on chairs G and J had brought, in the clearing under the rock-tower. Apparently, this building doesn't move, just as the gardens don't.

Starlight shattered through the trees and hit the grass like shards of broken glass.

"That Star is very large," I said.

"Is it? Oh. Yes."

He was uninterested. In the Star, in me, in everything. You could tell he was itching to get back into the tower, to be alone.

He'd sent the others off, in quite a friendly, relaxed way. When he turned to me, he was cool and distant.

The note he sent to me read "Until we meet." But it was now obvious he hadn't *wanted* to meet me. Either that or I was the most ghastly disappointment.

So—what was all this about?

"Prince Venari—er—Yill—er—" I tried.

"Call me Venn," he said shortly.

"—Prince Venn, why am I here?"

"Oh why indeed," he said, offhand, gazing away through the trees. "To be useful?"

"That's nice. In what way, and to whom?" (What excellent grammar! Didn't I dare not to speak properly, with *royalty?*)

"To me, perhaps."

"I see. And how am I meant to do that?"

"Well, Claidis," (*Claidis,* that was new) "frankly, I'm not at all sure. But there. You're doubtless a mine of information. You're like a book from the library. I shall want to consult you, I expect. One day."

"About what?"

"All the things you know."

"I don't know *anything.*"

He flicked me a glance iced with distaste. "You're too modest."

"I'm not modest; I'm telling you the truth. Who on earth do you think I am?"

He looked down his nose. He did it just as Argul does, when he's being—Argul. But this was—*Venn.*

"This is rather silly, isn't it?" he said.

"No. Or if it is, that's not my fault. Those men abducted me, dragged me here, and I want to know why, and saying I'm a mine of information is like saying—like saying *Treacle is chatty.*"

"I find all this rather dull," he said. "Don't you?"

I sat there, and my mouth dropped open, so I shut my mouth and thought, *I feel as if I'm going nuts.*

He just looked away through the trees. Then he glanced at the Star, which was now directly above. How fast it climbed—was it always so fast? Just tonight? Or had we been sitting here that long?

Then: "I hope everything is comfortable for you, Claidis."

"Of course it isn't!" I screeched.

He got up.

He's slightly taller than Argul, which of course makes him look too tall.

"Perhaps we should talk tomorrow," he graciously said, "or in a few days' time."

"Let's talk now." I, too, got up. "All right. I'm your prisoner. But I—"

He gave this soft blank laugh. As if I'd told a boring joke but he must be polite.

"Next month, then," he said.

The night breezes twittered and whined in the nonmusical air-harp strings. Monkeys bawled. And three or four nightingales chirruped as if they had hiccups.

"Wait," I said. And I heard Argul, oddly, in my voice, his authority. And it stopped this man a minute. (How old is he? A year or so older than Argul, probably. But he's like a man *much* older, *fifty,* say. Set like cold cement.)

"Wait for what, madam?"

"Why are you calling me that? I'm a slave, aren't I? You don't say *madam* to a slave. I was brought here, and I don't know a thing about anything—about the world—or about this place. I don't even know where I'm going to have to sleep."

"Grembilard will," he said, "naturally find you a suitable chamber. *If* you stay put this time, it will almost certainly not move. Of course, I can't guarantee it, the palace being what it is."

"This palace is *insane!*" I shouted.

"True. It was made to be mad, by my mother. One of her most cunning tricks."

The Star blared on the clearing. His face was blue-white. I expect mine was, too.

Then something growled, long and low, echoing and seeming not far off.

"It's only a vrabburr," he chillily (I think) said.

"Oh, *that's* all right, then."

"They don't come into the gardens. Stay inside the walls and you'll be perfectly safe."

"Oh will I? *Will* I?"

"I'm afraid, Claidis, I don't understand you," he said. "If it's all been so difficult, you shouldn't have asked to come here, should you?"

"ASKED???" That was all I could get out.

Somewhere or other, the safely-outside vrabburr (or another one) growled again. Which was the only reply I got.

Venn-etc. just walked off. He was on his stairs, going up, back to his room.

From the back, he didn't look like Argul, or Nemian—or anyone I'd ever met.

I sat down again on my chair; I was so stunned I didn't even try to think.

After a while Jotto appeared. He bent over me.

"Don't you fret, now," said Jotto. "He can be a bit—standoffish. His mother, you know. She was very harsh. Left him when he was only nine. Grem says the Rose Room will be all right. Come and see."

The west walls, which face west across the gulf, and the outer corridors there, and most of the rooms in these outer areas of the Rise, don't ever move. That is, they don't have the mechanisms and can't.

It seems that my yellow rooms, though in the west wall, do move—well, they did. But they hadn't for "years" and were thought to be "quiet."

The inner rooms of the palace can almost *all* move. They do it at will—only it isn't will—it's some clockwork thing, which makes them shift about, sliding and slotting around each other, but not in any real order.

Although Jotto told me that some rooms and sets of rooms do tend to "go wandering off" about the same times of day and night, and in the same sort of direction—"quite often."

He started explaining all this, or trying to, as he showed me the Rose Room. He was obviously trying to cheer me up, console me for Venn-etc. being unfriendly. But it just added to my feelings of utter furious, frantic bewilderment.

"The thing is, you mustn't go out of here until we fetch you. Someone will always come to *you,* if you press this carved flower, here. They may take a little while, though, so be patient, lady dear. Sometimes a walk of ten minutes can take all *morning,* the way things move around."

Apparently if a human presence—or even a clockwork one, as Jotto bashfully added—is in a room, it doesn't normally move but stays put.

Treacle had been left in the yellow rooms earlier, just in case, to keep them anchored. She only slipped out when I came in. Then, when I put one foot outside (twice), the yellow rooms "woke up." Perhaps they thought I'd gone. Anyway, they got frisky. (That was why Treacle had tried to stop me going out and jumped right at me.) After that, though, even when she and I stayed in the rooms, they took off. And the staircase had moved—hadn't it?—when Treacle left it.

Was I even listening to Jotto's explanation? I must have been, to be able to write it down now. Does it make any sense? I doubt it.

Finally I said to Jotto, who was by then artistically arranging some pineapples he'd collected on the way in a dish, "Who told Ve—*him*—I *asked* to come here?"

Jotto glanced at me. "Well. I can't say. Your companions, perhaps?"

"That Yazkool, you mean, and Hrald—?"

"Or it might have been in the flying letter."

"The—what's that?"

"Oh, just a letter, dear." Intent on getting the last pineapple *just* right, Jotto held up his hand for silence.

"Oh, blast the pineapples, Jotto. He has to be told—*now*—that I was brought here against my will. And I—want to go home!" I added in a wail.

But Jotto just positioned the last of the fruits and beamed at me. "There, isn't that better? Nothing like a proper display of fruit and flowers to make things civilized. Now don't you worry. You'll feel right as rain after a nice sleep."

"You don't believe me. *He* didn't. Of course I'd *have* to want to come *here,*" I sarcastically added.

"That's *right!*" cried Jotto, even his beam beaming.

I gave up.

This Rose Room is about twenty feet tall. Everything is roses, and rose-colored, including dresses in its closet. I hate it, naturally.

VRABBURRS AND OTHERS

I suppose another endless century has gone by. Haven't marked the days or anything. Days here are alike, and even weather seldom changes, except for a couple of insane storms. (You can see them *coming,* from the Rise.) I've counted twenty cats, all with domed foreheads. But since a lot are black or brown, and I haven't seen all of them up close, some might be ones I'd already counted. . . .

What to put down. I mean, things have sort of happened. Nothing much.

I'm supposed to stay in this big room, because it won't move about if I'm *in* here. And it hasn't. But I've been out, too, into the gardens, which don't move ever, thank goodness.

I fully expected the Rose Room to have taken off when I came back, so I'd taken everything I wanted outside with me. But the Room was there. Jotto says this R. Room is "sleepy." It hasn't gone anywhere for ages. I reminded him about the yellow rooms, also said to be quiet, which hadn't been. He seems to think that's different.(?)

Anyway, the R.R. opens right onto the gardens, so it's convenient for that at any rate. (Oh, Jotto keeps chickens, by the way. I'd wondered where the eggs came from.)

Lights come on in the lamps in here at sunset. The lamps are closed rosy glass roses, so I can't see what makes the light, which doesn't flicker, and it goes out when I lie down on the bed. (The first time that happened I jumped up again and at once the light returned.)

It's the old thing, isn't it? This whole foul business *is* an Adventure. I should be energetically exploring, making notes.

The more I find out, after all, the more chance I have of learning how to get away from here and back to—Argul. Somehow that was difficult to write. It's as if I've totally lost him. As if—I'd ceased to exist in Argul's world. I can't explain. But it's an awful feeling.

I *have* asked questions, of Grembilard, and Jotto, and of another one I call the Gardener, because I always find him in the gardens, neatly scything the lawns or restringing air-harps. I'm pretty sure the Gardener is a doll, but he's even more realistic-looking than Jotto, and he's sullen and grunts at you like a bad-tempered slave. Maybe he *is* a slave?

Grembilard, though a slave (the letter Venn sent told me he was), is obviously a favorite of Venn's. Twice I've seen them talking, all friendly and easy, in the distance. I never approached. The one time I came through a grove of strawberry trees, and there they were, strolling along, Venn's *face.* He looked almost *afraid* at the horror of Claidi, her appallingness. He gave me a brisk nod then turned and stalked off.

One evening, I saw a big pale bird floating over the gardens, and Jotto said, "There's the prince's owl."

He doesn't look so much like Argul. It was just that first time I saw him, somehow he truly did.

Well, he does, rather. Sometimes more than others.

Why does he?

All this is such a muddle, and I almost have this feeling they sent me on purpose to someone who looks like Argul, just to make things worse. But what would be the point of that? Then again, why did they tell him I wanted to be here?

And who are *They,* anyway?

Ironel? Jizania? The Wolf Tower?

Questions I've asked, about which I got no sense out of anyone here, are these:

1) Why am I here?
2) When can I leave?
3) Why did Venn's mother make the palace-cliff move around inside?
4) Who was Venn's mother? (Grembilard did say her name, but I can't remember it.) (Uzzy-something.)
5) Why did she go and *where* did she go? (Into the jungle, said Grem. That was all.)

6) What makes the hard, still lamplight? (The waterfall, Jotto said, on that occasion.) So,
7) How? (Jotto couldn't say. Grem couldn't or wouldn't. Didn't even bother to ask the Gardener, and of course not Treacle.)
8) When can I talk to Venn properly? By which I meant I'd make an appointment. (I dread this, but it's necessary. I have to convince him somehow. He dislikes my being here so much, *evidently,* he might help me to go?)
9) What is *scrowth-cha-chaari?* (The Gardener shouted this at three cats who were clawing some trees. Probably it's not polite. Jotto went very vague when I asked him.)

Bits of information I've received are these:

a) I should just "enjoy my stay" here!!! (Jotto said this. You guessed? He hasn't taken it in, and won't—like all of them—that I'm a PRISONER.)
b) That Grem set out from the gardens to fetch me from the other side of the gulf *two days* before he reached the outer corridors and could operate the bridge. This was because the rooms and stairs and halls and so on were all moving extra weirdly.
c) (And this may be interesting?) The cats here, which run about wild, all came from three cats originally brought here—when? With Uzzy-something? They haven't said—and the cats were ordinary then. But they have, over the years, developed thick bone ridges on their skulls! (!) To protect them when architecture suddenly shifts and they bang into things. Should I believe this? It's the kind of story I never would have believed—if I hadn't seen the cats.

Actually, lots of things here are . . . altered, or have been very changed.

Grem, for example. Real leaves do grow in his hair, which is anyway more like grass. How on earth can that be? (I haven't asked him. It seems—rude.)

And Treacle. That crying-which-isn't. She comes in and waters the indoor roses in pots, streams gushing from her eyes. Then she does a pleased little dance. I *did* mention her "tears" to Jotto. I asked, "How is it Treacle can cry like that?" Jotto said, enthusiastically, "Yes, it's *brilliant,* isn't it?" "No, but *how?*" "Well don't ask *me,* dear," said Jotto, as if thrilled to be ignorant.

He's always carrying on like that, but he's nice, too. And then again, look at *him*—he's mechanical—But.

Then there are those things that growl—vrabburrs—they don't sound right, either.

Argul, what would you do? It's almost as if I can't even see you mentally in my mind anymore. How long has it been since I was there with you, that morning in the Hulta camp? Months. Forever.

The Rose Room moved this morning. I was just getting out of bed and almost fell over. It didn't go far, only around the back of some Lily Rooms or something, according to Jotto, who found me after a quarter of an hour.

Anyway, once I'd gotten dressed, I put my stuff in the bag and went out through the corridor which now led from the door, I went into the gardens, and now I'm not going back.

He has rooms that don't move. If I'm stuck here, I, too, want a room that absolutely doesn't.

I've had enough of all this.

By late afternoon I hadn't done anything, hadn't seen anyone even. I *found* some lunch on a table, though I had to share it with six cats, some hummingbirds, and a bee, oh and a black-faced monkey that joined us halfway through. Food seems to get left out, here and there, I suppose by Jotto, who seems to do the cooking. (?) Sometimes silver covers protect it, unless various animals knock them off.

All the lunching animals were quite unaggressive. In these gardens, they seem used to people or dolls. The cats ignored the hummingbirds and bee in preference for the custard tart. (They don't seem to eat meat. No one does here. Maybe the cats have forgotten that birds are prey. But I'm not complaining.)

Later I found a wilder part of the gardens and climbed up and down through flowering thickets and came out on a ridge. I've found places like this before, here, but not one so high. From it I could see, not just for miles, but over half the world, it looked like.

On this side of the palace, the Rise mostly falls down and down through cascades of trees, until the jungle-forest wholly reclaims it. Then the jungle pours away and away, green turning to turquoise, and then to blue where it finally melts into the sky.

Wonderful views, these, but disturbing, too. The jungle really seems to have no end, no beginning now, either.

Then a storm started to build over there, in the great upturned bowl of the east.

Weather coming is always curious to watch from the Rise. With a storm, a sort of boiling starts on the horizon, then mountains of clouds block up.

The tops of the clouds, as they came massively and slowly tumbling toward the Rise, caught gold from the westering sun. The lower clouds were slatey-mauve. Lightning twitched inside them. But here the sky was clear.

It seemed to me I'd see all this better from the next ledge over. So I hefted my bag and climbed across through the stones and bushes, being careful not to tread on two sleeping snakes.

When I reached the next ledge, instead of looking at the gathering storm, I looked about and along. There was a wall there, which I hadn't seen earlier for the trees and bushes. It was an old wall, but sturdy, about ten feet high. And there was a gate in it, old warped wood, braced with iron.

I thought, as the thunder-light stabbed nearer and nearer, *I've got all my things. I've got a peach and some cheese and a cake left over from lunch.* I thought, *Well, should I try? There's a gate; there might be another road. And somewhere is the sea. There are other people, villages surely, towns, ships, chances.*

Such a lot of time seemed just to have dripped away. Suddenly I was crazy.

When I got to the gate, the distant thunder was starting to sound loud, as if the storm might mean something, wasn't just fireworks in the sky.

The afternoon went copper.

There was a ring-handle in the door. *It will be locked,* I thought—*or stiff from disuse.* I'd find a stone and bash it open.

But the handle turned easily, recently oiled, and the door parted from the wall, and there was a pale glimmering path going away and down, between tall trees.

I didn't pause. I just walked out of the gate, turning only to push it back flush with the wall.

Under the trees it was dark, but the path did seem to glow.

The air felt electric from the storm. Shadows massed against and through everything. Peepholes of metallic sky winked with lightning.

It came to me, Venn saying in his unbearable way, *Stay inside the walls and you'll be perfectly safe.*

Stay in this room, in that room. Stay inside the walls. *Stay inside the rules.*

The path swerved, and as I followed the coil of it, from a stand of eucalyptus a beast came out.

In books, I've read about being turned to stone, or ice. I *had* been.

There were lions at the House, I've said. And I've seen other animals. I've even seen pictures of tigers, somewhere.

This wasn't—it was—

Sorry.

What was in front of me was a tiger. That is—

It was big, about twelve feet long, if it had been standing on all four legs. It wasn't, though. Which was because its back legs were much heftier, and the front ones were smaller, and it held those up against its chest. It was tawny, and barred by black stripes—almost like a zebra—the way tigers are. Its underbelly was a creamier color, and all the fur was short, like well-brushed plush.

The head was more like a dog's face than a cat's. But it *was* a cat's, and from the mouth these huge canine teeth, white as peeled nuts, stretched out and over the lower jaw. It had little piercing brilliant eyes. They were palest blue.

A tiger's ears are small and rounded, almost toylike, I do remember that. These ears were tall. They were tawny and had paler fur inside. They had stripes. But they were the ears— of a gigantic rabbit. It was—a *rabbit.* A rabbit with a dog-cat's face and the skin of a tiger, and prehistoric teeth for serious rending.

And it wasn't funny. You couldn't laugh at it.

It was terrifying.

Then it growled. The sound went right through me, and I started to shake. Everything else seemed to, too. The leaves were shaking—no, it was a spatter of rain coming down.

That was jolly. It would rain while this rabbit killed and ate me.

You could tell it wasn't non-meat-eating, like the Rise cats. You could *tell.*

It dropped its top legs/arms down, and it was on all fours. This pushed its back end upward, and its head craned up to look at me on a too-long neck.

When it sprang, it looked just like a big cat springing, but like a rabbit as well, you know, when they bound.

You see, I was just rooted there, watching this monstrous thing plunging through the air at me. Where it landed would be where I stood. It would land *on* me, perhaps just breaking me instantly in two. That would save it some time.

God (that is a prayer, I think), God knows, I didn't have any thoughts. I just thought a scream. Though I couldn't scream aloud.

And then the tiger-rabbit came down, and it wasn't on me but about a yard away in a clump of hibiscus.

Cats play with their prey. Was it playing with me?

It was crouched there, on all fours. Its eyes glittered and its mouth was redly open. I missed something—its tail would be wagging—wouldn't it? But then, did it have a tail? If so, which sort—long and barred like a tiger's, or a powder-puff thing like a rabbit's?

Venn walked onto the path.

I said, "What tail does it have?"

"I beg your pardon?"

"Its t-t-t-tai-lll—" Suddenly I couldn't speak. I found I'd sat down, quite gracefully, on the path.

Venn made that *tstch* sound elderly people sometimes do when they're annoyed with you.

Thunder and lightning collided overhead.

In the flash, I thought the tiger-rabbit moved—but it didn't. The jungle went luminously black and again rain crackled through.

"Why isn't it?" I said. I could speak after all.

"What?"

What? Did I know what I was saying?

"Why isn't it killing me? Has it . . . gotten bored?"

But I could just make him out moving through the harp-strings of the rain, bending over—it.

"I did tell you," said Venn, with cold reasonableness.

"To stay in the gardens," I said. I said, "Is that—a vrabburr?"

"Yes."

I got up. The rain felt wonderful. The point was, I hadn't thought I'd still be alive to feel it. Coming over to the hibiscus, I looked and saw that the vrabburr had a tail. It was a tiger's tail, long as a bell-rope, but tufted with a black rabbit's puffball.

What was Venn doing? He was squeezing the vrabburr's right forepaw. Shaking hands?

"You were exceedingly lucky," said Venn.

"Hurrah."

It didn't have any smell, the vrabburr. And it was beautifully clean and tidy, even crouched there in the rain.

"It's a doll," I said.

"In a way."

I started to sing a happy song from long ago. Realized and shut up.

"You're hysterical," he remarked. Hysterical Claidi—how tiresome for him.

"Oh—*scrowth-cha-chaari!*" I shouted.

"That doesn't seem likely."

"Why not?"

"I don't eat much fur," he said. He went on squeezing the vrabburr's paw. I'd realized, this must be like turning a sort of key, to wind it up, but nothing was happening. Oh, it was my fault, no doubt. I'd ruined it somehow by not letting it tear me to pieces. Venn stood back. His curly hair was flattened and black in the dark rain.

I said, "What does *scrowth-cha-chaari* mean?"

"May you get fur balls."

The vrabburr blinked.

"It's all right now," he said, as if I *cared.* "We have about three minutes before it starts up again. You'd better come with me."

Humbly, I trudged after him, off the path, through the dripping boughs and vines.

"You often come out here?" *Why* was I trying to make conversation?

"Now and then. I don't go far."

"Are they clockwork?" I asked.

"What? The vrabburrs? No, not all. That's why you were so lucky."

Lucky me.

Presently—it was almost black as night, blacker, without the Wolf Star—we came up against a bank. Rock, ferns, bamboos, a door. Door?

Venn did something to the door, it opened, and he went into the rock. I, of course, followed. I sometimes wonder what is the matter with me. But at least we were out of the rain and horror-rabbit range.

It was a tunnel, lit by some other sort of magical light. Otherwise, it was a bit like the tunnels that led around from the House through the Garden. Like the one I used to escape through, with Nemian, which also went out under a wall.

Then, a hollow with an ironwork gate. I recognized it.

"You have lifters, like in the City."

"Lifts? Oh, yes."

He stood back gallantly to let me go in. I'd always hated the lifters in the Wolf Tower. I didn't like this one either. It was very bumpy.

Up and up we bumped. I thought, *Oh, we're going up into his rock-tower, under the gold globe, where he has that so-original oil lamp. I* am *honored.*

I was right, too. When the lift-lifter arrived, we stepped out into this eight-sided room lined with books, and with dark, old polished chairs and a table, and a stair going up into a high dome with a round glass window that looked like half a cut orange. The sky looked orange through the glass, too. And I could see part of the gold globe that sits on top of the rock.

It reminded me slightly of the black wolf statue on the Wolf Tower.

He was toweling his hair with a cloth. There was no light but the orange storm-light. He didn't look like Argul, or Nemian, or anyone. He looked like a young man who'd gotten rained on.

There was a wine-red rug. I stood and dripped on it.

Lots of books. And some little enamel figures. And a bird—I hadn't noticed it before—the white owl, on a perch, snoozing near the window with the famous lamp.

I have to admit, it was a good room. Interesting and lived-in. Comfortable, which surprised me. Not comfortable for me, of course.

"Oh, have this," he grudgingly said, handing me another mop-up cloth.

But the air was warm (even at night it's never worse than cool). My hair was already drying.

Above, around, the storm crackled and flicked its tawny vrabburr tail.

"I suppose you'll want tea, or a cordial."

"Will I?"

"At least you haven't fainted away," he disgustedly added.

This was the sort of thing that happened with Nemian, all over again. This fool thought I was *sensitive,* a lady, royalty. Claidis.

"Listen," I said, "it's time we got a few things straight."

He gave me that look again, *scared* of my time-wasting and annoyance-potential. He sat down in a big chair quite a long way off.

"All right. Let's get it over with."

I took a deep breath. "Someone you think is important obviously told you I wanted to come here, and they told you I was royal, too, called Claidissa or Claidis. You loathed the idea but couldn't say no."

"That's about right, yes."

"However," I said, "I'm not royal. Or if I am, only half, and anyway that may all be a lie. Let me tell you my story—oh, I'll be really quick, don't worry. It's soon said. I grew up in a place called the House, which you may have heard of."

"Yes."

"Good. Then you may have an idea what it's like there. Slaves, in the House, or in the City on the River, are rubbish. And I was just one step up from a slave, a maid-servant. Well, I left the House, helping a man called Nemian escape back to his City tower, the Wolf Tower. Heard of that, too? Thought so. For some reason I still don't properly grasp, they wanted *me* to take over control of the Tower Law. Only I wrecked the Law, destroyed it. Or, I hope I did—I meant to."

I paused to see if that got any comment. It didn't. I said, "I ran away from the City. I left with a Hulta leader, a chieftain, I suppose you'd say. We were going to be married. That was the life I had, and what I'd chosen. What I *wanted.*"

I had to hesitate again, to stop my voice going shaky. He didn't interrupt. I said, "On the morning of my marriage, before the wedding, I was grabbed by three City men, pushed into one of their hot-air balloons, taken to the coast, and thrown on a ship. Two of them—Yazkool, Hrald—brought me here. I thought originally I was supposed to be taken to the City, but now I'm not even sure of that. Yazkool and Hrald put me in that house across the gulf. Then you sent Grembilard and he brought me here, to the Rise. Which I'd never heard of, and which I'd never have wanted to come to if I had."

He just sat there.

I cried out at him, "I've *lost* everything I wanted. Don't you understand? I was happy. How would I want to be made a prisoner and forced to come here, with all these trees, miles from—away from—" I bit back the stream of words. But I'd clenched my fists, and my hair felt standing-up and bristly as hedgehog quills.

The rain had ended. The high window was clearing to its presunset spice shade.

"You expect me to believe this?" he said.

Yes, I did expect that. Why else had I made such a fuss trying to convince him?

"Very dramatic, Lady Claidis, if rather overdone. You're a good actress. They did warn me."

I managed to speak as level as a pavement.

"Who warned you?"

"I think you'd better see the letter. After all, it's about you."

As he went over to a carved cupboard in the far wall and opened its doors (I couldn't see inside), the owl-bird undid one eye the color of the sky. Then the eye and the doors closed, and Venn was offering me a sheet of paper.

Looking at this paper now, it's odd. It's not like any paper I had ever seen before—not, for example, like the paper in this book on which I'm writing, with my ink pencil. Thinner yet stronger. Very white.

And the writing is printed, like in a book.

Is this the "flying letter" someone mentioned earlier? I should have asked him.

What it said—I'll copy it down.

To Prince Venarion Yllar Kaslem-Idoros (So that's how it goes):

We trust you are in good health and pleasantly occupied amid your luxurious jungles.

It has become necessary that we ask your assistance. We must accordingly instruct you to accept, into your palace, a young woman of the towers. You will know her as the Lady Claidis Star.

It is our sad duty to warn you that she is an immature and excitable creature, given to rages, tantrums, and, shall we say, to *inventing* quite convincing stories of her own life. (She may even deny her own name.)

We are aware this is not the most suitable guest for you to receive, when, in any case, you are more at ease with the mechanicals and toys of your palace. Unfortunately we must insist. This Claidis Star has caused quarrels and upsets in several places, within the City and outside it. Her demands to visit the Rise, which she declares needful for her education, can no longer be ignored.

Our gratitude to you, Prince Venarion, we hope will offset, to some extent, this disruption to your personal routines.

We remain greatly in your debt—

I should have questioned him. Denied it. I don't know. There didn't seem any point. I certainly should have *demanded* (the letter says I do that, after all) to know *who* they were that sent it.

Because I saw the signature, and it's here, in front of me, but I was so destroyed by all of this, I just didn't—

I mean, after I read this, he showed me to the door, which opened onto the steps down to the gardens. He said, polite, "The rain's stopped." And I just went out and he closed the door, and there I was with this paper, stumbling down the stairs (and trying not to cry and feeling ashamed because I think I did cry)—and *desperate.*

To say *I* lied, and to lie about *me* like that.

As if they knew me and I was one of them and they'd been so kind to me and I'd been an evil troublemaker, and they'd *had* to send me here, where I insisted I wanted to go, before I did something even worse—

You see, I didn't know what to do. Don't.

So, I walked back across the gardens, and the sunset started and finished, then I got to the Rose Room somehow, even in its new place. The afterglow was dying on the walls, clashing nastily with all the curdled pinks in here.

The Star will come up soon.

These *lies*—

Oh, what am I going to do?

To be in this mess and to be blamed for it and to be lied about—

The signature. I didn't say yet. Well, this was how their letter was signed. It was signed "We." That was all. *We.*

MY ENEMY

Perhaps I could write some of it up now. I haven't been able to touch this, not for a while.

(Even now, with this book propped on my knees, I feel . . .)

After the Scene in his room, some more time passed, sliced into days and nights. I kept thinking now *really* was the time to go. After all I'd seen, it was simple to get out. But the vrabburrs and other possible *things* put me off. Which wasn't brave, but perhaps sensible.

I started to think about a weapon and wondered if there were any rifles or other guns in the Rise. But I can't fire a gun and anyway don't like the idea of shooting at things, even things with nine-foot-long pointed teeth.

Also I thought I was at my wits' end. If only I'd known—!

One thing. I said to Jotto, "I'm not comfortable in this room. It may move again, and all this pink is making me feel queasy."

"It *is* a bit ukky," agreed Jotto.

He was definitely more concerned about the color scheme than the moving-around stuff, and actually got down to it, and by that afternoon I'd been put into a kind of pavilion on the lawns, which is all pillars, and rather good tiles in the bathroom, and *always,* they say, stays still.

Treacle came at once and watered some pots of flowers on the steps (in the usual manner).

"I wish you could talk," I'd tactlessly lamented.

She just did her wriggle-giggle, didn't care.

That evening, which was four days after the Scene, Jotto brought me some supper.

"You're forgetting to eat. You're still in a mood, aren't you, dear?"

"You bet I am."

"Tsk," tsked Jotto. "And he's all funny and off his food, too. Like my chickens, frankly, both of you. It really is the end. It's so difficult, *getting* any food, and then making it look appealing. I mean, I could just slop it all down in a heap, but no, I *arrange* it in patterns, and put orchids (please note the orchid, dear) by the plates, and choose glasses that *match*—and what do I get? Does anyone swoon with joy? No. *You* nibble or gobble or sulk and won't eat it, and then the wildlife gets it. And now *he's* prowling around and around up there in his tower, and that owl ate his lunch—I *know,* I *saw* some nut-butter on its feathers—and it's not supposed to *do* that—Oh, it's too much."

"What a shame your prince isn't eating," I said sweetly. "If he ate something, he might choke on it."

"There you are, you see. This unfriendly *atmosphere.*"

I thought, *Venn's decidedly not upset about me, so what's getting to him now? Or is he just in a state because he had to* talk *to me for five minutes?*

Nothing happened that day. I just wandered about, climbing up small hills and peering into pools with golden fish in them. (Hrald would probably have run to get a fishnet.)

The gardens are beautiful, it's true. Like the House Garden, but better, more genuinely wild, more interestingly cultivated. I saw the Gardener once. He was shouting at some monkeys in the trees. Maybe wishing them fleas or something.

At dusk I saw a great trail of bats go over from the real cliffy parts below. Then, at twilight, the white owl sailed across, just before the Star came up, and blotted out everything with its too-harsh light.

I never thought I'd say a star was horrible.

But the Wolf Star is.

It's revolting. Too bright, too large, too *there.*

I've never seen it come up from the eastern horizon, always missed that. It's always suddenly just looming up over the gardens, slowly going on across the sky and away behind the Rise, and then gradually slinking back—it seems to set in the east, where it rises—just as too-big and too-bright in the last night hours. In the pavilion, whose windows are clear and only veiled with muslin, it woke me up every night.

If the moon is up when the Star comes, the moon looks like a poor blue ghost beside it.

However. After the owl soared off over the trees, I went in. I had another bath and went to bed because I couldn't think of anything at all to do. I didn't write in this book, hadn't written anything after the last bit. The bit that ended *"We."*

During the night the Star didn't wake me, coming back, for once. Instead, I dreamed that the owl flew in at a window I'd left open. It flew around the room, and I thought, *I'm dreaming about the owl flying around the room,* and that was all.

In the morning I did notice that a window I'd thought I'd shut was open. Then Jotto arrived, and I went out and had breakfast with Grem and Treacle and some cats under the huge flowering tree.

When I came *back,* I pulled the bag out from under the pavilion bed. I wanted something I'd left in it. I don't remember what it was, because I never found it. Which was because I didn't look for it. And that was because, in the bag, what I also didn't find, and that at once, was *this.* I mean this book.

I mean, it was gone.

Naturally I turned the pavilion's three rooms upside down. Even the bathchamber and the little side room full of old gardening things and a statue of a large porcupine.

I hadn't brought much with me, and most of that I'd left in the bag. I had this sense always now of just making camp, whatever room or apartment I was in.

When I'd looked everywhere, including pulling the bedclothes off and dragging the mattress onto the floor, I looked everywhere again.

Then I ran to the doorway and began screaming for Jotto and next for Grembilard.

Some monkeys answered from a tall tamarind.

After that I recalled a bell-pull thing in the pavilion, rushed back and yanked on it so hard that it broke and fell down.

I thought no one would come. (They'd all gone off after breakfast.) I started running about up and down outside the pavilion.

Now and then I've read of people "tearing their hair"—and I was. I was, as they say, beside myself. What I felt was worse than anything—even fear, although it was a sort of fear. Indescribable, or I could cover pages. Panic, loss, fright. And *shame.* Why shame? Of course, you'll see at once, although I didn't.

Then abruptly there was Grembilard, and Jotto, too.

"Is something wrong?" asked Grembilard.

I shrieked, "My book—my book's disappeared!"

"Oh my," said Jotto. Then, sensibly, "Don't fret, lady, we'll find it. What was the cover like, and what was the title?"

"Oh you—oh—it wasn't that sort of—it was—" I floundered. In my head I heard Nemian that time on our journey to the Wolf Tower patronizingly calling it my "Diary." "Diary!" I screamed, hopping from foot to foot. "My diary."

"Oh, um," said Jotto.

Grembilard said, "It can't have gone far, madam."

"I've looked—everywhere—everywhere—" I scrambled after them back into the pavilion. I stood cursing them as they wasted time looking carefully everywhere I had (including under the mattress and behind the stone porcupine). At the same moment, I was praying that they somehow *would* find the book where it couldn't be.

They didn't.

"Could you have left it under the tree at breakfast?"

I knew I hadn't, but I bolted for the tree. I rummaged around its roots amid fallen toast and flowers.

The monkeys yelled with laughter.

I *wouldn't* cry again.

"Well, lady, it looks as if it isn't here."

"Oh—*Jotto*—!!!"

"Perhaps, while you were walking, madam—"

Trying to be calm. "No, I did take the bag, but I didn't take the book out. I know I didn't—"

I wavered. Wondering now if I had. I hadn't trusted the pavilion to keep still, not really. If I was going to be more than a few strides away, I lugged that bag with me, and on every long walk. Tired, I'd sling it down and sit on it. I *never* took out this book—I hadn't wanted to, afraid of reading bits over and feeling worse.

But if I had, and had forgotten—maybe left it somewhere for a monkey to play with, *eat*—

All the things that have happened to me, and I'd kept hold of it. This book, which somehow meant and means so much, because I have filled it with my own truths, and almost everything that I've seen and felt. In this book I wrote how I first met Argul. I wrote about that first time

he kissed me.

I will NOT cry.

Some monkey has it up a tree. That's why they're making that terrible row. They've eaten my book, my *life*—and it's given them indigestion—

Or a bird's found it and flown—

I went completely still.

"Oops," said Jotto. "She's going to have a turn."

"The window," I said, staring at him coldly. "My dream. The *owl*—"

It was Jotto's mouth that dropped open. Why is he so human? Grem, the human one, stood there like a machine.

Jotto asked, "She means the prince's owl?"

"Yes I do. It was in my room. I thought I dreamed it. The owl took my book!"

I spun around and began to run again. The grass whirled by under my feet. I leapt over flower beds and through clawing bamboos. *They* cantered after me.

I was plainly heading for the rock-tower. His place.

"Don't," I grunted, "try to stop me—"

"But—but—" called Jotto, not out of breath, because he doesn't have to breathe, but still somehow breathless, "he's not there!"

I faltered, not meaning to, tripped on something, and flopped over.

Grem and Jotto helped me out of the oleanders.

"Prince Venn isn't in his room," said Grem. He shook his head to underline that.

"How—*convenient*—as if—I'd believe you."

"Look for yourself," said Jotto. "I carried his breakfast up all those stairs—and there he was, gone."

"I'll see for myself."

They let me, but escorted me. His door doesn't open unless it "recognizes" you. Like the door in the Wolf Tower. Jotto explained this.

In the eight-sided room, the thieving owl dozed on its perch. Red silk veils dimmed the windows. All those books. Were any of them mine? No, this book doesn't look like that. I wanted to search anyway, pull all the books down and open every cupboard and drawer. They wouldn't let me. I gave up struggling. Both of them are strong.

"Where does he go, then, your charming prince who steals things—gets his pet *owl* to steal them—things that belong to other people—where does he go when he isn't here?"

"He might be anywhere, lady," said Jotto, looking quite unhappy. "And if he's in the palace—well, with it always moving—"

I wanted to scream and scream. To behave the way the evil letter had said I did—and perhaps I do. Do I? But I walked out and down the steps. I didn't want to stay in his room. And the owl, though I could have wrung its feathery neck (well, I couldn't; it was an owl) had only done what he'd somehow made it do.

Why?

Why . . .

Was he even now curled up somewhere, a cooling drink in hand, reading my book?

Reading my truths, my life? About the House and the Law and Argul's kiss?

I threw myself on the ground. I behaved as they said, as I'd seen my foul mistress at the House, Jade Leaf, behave. A Tantrum.

"Oh dear, you've quite flattened this fern."

"Go *away.*"

"Poor lady. I'm sure he didn't mean to upset—"

I drowned him with my shouts.

But in the end I stood up. I shook myself, dragged my hands over my cheeks to dry them.

"Is she better or worse?" whispered Jotto.

"Worse, I think." Grem.

Treacle had crept up. She half hid herself behind a tree. I'd never seen her look so serious.

I said, quietly, "I shall look for him. I shall find him if it takes ten years. I shall kill him."

Writing that now, it seems absurd. In a way that puzzles me, too. My feeling was real, and justified—in a way. What Venn had done—it was like reading my mind—my *heart*—

Worse than anything, my sheer *embarrassment.*

You see, he wasn't—isn't—you.

You, whoever You are, are far away from me, farther away than the moon. And yet—nearer than anyone. Nearer even, perhaps, than Argul. If you've read my mind in these pages, I *invited* you into my head. And you, you had the kindness to accept and enter, and to be with me, through all of this.

Of course, I only made you up when I was alone. But no, I don't believe that. I believe you *are* there. Or you will be.

You're my guest, my friend.

Venn burgled me.

After my outburst, I sat down and said nothing else. I wouldn't answer either Grem or Jotto. Jotto went off and came back with some iced wine. I said, "Thanks." Didn't drink it.

They drew away. Well, they'd all been warned. I was "excitable" and "immature," given to rages, a liar.

I suppose it was the last straw. How many last straws does it take?

As I remember, I meant to rest and then get up and start my search. I madly thought that the calmer I looked, the easier it would be to get away from G and J, and maybe T, when the right time came.

I had no fears now of the movable palace, of vrabburrs, or of anything.

But the day, like the rooms, moved on and around.

The shadows had gotten longer, and an afternoon heat-stillness powdered the trees.

Then one of those yellow birds began to go *clink-clink.* I looked up, and Venn was standing there, just across from me. If I'd had any doubts, I needn't have. He was holding this book in his hand.

(In fact his name, properly spelled, is Ven'n—being short for Venarion with the *ario* left out.)

I got up slowly.

Grem and Jotto must have been there. I don't think I saw them, can't remember them. Really there was nothing, just a shadow-sunny static void, with Ven'n-Venn drawn like a dark line through its middle.

He was looking at me. I mean properly.

He was seeing me.

He said, "Grem says you've vowed to kill me."

"That's right."

"Suppose I didn't read it?"

"Why take it, then?"

"Well, perhaps I *meant* to read it—and couldn't. Your handwriting's pretty awful, Claidi."

I started at him. I don't know what I would really have done, and no doubt Grem would have stopped me anyway. Even Venn might have been able to. But in the rush of fire that was throwing me forward, I heard it again. My name. Not Claidissa or Claidis. *Claidi.*

So I swerved. I grabbed hold of a tree and swung against its trunk, and he said, "You have worse enemies than me, Claidi. Look."

And then he did something to this book, something to its back, and a little bright object, like a tiny flat button, dropped out from inside it, and he caught it in his free hand.

"What's that?" I stupidly asked. Claidi, always asking questions.

"That," he said, "is how the Wolf Tower tracked you and found you. By that private pool on your wedding day, where the balloon came down. *This* was in your book all the time. They could come and get you whenever they wanted."

"They—my book."

This book. They had found me because of something (scientific—

magical) put into this book. He couldn't really tell me how it worked, that is, when he did try to tell me. He said, Imagine a light shining miles away and you just go toward that light—and the thing in the book was like that, only it wasn't a light. If it had been a light, *I'd* have seen it.

But because of it, they'd found me. Taken me, brought me *here.* This book, too, had been—my enemy?

IN THE DARK

"What are you looking at?"

"I'm watching weather coming. Those clouds. The way you can see storms start long before they get here."

"Looking for the future, eh, Claidi? Perhaps you're looking the wrong way."

We just had that exchange, on this high wide balcony facing east. Venn and I. (We've been trapped here two days.)

He says clever things like that.

But he doesn't really talk to you, though. To one. I mean, he doesn't meet your eyes, when he speaks or as you do, or only for a moment, one huge gaze, and then away. Is it his disgust, or is he—afraid?

He hasn't known many people, apparently.

Says he prefers *reading* about people, even being *told* about people, to being with them.

He said, for example: "It's always preferable to read about a place rather than to go there. And reading about something, anything, is better than living the experience. One has distance, and there's time to examine the events. And if one needs to go over them again, there they are, the same, in black and white."

He then added, "After all, isn't that why you write everything down in your book?"

I replied bitterly, "Oh, I'm sharp as a spoon."

He'd blinked.

It's a Hulta expression, actually it goes "Hu-yath mai rar, ai: She/he's sharp as a spoon, she/he is." It seems funny, but Blurn once told me that, in older times, the Hulta used to sharpen the stems of their spoons, in case they ever needed them as weapons, so it's not as daft as it sounds.

I told Venn this.

He said, "You see, that's very interesting."

We had *this* conversation, if such it was, some days ago, in various parts of the gardens.

Before we got to that, though, we'd stood there in the afternoon, him still holding this book. And then he called Grem, who appeared. "Give her this back, will you?"

Grem brought me the book. I was able to take it from Grem. But then I just dropped it on the ground. It wasn't mine anymore.

Then Venn said, "Shall we sit down?" as if we were in a sitting room. And he sat on the ground, and then I sat on the ground, too, where I'd been before, with my back against a tree. Grem and Jotto—and Treacle—had vanished again.

He and I were about fifteen feet apart.

I'd needed to sit. Now I just stared at him, and of course he didn't even try to meet my eyes.

"I know how you must feel, Claidi."

"Do you? I doubt it."

"To take that, to read that—yes, unforgivable." I didn't say anything. (I didn't want to talk to him at all. At the same moment I wanted to shout at him on and on.) "You see, Grem mentioned you were writing something."

"*Did* he."

"I hadn't questioned him about you, Claidi. At that point I didn't want to know anything about you. I confess, that's why I half wanted you left in the outer rooms. Perhaps later I might have been interested to hear about what you did at the House, and in the Tower. But then, I wasn't sure what you'd tell me would be true."

I bit my tongue so as not to start shouting about the Letter.

Venn said, "Grem simply told me you kept busy and didn't cause any trouble. You walked a lot, and you wrote in a book. I realized it was a kind of diary."

"It isn't."

"No," he said, "it's more a journal."

I refused to like this much-better-sounding description.

Venn said, "Then, after we spoke last—"

"Is *that* what you'd call it?"

"I felt uneasy. Well, Claidi. I don't know people very much. There's Treacle, and Grem, of course, and there was dear old Heepo, before we lost him—"

(??)

"And my mother, I suppose, if I can count her. She was very stern and distant. She went away when I was nine. . . . Anyway, how could I judge you? You seemed genuine. But I was in the dark."

I sizzled. Tried not to.

He gave me one of those quick wide glances and said, "I thought that if you kept a journal, you might have put the truth down in it. Of course, I could be wrong there, too. Maybe your journal is all lies and dreams and mad made-up nonsense—"

I yelled then. I yelled quite a lot.

He looked alarmed, and then he just sat there, looking at the broken-off fern frond he was turning in his fingers.

What did I say (yell)? Can't remember. (He's right. I should have written it down and *then* yelled it.) Somehow I'd forgotten about the sinister button thing in the binding. What I said was all about truth, and my being truthful, about that Letter, what he'd done, and I must have gone on for a while.

In the end I just didn't have the energy to continue. There was a long silence.

"God, Claidi. Yes, I'm sorry. Sorry. I should throw myself off the Rise."

"Why don't you, then?"

"Because I'm a coward," he said. Just that. And then I saw—well, he was crying. I mean, it was almost like Treacle. Tears just ran down his face. And then stopped. But unlike Treacle, he had for a few seconds that cold-in-the-head sound one has if one cries.

In this voice he said, "Please understand, I don't expect you to forgive me. This isn't an excuse, only an explanation. I just didn't know any better. I don't know how I should behave to another person. Not really. I've never had much chance to find out." By then his voice had cleared. He said, crisply, "They'd told me you were—well, you read their letter. But I started to have doubts. I thought your book would prove it one way or the other. It has. *They* lied. *Not* you. And you—are *you.* And because you are, I am *ashamed.*"

I got up and walked off. Somehow I'd picked this book up, too, and I took it with me.

He let me go. No one followed. I ended up quite lost in the gardens, in a jungly bit (like "dear old Heepo"?).

I raged, naturally. How could he act so wickedly and then *cry*—but I kept thinking, it was just what a very young child might do. A kid who did something bad because he didn't know any better. And then saw the damage and got upset. I mean, he wasn't crying for himself. What had *he* to lose? He was crying . . . because he'd done this to me.

But then I thought that maybe he thinks everyone has to love him and think he's nice and wonderful, and he cries when he does something unspeakable so we'll say, Oh, poor Venn, look how sad he is. Better forgive him, he didn't mean it.

Sunset arrived.

It was when the awful Star rose that I remembered the bright awful thing that had fallen out of the binding of this book.

I decided I'd go and find him after all and demand what that was all about.

But next I ridiculously couldn't find a way out of the jungle area, especially in the dark as the Star moved on.

Finally I heard Jotto calling in a timid voice. I let him find me.

Jotto said, "Er, lady dear, there's some lovely supper, but he did say—um—would you sit and eat with him—outdoors?"

"Oh, all right," I graciously barked.

Supper was under the flowering tree near my pavilion. (The flowers give off a marvelous perfume at night.) Several cats and other things soon arrived. They always do. (Jotto says a monkey can hear a pie or a mango being sliced from half a mile away.)

Deeply dark black sky and the stars and moon looking washed and shiny, since the Star had moved on. (It seemed to go faster that night.)

I won't put down all the conversation. I couldn't follow all of it anyway, the things he "explained."

And I still don't know what I think of him.

He looked all right. He had on this white shirt with fringes on the cuffs.

Oh, anyway.

I will make a note of the supper; it was—well, under other circumstances I'd have been fascinated, delighted. Not so much by the food, though that was delicious (it usually is, here). How it was served.

I thought Jotto was going to serve it, as he normally does if he's around. But he sat down by Grem. Treacle was there, too, with her spiky black hair brushed up spikier, and long gold earrings. (I was the only scruff-bag, in my now worn-out dress from the Rose Room.)

Tall candles burned in globes of pale amber. By this light, up a strange little ramp I'd been wondering about, the first dish was drawn onto the table.

It was a big silver dish with a fresh salad arranged like jewels by Jotto. But the dish was attached by a harness arrangement to a team of tiny black-and-white rabbits! I do mean tiny. They were each the size of a *mouse.* There were ten of them in all. They galloped forward and pulled up to a perfect finish. Then they stood there until a beaming Jotto (saying "Aren't they *sweet?*") unharnessed them.

Then other dishes came in procession. Five blue hippos, about the size of kittens, brought vegetables. Ten black-necked geese, the size of sparrows, brought a train of hot sauces. Two very strong little tigapards, each as big as a blackbird, hauled up a large pie on a gold tray. Three fat mouse-sized mice that also looked like *pigs* (they had curly tails, and snouts—perhaps I'll call them *pouses?*) brought a china castle of assorted nut-cheeses.

They all managed faultlessly, except for the tigapards, which, as soon as they saw us all, promptly sat down and had to be helped to lug the pie by Treacle.

Once released, all these creatures ambled about the table, playing with each other and accepting pieces of food, but only when offered to them. Well, one of the pouses (pice?) did drag a banana away behind the salt cellar, but never mind.

They really were lovely, these little animals.

When I asked, they told me—Venn told me mostly—that they're not dolls, are quite real. They'd been bred, like the vrabburrs. "Not everything she did," said Venn, meaning his mother, "was dangerous."

"Where do they live?"

"They have a big hutch and enclosure in the gardens," said Jotto. Grem added, "They're taken in at night."

The supper was relaxed. It was hard to be nervy and angry, with mouse-sized rabbits playing kick-ball with a radish, and a miniature tigapard purring in your lap.

I did think, *This is clever. I shouldn't fall for this.*

But I fell for it.

The wine was pink, in rose-amber glasses.

I heard myself laugh at something Jotto said. And then he, Venn, laughed. As if I'd said he was now allowed to.

I've wondered about him and Treacle. He's grown up with her, seems fond of her. But she's a wild thing, Treacle. She's called that, they say, because she always liked treacle.

He doesn't treat any of them like slaves. That says something about him. Maybe?

They all *know* each other. They know Jotto, though he was, obviously, always an "adult," even when they were kids.

What was that like, growing up in this bizarre place?

Venn says his mother was close to him only when he was very small, and he remembers being two years old, because he has a clear picture of walking in the gardens with her, and she said to him, "You're two now, Venarion." And after that, she changed.

"She didn't touch me anymore," he said. "She used to hug me before that." He was drinking the wine, seeming so casual, but I knew he wasn't; it still distresses him. "She became cold and uncaring. I seldom saw her. Before, she used to read stories to me. When she changed, I had to read them myself. Grem would help me hold the books, they were so heavy."

He could read at two years old!!

"I bored her," said Venn, laughing again. "Well, she was a very clever woman. A scientist—what your Hulta would call a magician. She did all this. Made the rooms move, bred the animals—the cats with the plated skulls, the vrabburrs, these little ones on the table. She did other experiments: Grem's hair, for example. And Treacle's tears." (I wondered if they minded, but they didn't look bothered.)

Jotto even said, "Don't forget *me.*"

"Yes, of course, Jotto, the most brilliant of all mechanical dolls. The other three, across the ravines—they weren't so good. But Jotto's magnificent, aren't you, Jott?"

"I am," said Jotto, "though I say it myself."

"In a way," said Venn, cheerful, smiling at the moon, "I'd say I was her experiment, too. After all, she made me, didn't she, even though I'm only flesh and blood. Her son. So I think I was the least successful experiment of them all. The only one that didn't work as it—I—was supposed to. Then, anyway, she got tired of all of us."

He'd gently lifted up a pouse, and I thought he was going to dunk it in the sauce by mistake. But he realized in time and put it carefully back on the table.

After that, they changed the subject, all four of them, the way a family can do things like that, acting as one.

We played clever word games. Grem sang a very funny song about earwigs, and Jotto produced a flute and started the nightingales singing. (Some of the nightingales are clockwork, too. Put there to "encourage" the others.)

Later, Treacle and Jotto were running races. They were always neck and neck. And Grem strolled off to talk to the Gardener, who suddenly appeared like a grumpy phantom across the lawn.

Venn looked at me, slightly longer than usual. So *I* looked away.

He said softly, "You know, I really couldn't read a lot of it, Claidi. Your handwriting—is a little like another language."

I frowned. "Just tell me about the *thing* in the book."

"It's a Tag. You've been patient, waiting so long to ask me."

I'd forgotten, actually. Incredible, but a fact.

However, now he said he'd answer whatever he could, including the questions I posed in my "journal."

And when he said that, for a second everything seemed much easier, *because* he'd read this book. How strange. How awful. But it did.

THE QUEST FOR THE LIBRARY

Her name is (was) Ustareth. His mother.

That was question number—let me look back and see—No. 4, or part of it. As to who she was, no one *I'd* know, it goes without saying.

I think I'll answer these questions here, in the order I put them before. (He would approve of that, writing it down and then writing it out again with the solutions, in the right order. I'm not doing it because he would approve.)

Here goes:

1) Why am I here? *Not* because I asked to come here. He doesn't know. He said this: "They sent you here to worry me, I think. I don't—didn't want visitors. But mostly they did it to punish you. You messed them about. So they've messed *you* about."
2) When can I leave? No, he didn't answer that. I didn't *ask* it, in fairness. Because now there seems so much to sort out here, perhaps I have to stay a while.
3) Why did V's mother—Ustareth—make the rooms move? Her experiment. To see if she could. To have fun. To stop herself being bored.
4) Who was she?—answered. Or as much as I can, so far.
5) Why did she go and *where?* He'd said because she was fed up with it all. Into the jungle, so presumably *through* the jungle and

off to somewhere else? But he looked very odd over this one, which is reasonable. Didn't press it.

6) and 7) The hard light in the lamps—Yes, the waterfall creates the power for this, as it does for some of the clockwork, and for certain other things. . . . We didn't somehow quite sort out if this included the food. But it turns out Jotto doesn't always cook; he simply has to go and collect it—? Then he arranges it and brings it. I'll have to go through this one again; I didn't follow it really. Oh, and the waterfall power thing is something about hydro-something. No, I didn't understand that at all, though Venn went over it two or three times. It works, though.

8) Talking to Venn. I am.

9) That question about the fur balls. (V says what the Gardener shouts at the monkeys means "May your fur turn to iron.") (Fine.)

We talked a very long time before I went off exhaustedly to sleep.

The worrying thing is, because he read this book, or some of it (most of it I suspect), he partly knows me.

But I don't know him.

And yet—I almost feel I *do*—also because he read this. And that I can't explain to myself.

As if in exchange, he did say a lot about his childhood. In clever, offhand sentences. It sounded, underneath, miserable, but also—glorious. All that freedom. But the not having a mother.

He knows I didn't ever know my parents.

He said, "We have to go to the Rise library. There's information there, things about the Tower Families, the history of the Towers, and so on. It might help you. The trouble is, of course, *finding* the library. It, naturally, moves, too. And quite randomly. It'll be murder."

"Tell me about the flying letter."

"I don't think I can. I mean you won't understand."

"Try."

"Claidi, I mean *I* don't understand. I never have. And I've only ever gotten three. Four, counting the lying one about you. They just—appear—out of the wall."

"Oh."

So the flying letter and the thing, which Venn calls a Tag and which they put in this book, remain a mystery.

Who put the Tag into the binding, though?

Probably Ironel Novendot. But I suppose even Nemian could have done it. To make sure that I didn't stray. Perhaps when he saw I was getting interested in someone else, in Argul. Perhaps Nemian slipped the Tag in under the binding as we traveled. The book wasn't always with me, but in a wagon.

It left no mark I could see. But then the book was already a bit travel-worn. And how would I ever think such a thing was possible and so look out for it?

"I've seen such things before," Venn said. "So I checked. It didn't surprise me to find it."

The House had candles and oil lamps. And Peshamba had crystals that watched you, and dolls—but not like Jotto. The City on the River had nothing much . . . just watchers, lift-lifters worked by slaves, and balloons. And the doors could recognize you. And they had the Law.

"They all have the Law," said Venn. "In some form. The House had all those rituals you disliked so much. And there are other places, with other rules."

I said, "What about here?"

"No, there's nothing like that here. Perhaps my—when she came here, Ustareth, she hoped to escape the Law and the rituals."

Something nags at me. If you dare read this again, Ven'n, though I don't think you will (I hope you won't), then here it is: The Rise does have its own version of the stupid and mindless Law-type rituals and rules, designed to get in the way and make life difficult and chancy. It's the *rooms moving about.* Isn't it?

We prepared for the trek solemnly and with care. As if for a great expedition into unknown lands.

Jotto and Grem were to carry a lot of things, including water bottles—there are bathrooms everywhere, but you can't always be sure the water is drinkable.

Treacle also carried some stuff, and I volunteered, too, but they didn't give me much.

I'd packed the pink dress with my WD and wore this grey-white one I brought from the House over the gulf. (And I packed this book, although I hadn't written in it and thought I might not again. But, as you've seen, that didn't last.)

Venn also carried things in a bag on his back.

The funniest thing was the team of six cats Jotto and Grem rounded up and harnessed to a sort of sled to carry light bedding and other bits and pieces.

Venn drew a rough map before we started.

"The library is often *here.*" He pointed at the spot he'd marked in a tangle of squares and circles and snakelike coilings that were apparently rooms, corridors, courtyards.

Jotto particularly looked glum.

"Only doubtless it won't be there," Venn went on. "It had a phase," he added, "of traveling east then south, then back north and west. So we could try for that, to start with."

"But what about the time it just kept going up and up?" said Jotto. "It was on the sixth gallery once, rumbling about between those towers—"

I stopped listening really. It sounded hopeless, frankly. Why were we doing it? For me, it seems . . .

We left the gardens about midmorning.

The cliff-palace loomed over us, swallowed us up in its caves of painted stone.

For about an hour we walked steadily, and although we heard *sounds* of parts of the Rise moving, everything around us stayed still, as it was once supposed to when someone was there.

"Though just walking about in a room can set it off now," said Jotto. "I should know. The times I've been trapped for *days.*"

Once or twice peculiar mechanical things appeared and went rattling past. That is, they went *past* because we all quickly got out of their way—they seemed likely to knock you flying otherwise, and some were as large as a sheep. They are cleaners, Jotto said, sniffily. Once, too, there was a sort of spider thing, crawling over a ceiling, touching up the paintwork.

Soon, however, we were just going out through a wide arch when an enormous staircase came pouring out of a wall. It rolled right at us (reminding me of the storm-waves on the ship) and stopped with a thud only when it had blocked the arch. Meanwhile we'd scattered, yelling, and the cats had overturned the sled.

Jotto and Treacle and I gathered up sheets, and Grem mended the broken harness.

"We'll have to go *that* way instead," said Venn, waving the map.

This became the chorus to our crazy journey. Oh, this way's now impassable. We'll go *that* way, then.

But *that* way was often found to be blocked, too, or had gone off itself somewhere else.

Four days went by. And *four* nights. Unbelievable, I know, but worse was to come.

Books at the House were sometimes adventures. Some of them had titles like *Hunting the Treasure Hoard* or *Quest for the Emerald Queen.*

Well, this must be the *Quest for the Library.*

In a sane book, one would travel over plains, across mountains, through deep woods. Here we slog on and on through this ghastly palace. In the book, probably we'd be getting somewhere. Here, we're always miles away. I do mean miles.

On the *fifth* day we got stuck. In here.

We'd gotten caught before, once, on day three, when an apartment we were crossing abruptly took off—so fast that Treacle and Jotto and I fell over!

The apartment, which had several rooms with inner curtained doorways—if there are no closing wooden doors, the whole thing tends to move together, Venn said—rushed around for nearly an hour and then stopped dead in an area dark enough that the hard light came on.

When we looked, there was no way out. The three outer doors were blocked by walls now directly outside. Luckily, after only ten minutes the apartment went off again. As soon as we could, we all charged out into a stone courtyard with a statue (of a huge rat or something). We only just made it, too, before the apartment swung away again. (We walked past this same apartment the day before yesterday, I think. It looked the same. Fortunately we didn't need to go through.)

Anyway, the evening of the day before yesterday, we made camp at dinnertime facing the foot of a vast staircase. We left quite a gap between us and it, of course, in case it suddenly moved. It didn't move, though. Jotto set up the brazier and Grem lit it, for tea.

It's extremely weird. Unless there are the lights, which often there haven't been, sitting around this kind of brazier-campfire, late at night, in the middle of a *building.* Shadows gather blackly at the edges of the light, just as they do outdoors. Even eyes sometimes gleam there, watching cats or other things (?) that Venn says live in the palace.

In the morning we were woken about dawn by the rooms behind us thundering off like a herd of rhino.

Venn consulted his map and said we ought to climb the staircase. This obviously was tricky, especially for five of us and six cats pulling a sled.

He said we'd do it this way: me and Jotto together, then him, Treacle, and Grem (carrying the cats and the sled). This way, even if separated, no one should be stranded totally alone.

I was jittery, climbing that stair, I can tell you. But we all made it—almost.

Treacle, clutching three cats, was on the last landing when the *lower* stair split away. It was a fearful sight. She seemed to be hanging in space, but then her piece of stair just rose gracefully upward. As it sailed past us, she was able to jump off into Grem's arms. One of the cats bit him in the excitement.

Leaving the stair-top soaring on up into a dome, we came out into a massive hall with cream-yellow walls, a gallery, and a gigantic window and balcony facing east.

There were books in stacks built into the walls.

"Is this the library?"

"No," said Venn. "It's the Little Book Room."

"I see." It was about a hundred yards long and about the same wide.

We had a late breakfast in here. (Jotto kept muttering about his chickens, which he had left the Gardener to feed.) Then we had a look at some of the books (most of which seemed to be written in different languages).

I climbed up an inner stair to the gallery and went out onto the balcony. I was admiring the view over the gardens—the descending jungle-cliff beyond—when the Little Book Room began slowly moving its Little self. It was so gentle, it really didn't seem much to worry about. From the balcony, it was quite fun.

The LBR glided along and along the third story. Trees went by below, some with monkeys staring up curiously. I even glimpsed the Gardener, bending in an annoyed way over a lotus pond. *Then* the LBR began to *rise.* This, too, was smooth enough, but we went up and up, and where we settled, I'd say the ground was—well, a very long way down.

Behind us, the only exit has been closed off by another wall.

At first we all waited for the room to move again, but it hasn't.

Two days later, we're still here.

It wasn't a storm I saw gathering, from the balcony, just bubbly clouds. It's getting on to sunset now again. Jotto is stoking the brazier. Four of the cats are having a pretend-fight.

There are two bathrooms off of this room. I had a bath in a yellow marble tub and washed my hair. For something to do. And to avoid Venn.

It's all right when we're traveling, or eating or something, but when he seeks me out, as he did on the balcony . . . it makes me uncomfortable. And his clever remarks—*"Looking for the future."* He also said there are ghost mice in the library that eat the pages, and that have "eaten more than we can ever know."

I wrote a lot of the last section locked in the bathroom while my hair dried.

There's a bedroom, too, very small. Lemon-curd silk and white wood furniture. He avoided it, and Jotto whispered to me, "*She* used to sleep there a lot, at times."

She—Ustareth. Venn's mother.

I was nosy. I tried to open the cupboard doors and drawers, but none of them would. I thought—was I being as bad, doing that, as he was, reading my jour—my book?

He's made me feel I need to know things. This whole trek is supposed to be so I can learn more about the Towers. The Wolf Tower—the Law, the rituals, what *They* (?) are up to. But honestly, I don't want to know. Not really. But he's made me feel now that I *have* to—or somehow I don't have a chance.

How has he done that?

I am so aware of him all the time.

This huge room is too small for both of us to be in at once.

"The food's going to run out," says Jotto, looking peeved. "And I packed such *masses*. Look at this bread! And these pomegranates are all runny and squidgy."

This is stupid. We're trapped miles from anywhere in a *room* in a *building* and we're going to *starve.*

Venn said, as if he didn't care much, "She knew ways of making the rooms shift, if this happened."

"Who? Your mother?" I asked, furious. "Didn't she ever tell *you?*"

"She never told me anything after I was two."

"And you never tried to *learn* anything after you were two," I nastily said.

Jotto looked upset and I wished I hadn't.

But Treacle turned a cartwheel, revealing she was wearing red-and-gold-striped underpants. Which made us all laugh, for some reason.

After lunch or tea, whatever it was, I walked off to Her Room, again.

I did something awful. Maybe it wasn't. She's long gone, and if she'd cared about any of it, wouldn't she have taken it with her? Using a knife and fork from the meal, I started breaking into the drawers.

She could have fastened them by some *scientific* means, anyway. And she hadn't. No, I got them all open after about half an hour. It made a mess—chips and splinters and curly gilded locks all over the floor. (No one came to see what I was doing, though I hadn't been quiet.)

There was some jewelry. Very beautiful. Long teardrop pearls and a necklace of transparent, polished green stones. A topaz in a ring.

When I saw the ring, I thought of what Grem had asked, about *my* ring, if it was my mother's, because it had "properties." Venn knows now that it doesn't—because of course my ring came from the Hulta. But does this topaz have them? I picked it up cautiously. I even put it on my middle finger—it was quite a bit too big.

Then, I stole it. I do steal things. I stole this book. In the House, you only ever got anything by stealing.

But I felt guilty, even though I know I took the ring in case it's going to have some magical-scientific use.

It's in my bag, tied up in a cloth from the bathroom. So if you read this, Venn—you'd better not—then you'll know.

Apart from the jewelry, I didn't find much. Most of the drawers and little cupboards were empty, just dust and sweet-smelling powders in the corners, and in one, a little black key and a scrap of paper with nothing on it.

There was a closet that had only one door, and the door had a bird painted on it. I didn't need to break in—the little key worked. The door opened. And there was this dress. Ivory satin is how I'd guess it should be described, thickly sewn with pearls.

I pushed it aside, and in the back of the closet was a lever with an enamel handle.

They used to say I had moods.

I'm in one.

I reached in and tried the lever, and when it moved, I made it go over as far as it would. When I did, there was a really frightening noise—like hundreds of bricks crashing away into a bottomless pit. Perhaps that's what it was, because the back of the closet was now open, and beyond was another stair, narrow and dark and completely uninviting. It went down and down.

Although no one came to see before, this noise was so extreme, they all had, now.

They stood there, gaping. But Venn wasn't gaping; he looked paper-white. He said, "I remember that dress."

I said, "Do you remember these *steps?* Are they safe? Do they go anywhere?"

"Yes . . . I think that's how she used to leave this room, or come up here, sometimes. I seem to recall that, how she'd just disappear; I couldn't find her. . . ."

He turned as if to go off, but Grem caught his arm. Then they walked off together, and Grembilard had his arm around Venn. And I felt as if my stomach had turned to boiling soup, and I could have slapped both of them. And me, for being so unkind.

* * *

Anyway, they've decided now, about—it seems—six months later, we'll all use these stairs behind the closet to get out of here. They "think" the closet stairs don't move. Let's hope they don't.

They did. *Did!* We're all separated—I'm LOST—in this hell-palace-Rise—I haven't a clue what to do—

LOST IN THE KITCHENS

Night's arrived. Hello, night. It was already sunset when we left the big Little Book Room. So, yes, it would be night now. The windows are all high up, and all I could see was fading sky, and now it's black sky, and a couple of stars. Not the Star.

Some lights came on, rather cold, and of course, still and hard.

I'm writing by their glare, sitting on an old table against one wall.

Even before Argul, I haven't been alone much. I used to share a room with Pattoo and Daisy in the House. And a wagon with Hulta girls in the camp. I was alone a lot on the journey with Nemian, and when I was dragged here. But there were always people about somewhere near. And in the Tower, I *wanted* to be alone, to get away from the people.

But I'm alone now.

What happened?

Venn went down the stair first, to try it. And he said Grem should come last as backup to the rest of us. Jotto, Treacle, and I were in the middle. The cats—J and G and I tried to carry them. They got away, though, and rushed down ahead of us. I thought they would be all right. (Jotto said cats are always coming into the palace yet always managing to get out again. They can get through tiny holes, and they also leap, vastly better than any of us.)

We shared carrying the baggage, and I had my bag. I was also carrying a pillow—but it fell away from me when the stair broke up.

I didn't like that stair. Even though I found it. Maybe it had it in for me. That's silly. But who knows.

At first we moved down with no problems at all, and although no lights came on, Jotto lit a candle under a glass bulb. It flickered a lot. And the stair started to curve around to the right, and then it was like a corkscrew.

Then it straightened out again, and it and we emerged into an open space, with a tile floor below gleaming in the last of the sunset.

"Thank God," said Venn. He sounded strained.

Perhaps it was his voice—or even some of the cats' voices, since they were sitting in the red pool of light meowing up at us.

The stair *shook itself.*

Treacle and I grabbed for each other but were dashed apart. I fell to my knees, and little sharp splinters in the stair bit into my knees (insult to injury!).

I saw, and couldn't do a thing, Venn and Jotto and their piece of stair going one way—left; and Treacle spinning off on hers to the right.

Behind and above me, Grem called, "Catch hold of me, lady—" but as I turned and tried to, it was too late, and his stair-segment was flying him up into the ceiling, which opened to let him through.

And I—I was dropping fast toward the floor—and I screamed, but the floor opened wide, too, and I plummeted down and forward into darkness and the smell of old water, moss, and rust. The floor above closed up behind me.

When the stairs stopped, I slid off and stood up in blackness. Was it a cellar?

No. As my eyes adjusted, I made out the first line of high windows, their glow just fading.

I stood staring at that until it was all gone.

Then a light popped on.

Somehow it took me ages to realize I was in a sort of kitchen—kitchens—room after room. They must go on, like everything else here, for miles.

Tried to recall what Jotto said about the food. (I apologize for not noting it down properly before, but a lot's been going on.)

Jotto said, I think, that the kitchens now make the food, or a lot of it. And he said he meant machines made it, but *in* the kitchens.

These must be the machines.

Up near the ceiling, tanks and bulges and long sprawls of pipes. Which make noises—gurglings and thumps and skinkles.

I don't understand, of course. Maybe you do.

Venn—if you ever read this—I don't mean *you.*

The thing is, I don't think anyone ever needs to come all the way down here. You can fetch the food from somewhere else. So the actual kitchen rooms below and around are just unused, and falling apart.

There are old fireplaces, some in walls, some in the center of floors with hooded indoor chimneys hanging over them, all ready to suck away smoke that never happens.

There are black stone ovens, and great rusting kettles, and pans and cauldrons, and spits to turn meat—thick with cobwebs and greasy, ancient dust.

And tables and cupboards and benches and broken bowls and enormous spoons and ladles.

Abandoned.

The smell is overpowering in parts. Of rotted vegetables and cold fats that are perhaps twenty years old. (More?)

A sorrowful, sooty place.

I've even found an old book of recipes, some in other languages, some in mine, some oddly spelled.

"How to make a cinnamon toad"—!? Ugh!

I wandered for ages. Water dripped down, and the pipes and vats above made noises. (And also sometimes dripped sticky slimes, so I'll never be able to eat anything from here again. If ever I get the chance.)

It's eerie, too. Because of the light and dark, the sounds. Easy to imagine there's something else here with you.

I must find a way out.

So far I haven't found a way out.

I've gone around in circles. I know I passed that big barrel before, oh, about two hours ago.

They don't seem to move, the kitchens. Perhaps they're not allowed to, for fear of disarranging the cooking pipes. Or they do it on the sly, to confuse people trapped here.

I dozed off in this corner. (It's hot, damp, and airless.) When I woke up, I heard *something moving about.*

It's an echo, of course. Or mice. Rats even. Rats are all right. There's lots of spilled stuff for them to eat.

It didn't sound like rats or mice.

My imagination.

* * *

Something is down here. With me.

Help.

What I'm going to do is find somewhere to hole up until daybreak. Some light will come in here from the high windows. I think that may be safer than this false light, which whatever is down here obviously doesn't mind.

I definitely just heard it.

What *is* it?

A sort of fluttering soft rush—and then—almost skittering—

The rush was like wings. Big.

So I wo———

That was where I got up and ran, dragging this book and the bag and everything with me.

I plunged down a corridor and through some more kitchen rooms, which I may have gone around already. Then I was in a long room more like a very wide passage, with great basins against the walls. A lot of water was on the floor, splashing up as I ran.

The bad-vegetable smell came strong and repulsive. No lights worked; only a dim glow filtered through cracks and holes from other places, casting thick shadows. Things lit up strangely. I kept seeing *eyes.* Perhaps, I thought, they *were*—

And then I realized I wasn't fighting my way through old dishrags or torn curtains.

Plants grew there, in the half-dark—tall, slender stems and drooping flags of leaves, some of which broke as I pushed by. There were spongy mosses, too. I kept treading on them, and huge funguses like dissolving statues, some of which were luminous.

Despite this, I wasn't prepared for what I saw next.

I'd burst into a *wood.*

That really is what it was. An indoor forest.

There were *trees*, twenty or thirty feet high, their tops crushed against the high ceilings and then spreading and looping over. In places, they'd cracked the stone and forced their way through to higher kitchen rooms above. As in the jungle beyond the Rise, creepers roped these trees. There were shrubs that thrust up from the paving. And the funguses, which seemed tall, were now taller, trees themselves, like oaks made of yellowish candlewax. The rest of the vegetation was a pale swimmy-green, or oily-black. . . .

The smell was thicker, yet less horrible. It was more natural, I suppose—earthier.

"Fruits" and "flowers" grew here, too, none very recognizable or tempting. (Fruit like long-fingered gloves, flowers like white spiders—yum.)

Lots of water, spilled from old taps and cisterns, or dripped through by rain.

The food pipes twisted about through all of this. I think their leaks have caused these things to grow, plus, too, ancient leftovers, maybe from centuries before—cheeses that have become quaint molds, or apple cores mixed with other stuff, which may have bred those things like umbrellas with fruit like frogs.

I stood there in the middle of it, uneasy and not liking it, yet impressed. It reminded me of the vegetable forest on the way to Peshamba, where we'd seen the monster—

Then I glanced up and saw, hanging from one of the food pipes, a heavy long thing, some vast knot of creeper or fungus. It had ears. Eyes. The eyes, cool and slitted, were looking at me, still and thoughtful.

Now that I could see, it hung upside down from a long hairless tail, which was curled over and over the pipe—the way a bat hangs, though a bat doesn't hang by its tail. . . . How big was it? About my size. Bigger . . .

It will just uncurl its tail and spring.

But it didn't. The eyes closed up.

And then I heard that rush-flutter sound. It went directly over my head, and a raw compost-heap-smelling wind fanned me.

Another of them—and it was *flying.*

Not wings. Its stunted little arms were held out, and broad flaps of skin stretched between them and its hairy body, carrying it in a long glide, downward.

They were flying rats.

A flying rat landed near me. It stared at me from grey eyes that didn't reflect enough light to go red. Then it lowered its snout and drank from a pool of rainwater.

I turned my head so slowly that I felt my neck creak.

They were all around me. Fumbling about, searching over the mosses for parts they liked to eat. They made the skittery noises when their hair scratched through leaves and fronds.

They must live here, but also, they're all through the kitchens. I'd passed by them. Shadows, smells, eyes. *Not known.*

Why hadn't they attacked me? When would they decide to?

Oh, now, probably. Two or three were edging up on my left, and one was pottering along from over there. Some were smaller or bigger than others. That one looked the size of a large dog. *That* one, when it stood up again on its hind legs, was about as tall as a man.

I wanted to scream my head off.

Instead a thought came into it, sharp and bright. Of the ring in my bag, the topaz.

Properties. What Grem had thought my Hulta ring had, only it hasn't. Does Ustareth's ring have them? Was it, in any way, "magic"?

I crouched and fished in the bag and scrabbled out the ring. Nearly dropped it in a swamp of water and mud.

It would only fit on my right thumb. I eased it on. The yellow stone gave a flash.

What should I do?

Obviously I'd done it, because, look, the rats had stopped advancing; they were just shambling away.

The ring was burning like a lamp—that flash wasn't from any light; there isn't any proper light just here.

A great gold blaze goes up from Ustareth's ring, and I'm safe.

There's another light, too, though. White. What's causing *that?*

Above, in the mossy wall, a door flies open with a crash. The rats lumber away, but not as if afraid. More as if they're shy, irritated, don't want to be disturbed.

"Claidi!"

He leaps down about fifteen feet into all this muck and squelch. It's Venn. He throws his arms around me as if I matter. And I'm clinging to him as if he's my oldest friend. As if he's Argul.

BETWEEN THE SUN AND THE MOON

In the morning, we saw Jotto, and later Treacle, waving up at us from the groves far below. They'd managed to escape back into the gardens.

It was a sunny morning. Always is, here.

The night before, after Venn so dramatically appeared, Grembilard leaned in through the door. There was a strong rope, part of the supplies we'd carted about with us all those days. Grem had attached it to something, and now first I, and then Venn, were hauled up to the place above.

The door was really a window. This part of the kitchen had sunk. A lot of the kitchens anyway lie outside the main building, in various courtyards. This one led up onto a terrace.

The rat-creatures didn't pay much attention. A few glanced up as we closed the window—glad to be rid of us.

"They wouldn't have hurt you," said Venn.

"No?"

"They're timid, don't like strong lights—even what you call the hard light, though they're fairly used to that. They wander about the lower parts of the Rise at night. Sometimes you see one being chased by a cat."

"What happens?" I asked dubiously.

"The cat works out the size difference and loses interest. The rat goes off about its own affairs."

"Did *she*—I mean your mother—?"

"No, she didn't breed those. They've just got like that by themselves over the past twenty years."

We camped above the terrace. Dark rustling trees crowded close, grasshoppers chorused, stars winked as faint clouds drifted over. The Star had gone off to the west and was hidden by angles of the cliff.

Grem fried vegetables over the brazier.

Venn and I were rather embarrassed.

We didn't speak about hugging each other, or sit at all close.

In the red brazier light, he looked now very familiar, but not like Argul at all.

I showed him the topaz ring.

"Yes," he said, in that cold voice he so often goes back to, "she said she left that somewhere, I think I was meant to search for it. A little extra test she set me when she left. I didn't ever bother. I suppose it was in her sleeping-place off the Little Book Room."

"In a drawer, with some other jewelry." I explained why I'd taken it, because of Grem's question about my own ring, which made me think Ustareth's one had powers.

"But if it does," I said, "why did she leave it behind when she left?"

"Perhaps she was as sick of fiddling about with science as she was of meddling in everything and everyone's lives," he rasped.

So there was a tense gap, and we ate some of the food. Finally I said, "But does it have properties—powers—"

"I'd expect so."

"The stone—the topaz shone out in the kitchen. And the rats backed off. I thought—"

"They backed off from the flash of the ring. Some reflection it caught. I told you, they don't like strong light much." He was snappy now. So I left it.

It was as if he didn't like me again, or liked me even less because, for a few minutes, he *had* liked me.

Whatever else, I thought I had better give him the topaz ring. But when I did offer it, he said, "You keep it. You found it."

"But—"

To which I got a furious: "Oh, just keep it, Claidi, for God's sake. Why must you keep *on*." Followed by Venn getting up and stamping off for a walk in the trees, scaring all the grasshoppers into dumbness.

I asked Grem about Treacle and Jotto, and Grem said he thought they would be all right—which of course we now know they are. Then I curled up and tried to sleep.

I hate the way, once you start to know someone, care about them, their behavior can distress you, even when it's unreasonable and not your fault, even if you were really trying to be careful, tactful.

So, apparently I must care about Venn.

I wish I didn't.

Next day, after we spotted J and T, Grem, who had been out and around, reported that the main library had appeared directly above us, on the "ninth level," as he said, with the moon and sun towers.

"Yes," said Venn, who was now being distant and vague, "it does tend to go there, doesn't it?"

"Generally it then stays in place there for several days," added Grem. (As if they were talking about something painfully ordinary.)

"I hope you're ready for a long climb, Claidi," said Venn, now distant, vague, but hearty.

"Not really."

"Oh, well, that's tough, madam."

Scowling, I now concluded they'd want me to climb with them up the side of the cliff-building—by ropes—hanging on to the odd statue that stuck out, or wobbly windowsill. And I was getting ready to refuse point-blank.

But we walked along around the cliff, through the trees, now and then into a dip and up again. And so reached an *incredible* staircase.

"Before you ask, Claidi, it doesn't move; it's outside the outer wall."

It was a *mountain* of a staircase. I didn't try to count the steps, but looking up and up at it from its foot, I guessed there must be hundreds upon hundreds. Thousands. It was far higher than the highest towers of the House. Perhaps the Wolf Tower.

The staircase was also wide, oddly ornate, with carved handrails and marble lions at intervals. (I think they were lions—they were very weathered and mossy.) (Could have been badgers, really.)

Anyway, we started to climb up.

After thirty solid minutes, it was getting slightly exhausting, but then there was a broad terrace or landing before the next flight. These landings happen at intervals all the way up. Some even have drinking-water fountains.

The stairs were also crumbly in parts, and were cracked where trees had rooted and pushed through. On the seventh landing, I think it was the seventh, when the world seemed already fallen far, far away to a green-blue ring, some big purplish monkeys were thumping about, and threw nectarines at us—until Grem made a loud whooping noise and they fled, leaping off the stairs into space, catching backhanded on handy neighboring boughs.

Neither Venn nor Grem seemed tired. *I* tried not to seem tired, ashamed of my feebleness. I'd thought I'd hardened up a lot, walking and riding with the Hulta. But climbing stairs isn't the same.

We stopped for a longer rest, thank heavens, on the fifteenth landing, or whatever it was. We sheltered from the noon sun under a spreading melon tree. (Grem watered his hair at one of the fountain-taps.)

The view was awe-inspiring but repetitive. All you could see by now were things tapering away, getting smaller and smaller. The far blue world, the high blue sky.

A large bird flapped across on ragged wings.

Lucky thing.

We got there in the afternoon.

Out of the cliff, these two brown stone towers—not that tall, and without any real distinguishing marks, just a few scattered indigo roof-tiles left. Windows without glass. Shadows running sideways.

"Sun and moon," said Venn.

"Why?"

"I haven't a single idea. Do you, Grem?"

"No, prince."

Grem (and Jotto) call him "prince" as if it's an affectionate nickname.

Wedged between the two disappointing towers was a huge block of building with long glazed windows of colored glass. It had a vaulted-arched doorway, with its own (yes, more of the things) steps, guarded by two beasts that were like pigs more than anything.

The Library.

We—I—crawled up the last steps. *They* walked.

It was cool in the vault of the doorway.

I thought, *Even if it takes off right now, and goes rambling back down into those kitchens and won't come out—I don't care.*

Venn was looking at the shut door. He said suddenly, "Try her ring, Claidi."

Oh, so now we could talk about Her Ring without him going loopy.

"I've put it away," I said huffily. But I was curious. I walked right up to the door and started digging in my bag for the topaz.

I hadn't even found it, let alone brought it out, when the door opened. Wide.

Inside looked cool, dust-moted, and calm. It had that smell libraries always have—well, so far as I know. Of new paper and old paper, of bindings, and the powders of books.

In the high ceiling was one of those skylights, and patterns of sky scattered over the old, dark-tiled floor.

"How did it—?" said Venn.

I realized the door hadn't been meant to open like that.

"It *recognized* you," I stated.

"Yes, it does recognize me—but not you. Not even Grem."

"Well, I probably touched the ring in the bag—"

"You'd have to be wearing the ring, Claidi."

I thought of the Old Ladies in the House, who had had such authority. Especially wonderful (untrustworthy) Jizania. I said, cool and calm as the library, "But I'm not. A mystery, then. But what isn't a mystery," I added in my best Jizania voice, "is that I'd like some hot tea, now, as soon as possible. Thank you."

They stared.

I walked on into the library coolness, head high. Secretly frantically hoping they'd hurry and follow, in case anything moved.

And they did. And five minutes later Grem handed me one of the traveling cups full of hot spicy tea.

Really, after what he did (reading *this*), I shouldn't have any feelings for Venn but contempt, distaste. Hatred.

None of that applies. I've tried to feel like that. It no longer works.

Instead I feel so sorry for him sometimes I could howl. At other times I want to kill him. Then—he does something that charms me, turns me around. And then I remember how he held me in his arms when he found me in the kitchens.

Of course, I don't *want* to feel close to him.

It's the old thing, that thing that happened before. I fell for Nemian (who Venn is sometimes *so* like, not to look at, but in his manner. Even the sudden charm). Then I met Argul. And Argul was *right.* He was meant, and *I* was meant.

But now am I just swinging away toward the nearest new attractive (he is) man—a new friend, a new interest. I don't trust myself.

No, I don't feel for Venn the way I feel for Argul—even though I feel I've *lost* Argul, somehow—

No, it's not the same.

And yet—

Oh, Claidi, you absolute hopeless dupp.

Who can I rely on if I can't rely on myself?

(And now I half want to tear this page out—in case *he* reads it.)

I only want You to know. Well, I do trust *you.* We've never met. Probably never will.

So is that why I trust you? Is that all it can ever mean? So long as one never meets another, one is *safe?*

This isn't getting me anywhere. Except over the page. My "Journal"—how many pages are left? Just checked. I've filled over three-quarters of this book!!!

As I drank my tea, enjoying every gulp, sitting on a marble bench, Venn came up to me.

He stopped before me and bowed low, sweepingly. It made me laugh, and then he smiled, as I've only really seen him do with the others until now.

It's a nice smile. The long mouth and white teeth, and one lower one with a tiny chip off the top. How did that happen?

"Claidi, I apologize for my temper and moodiness. Can you forgive me?" (Just like Nemian.) (But then, not at all like Nemian, that practiced girl-dazzler.) "It's odd, isn't it, you're the first woman I've ever met—apart from my mother, and Treacle."

I didn't reply. What could I say that wouldn't cause a problem?

He sat down, quite a way along the bench, gazing, not at me, of course, but up at stacks and stacks of books. There are three galleries, one above the other, mounting to the skylight.

"Claidi. I'd like to try an experiment. I don't want to explain, because that might somehow affect what happens. Would you just do what I ask?"

"You want me to jump out of a window?" I inquired blandly. It was sort of a joke, but he swung around on me.

"Oh—you're joking. I'm sorry. No, no windows. You're not wearing my mother's ring?"

"You can see. It's too big for me, even on my thumb. It's in the bag still."

"Then, when you're ready, would you stand out on the floor and ask for a book. The same voice, I think, in which you gave us the order for tea."

Puzzled, I asked, "Which book?"

"Anything. Something you'd like to read. Something about the City Towers, I suppose."

I shrugged. I finished my drink and put down the cup. I walked out onto the tiles.

Clearly I announced, "I'd like a book about the Wolf Tower." The very *last* thing I'd want in the world, frankly. A pity, that, because presently I got it.

Standing there, I felt the vastness of the library, its height, the shafts of dusty sun. All those books straight-backed like bricks. Others just in paper form, or scrolls rolled on two bits of wood, or tablets of wood *carved* with letters—

Then I heard a ticking begin, all along the shelves. It sounded like dozens of clocks starting up.

I thought of the ghost mice who ate the books, eating more knowledge than he or I could ever manage to read.

Then there was a louder click. All the other ticking stopped. And *then,* down through the air, came drifting, light as a cobweb, this silver thing like a sort of ball of hair. It was all tendrils, and wrapped up in them was a large book in black covers. It was bringing the book from the highest gallery.

The hair ball laid the book at my feet, detached itself, and swam weightlessly off.

Venn picked up the book. He showed me the cover, on which, in dull gold letters and in my own, the City's, language, these words: *The Towers.*

He put the book on a nearby table.

Then he just stood there.

Then he came over to me and grabbed up my left hand.

"It's you—it's *this.*"

"What? Let go of me!"

"Claidi—your *ring.*"

"I'm not wearing it—oh, this one. But this one is a Hulta ring—"

"I know. Claidi, I'm sorry, but remember I read your journal." (As if I could forget.) "I know about your ring. Argul gave it to you. You told Ironel in the Wolf Tower that it had been your mother's—" Venn hesitated. He said, "I know you think Ironel wrote to me. She didn't. I've heard of her. That's all. It was Grem who asked you about your own ring. You don't know why. It was because of the dolls in the other house, back across the ravines."

Totally perplexed, I said, "Dolly and Whirr and Bow?"

"That's what you called them. You see, they didn't speak, couldn't anymore. But when you were there, they started speaking. Even poor old Whirr was trying—that's why he *whirred.*"

"I see," I said. Didn't.

"There were other things. On the bridge—do you recall when you looked over and down?"

"I'll never forget."

"The bridge tried to move. It steadied, but for a moment, Grem said he thought you'd both be shaken into the ravine."

I'd thought that feeling of dizziness was just me.

"The rooms move more, now that you're here," said Venn. "They always have, but it's worse. The Rose Room, for example, hadn't shifted for about three years. But when you were in it—suddenly it was off, if not very far. As for the first apartment you were in—those yellow rooms—I don't think they'd ever moved, or hardly."

I stood there in my old familiar enchanting pose, my mouth hanging open.

"But, Venn—"

"Then there was the vrabburr—the clockwork one. Claidi, it would probably still have killed you, but it got switched off. I thought then it might be the storm affecting it. But now I think it's your diamond. Yes, I'm damn sure it is."

"How?"

"Your journal says Argul told you his mother was a scientist. The Hulta called her a magician. The"—he faltered, had the grace to look uneasy—"the glass thing she gave him that told him how important you were . . ."

I said firmly, before I could even think, "Argul's mother had nothing to do with the Towers. He never said that much about her, but from what he did, she was great. Wise and kind and funny. He loved her. She died when he was a child."

"I know. She had to leave him because she died. As opposed to leaving him as a child because she got bored with him, like *my* mother with me. *Ustareth.*" Poison in his voice as he said it. His eyes bleak as a desert. "Claidi," said Venn, "I envy your Argul. In several ways. He's the sort of man I'd have liked to be—heroic, and yet casual. Honest. Good. Brave. *Loved.*"

"Yes," I said, humble before this praise of my Argul. My lost, almost-husband. Then I said, quite rudely, "But come off it. Why would anything Hulta have power *here,* in *this* place?"

"Because it's strong," he said.

I remembered then the white light I'd glimpsed after the light from the topaz, in the kitchens. It hadn't come from the opening window after all. The ring. Mine.

I stared down at it, bewildered.

The ring had powers I'd never known. Could I have learned to manage them and used the ring to escape, long before all this entanglement happened?

He was envious of Argul.

Venn said, "I'll bring that chair over, Claidi. Sit down and read the Tower book for a while."

"You know, Venn, I really don't want to know *anything* about the rotten ghastly towers."

"Yes, Claidi, I understand that. But maybe you must."

"Why?"

"I knew you were the daughter of Twilight Star from that flying letter."

"I may not be her daughter."

"How can you know, until you find out more? Twilight might be mentioned in that book, at least as a child. I've heard of her. She fell in love with her steward, who'd been a slave."

"You know that from my book, not—" But he hadn't. Even I hadn't known my father—if he was—had been a slave.

And Venn was saying, "I know it from my mother, Claidi. She'd heard of *your* mother. As I said, she told me stories, before she changed to me. One of those stories was *about* your mother. I know you're younger than I am—when I was two, you weren't even born, were you? But Twilight and your father—they were together for some time before you arrived. I can't remember his name. She must have said. But she did say this: Twilight was strong, clever—different. That's why Grem and I thought Twilight might have made your ring. . . . Ustareth used to admire her. Ustareth said that Twilight 'broke the rules.' I can recall Ustareth saying that, and her eyes were bright. *She broke the rules, thank God for her.* That's what she said."

He glanced at me. Away.

"Claidi, a daughter might be like her mother. What did *you* do?"

I was trembling.

Slowly I answered, "I broke the rules."

Before I started, I wrote everything up. Mainly to put off opening the black book. *The Towers.*

Scared.

Afraid of my ring, too. My beautiful ring that Argul tried to give me in Peshamba, then gave me in the City.

Argul's mother was Zeera, a real Hulta name. And she *was* Hulta, wasn't she? When I was with them, a couple of the younger women had that name, too, named after her, I think.

Somehow it's disturbing to think that she died when Argul was ten, just as Venn's mother vanished when he was nine. Even so, Argul knew Zeera all those ten years. Venn only knew Ustareth before she changed toward him, stopped loving him. I keep thinking about this. Even while I'm getting ready to read this black book.

Before leaving me, going off into the depths of the library, I think he was looking for something himself—Venn said this:

"Strange, Claidi. Where the library is now, between the sun and moon towers. There used to be an old expression; *she* used to use it. Being between the sun and the moon. It meant being between two vital things. Having to make a decision, a choice."

As I am? Between my freedom and Their Law? Between my future and my past?

Between Argul . . . and Venn?

I just now opened the black cover of the book, and the first thing I saw was a printed drawing. Of a huge tower.

Not like these. Like the City Towers.

Like the Wolf Tower I thought I'd never see again.

Have I learned anything?

I've sat here, more or less, reading for hours, almost all the long second half of the afternoon.

There are two bathrooms in the library (old cracked baths on rusted, gilded feet), cupboards stuffed with ink pencils (I took one), closed wooden boxes, and brooms.

There's a kitchen still attached that opens into a run-down yard. . . .

It's silly to start describing all that. Basically I still don't understand much about the Towers.

Though not very old, the black book is one of those books that read like this: "And thereinunto they have done that which verily it please them that they do muchly." (!) (Sigh). No, I'm not myself muchly pleased. So my dread has turned to exasperation.

Venn has vanished. There's a high roof-terrace or something. I think he's gone up there.

I wish he'd stayed to help with this.

I'm glad he's gone away.

I'll read a bit more.

The Towers weren't there first. The Families were.

I remember those names, which I see again here. Wolf, Vulture, Tiger,

Pig, or Boar. And once there was a Raven Family and a Raven Tower, but they were destroyed.

Historically, the Families fight together. Then they pal up. They make alliances, swearing eternal friendship, and sons and daughters of one Family or Tower marry into another, to tie everyone together neatly. But then another quarrel starts, generally over something mind-searingly unimportant, and they're off again, using cannon to blow each other's Towers to pieces.

They were always fighting. In the end they were sick of it, and the harm they'd done to each other and themselves.

So then they thought of the Law.

The Law isn't the same everywhere. I'd already realized that. At the House the Law was that we had endless stupid rituals that *had* to be followed.

According to the black book, there are other cities, other grand houses or palaces—some called things like the Residence, or Sea-View. The Families, in one form or another, are scattered about through these places. They all have some type of the Law, which must be followed. But not all of them call it Wolf Tower Law. Despite the fact that the Wolf Tower seems to have ended up the most powerful, and the WT Families are therefore the most important. (I remember the authority Nemian had for Jizania, once she knew who he was.)

If I have it right, the Law, in whatever form, is there to use up the Families' "fighting spirit." Turn it away from war and argument. The Law seems to have been invented to stop them from having the time or energy to cause trouble otherwise.

But of course, they do cause trouble. The Law itself causes trouble. (I'm truly afraid now that I won't have stopped it properly, in the City, and even if I did, only in that one place.)

The black book doesn't say that the Law is, ultimately, just as cruel and senseless as war-making. The black book is all for the Law. *This cunning and most absolute Notion* is what the book calls it.

I don't know. I don't want to write any more about it, and there isn't much more. It just goes on and on—endless histories of these impossibly terminally useless mighty lords, ladies, princes, and princesses, flomping about, basking in how fantastic they are.

But. I did finally find something: two Family trees, tables of who married who—the "m" means married, so far as I can gather. And what children were then born.

I'll just copy it in.

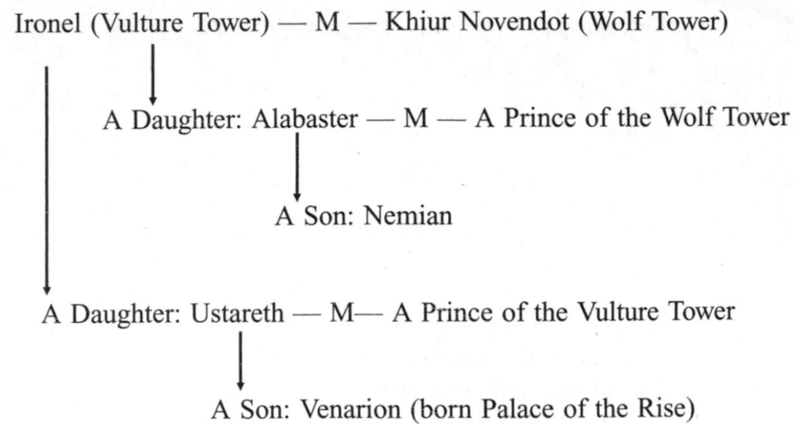

(Something I noticed from this one at once was how they hadn't bothered to name two of the three fathers, only Ironel's husband—Ironel married!!!!!—and the two sons.) Does Venn know she's his granny? And Nemian—is Venn's cousin! No wonder they sometimes have nearly the same voice. And Ustareth is Ironel's *daughter*—one more unbelievable thought.

But then I saw the second Family tree, and my heart jumped and hit its head on the underside of my chin.

Jizania Tiger (Tiger Tower)—M—Wasliwa Star (the House)

↓

A Daughter: Twilight Star

THE ROOF

"No thanks. I really don't want anything else to read just yet," I said, as Venn held out a slim pale-covered book the moment I emerged on the library roof.

I'd climbed up the stairs from the galleries, and now that I was there, I stretched, shook my hair about, glad to be in the fresh air again. The sun was low. It would be a spectacular sunset from up here—the highest point now, from the look of it, of the whole Rise. I could even see the waterfall a huge distance off, at the other end of the cliff, shimmering like a curtain of lights.

"This is different."

"It's a book, Venn. That other book has probably put me off reading forever."

"What did you learn?"

Cagily I said, "Not much. Couldn't understand most of it." Then, "It did list Ironel Novendot." When he didn't react, I announced, "She's your grandmother, Ustareth's mother."

Perhaps I shouldn't have been so blunt—nor surprised when he laughed.

"*Is* she? What horrors I've been spared, never meeting her."

"Did Ust—did your mother talk about her?"

"She must have, a little. Never as her mother. I'm just going on your own intense description of the Old Lady."

"Right. Of course."

"Did it list your own mother?"

"As I keep saying, *if* she was. Yes."

I was sullen, and half turned from him. He knows too much about me. He has no right to know *this.* Which is unreasonable. He'd only have to fetch the black book himself.

"Was it of any help?"

"No."

"That's very positive, Claidi."

"It's very true."

"Try this, then."

"I don't want to. What is it?"

"Look and see."

Nosiness—my strongest characteristic?—won over everything else. I took the pale book.

The instant I opened it, I saw it was another Journal. Not like mine. This one was hardly filled, mostly only a few lines or paragraphs here or there, then blank pages. One line was *Why am I here?* That *did* catch my eyes. Another: *I'm tired of waiting.*

Then a full page. I couldn't read a lot of it—the light was going, but also the handwriting . . . and he'd dared go on about mine.

But, it was a woman's handwriting, I thought. Who was this?

Over the page: *I shall go tomorrow.* And then nothing. The rest of the book, empty.

Ustareth?

Then I tried quite hard to read what she'd written. She was impatient, you could tell. Her writing was educated—she was a princess, a lady—but untidy and scrawly with anger and hurry, or perhaps tiredness.

I sat down, my back against the high railing around the roof.

I didn't copy down what she wrote—there was too much anyway. I'll just say what I found out.

She'd been sent here by someone she didn't name—Ironel? Or the weird and worrying "We" . . . She'd had no choice. Nor in her marriage. It was the *Law.* Her husband was called, I think, Narsident Vulture-Ax, from the fed-up scribble. (As I often do, she soon reduced him to NV.)

In the unhappy, forced marriage, she made "scenes," so they'd sent her off here alone, to do "something." She was, at the time, pregnant with Venn. Imagine that sea-crossing. She said she had to travel by sea; they didn't trust the balloons over water. (I'd always rather wondered about that, why they'd put me off onto a ship.)

She didn't say much about anything. She didn't complain, although now and then she wrote some simply explosive swearwords (typical of royalty). But though you couldn't always read the rest, *these* words were always printed carefully, even sometimes ornamented with curlicues. . . . I have to admit, I smiled once or twice.

The birth of Venn was by itself in the middle of one page. It said, "Free at last. I had the boy." (She knew he'd be a boy?) "My mechanical servants were useful, better than those idiots in the Tower."

That was all.

I thought of Venn, reading this.

As he may have done, I scanned the next pages, which obviously covered months, years, for any comment on him at all. There was only one. "He's intelligent." That was it. I suppose she did mean Venn?

Had she *ever* loved him or been interested in him?

She hadn't wanted him.

This is all rather—I don't like putting this down. In a way, he's let me pay him back for reading my own book, letting me see this.

From what I could make out, no one was at the Rise but for her, and her servants, though Families of the Towers had been living there in earlier times. There was one mention of local people—"Otherlanders"—arriving on a sort of visit. She made no comment.

On one page there was a beautiful, involved description of a new plant she'd somehow grown, a mix of a lilac and a pear, that produced fragrant purple fruit. She cared about that. Then again, three pages later, she just says, "Mauve thing died." So. (Where are her other notes on her endless experiments—the vrabburrs and dolls, the moving rooms?)

But there was one long passage that may have been why he gave me the book to read. It isn't about him, or about her. It's about what she was sent here to do, twenty years or so ago.

I read it and thought she'd made it up, or was talking in some clever way that wasn't meant to be taken seriously.

But then it seemed she did mean it, so she must have been mad.

Then again—there are things here—if I hadn't seen them, I'd have thought they were all lies.

He was leaning on the railing a long way off across the roof, looking out toward a deepening red sunset.

"Venn . . . may I ask you? This stuff about *creating* the jungle—these things about plants and animals being bred here and then taken away to the Towers and Houses and so on—as if this was a sort of farm, or workshop, for the benefit of the places back over the sea—It isn't true, is it?"

"Yes," he said.

The short sunset was already ending, and I'd missed most of it. I'd really wanted to see it from up here, too—after all, the library might not still be up here tomorrow, or we might not. (We won't be.)

"But—she seems to say they sent her here to *make* the jungle—where there was mostly a *desert waste*—"

"Yes. That's why they sent her. Apart from punishing her, of course, for irritating them all."

"How could she do that? *Make* a jungle?"

"How could she do any of it? Think of the animals. Think of Jotto."

"But the jungle-forest is *immense*—and natural."

"She was very clever and she worked very hard. And she had lots of machines she herself invented, to help her. Planting and sowing, working out systems to water everything or bring rain—she did most of it in the first two years. Then, because of how she'd arranged it all, the jungle grew and spread *itself.* I can remember bare places, long areas of sand, even when I was seven or eight, that grew over, filled up. I used to like all that, before I got used to it."

The red was maroon now, and going out. Soaked up by the vast sponge of the *jungle.* In the afterglow, a white ghost came wheeling through the sky below, on two wide sails.

Venn held out his arm, and the owl veered slowly in and alighted on him, folding its vast ghostly wings. "Hello, owl," he said to it, and it turned its head, that way they do, almost all around, like a stopper in a bottle, to look at him.

"Even the owl," said Venn.

"What do you mean?"

"You think he's quite real, don't you?"

"The owl is a doll?"

"Yes, Claidi. Once a month, Jotto or Grem or I undo a little panel—look, under the feathers, there—and oil him. He's two years younger than I am. She made him for me and gave him to me that day when she said, 'You're two, now.' The day she changed."

"But—he *eats* things!"

"But he's not supposed to."

The owl settled. It closed its eyes and all the light went from the sky.

"I missed the sunset, reading her journal," I said lamely.

"Never mind. You'll see the Star come up in a minute. I wanted you to see that, Claidi, from here. Let's go over to the east side of the roof."

Down and down, the miles and miles and miles of now-dimming forest. The huge, sky-touching trees and knitting of creepers that cover and devour everything—roads, statues—vegetable lushness and life.

Ustareth made all that. Can it be possible?

Venn must hate his father, too, this unknown prince with the ugly name—*Narsident,* from the Vulture Tower.

"She doesn't," I said, "say much about her experiments. And—did she have a special room in the Rise where she worked?"

"No," he said. I was going to say, *Then where?* but he said, "Come here, Claidi. The Wolf Star's coming up. I want you to see."

"I don't like your Star."

"You said. It isn't mine."

We stood there.

There was a gleam, in the distance, and down. I thought it was a lake or something I'd never been high enough to see before, catching the rays of the Star—which I couldn't yet see either.

But the glow got unbearably fiercer and whiter, until it was almost blinding.

"You're not missing that, are you, Claidi-Claidis?"

"What is it?"

"What do you think, madam?"

"Something's on fire—white fire."

"Almost."

And then the scorching blaze began, inch by inch—in fact, mile by mile—to *rise.* Up out of the forests. Up into the eastern air. Up and up. It was clear of the land and into the sky now.

"The Star—" I said.

He said nothing.

"But Venn—it didn't come over the horizon the way a star would—"

"No."

"It came up from the jungle!"

"Ustareth made that, too," he said. Already the blue-white glare had drained his face of any color. "It's called the Wolf Star, but it isn't a star."

"What *is* it?"

We watched as *It* went on rising into the height of the east and at the same time drew nearer.

"I don't know, Claidi. But she used to go there to do her work. It's on the earth by day, on a high plateau in the jungle. By night, up it goes, as you see, moves around the sky, returns in the morning before sunrise. She'd be gone for days. I mean, when I was an infant, and the rest of the time she was with me. Days and nights. So she must have also traveled in it. Up *there.* It goes much higher than a balloon; do you realize that, Claidi?"

"Yes."

"She never took me to see it. Let alone sail in it. But she talked about it, once or twice. It sounded magical. It's only mechanical. All the mechanical controls are in it that make the Rise—how shall I say?—*run.* Things to do with the food machines, even the way we use the waterfall for power. The rooms moving, that, too. All are somehow worked—from up there."

"Do you think—does she *live* on the Star?" I gasped.

"She might have. But no, I think eventually she just arranged it to work by itself, like everything else. I think, when she left, she went far away. As far as she could get."

Our heads were tilting back, to watch the Star rise ever higher.

The owl, turned to silver, slept. Only—it didn't. Dolls don't.

(I'd puzzled over how he'd trained it to steal my book. Obviously, he'd only had to *set* it.)

"Why are you telling me all this, Venn?"

"You break rules," he said, dreamily. "You break machines, don't you?"

He meant I'd broken, defaced the dice in the Wolf Tower.

I went cold.

"Why would I?"

We were looking at each other. Straight into each other's eyes.

"To find your way home. To get back to your Hulta people. And *him.*"

HOW WE LEFT THERE

We got out of the library soon after and went down the great stair to the first landing. The black book was left behind for the hairy machines to replace. Venn brought the other book—hers.

On the way down, the owl flew around him twice. Then flew away.

Grem cooked supper on the landing. Fireflies appeared from nowhere, as if attracted to the brazier flames.

"We'll have some sleep. Get up and go all the way down when the Star comes back over, before dawn. An early start. Then we can arrange things. For the journey." Venn. He was very organized. In control. It was all his plan now, and Grem and I were just being swept along. Perhaps that was fine for Grem.

"I want to talk about this," I said.

"Do you? What's to talk about?"

"All of it."

"Claidi, you've never struck me before as painstakingly slow and thorough."

"Haven't I?"

"All right. Say what you want."

"Well, thank you." So I said what I wanted. I said that he seemed to think we could set out from the Rise, go through the jungle, find the Star (handily parked on some plateau or other), hop into it, get me to smash it up—because I'm good at that?

"Is *that* what you thought I meant?"

"Isn't it?"

"Not quite."

"If," I said, "the Star is some sort of sky-ship(?) and has machines in it that somehow work the palace, won't they be difficult to damage? Besides which I don't see myself doing that, somehow. In the Wolf Tower, I destroyed—or tried to—the dice and records of names for a purpose. But if the things on her ship-star are broken, what will happen here?"

"The rooms will stop moving about, at the very least."

"The food machines may stop, too—the light. Even the water may be affected—"

"How housewifely you are," he jeered.

"*Human* is the word you're looking for."

"Oh my."

"No, Venn. What about Grem and Jotto and Treacle—and all these animals that come and go—"

"Not everything we eat comes from machines. Haven't you noticed that the gardens are bursting with fresh fruit and vegetables? There are even tea bushes, and Treacle is an expert at picking and drying the leaves. Jotto is a master cook, despite anything he says. Even I can bake bread. As for the animals, they really don't need us. They're terribly good at surviving *without* people."

I said, "What about the little animals in the enclosure?"

"You thought they were cute? They get out all the time. Jotto goes mad finding them. They're happy in the gardens, and I've seen them band together and frighten off a monkey. People—well, in fact, people rather cramp an animal's style."

I decided not to hurl my plate at him. (Grem came quietly and took it from me anyway.)

"As for the light, we have lamps and candles. As for the water, most of the taps run straight off the waterfall. Apart from that, none of us might want to stay."

"I see. So after I ruin the ship-thing for you, I'm to take myself off *home,* as you put it, though I don't see how. While the rest of you bounce away in other directions. Is that it?"

He laughed, that way he does, low and soft. Somehow it ended my anger.

"You haven't seen what I mean, Claidi. I explained all wrong."

"I haven't, no. No?"

"I didn't really mean smash the Star machines. Just—break their routine. Use them. Think about it. Apart from anything down here, what does the Star actually do?"

"Rises and goes down."

"And crosses the sky. Both ways."

I thought. "Oh," I said.

"Yes, Claidi. Perhaps it's possible to make it go another way—any way you want."

"Across the sea—"

"Why not?"

"How?"

"I don't know. We have to get there, get into it, and see."

"*We* have to."

He sat back, clasping one knee. His legs are long. Nemian used to sit like this, looking like this. And Argul. Probably lots of men, and women, do. Why do there only seem to be these three men in the world?

"Well, Claidi, if I asked you to stay here, with me, you wouldn't want to, would you?"

A long silence.

The fireflies had gone. Down in the jungles his mother made, monkeys abruptly began hooting, as they do now and then at night, scaring you witless.

Then again, the long silence.

"I didn't think," I said, "I had a choice."

"I've shown you that you may have one. *She* didn't want to be here. They made her. She left. You're the same."

"Then you—"

"Oh, I won't go with you. To the Star, yes. The country down there is full of tigapards, and all the rest of it: her bred animals; the *real* vrabburrs—you'll need me to help you reach the Star. No one else. I wouldn't risk Jotto or Treacle in that mess. I shan't ask Grem."

"You're saying you'll see me to the ship—if it is one."

"And then I'll come back here."

I looked at him under my lids. He was staring up at the sky above, from which the Star had by now moved away.

"You said you might all leave."

"We might. But not with you. We—I—don't belong in Claidi's world. Though . . . you could have been welcome in mine."

A rush almost like tears closed my throat, so I couldn't or didn't speak.

I thought, *This is crazy.* If we do this, we'll be eaten alive by vrabburrs, or something else his awful mother made or bred. Or we won't find the Star at all. Or we won't be able to get into it.

We'll end up back here, both of us.

So it's unwise to start dreaming myself back with Argul. Or being afraid of this good-bye. Afraid of something I don't understand and can't recognize.

I couldn't stay with Venn. Not if I have the choice. Argul is the one. He always will be the one.

And yet—

"There's a firefly in your hair," Venn said in a hushed voice.

I became aware of the green-gold spark only in the instant it zigzagged away.

When I looked up, he said, in the cold arrogant voice, "And the rings might work against any dangers. Hers or yours. So let's stop *chattering* and get some sleep."

It's so sudden, happening so fast. Too fast.

They've waved us off. They did wave. Jotto had his favorite chicken under one arm for comfort—a smart chicken with white stripes.

I feel as if I've lived here a long time. Not a month or so—many years.

All such a *hurry.*

I wish it hadn't been. I wanted to go on that walk again, that long one under the trees with blue flowers, and that pool with the big fish, and the hydrangeas. . . . I liked that game Jotto taught me—did I ever say?—with the little painted squares. And Treacle watering the pots of flowers from her eyes, which, saying farewell, were *dry,* though she looked sad and stern. Perhaps, if she really does ever cry, her real tears *have* to be made of *nothing*—

She's frightened for him.

I've never asked where they're from, Treacle and Grem. The children of Ustareth's slaves—or free people from the neighboring lands, which were then a waste. How did she make them have leaf-hair, watering-can eyes? How? (And how could she?)

Grem kept flatly saying he'd come with us. Was refused. And Jotto offered, very bravely, because you could see he was appalled at the thought of the jungles.

I liked living in the pavilion. I did. And the statue of the porcupine I found in the back room. Jotto and I had planned to move it out under that big tree. He says he will, anyway.

I'll never see it there.

I'll never see any of it again.

The gardens are beautiful. They looked wonderful in the dawn as we came down off the stairs and then into them from the terraces. Mists of trees floating in fogs of light—

Seven cats washing each other in the shade.

The Gardener cleaning out a birdbath, turning his back on us. He certainly doesn't care if any of us stays or goes.

Those little animals, the tiny ones, hippos and rabbits, pouses and geese and tigapards. We could have had a last dinner, played with them. Or just gone and seen them in their enclosure.

And the waterfall, it was so splendid—

I'd have liked to go and look at it at the other end of the Rise. I've gotten so used to the sound that I don't hear it. It's going to be odd, really, *not*-hearing it.

And the rat-beasts in the kitchens, poor old things.

And just being able to reach up and pick a ripe peach or orange, whenever I wanted.

And all the colored windows glowing from the cliff in the dusk after the swift sunsets.

And the infuriatingly blinding light of the Star.

The Star.

Stop it, Claidi. Just stop.

I'm just nervous about going into the jungles again. Especially now that I know about them. And what's in them.

No, that's not it.

We'd packed. I didn't have much and offered to carry more, but I also got refused. (No one can refuse like Venn!)

Treacle brought me some different clothes to wear: smooth silky trousers and a tunic, and high boots because of snakes (which, until now, I've only admired and not bothered about).

He has a rifle. And bullets.

He took her ring, too, the topaz. Put it on (it fits him; perhaps she made it for him, anyway). Then he looked uncomfortable, kept pushing it and turning it as if he wanted to drag it off.

Jotto brought us food in little waxed-paper boxes, and water bottles. I did take some of those.

My bag feels heavy. Like my heart. Oh, what a line, worthy of that awful writer Lady Jade Leaf, at the House.

They were on the lawn under the tree with flowers, where the porcupine may go, when they waved.

Grem embraced Venn. Then Jotto embraced him. Then Jotto embraced me. Jotto looked tearful, but like Treacle he can't actually cry. (*She* might have thought of that. If she gave him the emotions, she might have made him able to express them.)

Treacle turned one solemn good-bye cartwheel. Today her underpants were scarlet with blue dots. This almost seemed the saddest thing of all.

I hated coming here. I was terrified and raging. At least I didn't cry as we marched away.

And I'll be alone with him now, as never before, in the depths of the jungle-forest.

Her forest.

HER FOREST

Trees. Shrubs. Shadows.

Glittery strings of water falling from high rocks smothered in vines.

Flowers without color or scent.

Flashes of parakeets high up in the canopy.

It's the same way it was coming here. There's no point in going on about it again. The only difference is knowing she planted it and made it grow. It was her talent for science that enabled everything to grow so quickly, so lushly. And so tall.

This used to be a desert waste. Like the one that surrounded the House. Dust and buried ruins and mostly poisonous wells. And now, it's this.

Trees, shrubs . . .

Glittery strings of water . . .

And vast silences, now that the waterfall thunder has died away.

I'd thought we'd be awkward together, or I would, but while we're on the move, of course, that doesn't come into it.

Venn has to hack our way through, and so do I as much as I can. The faintly shining path I'd seen before keeps on, descending from the Rise, now coiling to the left or right around things, and in parts smothered. It's exhausting. When we rest during the day, we sometimes just drink some water and then fall asleep. Neither of us is used to this sort of thing. No proper stamina.

Often at night, though, we can't sleep. The Vast Silences get shattered all the time by yowling monkeys, or deer (he says they're deer) abruptly crashing by through the undergrowth. Once something leapt right over us, a living arc with legs and *eyes.*

Tigapards prowl. We hear them. They don't come near the fire, or do our rings keep them away? (I've recalled that time on the beach, after I'd just gotten off the ship, when the tigapard behaved so oddly and never came near me.) So, my ring is as powerful as Ustareth's? This still seems wrong. How could it be? Was Zeera as powerful as Ustareth??? She didn't sound that way. Zeera was kind. She *looked after* people.

We did see a vrabburr, the very first morning.

We were on a steep part, and I'd gotten tangled in a creeper, slashing at it, and Venn said, "*Ssh.*" I had the sense to realize it wasn't him being moody again.

When the vrabburr appeared, it was a few yards away—that area was abnormally clear, or we wouldn't have seen it.

Vrabburrs kind of lope. Very unevenly, because the front paws are so much shorter than those great, heavy back legs. It fallollopped across the path, and shouldered, if you see what I mean, through into the rest of the jungle.

It hadn't scented or seen us, or whatever. He said, "It must have been clockwork, that one." So maybe the clockwork ones can't even scent or see you, unless you're very obvious and close. I haven't asked. I'd rather not know, really.

Anyway, he says—now that we're out here, so perhaps he's only lying to reassure me—that the vrabburrs are fewer in number now. The clockwork ones run down (why didn't he leave that other one to run down, then; why wind it up again if they're dangerous?), and the real, bred ones have spread out into the farther jungles. Lucky old farther jungles.

As I say, at night we stay awake a lot.

We sit, or lie, a great space apart across the fire, usually turned away and not looking at each other, and we talk.

Argul and I used to talk for hours when we were alone, but not yards apart. And even our most serious discussions were full of jokes. We didn't seem to talk much about the past, either. It was sometimes about that evening, or that day, but more often about tomorrow. Next month.

Venn and I talk mostly about the past.

"I remember that tree over there, Claidi. Do you see? Yes, that palm. She used to bring me to look at it. I was about one and a half."

"You remember a lot from when you were very young. Most people don't."

"That's because most of my life happened to me before I was two." I digested *that,* and he said, "To start, it was only a little plant, the palm, in the middle of nothing. All this was bare. Sand, with just a bit of water welling up around a stone. But when she brought me next, the palm was already taller than I was. And there were other things growing everywhere. All about thirty feet high. Look at it now. Tall as the sky. I thought it was magic, what she could do. I still do, in a way. Well, in a way, it is."

Odd. I could just picture Zeera at that moment, with *Argul* as a little boy standing by her, and the palm tree growing. "So you think she did *some* good, then?" I said.

"Oh yes. Great good. If I think about her now I'm an adult, well, she must have been very unhappy. I remember something in her book, the one I showed you—did you read this bit? About how she quite liked Narsident, my father, when they first introduced him to her."

"I don't remember reading that, I couldn't read parts—"

He opened the larger bag and produced the book (he's brought it with him). I wished he hadn't. Her book makes me uncomfortable. But I suppose, once he found it in the library . . . didn't he ever look before? . . . it's all he has left of the real Her.

Anyway, he read me this thing about how she thought at first her husband was handsome and noble, and then found out he was awful and she hated him. But it was too late by then. Then Venn read a sentence in which she added that she thought everyone should have some way of telling if the person they were attracted to was really right for them.

Of course, I thought at once of Zeera's glass charm she gave to Argul. The thing he'd looked at when he met me. The way he could be sure *we* were right, that he truly did want *me.* (Had Venn thought of that, too?)

Strange.

Venn sighed and said, "She wasn't so bad, you know. I'm not fair to her."

"Well, she left you."

"She wasn't so bad. At least, not to other people. She helped the local people, Otherlanders, she called them. If they got ill, or their crops failed. They'd bring people to the Rise with a broken arm . . . and she'd make them well. Or—she did that until she changed. After that, she wouldn't see them. She'd hardly see *me.* She preferred her mechanical dolls."

(I heard Argul saying to me, ". . . My mother told me about Peshamba." Peshamba, the city with mechanical dolls.

And, "She knew such a lot. Herbs and chemicals.")

I said, "Venn—"

"Yes, I know. She was a terrible person."

"I was going to say, in some ways she sounds—like Argul's mother."

"I know. I caught that when I read—your journal. What you wrote that he said about her. And about Peshamba, too. My mother could almost have invented and made Peshamba."

"But it's coincidence. Zeera was Hulta. And anyway, she was there with them, long before Ustareth left the Rise. Argul's eighteen, two years younger than you—"

"No, three," Venn corrected me. (Hadn't realized Venn was as old as that—)

"Three, then. But that would make *you* three when Argul was born—and she didn't leave here until you were nine. Is it possible somehow, later, she and Zeera could have met?"

"If they had, Ustareth would have thought Argul's mother was a barbarian."

"And Argul's mother would have thought Ustareth was a tronker!" I flared.

End of discussion.

Although Venn hates her himself, he doesn't like anyone else to insult Ustareth.

It's quite difficult trying to see to write by dying firelight.

Actually, last night (after the deer or whatever leapt over us), I asked Venn about the two men who abducted me, Hrald and Yazkool. It was to make conversation, really.

Venn said he didn't know them. So I asked what Grem had thought. Venn then said Grem hadn't seen them; they'd been gone when he crossed to the house.

Something in that seemed weird, and I thought back to that morning. Bellowing monkeys, smashed plates on the terrace and upturned chair, a breakfast started and left. How I'd thought H and Y had been thrown into the gulf. "They left in a hurry, then. I thought you paid them?"

"Oh, I'd sent a courtesy payment, with Grem. He didn't see them so he just brought it back."

"Why did they rush off?"

It seemed he wasn't going to answer. He didn't.

Then, somewhere in the dark I heard him say, "Those two ruffians. It's possible something carried them off. It occurred to me when I saw what you wrote about it."

I'd been drifting to sleep. This woke me up and no mistake.

"I don't know if I should tell you," he said. "I know you'll get anxious."

"And my life otherwise is such a serene sea of calm."

"Claidi, you *deserve* to be told. Yes, something may have taken them. They were on the roof-terrace. Something like this happened once before."

"When? Who?" I gabbled.

"A servant of my mother's. He was old, and very gentle. Heepo. He used to talk to me a lot after she stopped talking, find me things to do that I liked."

"And—?"

"Well, Claidi, when I was about seven, Heepo was out on a high balcony of the room where I was playing. It was noon. A sort of shadow flicked over the light. I didn't bother for a moment, and then I looked up. Nothing was there. And neither was Heepo. I thought he'd gone out of the room, not telling me, which wouldn't have been like him. I looked for him, couldn't find him. Then Grem looked, too, and Treacle. I even got my courage together and went and disturbed Ustareth. She didn't say much. Just, Yes, never mind, or something, as if I'd lost a toy. But we never saw Heepo again."

"You're saying something *swooped* down and took him off the balcony—without even a cry—"

"Without anything. Just that flick of shadow, which I didn't look at. It was too fast, you see. It was just *there*—then gone. He didn't have time to call. And neither did those two—Hrald and Yaz-the-fool. But the monkeys must have seen something, and it scared them badly."

"What *was* it?"

"All our talks circle around Ustareth. She bred a lot of birds here. Perhaps some very large bird, very fast, predatory."

So, one more delightful menace to look out for.

I'm so *pleased* I never knew this at the Rise. All those high places I sat in the sun, those landings on the great outside staircase—the roof of the library!

The path stopped this afternoon.

We were far down the cliff, jungle looming above and falling away in front, never able to see far. Mist of blue distance through leaves.

When it went, we searched for a while. But this time the path hadn't been covered by vines or broken up by bushes. It wasn't there anymore. No more path.

"She used to bring me this way," he said, angrily. "And the path went on much further. Right to the base of the cliff, and then there was a deer path—"

He was irrationally furious—with rational good reason. I sat under a tree while he raved.

Then he growled at me, "Come *on,* then."

Whenever things don't go right, I get this impression all this is my fault. The journey we're having to make, I mean. But really, I never wanted to do this. I'd have gone the other way, if I'd made the choice. The way I was brought here. Used the road, tried to find a place on the coast with ships—

But now it all seems: Well, I'm doing this for *you.* So the least *you* can do is keep up/cut a way through faster/not want to rest or to have a drink of water.

Or a pause for lunch.

I'd been thinking, at least he talks to me now like a normal person. Huh!

He's strong after all. He kept tearing on, kicking and chopping stuff out of the way. Birds flew up screaming.

Finally, late in the afternoon, I said, "I can't go any farther without a rest. I'm sorry."

And he heaved a great sigh. "Oh, all right, all right. In about ten minutes, once we get down to that wild fig tree."

It doesn't seem any harder without the path, anyway.

He's gone to sleep, leaning on the fig tree.

We've been here three hours. Lost all the time we gained in the mad scramble.

When the Star comes over, even through all these leaves, jagged pieces of light drop through.

I mean, I'd never have chosen to go this way, toward her Star.

Breaks in the tree line. Looking into the forest below he showed me a *lynx*—a small, catlike creature, tufted ears, very pretty and not friendly. Later on, as we were trying to find a way down, I saw another lynx—only it wasn't. This one (it had a spotted coat, grey eyes gleaming in the jungle-dusk) was a jaguar.

I asked him, after we *got* down, and when we eventually made our "camp" for the night, if the animals at the House, the lions and hippos, Jizania's blue bird—if originally they came from here.

"Possibly," he said.

He doesn't say much at the moment. Even showing me the lynx was: "Look. There's a lynx."

He's in his Nemian-phase. The noncharming one.

It's when he's in an Argul-phase—not that he's like Argul, just looks like him and is efficient, leaderly, funny, and helpful, like Argul—that's when I really should be most wary.

I should be glad he's being a pain, glad I don't like him or feel close to him. At the moment.

We're all the way down the cliff. It towers behind us, a dark green living wall. (The Rise is invisible.)

We march (stumble, hack, claw) a way onward.

Saw another of those strange old statues today; we passed quite near it. It seemed to be of a bear, like the one near Peshamba. Not really the same sort of bear, though. It was carved very shaggy and had huge teeth, with flowers growing between them, as if it were eating them. But I suppose they, or their bush, were really eating the statue, rotting it away.

He has been THE END all today.

I shouted at him, Why had he made us do this?

He shouted, Because he knew I couldn't stand it at the Rise, kept on "whining" I had to get back to my "people" (the way he said it!), these "barbarians," and to my "barbarian chieftain love."

I yelled that my BCL was worth ninety times ninety of any City-bred fool of a prince.

We both ended up suddenly laughing. Both apologized.

But it isn't comfortable.

The worse thing is feeling that we are never going to get anywhere.

I mean, we can't see where we are or where we're going, although sometimes there are breaks in the trees, glades where he takes a "reading" from the sun or stars.

We saw a ruined building yesterday, near sunfall. Crimson-and-yellow parrots were flying around it; they have nests in the broken roofs. He said it was a temple. It had been here since the time of the waste.

A temple to what?

"To God, in one of God's many forms," he replied sweepingly. "I think this one was a parrot."

We did look in at the great open front, but lots of the temple had fallen in, pulled down by creepers. A white monkey sat claw-combing his fur.

An abandoned overgrown village. We more or less fell right into it. A mat of moss and vines gave way, and we nearly dropped into a sunken house six feet below.

"Damn," said he. "I remember her mentioning a village near the plateau. I hope this wasn't it."

"You wanted to see the village again."

"I never saw the village. Don't be absurd, Claidis. I thought they might help us get to the Star."

We don't talk now at night. He gets either very polite or surly.

I expect I do as well.

(Sometimes he forgets and calls me "Claidis.")

Although we were in a clearing after dusk tonight, the Star didn't go over. We haven't seen it for a few evenings now. Are we off course?

"Something is tracking us," he said.

"Excuse me?"

"*Tracking* us. As in hunting us."

"?!!"

He stopped and checked the rifle. I don't like guns. I always think of the brutal House Guards when I see them. But the Hulta had some. Peshamba did.

"What is it?" I asked.

"For God's sake, Claidi, your eternal amazement about wildlife is ridiculous. Does it matter *what* it is?"

"Yes."

"Why, for heaven's sake?"

"Well it might not be dange—"

"It is. It's something big, powerful, and intent. A carnivore. Yes, all right. It's probably a vrabburr—a real vrabburr. Even a pair. They'll sometimes hunt together, a male and female."

I felt sick.

He said, "Walk in front."

"I don't know the way—"

"*Claidi!* I'll strangle you. Neither do I. Go *in front.*"

So I crept rapidly forward, or tried to, cutting vines and things out of the way as quietly as I could.

I hadn't heard anything, suspected anything. He knows this place and its beasts better than I do, of course.

As we went on, I was aware of how much noise *we* made, though.

And then we were on the edge of another clearing, a very wide one, with spires of pink flowers and swirls of hummingbirds in sunlight.

Venn spoiled it. He said, "Stay dead still, Claidi, and listen. They—there *are* two—are right behind us. In the clearing there they'll have the chance they want. There's room for them to race and they're fast. What you do is this: You go down into that shadowed area. Stay there and wait.

I'll shoot them if I can. If not—when you hear the first shot, run, and keep going. Get as far as you can."

"What about the ring—rings?"

"Either they don't work or they haven't. I don't know how they work—do you?"

"No—but I can't leave you—"

He turned and glared at me, white-faced. As if he'd happily kill me himself.

"The other village is somewhere here," he said. "You've got a chance."

"I mean—*you*—"

"Oh, me. So what, me."

"Venn—"

"I ought to feed you to them. Go—*Guljurri ban!*"

It was a dreadful curse of some sort. I *felt* what it meant, even though I didn't know. It had nothing, I bet, to do with fur balls.

Confusedly I thought, *He's going to let them have* him, *if he misses with the gun. He's frightened and trying to save me—this is all wrong—but I'm making it worse.*

So I slipped away from him without another word, into the tangled shadow between the trees. I hid, as he'd told me.

I was frightened daft myself, but somehow it didn't seem real, and I thought, *Nothing will happen.*

Then, the vrabburrs came.

PEARL FLAMINGO VILLAGE

They were very big, that was what I thought first. Then that one vrabburr was larger than the other. A parent and child, perhaps. Daddy or mommy vrabburr teaching baby vrabburr how to hunt.

Sunlight shone on them, but also they were all part of the forest, its bars of shadow and dull highlights on their pelt. So in a way, the forest, too, seemed to be stalking us, had *become* the vrabburrs in order to attack us properly.

They'd halted, a short distance from Venn. We'd made a tunnel through the foliage, and they could see him clearly, with the loaded gun pointing at them. His arms *looked* steady. He looked immovable, heroic. (Hopeless?)

One, the bigger one, lowered its awful dog-rabbit-tiger head and savagely tore up a mouthful of moss. (So they're vegetarian *as well!*) The other sat there on its fat haunches. It would have looked amusing if it hadn't been what it was.

And then this smaller one just *launched* itself at Venn.

Yes, it was racing, and the speed—two flying *hops*—grotesque and terrifying—and it was there—it was against him—on him—he was lying under it—and I'd heard the gun fired, the shot had split the sky—but it hadn't done any good—

The other one was coming in now, too, racing and hopbounding.

I'd forgotten the rings. As he said, we didn't know if or how they worked—and they hadn't—

This is perhaps the most stupid thing I've ever done. So far. I ran out of cover, which he'd risked his life to send me into. It wasn't bravery—it was terror—and stupidity.

I started screaming and shouting. Every bad word, every mad word—and everything ending *Vrabburr! Vrabburr!*

And I rushed toward them, yelling and shrieking and waving my arms—

The bigger one hesitated. It sat back, and reared up, with its ghastly rabbit front feet—with a rabbit's huge digging claws, I now saw—half raised, as if ready to slap or punch me.

But I'd gone nuts. I know I had this image in my mind, not thought out, just there, just what was going to happen, of running right into it, thumping it in the chest, bashing it on the nose if I could reach high enough—

Oh, it wasn't just for Venn. It was for everything.

I was nearly there—and the one on top of Venn was horribly growling, so I thought the worst, and he was *silent*—and I was yodeling something about man-eating marmalade (I suppose I meant the color of their pelts)—

When—

The standing-up, ready-to-box vrabburr abruptly toppled over. It fell, like a striped velvet cushion, and lay on the moss.

Venn had shot it after all, and it had only just realized?

But then the other one, the one sitting *on* Venn, rolled tiredly off him, as if it just couldn't be bothered and preferred to take a nap.

He couldn't have killed both of them with one (delayed) shot.

I pulled up, coughing, breathless.

Only then did I hear a strange thin buzzing sound, which I now understood had made all the fine hairs rise at the base of my scalp.

What now? Some murderous insect, or swarm, perhaps?

Wildly, I looked up and around. Nothing. Even the hummingbirds had wisely fled.

Venn sat up. His jacket and shirt were torn, there were scratches on his neck and cheek, bleeding, but they didn't look very deep. He looked quite green, but it may have been the green shadow.

"Venn."

"Feigned dead," he said, offhand, although I could now easily see him shaking. "It's the best thing, if they get you. Slows them down. They don't like dead meat, much. They can't decide, you see, if you're still worth eating or not."

"Oh, I see. That's clever. Very cool of you to do it."

We sounded as if we were at a tea party. "Oh, hello. I've just been pretending I was dead as a vrabburr tried to eat me." "Oh, hello, how fascinating. Well done."

But I kept rubbing my ears, trying to clear the noise out of them. Venn was starting to do the same. And both vrabburrs lay there, like heaps of orange-and-black plush.

The people stole across the glade, and I thought they were only shadows, disturbed by tiny returning birds, or the sun and some nonexistent breeze moving things.

And then there were several of them, men and women, a group. Standing there, just below.

The five at the front took the pipes out of their mouths, and the buzzing whine ceased.

Dark, dusk-colored people, a skin shade I think is brown but looks almost blue or green in the forest. Light clothing almost the same color.

Three ran past me and bent over the vrabburrs, stroking them, putting some loose things around both their necks.

Another one stood there, bowing gracefully to me and to Venn.

This man then spoke in another language.

But Venn answered, saying something like, "Howa drah b 'doo?"

Then the graceful man turned to me and said, in my own language (accented but clear), "The vrabburrs are not harmed."

"Oh, *good*—I'm so *thrilled*—my *main* worry—"

"Shut up, Claidi," said Venn. But he was grinning. He spoke some more in the other language.

The rest of them were helping load the vrabburrs on a sort of tray, which they then, eight to a side, lifted. They must be strong.

Venn said, "They think all life is important, Claidi. They heard us, he says, and came to save us, but also to save the vrabburrs."

"Now what? Are they taking them off to make them into attractive rugs?"

"Of course not. They like them. They'll keep them in the village a few days for the children to see, feed the vrabburrs, clean their teeth, and check their general health. Then return them to the jungle."

I gaped. Well, anyone might have been surprised.

"My mother," said Venn, "taught them all that. They're from the village I told you about. So I've gotten you here, at last."

Their pipes make a sound that just knocks vrabburrs, tigapards, jaguars—that sort of thing—out. It doesn't hurt them, though.

I've been told, by Shrin, that the air-harps in the Rise gardens have a similar purpose—their sound, when they make it, warns off the vrabburrs, and other bigger outside animals. They just don't like it. I remember now, even the larger monkeys would sometimes go all funny when breezes blew through the harps. I'd never linked the two facts up. (Am I just very slow? Well, I had things on my mind.)

Outside, beyond the veranda, is the village. Small houses thatched with leaves. Carved wooden pillars, painted. The lake is the curved shape of a bean, so Shrin said.

I thought it was blossoming trees growing in it, all that silvery pearl pink. But just before sunset, we walked down, and its hordes of pearl-pink flamingos, which have given the village its name—Pearl Flamingo Village.

I've seen flamingos here and there, but never so many. They say there are two thousand on the lake. Sometimes they suddenly fly up, and there's a sort of soft lightning in the air as all their wings turn and catch the sun.

Shrin is the wife of Burand.

Burand and Shrin are the only ones who can completely talk the language I speak. (They learned it from their parents, who were taught by her—Ustareth—and her machines.)

Everyone is still very respectful about U.

Why? She was—

Anyway, beyond the lake is a cliff. It's not nearly as massive as the Rise, but up there *is the Star*. It's absolutely true.

This evening, as the sun set, out of the jungle along this little cliff-top, *It* rose.

From here it looked more than ever huge and overpowering. It caught the last rays of sun, blistering. You can see it has points sticking out of it all over—like the spines that stick out of the green case of a chestnut. Just like a star.

It *is* a star. Only it isn't.

The Pearl Flamingans come out, most of them, to see it rise. (Its return in the last hours before dawn tends to act as their general wake-up. You see, here it's blinding. Sunrise in reverse, and after it's down, the sun comes up not long after.)

Shrin says they all like the Star; they enjoy it—rather as I recall how the Peshambans liked their Clock, which they worshiped as a god. But the Clock was much more civilized than this Star.

Venn has explained to the village that the Star may be going away.

They looked shocked—then resigned.

Burand said they'd always expected this. Ustareth had told them that probably one day it would.

Had she meant to use it herself?

* * *

Tonight we had dinner on the veranda with Shrin and Burand and their seven children, and all the household dogs and cats, monkeys, mongooses, lemurs, parrots, lizards, and snakes. The noise!

They encourage animals of all types. The animals know it and take great advantage.

I shared my meal with two cats (*not* the dome-headed variety) and a tortoise—the oddest creature, with a wrinkled, kind, old face, and in a shell!

Lemurs swung from pillar to pillar. Tails in everything.

A snake kept coiling around our feet and ankles. They call it Flollu—which means Nosy. It is. (It visited me during the night, stayed a whole hour, taking up most of my bed.)

I have to admit, I love it here.

Venn's being nice.

I am.

These people are *good.* I know I make mistakes about people (the Sheepers and so on). But this village is just—I'm not sure there's even a word for it. But it's great. And apparently, from all they say, that is because of Ustareth!

Venn looked stunned, the more they went on about it, what she taught them, how lovely she was. He muttered something about they were trying to please him by lying. But then he muttered no, he didn't think it was that.

They have the light, the sort the Rise had. It's from some dam(?) around the far side of the cliff in the lake. They have running hot water.

The knockout pipes were given to them by U, as well as the collars that they use to keep beasts like vrabburrs happy while they check them over. (I've seen "our" vrabburrs in a big garden place. They're free to wander, just in the collars. Children feed them vegetables and pat them. The vrabburrs look just a bit puzzled. No doubt thinking, all these juicy kids, why aren't we biting into them?)

There are other things. Foolproof medicines, vast crops that never fail.

They say that in return Ustareth left them the job of looking after the jungle-forest. So they do. They like doing it.

They know who Venn is, though he's never before been here. One old man came along after supper and shook Venn's hand. Said he'd known Venn "as a puppy" (translated Shrin). And how were Jotto and the chickens?

This morning I was down watching the vrabburrs, when I saw two girls, both with flowering hair. One had white flower hair, one blue.

I saw another cat, too, with markings around the wrong way—white with a ginger understripe and tail.

"Shrin, she experimented here, didn't she?"

"Ustar?" (That's what they call her.) "Yes, she did. The village has many abilities."

"*Abilities?* Flowers instead of hair—"

"*With* hair," said Shrin firmly. Then she took me over to a neighbor and said something laughingly to this woman, who in turn laughed.

And then this woman—

This woman cleared her throat—I'd heard her speak; she sounded quite normal—and then she sang like a bird. I mean birds. I could hear finches and blackbirds, nightingales, larks—and other things, all *going at once,* even those yellow birds that go *clink.*

We've been here two days. Venn's been talking a lot with Burand and the elders of the village, Old Ladies and Gentlemen.

I wanted everything to drag on anyway. No rush to get to that Star.

Then Venn came in, just before supper, to my little room, where I was talking to Flollu.

"Claidi—may I sit down?"

"Try that stool carved like an anteater—*What is it?*"

He looked awful. As if all the good stuff of the village had been drained out of him very fast. And a lot more with it. He looked—looks—empty. And afraid.

"You don't understand the language here. I've kept hearing them say things like *When she was here, and then when she came back.*"

"You mean your mother? Well, she came here a lot, came back a lot, when she was working on the Star—"

"No, not like that. It's their tenses."

"Sorry, what?"

He scowled. The scowl faded. He was too distressed to be annoyed with my lack of education. "Past, present, that sort of thing."

"Mmm?"

"Claidi, they said that she came back. I thought I hadn't understood, myself. I'm rusty with their language. But I had. Came back in the sense of stayed. Not left."

"What?"

"Is still here."

We both sat there, staring at each other.

At last he said, "What I haven't grasped is if they've told her I'm here. I get the impression they haven't. *Can't.* But when I got it straight, I said,

Let me see her. And without hesitation they said, Yes, when would you like to?"

The warm evening was cold, for me.

"Is she in the Star?"

"No. It's a building on the flamingo lake."

"You're going?"

"Wouldn't you?"

Would I?

"I don't know. I never knew Twilight. I'm not even sure she *is* my mother. But if she was, she left me because she had no choice. I don't—I haven't a quarrel with her."

He put his head in his hands.

Then he got up and walked about such a lot that the wooden floor groaned, and Flollu gave a sort of snake sneeze and rippled out.

"They said they'd row me out tonight, after supper," Venn said. "So I won't be eating supper."

"No." My stomach, too, was churning.

Ustareth—*here.*

The Ustareth.

"Claidi—will you come with me?"

"Me?"

"For all the worst reasons. I'm afraid to meet her. Afraid of what I'll say and do—what I'll feel. Afraid I won't believe afterward I saw her at all."

"Isn't there a chance you and she might—make up?"

"No," he said. No rage. Just—an empty space.

HER

A tall villager rowed us over through afterglow and matching flamingos.

The water here was as thickly smooth as milk.

It was an island, small. Trees already heavy with night, and a house only visible between them. The house had a pointed roof, with indigo tiles, now turning black. No lights, no lit windows.

"Is she there?" Venn asked.

"Yes," said the villager. I knew that word by now at least.

"She doesn't put on the lights—or light a lamp."

"No, Venar Yllar."

Venn was like stone. Stone-voiced. Inside, I thought, churning like I was; worse, of course, much worse.

The boat scraped in on pebbles. Two or three more flamingos flushed up from the shore and flapped away.

We got out.

"Better wait," said Venn to the villager.

The villager shook his head. He said something and Venn said shortly, "Oh, all right."

"Where's he going?" I asked, as the man rowed off.

"He says he'll sit on the lake in his boat. Come back when we signal. Our meeting is to be *that* private."

The Star had risen. It was already going away, in over the jungles, toward the Rise. Shadows lengthening and closing like doors.

Venn turned and strode up the shale toward the dark house in the trees.

* * *

There *was* no door. That was the first thing. All the windows were one story up. Then, around the far side, fumbling now in blackness and starlight, there was a stair, which led up to one long window above. He put a foot on this stair, and the hard light came on, blinding us both.

Perhaps I should just have kept quiet, but I thought I ought to suggest this: "Venn, if we get in, and it's *her* house—suppose the rooms move?"

"Bar jar, lak sush," he grated.

I'm fairly sure this means "Shut up, you *@!# fool." So I shut up.

The light was in a glass tube by the window, and we went up to the windowpane and looked through into a dark hollow with a floor that gleamed like water. There was no furniture in the room, but a big something crouched there.

"What's that?"

"Claidi. It's a box."

There was no handle on the door. But after he spoke, the door just opened itself.

"It responds to a voice," he said.

"*Your* voice."

"Perhaps."

He walked in as I hung back, but then I thought the door might shut him in and me out, so I dove after him.

I expected a vrabburr or something behind every object, every curtain or screen, or chest. Nothing was there, though, not even a mouse, or a spider in a web.

Lights came on, and went out, as we moved from room to room.

All the rooms had only bits and pieces in them. They were clean, without dust, yet unlived in.

We did pass a bed, or a bed frame, in a side chamber. And in a bath-place, a long towel trailed over the side of the tub. Venn half went as if to pick it up, then moved quickly away. Probably she must have used it. *Her* towel.

But she was gone, long gone, as she had been from the Rise. Of course, I'd known it really, and perhaps so had he.

We wandered around. There was a wide room with lots of windows, and in the floor a pale burn. "I bet she worked in here, too. Spilled something," he said.

We stopped under a kind of tree, which was a lamp stand with many hanging china globes that didn't light up.

"This is pointless," he said. I didn't argue. Nor when he added, "But I'll just try up those steps there. . . ."

The steps wound around, and I kept thinking they'd suddenly lurch apart, like that stair behind her closet. But they didn't.

We came out into an annex, and there was a big wooden door ahead.

He and I stood looking at the door in the hard light.

"Might as well," he said. But he didn't go forward. "Claidi, Burand told me something—about this ring, the topaz. He said it could have done what their pipes did, to the vrabburrs."

"Why didn't it, then?"

"One has to—think *through* it—I wasn't sure what he meant. But it may be the same with your own ring."

"My ring wasn't made by Ustareth. It was Zeera's."

I thought, anyway, my ring hadn't helped me. When I was kidnapped—nothing.

Venn crossed to the door, opened it—it had an ordinary door handle—and walked into the room beyond.

I couldn't see much into the room. There was a brocade curtain hanging just inside. But a softer light had come on.

I'd just wait, until Venn came out, said, *That's that, then.* And we'd leave.

He didn't come out.

Had he found something fascinating after all? Something of *hers?*

After a couple of minutes I called cautiously, "Venn?"

But he didn't answer.

The sensible thing, of course, was not the thing I did. I ran forward and burst through the curtain.

There was a bench, and he was sitting on it. But I didn't really take that in.

Across the room, under another of the tree-lamps, this one all lighted up, sat a woman in a black chair.

She was dark; she had a smoky skin. Very dark hair in a long, thick braid, that fell over one shoulder and then hung to her ankles, ending in a golden ball. An ivory satin dress sewn with pearls. Which seemed familiar . . . No other jewelry, no rings on her fingers.

Ustareth wasn't beautiful; she was magnificent. She was like a dark lion.

I just stood there, in this scene to which I felt I didn't belong.

Then Venn spoke to me. Or to someone.

"She mostly used to wear plainer clothes at home. But I remember this dress. She wore it the day she left. I mean, left forever. She's wearing it now. That's what threw me, when you found the dress in the closet; in her room off the Little Book Room. How could it have been there, when she'd worn it the day she went away?"

The woman in the chair said nothing. Her night eyes burned, unmoving, unblinking. I had to look somewhere else.

"I thought then," said Venn quietly, "that she must have changed into other clothes somewhere in the gardens, and Jotto had brought the dress back to the palace, put it away, and forgotten it. After all, it's not what you'd expect a woman to wear traveling down through a jungle, is it?"

"No."

"Why don't you go over and meet her, Claidi. My—mother."

"Venn—"

"Go on. Shake her hand. I'm sure she won't mind."

I glanced back at—*her.*

She didn't look as if she minded. I stared, and I took a step forward. And then I somehow saw that what seemed to be slight movement in her was only my own swaying about. I saw she really didn't blink. She didn't even breathe.

She was dead!

No. Not dead. She'd never been alive.

I did go forward then and walked quickly over to her, all the time still expecting her to abruptly stop me in my tracks with some crisp comment, some regal gesture.

But she didn't. When I was inches away, still she didn't. She did look very—totally—real. Her skin, hair. Her eyes did, too, except for not moving. They shone so brightly. There was the faintest scent of perfume. And something chemical—as if she'd been handling things like that.

I could remember Argul saying sometimes Zeera's hands would faintly smell of herbs she'd mixed up, or even chemicals. He didn't mind, even when the herbs were bitter. It was her trade, her gift. He was proud of her.

Shake her hand, Venn had said.

So I leaned forward and picked up her hand. She was a little stiff, the way her arm moved. The lake damp must have gotten to her.

"She's a doll, isn't she?"

"Yes, Claidis."

"How vain," I said, scornful. "To make a doll just like herself—it *is* just like her, isn't it?"

"Exactly."

I let go of the doll's hand and looked at Venn.

"But it wasn't, Claidi, all that vain. Just common sense. Since the doll took her place."

"Yes, I see. You mean here in the village."

"No, I mean at the Rise. I mean . . ." He got up but didn't move forward. "I mean when she left. She left *this*—in her place."

"But you'd remember it, wouldn't you?" I said.

"I do remember it," he said. "I thought it was *her.*"

The roof might have just dropped in on me, on us. Or the whole room rushed off in a circle after all.

I jumped away from the doll of Ustareth in the chair.

"But how could you ever—she's a *doll*—"

"Think about Jotto," said Venn, stonily.

"Well, yes—but—"

"Jotto was an earlier model. With *this* one she got it perfect. Remember it—she—moved about. She spoke. She blinked her eyes, and *breathed.* And it was all mechanical."

I shook my head. To clear it mostly, which didn't work.

He said, "And she never let me near her after that. Never touched me. Most of the time I never even *saw* her—she'd speak only about seven words a month to me—only that wasn't her—it was this *thing.* Claidi—*this* even fooled *Jotto*—"

"Venn, if it's true—"

"It's true. Of course it's true. Her final joke on me. Not only did she leave me, but she left me—with *this* for my mother. I got the idea from the dress, you see," he said. "It's a little clever extra thing she did, to show me how to work it out. The pearl dress went with her, yet an identical *copy* of the dress was still at the Rise. Just like the identical copy of my mother."

"Venn—Venn, listen—you said it all happened—that she *changed*—when you were two—"

"It did. *You're two,* she said, and off she went, and I had *this.*"

"Venn, she left you when you were *two.*" I was so excited I couldn't stop the words. It wasn't the time to say them, but they had to be said, and probably no time would ever be right. "Venn, she's *Zeera.* She's Ustareth, and Zeera, too. She was your mother, and she was Argul's mother—you and he—you're brothers!"

"What?"

He'd turned toward me, stared at me now as I stared at him. I repeated what I'd said quite slowly.

Then I pieced it together, there in front of him, as we stood in the room on the lake, with that seated doll, whose clockwork had at last run down.

I didn't say everything I'm putting here, but he knows, of course. It was obvious enough.

She hadn't wanted her Tower husband, Narsident, and she hadn't wanted Venn, or she came not to want him. What she wanted was to escape the Rise, and the Law, and be free. So she did everything They'd said she must—grew the jungle, bred the animals. And for herself she made the doll.

I think perhaps she did wait until she thought Venn was all right. He was an extremely bright and clever little kid. She thought, *He can cope now.* And also she did something to the doll so it would run a lot longer. Seven years.

When it started to run down, it would leave, so Venn wouldn't see. Possibly she thought the doll would just stop somewhere in the forests and never be found. Or she made it come to Pearl Flamingo Village so that one day Venn might come across it and learn what she did—maybe she felt her lie had to end sometime.

She came here, I'm certain, on her real journey away, when Venn was two. At first I couldn't think why she hadn't used the Star to leave in. But anyway, she did leave. She reached the coast and went back to the land across the sea, the land she'd come from.

And somewhere there, she'd met, that year, the Hulta. She met Argul's father.

Venn's father was the man she didn't want. Argul's father was the man she chose. All I'd ever heard of Argul's parents had been how well they liked and loved each other. And if Venn was the son she didn't care about, Argul was the son she valued.

Venn knows that. I went all around avoiding it in what I said, but it's a fact. It must be.

She left Venn as soon as she could. Only death took her away from Argul.

Oh Venn—

Oh, Venn.

How I wish I could make it different, or at least lie really well and fool you.

And what do *I* think of her?

I can only say this: I despise Ustareth, fear and distrust her, yet I feel sorry for her. And Zeera—well, I've always loved her. She brought Argul into the world. And Ustareth and Zeera are the same person, but not for me. Not for any of us. Perhaps not even for herself.

It was when he said suddenly, shrugging it all off (which convinces me it's gone deep as deep inside him), "Why didn't she use the Star to get away?" that I did think of something else and say it.

"To start with, she left it here to go on working the Rise—the rooms, the food, and everything. But I think she thought you'd leave the Rise one day. I think—I think she left the Star for *you* to use—I mean, the window opened for *you.* So maybe"—I chanced it—"the Star was left for you to follow her."

"Well, it's too late for that, isn't it?"

"Yes, but—" It was truly difficult for me to say what I said next. I'm not sure why. "There's Argul," I said. "You're half-brothers. Oh, Venn, you look so alike."

"We don't." Haughty.

"You *do.* Your coloring is different, yes. Not your eyes, though—and so much else—I kept seeing it and didn't know why—"

Venn had said once that Argul was someone he'd *wished* he'd been like. Now Venn looked down his nose (like Argul). *I?* I, Prince Venarion Yllar Kaslem-Idoros—resemble a *barbarian?*

There seemed no point in going on with it.

I cast one last look at—*her* and went out.

I lingered by one of the other windows until Venn followed me, about an hour later.

We went down through the house.

Lights blazed on, blanked out.

"I hate this kind of light," he said. "You see too much, but it never looks real."

The door, which had shut, opened when he spoke to it, and closed again when we were outside.

A moon was rising, shining on the lake, turning the flamingos to snow. We could just make out the boat, with the man sitting, waiting.

What do the villagers know about all this? Are they in on her trick? I don't somehow think so. To them, she was always mysterious, a scientist, magician. They must have realized the doll isn't her—and yet, in some magical way, it *is*. Maybe for them that makes sense, and they think it will for Venn. Because they're not bad, not underhanded themselves, or cunning. So maybe they don't see it in others.

"Tomorrow," Venn said, "we'll get up to the plateau on the little cliff. Get you to the Star."

"Er, yes. Thanks."

Should I have said, *then,* "If it *can* sail, the Star, please come with me. I'd like you to. You're important to me, even if you weren't to *her*. And he will want to know you, too—"

But it seemed, then, that Venn might have said, "I'm only important to you, Claid*is,* since I remind you of him. As for Argul and myself, we'd probably kill each other on sight."

Actually, I brilliantly said, "Oh look, the moon's coming up."

And Venn carelessly replied, "Moonlight. Now there *is* a light."

THE STAR

Two hours before dawn, we set out.

It—the Star—hadn't yet reappeared above the village. (The time it took did vary, no one knows why, or seems to care.)

Venn said, "I want to be up there, on the plateau, ready, when it lands."

I didn't, really. But then, I was afraid of it.

And he was, too, and that was why he wanted to confront it. Because it was too late to confront *her.*

The village had been very silent. No one much about.

If it was possible, I'd be robbing them of their Star. No one had said anything about that. Shrin kissed Venn on the cheek. But Burand bowed.

Flollu the snake was in his basket (yes, he had a basket). He didn't open an eye when I said good-bye to him.

We'd had about three hours' sleep. Well, I had. Maybe Venn didn't sleep at all.

I expected him to be bad-tempered and unpleasant, like before, but he wasn't. On the rough bits of the climb he was patient and helpful. Gentle. He didn't say much.

I'd thought it would all be a tough climb up the little cliff, but there was a paved path, some steps, also level places where you could just walk normally.

The Pearl Flamingans had been here for days, though, apparently clearing away undergrowth to make it easy for us. Generally they didn't ever go up there—it's a sort of sacred spot. Even that morning, the very last part of our climb, Venn did have to cut a way through. The helpful villagers still hadn't gone up beyond a certain point.

We emerged at the top, and the sky was pale, and some birds were calling. The lake spread far below, spoon-silvery. A big wave crinkled there—flamingos.

"Here it is," he said.

So I had to look upward instead. The predawn sky was so pale, too, from the return of the Star.

It was stealing in across the vast clearing where the village lies, and it hung quite low. It cast not only light but the shadow of itself, like a ghost. This slipped over the trees, the roofs, over the water. . . . Soon it would fall on us.

I'd been looking down again.

I looked up. Was shocked.

Now it was the size of all my hand, when I held my hand up to see. And now—already it was bigger. It was so bright—the hard light Ustareth had made must fill it up inside.

All the chestnut-case prickles on it looked sharp as knives, but other things stuck out of it, too—bright rods and curved bright sticks and things like little shiny saucers—but they must all be much larger, if you were close.

They were.

The Star was sliding home now into the sky above the plateau. It was growing ever bigger.

And the shadow covered us, very black, all the light left out beyond the shadow's edge.

Only when the shadow shifted did I admit I'd thought we were going to be crushed and that Venn wouldn't move in time—

The Star sank, weightless as a ball of fog. As it met the cliff-top, a slight vibration ran through the rock under our feet. That was all.

It was about—a hundred?—feet from us. Now I saw that it was, after all, only about the size of a small house—smaller than the one on the island.

And then, to me the weirdest thing of all: all its light went suddenly out. The whole Star had been switched off, like one of the Rise lamps.

"Let me go first," said Venn.

"Why don't we walk together?"

"And why can't you act more like a lady?" he asked sadly.

"I've said, because I'm not a lady."

We strode boldly forward, trembling.

About ten yards away, and with no warning, a round opening happened up in the side of the Star.

Venn and I both stopped dead. And I'm afraid I squeaked.

"Get behind me, Claidi."

"Why?"

"*Claidi*—"

It was too late anyway. There was a kind of ramp coming out, and something was coiling down it, out of the Star.

"Oh, it's only a snake."

"Claidi, don't be a complete—it *isn't* a snake."

"But it's just like a—"

Well, it was. A bit.

A dull-silver, flexible, legless thing, snake*like* (like Flollu). But now the head was raised, and two dawn-pale eyes regarded us. The head was human, almost.

"Dowth ti nali?" asked the head.

In Pearl Flamingan, that means *Can I help you?*

Venn said something to it.

"What did you say?" I hissed.

"I asked if it was friendly."

"Suppose it says it isn't?"

"It's a machine. If it says it isn't, we can believe it. And the opposite."

The machine-snake spoke again, now in crystal tones, the language of the Towers; the Rise; the House.

"Good morning, lady and gentleman. I am perfectly friendly, also indestructible. The Princess Ustareth made me. My name is Yinyay. Would you care to visit the also friendly and indestructible ship?"

Yinyay is a doll, a mechanism, obviously. The voice is slightly more female than male. Faultless. It even pauses as if taking a breath—as Jotto did. (As the Ustareth-doll must have done.)

The face of Yinyay is quite beautiful in its way and is surrounded by a long silky mop of tinsel "hair." The hair is part of the mechanism. Sometimes it grows very long, shoots into a corner (the corners are rounded, but never mind), delicately pulls out a tiny beetle or snail, which has accidentally gotten into the Star (ship), then carefully puts it outside.

It chases moths away from the light the same way.

Venn and I both felt funny about going after Yinyay up the ramp, into Her Star-which-is-a-ship.

"Would you like some tea?" asked Yinyay.

"No," said Venn.

"Thanks anyway," I said.

"It's a machine," said Venn. "You don't have to be polite to it."

"What about Jotto?"

"That isn't the same."

Yinyay waited without comment as we argued, still on the threshold. Then it glided back inside the Star.

We stayed at the top of the ramp, staring in.

I'll describe the Star now; I might as well.

Really it is only about the size of one very large room, that is, the top half is, but there's the lower part, underneath, where machines are stored and the stuff that makes the Star able to move, to rise and "set."

The upper room is mostly what Yinyay has said is the Deck (like on an ocean ship). It's all made—walls, floor, ceiling—of this pearly metal. I think it's metal, I haven't asked.

The space is circular, and around three circular "sides" are padded benches, with sort of metal desk-things against the walls. These are—or have—"controls." Yinyay controls them . . . or they control themselves?

You can maybe almost guess that I don't understand at all, really.

Ustareth had a room here, too, to conduct her experiments—I don't know where that was. In the lower half, perhaps. Unless it was all done at her house on the lake.

The strangest thing of all is that you can see out of the three round sides above the controls, but only when Yinyay does something to them. It's possible to make them respond to just a voice, Yinyay says. At the moment they don't.

When Yinyay told us this, it seemed to gaze expectantly at Venn. I asked myself if Yinyay somehow knows Venn is *her* son. I didn't feel I could ask.

On the fourth rounded wall are doors that open when you go up to them and say "Open!" These doors run sideways into the walls. (I'd never seen a door do that.)

Behind is an area with a couch, and something that supplies food, and a bathroom area, and some cupboards with books in them, and also "instruments"—all of which look like nothing on earth to me. But Venn took ahold of one weird thing and exclaimed, all pleased, "An Astrolabe!" However, I've no idea what he meant or what it is, or even if I've spelled it right.

Altogether, though, there wasn't that much to see, once we'd forced ourselves to go in.

Venn began to ask about the lower part under the floor (if it is a floor) and could he go down and see the machines in there. But Yinyay said it was sorry, but only *it* could worm through a special hatch. "The magnets are located there," announced Yinyay.

I have no notion what that is all about. But it seems the magnets make the ship able to "fly" and to land.

Venn appeared to grasp this. No one explained. (And if they had, I doubt if I'd have understood, so I didn't nag.)

Then Venn asked the Huge Question.

"This craft—can its direction be altered? Can you guide it across the sea, for example?"

"Of course," said Yinyay. "That is this ship's main purpose, Prince Venarion."

(So Yinyay did know who he was. A little later, Venn said to me that Ustareth must have stored such information, and recognition, in the Star, and/or Yinyay.)

Mostly, though, we were just astounded. Floored by the frightening simplicity of changing EVERYTHING.

As we were standing there, gawping at each other, Yinyay said it would now go and see to the something-or-other, which I can't remember properly. It glided off. Yinyay is also *sensitive,* I mean to human moods.

(I can't go on saying "It." Apart from anything else, it's confusing—see what I mean. I'm afraid I refer to Yinyay as "she," so I'll write Yinyay as she.)

Anyway Venn led me over to one of the benches and we sat down.

It was very quiet, but for birdsong outside. Below the ramp, through the opening that Yinyay hadn't closed up, we saw that the sun had risen. Little sparrows were pecking about only a foot or so from the Star.

Before Venn could speak, I said, "Could it be lying?" (Yinyay was still *it,* then.)

"The machine? No."

"Then—she did mean you to sail—fly—on this Star. She must have done."

He looked at me. One of the long looks that sometimes he gave me, long, long looks, to make up for all the quick looks, the sidelong glances.

"If she wanted that, it hasn't happened."

"You don't trust the Star."

"Oh, I trust the Star completely. And this doll-snake. I trust Yinyay."

"Then—"

"For you. With you. I'd trust you to be safe. It'll take you—home, Claidi."

All this time, I hadn't felt that. Probably I hadn't believed it could happen. And even now I didn't. Yet my heart sort of woke up and shook itself, with one great thud.

Home. The Hulta.

Argul. Argul.

I felt hot with joy, and then so cold, as if a fire had gone out inside me. I saw I was afraid of going back. Not the journey—but afraid of going back to my life as it had been. To him.

But why—why—

Why am I so afraid half the time. I just *won't* think of it. So I imagine seeing Teil and Dagger, of riding Siree, of laughing at some witty put-down of Blurn's. But Argul—isn't there. . . .

I now know that he, too, astonishingly, has Tower blood. He's related to *Nemian*—to *Ironel*—another of her grandsons! But it isn't that. Somehow that's easy to ignore.

Even in my head, I can't quite see him. It's like how, sometimes in the blackest of nights, you catch a glimpse of something out of the corner of your eye, but when you turn, you can't make it out at all—

"Come with me," I said to Venn. Boldly, as I'd strode up to the Star—and shaking like then.

"No, Claidi."

"Of course, you don't want to leave the others? If the Star can be made to do different things, we can land it at the Rise, pick them up, too—"

"No, Claidi."

"*She* went over the sea, Venn."

"And I shan't. Can't, Claidi. I can't."

"Why not?"

He shook his head. He looked away. Then he said, "When I wickedly stole your book and read it, I came to know you. In the only way I ever can come to know anyone, now. By reading about you, you became real for me. And—more than real. I've behaved like a pig all the way here. Do you know why? Of course you do; it's the only reason you put up with me. I don't want to lose you. To be without you."

"Then—"

"But worse than that fear is the other fear. The fear of a world—of people. All of them real. And no book to read on them to put me right."

I said, "But it won't be like that. Not once you—"

He said—with his black eyes, Argul's eyes, on the desk controls that neither of us really understood—"I'm the unreal one. Just leave me where I am, where I can get by."

I said, not meaning to almost, "Argul—"

"Oh, Argul. Yes. And Argul is also the best reason of all for my staying here."

"Why?"

"Why do you think, Claidi?"

"But—"

Then he met my eyes. His did what they do in books: they *flamed.* "You both preferred Argul. Ustareth *and* Claidi. I can't—I damn well *won't* try to compete with *that.*"

Then he got up.

And I jumped up.

"Don't leave me here—not yet—"

"No, I'm going to talk to it—Yinyay. It's all right."

And he walked to the doors that open when you say "Open!" and went through, to where Yinyay was all coiled up around one of the cupboards, her hair in the ceiling (dusting?), and the door shut.

Everything did change that night. For everyone. In the village. At the Rise. For us. For me.

Yinyay served tea in a while, without anyone saying how thirsty we were. And some cakes and fruit, too.

She, Yinyay, sat coiled by the rest-area table, and when we reached for anything, a tinsel strand of hair would get longer and lift the plate or pot and serve us.

I can't remember what was said, much, at first.

He and she talked a lot about the ship which is a Star. Sometimes Yinyay showed how things worked, and I tried to concentrate. I might need to know.

I was angry with Venn. And that wasn't fair.

And I was sorry.

And.

Presently, in a silence, I asked Yinyay what would happen to the mechanisms at the Rise. No one else had bothered.

"I shall alter the circuits," said Yinyay. "Nothing need be upset at all."

"One thing, please," said Venn. "*Please* upset one thing."

Then Yinyay said, "You want to stop the rooms of the palace moving. Nothing easier, prince. Princess Ustareth left memory for me that it might be required."

And I said, "What else did she leave as memory—about Venn?"

Perhaps I shouldn't have. It wasn't my business. Venn wouldn't let it be.

And Venn said, "Yinyay, I don't want to know. *Nothing* about Ustareth. And I don't want Lady Claidis to know, either. Understood?"

Yinyay's hair fluffed up, then settled.

"I have wiped it away," was what Yinyay said.

A doll-machine—so calm. I felt my eyes bulging with a cry I didn't make.

Venn only said, "Yes."

Yes.

So he'll never know, and I won't. Not from Yinyay or the ship.

But as for the Rise, it seems everything will be as before—except the rooms won't move again. Which seems peculiar, I'd gotten so used to it.

Then Yinyay made a suggestion. (She does sometimes.)

"Since the ship is now to go elsewhere, there's no need to observe the circling route tonight. Would you prefer that?"

So the Star could stay on the cliff. This one night. And at the Rise, when they saw it didn't come over—they'd know we had found it. Know I would go away. Although maybe they'd never doubt that Venn wouldn't go with me.

He'd said that the villagers would see him back to the Rise. They could travel the jungle-forest in safety. He was glad, he said; they might start to visit the palace again, as they had in his childhood.

Doesn't he see, the villagers are people, too—and he isn't nervous with *them.*

But then, they're not the Hulta. Ustareth left the village, too. That must make the difference.

He stayed and dined with me on the Star. Neither of us ate much, but it was a nice dinner. Even if all the dishes came out of a slot in the wall.

Moths rushed to the cool light in the ship, and Yinyay's hair fluttered them out again.

The village, too, would miss the Star rise tonight.

After we ate, he took me for a walk along the little cliff-top.

"Stretch your legs while you can. Yinyay says it will take ten days at least to get you back."

The Star won't be fast. Slow, gracious travel. They've decided that will be more comfortable for me.

We didn't discuss what I should do with this ship once I arrive. That is, once I've found the Hulta—who may have gone anywhere, particularly if they're searching for me.

I *tried* to ask Venn what he wanted me to do with the ship.

He wouldn't talk about the ship.

He kept on telling me things about the jungle. What tree that one was, over there. And that huge moth, and that flower, which had opened on the rock, and smelled of caramel.

All day we'd been in the Star. Now he showed me the stars above.

"That one's called the Queen," said Venn.

It wasn't that large or bright, but unusual; it had a violet glow.

Then he said, "Ask Yinyay to show you the portraits, from the memory bank."

"Whose portraits?"

"Anyone's."

I thought nothing could be further off from mattering.

All the while we were there, walking about, and inside the ship before, I had this ache of tension, knowing any second he'd say, "And now I'm going down the cliff." He'd say, "And now I'm going, Claidi. Good-bye."

And then, under a tree, the ship-Star gleaming not far off, and the mauve star overhead, he said, "I'm going now, Claidi. Good-bye, Claidi."

I took a breath. I turned to him and held out my hand.

He took my hand.

Then he leaned and kissed my cheek. (The way Shrin kissed him in the village.) His hair brushed my skin.

"Farewell," he formally said. He turned and walked away. At the beginning of the path down the cliff he turned. "Claidi!"

I couldn't answer.

He called to me across the dark, "*Break the rules!*" And was gone.

How happy I should be. I am. Sort of.

It's been three days now, just time enough, as we sail-fly, to write everything up, sitting in the sunlight through the three cleared walls, as blurred, green ground and blurred, pleated emerald sea flicker, miles and miles below.

Yinyay does everything. Is even all right to talk to. When I want to talk.

I did ask to see some portraits, that first night, when I couldn't sleep.

Millions of pictures—like paintings, but not quite—passed before me on a kind of stiff sheet that ran up from the floor. Wonderful-looking people in fabulous clothes and jewels.

Who were they all? Families of the Towers.

Eventually I did think and asked to see Jizania from the House. And so I saw Jizania as a young bride, in her wedding dress of gold, with Wasliwa Star, her husband.

Do I wish they *were* my grandparents?

Well, yes. I'd be crazy not to.

She got more beautiful when she was old, but even so, she had a lot of style as a girl, Jizania Tiger. Her hair was fine and golden, like her dress. Wasliwa was a handsome, impressive black man—nearly seven feet tall! He towered above her in his garments of russet and thunder-blue, his head shaved like polished mahogany. So I wondered if her baldness was a tribute to him, in the House when she was old. (If I *am* her grandchild, she must have been so *old* when she had my mother—it doesn't seem likely.)

I can't claim they are my grandparents. I don't know who I am.

There was no portrait of Twilight.

I've taken off Argul's ring.

I feel awful about that. But the ring itself *worries* me now. Ustareth must have used it to get through the jungles. What powers does it have? And on this, Yinyay was hopeless. Didn't know a thing—of course, thanks to Venn, since helpful memories of Ustareth have been "wiped away."

I keep the diamond in my bag. It lies next to this book and the new one Yinyay produced for me yesterday, seeing me writing, and how near I was to the end of all the pages.

Which in a way is the oddest thing of all. That my life has now filled it up. This entire book.

And I thought before, after I escaped the City, everything had been sorted out, and I wouldn't write anymore.

Now I'm glad I have the other book. The new book . . . ready. (I got Yinyay to check it for Tags. Unnecessary, but I was glad she did.) Perhaps tomorrow I'll start on it. Describe the journey back. Try to find something interesting to tell you, my poor friend, who I've dragged all this great distance.

Yinyay just came and said it's dinner. (Rather like a mother, in some way. But I never knew my mother, so how can I be sure?)

I shall squeeze this in. There's no room for more than a few lines.

We'll reach the land I came from. I'll find the Hulta. I'll find Argul. Maybe I'll see him from the air, even, riding his horse, his black hair flying back like wings, and his fierce face, which I can't quite remember, raised to meet this falling star.

And once he sees me, too, once our eyes meet, then—then it will be all right. Despite the Towers and the Law, and despite Ustareth who was Zeera. Despite Venn. Argul is my family, all I need. Once our eyes meet, I'll be home.

Wolf Queen

To Beverley Birth—
who has been a best friend to these books

UP IN THE AIR.

Traditional

CONTENTS

THIS NEW BOOK

The world is so far below, down there.

Sometimes I feel this ship will never land there again.

It's the first time we've *crossed* land for nine days. Before that it was just water—the ocean, day after day and every night. And this is the first entry I've made in this new book, which is to be my new diary-journal-whatever.

There's a sunset starting now. The sky is a deep *sky*-blue, with biscuity-gold high clouds above, quite still. But a wind from the land has blown one different, low, large red cloud toward us, and now the cloud has wrapped right around the ship. We've been in the cloud for several minutes, since we sail-fly very slowly. It's like being in a rose-red fog.

When I was writing on the last page of the *last* book, I said I'd describe my journey in this Star—this sky-ship.

Only, as I say, until now there wasn't much to see. Only the water. Too high to make out anything definite, except, sometimes, in sunshine, altered colors in the sea like drifting dyes.

Before the sea, there was just the top of the jungle.

This coast, when we reached it, looked bare and bleak at first. Then there were forests—Yinyay says that's what they are.

As the light goes, the forests seem to be separating.

A broad river flashed below in the last twilight gleam. And—how odd—I saw the small shadow of the Star, in which I am, pass over the river's surface.

The main thing is, I have to find Argul. Which means finding the Hulta.

And then, once I've told him properly what happened, well I—we—have to think of some way to be safe. Because if the Wolf Tower sent kidnappers after me once, why not a second time? Or will they just think now I'm too much trouble, not worth the effort, and leave me alone?

Somehow, leaving the Rise, I never thought about this possibly ongoing threat from the Wolf Tower.

But I was very muddled, particularly about Venn.

I'm still muddled about Venn.

He's Argul's half-brother. I keep reminding myself of that. That's why they look so alike, and that was why I sort of fell for Venn. Yes, I did fall for him. (Can say that now he's miles away.)

But there was absolutely nothing between us, beyond the polite good-bye kiss he gave me.

I kept wondering today if we would miss signs of the Hulta, because we're up so high. But when I spoke to Yinyay, she said the machines on the Star will spot the Hulta instantly.

"How?" I asked.

"You have told me a great deal about them," said Yinyay. "This information is fed into the ship, which, even now, is alert to seek and recognize them."

"Even from up here?"

"Of course."

The Star-ship is incredible and can do so much—rising and landing, lighting itself at night, making food, judging a thousand and one things perfectly.

And Yinyay herself, being mechanical, is sort of part of the ship—*linked* to the ship, the way Venn's mother, Ustareth, made her to be. Though Yinyay looks like a silvery doll snake (quite a large one, standing on her tail taller than me) with a sweet face and voice, and though she does nice, helpful, funny things, like handing you a cup of tea held in her extended hair—Yinyay is massively powerful, too. *Reliable.* So I believed her. If the Hulta are down there, the Star will "recognize" them.

Later she even said something about the Star's having worked out the most likely places for the Hulta to be, right now, taking into consideration what had happened, how long I'd been gone, and their ways of traveling generally. Which means we stand an even better chance of tracking them down.

So, nothing to worry about at all.

Dinner just came, as always, out of a slot in the silver-pearly wall.

It's dark now, that red cloud left far behind.

Through the cleared curved window-walls at the "front" of the Star, I can watch all night, if I want, while sitting on a comfortable padded bench.

Maybe I'll see the tiny lights of settlements, towns, or villages down on the ground. Maybe I'll see—the lights of the Hulta camp, the little fires and lamps, and the big central fire where they hold their councils, and maybe even (unseen by me at this distance) Argul will actually be standing there, their leader, tall and straight and bright with gold, his long black hair gleaming.

I have found Argul! We are together again! Perhaps the very next thing I write here will be that. Why oh why don't I think it will be?

HULTA WELCOME

It was the Star, of course, that found them. I wasn't even watching at the time, but in the bathroom, soaking determinedly in a warm, scented bath. (Trying to calm down.)

I shot out when Yinyay told me, didn't wait for the warm air-jets to dry me properly, flung on clothes and ran into the main area with my hair wringing wet.

"Where? Where???"

This was three and a half days after my first entry in this book. It was afternoon, and below lay a sunny flatness, a plain, with occasional greenish puffs that must be woods, or the last of the forest.

"Wherewherewhere— "

"There!"

I couldn't see anything that made any sense. (It had also been mostly impossible for me to see anything identifiable, by night or day, even lights, unless there were hundreds of them together.) However, Yinyay now guided me, and then I saw a far-off splodge, like more woods only browner.

"Is that—?"

"That is."

The Star began to descend, a little slantingly, toward the splodge.

The splodge in turn began to excite and upset me so much I was shaking, and water drops spun off my washed hair all over the room, so soon it looked as if rain had fallen.

Yinyay extended her own tendrilly hair, which can do lots of useful things, and soft drying waves of heat played over mine. But I couldn't stay still.

I ran about, from curved window to window. And then I ran away, thinking I ought to fetch something—what?—and then back again.

All this while, the Star flew on and down nearer to—

The Hulta.

I could see licks of color in the brownness now, suggestions of movement—the roll of wheels and wagons, trot and pull of horses, running of dogs and children—

Oh God. At last. But—I wasn't ready—

"How long do I have?" I cried. "I mean, before we get close—land—"

"Some twenty and one-quarter minutes," said Yinyay, precisely.

"Oh—no—that's not long enough—I must—I have to—"

What did I "have to"? Nothing. I had packed my bag; even this book (and the last book) were in there, and about nine million ink pencils of various kinds. And anyway, nothing had been said about the Star's rushing away the moment I stepped out. Yinyay had already told me the Star would simply land and wait, until I came back and told it what I wanted next.

What would the Hulta think, when they saw the Star, a great spiky starry thing, bowling along the sky, by day, violently sparkling from the sun, a planet presumably come unfixed from outer space?

Would the kids be scared? The well-trained, well-loved dogs start howling? Would Argul ride between his people and the Star, strong and wonderful and *good,* to protect them, with Blurn, his second-in-command, black and handsome, wild, brave, and over-the-top, at his side?

"Can't we go any *faster?*" I now blathered.

"It's best," said Yinyay, gently, "not to descend too quickly. The magnets are most efficient when at leisure."

The magnets are how the Star rises and descends. Have never understood this—and right then everything Yinyay said sounded ridiculous.

But I just rushed away again and then rushed back again.

And then I just kneeled on a bench, craning over the steely desk that has controls in it, and peered down and down at the splodge getting bigger, and becoming the Hulta.

Suddenly, I could see it had *become* the Hulta. There they were. Tiny as fleas, but really there.

Then I even made out some of the wagons I knew, from various marks. Like Badger's wagon, which had a long patched tear in the leather top, where a bough once fell in a storm, and one of the women's wagons, too, which I'd once shared, and which was painted across with stripes.

Obviously by now the Star had been seen in turn.

Face upon face, small as grains of rice, staring up. Kids I could just see, pointing. Riders riding in to form a kind of ring around children and animals, An abrupt spark here, there, *there*—which were sun-catching knives being drawn, and bells and disks shaken on bridles as horses reared.

Yes, I'd been stupid.

"Yinyay, can we stop, please, I mean stop the Star."

Yinyay did something with her hair on the desks. We stopped.

"I don't want to go any closer like this. It's scaring people and causing too much bother. In fact—Yinyay, sorry, but can we back right off?"

We were lifting, ascending, retreating.

The crowds of rice-grain faces were folding back into—a splodge.

"Let's come down—say, over there? Is that all right? Then I can go across to them on foot. Look, it's downhill. It'll only take me half an hour. And . . . I could do with a walk."

I tried to sound organized and efficient. I was cursing myself for my selfish idiocy, putting myself first, not thinking. Frightening my friends with this big, terrifying sky-object.

In the confusion, I hadn't had a chance to find Argul, there among all those toy wagons and toy humans. If I had, would he, too, have looked only like that? Like a tiny, moving toy?

We landed, smooth as silk. Inside ten minutes I was walking downhill, through some rather odd trees with no leaves, but covered in something like green foam—

Then I met the Hulta head-on.

That is, I met twenty Hulta, seventeen men and three women, on horseback and with drawn weapons. The front four men had rifles, pointing ready at me. And the first of these men was Blurn.

"*Clll—aidii*—oh yarollakkus," said Blurn, on a long, astonished, sighing-boom.

I thought, I've never heard *that* before, yarollakkus. Probably rude. I didn't ask.

"Hi, Blurn," I said shyly. Feeling a total fool. Back five seconds, and already I'd caused all this fuss.

Over their shoulders I could see the Hulta wagons down-slope, in a defensive huddle.

"What in—what are you *doing* here?" asked Blurn.

"Blurn, I'm sorry, it was stupid to arrive like that. I was rattled and didn't think. *Sorry.*"

He gaped at me and I at him.

"What do you mean what am I *doing* here?"

"I mean what the hell are you doing here."

Something reached me then, at last.

Something I had never felt from, or among, the Hulta, not even at the very start, although, at the very start, I hadn't known I hadn't. What I mean is, I had thought, when I first met the Hulta, they were murderer-bandits and insane. (None of which was true.) But I'd assumed they would therefore be dangerous. Half-imagined they were, until I learned otherwise.

Now—they *were* dangerous.

I looked at them, and all at once I saw how it wasn't any more simply that they'd been unnerved, expecting to have to fight and guard their people from a skyborne alien threat. It wasn't even astonishment at my abrupt return, or annoyance at my thoughtlessness.

No. It was—

It was dangerous, unliking, *angry, hating* hostility.

"Blurn . . . ," I said, uncertainly.

All right. All right, Claidi. Hey," said Blurn, turning back to the others, "how about giving her and me a bit of room?"

And then one of the men spoke.

Most of the men there I didn't know that well—I'd looked in vain for Ro or Mehmed. But this was Badger, whose wagon I had seen. Badger, who I did know quite well.

"Don't trust the rotten little okkess," said Badger, giving me a *look*—what a *look*—and then turning in his saddle and spitting on the ground.

I went cold as ice. It wasn't from my wet hair.

And, well, I knew what *okkess* meant. Not many women would want a friend to call them that.

I just stood there.

Blurn said, "I said, I'll deal with it. Claidi? Walk over there with me, will you?"

They sat their horses and watched as Blurn dismounted, and he and I walked aside along the slope. Some of them kept their rifles pointed at the place where the Star had landed. One of the women stared at me, and when I looked back, I saw it was Ashti, Blurn's partner, who had always been so nice to me. Who had gone to the pool with me that morning of my wedding day, the day when I was captured and carried off—and Ashti's face was like a dark stone mask.

Her face was worse than the name Badger had called me.

I felt sick. But I didn't know why I should.

So I halted and turned and caught hold of Blurn's arm. And he picked my hand off with dreadful quiet strength.

He still wore his hair in all those scores of glorious braids. His eyes were like polished bullets.

"Blurn, I don't know why you're acting like this." He just looked at me. "Why is everyone—like this? Is it because of the Star—the ship—I said I was sorry—"

"*That* thing," he said, as if I'd mentioned some old wreck of a wagon I'd arrived in.

I hesitated, swallowed. I said, "All right. Just take me to see Argul."

Then Blurn flung back his head and he laughed. He laughed like crazy, and the sky reeled.

"Argul is not, at present, here."

"Then where?"

Something seemed after all to break through his eyes. He said, "Claidi, are you really so tronking daft that you don't know what you did to him?"

"What?—what *I* did—"

"Left him. Like that. You couldn't even tell him to his face, could you, that you were through? Did you think he'd attack you? He wouldn't have gone near you. You're stupid all right. Real stupid, Claidi."

I stopped looking at Blurn because that wasn't helping. Looking at anything was a problem. The trees were all covered with this bubbling frothy stuff And the Hulta were bursting with hatred. I shut my eyes and said, "Look, Blurn, I didn't *want* to leave Argul. Some air balloons came over and some very big men in uniform, from the Wolf Tower City, grabbed me and dragged me off. I did my best, but there was no one who could help. Didn't Ashti tell you? She was *there.*"

"Yeah. All the women told us. The balloons and how you all ran. Then they thought you'd got left behind."

"I *had* been. In a net. Then I was tied up in the balloon and up in the sky. I'll tell you the rest later."

"No, thanks. We know the rest. A friend, you see, of your *best pal* from the Tower—he told us."

I tried to hold on. "I don't have pals from the Tower. Who was it?"

"Look, girl," said Blurn, "in a minute they're going to come over and skin you. Get in your flashy star-thing and go away."

I'm hardly brilliant, but even I could see something had seemed to happen that hadn't. But I was shocked—so shocked even the panic wasn't boiling up in me yet. I sounded nearly calm as I said, "At least tell me where Argul is."

"Could be anywhere. After you dumped him, he left the Hulta in my charge and went off by himself. That was months ago, Claidi. None of us have seen him since then."

Calm went. "But didn't you try to stop him?" I screamed.

"You couldn't stop Argul, when he'd really decided. Besides, Hulta law says that if a leader doesn't want to lead anymore, he gives it up. So I'm leader now, which I never wanted. He was my friend!"

Away along the slope Ashti called suddenly in a clear stone voice, "Do you want *me* to see to her, Blurn?"

He turned and shook his head at her. To me he said, "I tell you, Claidi, I was surprised at you. Going off with that okk Nemian again, after the way he was last time."

I nearly jumped out of my body into one of the weird trees. I spluttered. I cried, *"Nemian*—I wouldn't touch Nemian with a six-man-height-length flagpole for goodness sake—Is *this* what you think? I ran off and left Argul on our wedding day because I *wanted* to? Wanted to be with *Nemian* in the *Wolf Tower?* Are you *mad?"*

"Are *you?*" he said.

I shivered.

"I think you must be. Look, I *know,* so there's no point you lying. You see, this dupp from the Tower turned up soon after you went. He swanned in with his little escort and told us the lot. He said you were done with us. And if we didn't believe him, look in your diary-book, which you'd carelessly left in the rush to get back to Nem. And yes, I've read your book. You'd written it out plain enough. On and on about how you really wanted Nemian, couldn't stop thinking of him, and Argul was all right, you'd put up with him. Second best. And then you just couldn't help it, you sent this loveletter to Nemian—"

"I NEVER sent any—"

"And they got you word he'd send someone along. And how you wanted to go to that pool because you knew the balloon could get down to you there easily, none of us around to get in the way. Pity you left the diary, eh? Or we'd never have completely believed a story like that."

"I didn't leave my diary behind. It went with me. So what *diary* are you talking about?"

"The book you were always scribbling in."

"What you found wasn't that—wasn't *mine.* I can *show* you my diary. They must somehow have made one like it. Dropped it in the right place to be found."

"It was in your writing. Even I knew it. And Argul certainly did."

Argul—I had to do something—but I was shaking so hard suddenly that all that came out was stammering.

I was trying to tell him that the Towers, the Rise, could do incredible things—make copies probably of handwriting, diaries that would seem to be the original diary. And it sounded lame. Absurd. I knew he didn't believe me.

Blurn folded his arms. It was like gazing at a bolted door. He said, "Where's the ring Argul gave you?"

I stood there and said nothing. I knew I couldn't explain to him why I had taken the ring off. He wouldn't believe that either. Anything I said, he wouldn't believe, even if I said the sky was blue.

I felt as I sometimes had when I was quite little, in the House. Utterly hopelessly powerless. At the mercy of rules I didn't understand and people who didn't ever want to bother to understand me. It was like that. And worse, because Blurn had been my friend, and Argul's friend, and Blurn hated me. And I couldn't find any more words.

"I've had enough of you, girl," he said then. "If that star-ship junk isn't going to bother us, get back in it and clear off."

He turned. He strode along the slope, making as he went a sweeping signal to the others.

I watched them go, without a single backward glance at me. And there I was alone, under those disgusting frothy trees.

MIDNIGHT DAGGER

Someone else has read my diary. Like Venn did. Funny really—since this time, it *wasn't* MY diary at all.

I have been trying and trying for hours, crouched here in the closed-off area of the ship, to put it all together.

The Wolf Tower grabbed me so they could punish me, then they were double-crossed by someone else, who captured me instead. Either way, it was against my will. I was shipped (by a real sea-ship) to the Rise, and stuck there, till Venn helped me reach this Star and come back here.

Blurn and the Hulta, though—and that means Ashti, Teil, Toy—all of them—think this: I left willingly to go by balloon back to Nemian, that utter creep, and live in his City with him.

And someone—the Wolf Tower—or that other unknown lot who took me away from the Wolf Tower's men and sent me to the Rise—left a diary so like mine it convinced even Argul. Argul has never read my diary. But he often saw it. Saw me writing in it. Knows my writing. And this *fake* diary is written in my writing—or so near, they didn't see any difference.

And the fake diary says I loved Nemian. Wrote to Nemian and told him so. And he arranged for me to be with him.

Next thing, I appear again, in the Star, which I suppose the Hulta think is also from the City.

And Argul—

Argul thinks I am with Nemian, whom I love.

Oh no.

They all hate me. And—it's all because of a lie.

This is like the Rise, when Venn believed their lies about me—the lies of the Tower, or someone who signed themselves "We."

Also, it's much worse. Because these people were my friends. They were the first and only family I ever had.

Am I guilty in some peculiar way? Is it . . . because I fell—not for Nemian—but for Venn?

No. *Rubbish.*

I didn't fall for him *that* hard.

Why does the Wolf Tower, or whoever it is, *want* everyone to think I've done these idiotic and horrible things? Just to pay me back?

Where is Argul?

I'd actually fallen asleep, curled up on the bed-couch by the wall. Was having a nasty dream about something, I forget what, but it left a bad feeling all through me.

". . . What?"

"Someone is here, Claidi."

Yinyay's sweet face floated over me on her mechanical serpent-like body, in the Star's dimmed lamps. Was it midnight? Felt like it.

"Who? Aren't they—?"

"Armed," remarked Yinyay mildly. As if it didn't mean anything much. "She was requested to lay down her weapon and has done so. She will do you no harm. She's been told, the ship protects you."

Of course upset, but puzzled, I got up and wandered out into the main chamber. No one there.

The opening stood wide in the ship's side. I looked through and down the ramp, and out at the night plain.

"Dagger."

" 'Lo, Claidi," said Dagger.

She stood there, grimly planted and gazing up at me.

She was just eight when I went—was taken—away. Halfway toward nine now, I supposed. But she was always like someone much older. Older than me, definitely.

"Er, Dagger. Er, what . . . ?"

"I'm not coming into that machine," said Dagger. "Will you come out? I won't hurt you. I gave that snake-thing my Hulta word."

"Oh—yes."

Yinyay was there at once. She slipped a coat around my shoulders. She can be (occasionally, oddly) motherly. (But then, I've always thought

Ustareth designed Yinyay to care for Venn, when he was quite young, in case he had found the Star then, gone traveling in it.)

"Thanks. . . ."

On the ground. The night was chilly; I was glad of the coat.

Dagger herself wore a jacket and long waistcoat and a cloak.

"What *is* that thing in there?" she asked. *"Is* it a *snake?"*

"No—a sort of mechanical doll—like at Peshamba."

"Doesn't look like that."

"No."

Dagger said, "Don't you want to know why I came up here? No one else would. And if they knew *I* had, they'd say I was a right dope."

Surprised, I realized Dagger wasn't swearing in her usual vivid manner.

She had been with me, like Ashti, Toy, and Teil, by the pool, on my wedding day. My *un*-wedding day.

"Then why did you?" I asked humbly.

"I want to ask you, Claidi, if it's true."

"Which bit?"

She scowled but said, "Did you dump Argul and run off to that twit Nemian?"

"What do you *think,* Dagger?"

"Well, it looks as if you did."

"Yes, doesn't it. Well I *didn't.*" Something in me flared up all at once, and I began to rant on and on, all the things I might have shouted at Blurn. How I would *never* have left, and if I had, I'd have done it differently—didn't any of them remember me at *all?* Did they really think I was that foul?

I said I loved Argul and only wanted Argul. I told the story of what had happened, the abduction, balloon, ship, the jungles, in rather more detail than I'd been able to offer Blurn. I didn't say much about Venn. Just that I hadn't at first been able to escape from the Rise, and that as soon as I could, I'd come back.

Dagger stood there, frowning. I could make this out by the faint Starlight (from the ship) and the broader starlight of the sky.

"You mean you were just stuck there, in this palace place, and all that time, and you didn't try to get away or *do* anything?"

"It was impossible, Dagger. Really it was. I couldn't see where to go—I didn't know what to do."

"Doesn't sound like you," she said, damningly.

"Well it *was* me. I'm telling you. And the other stuff about running off to Nemian *wasn't* me. Wasn't. Isn't."

"Yes," said Dagger. She stared into the night.

"Look, Dagger, if you don't believe me, then just go away."

"I believe you."

"Because this is bad enough without—yes?"

"I believe you. Sounds all wrong and mad, but then you running off like that 'cos you *wanted* to was madder and wronger."

I felt sick now with relief. Couldn't speak.

Away through the distances of the night, sliced over and over by the thin stems of the froth trees, veiled by their almost transparent foliage, I could make out the glow of the great Hulta campfire, maybe a half-mile off.

"Is there any chance anyone else might believe you?" Dagger asked my yearning unspoken question. "No chance, Claidi. They can't see it somehow. Don't know why not. Argul going away like he did probably put them off you."

"Why did he, Dagger? Why couldn't *he* see, if *you* can—"

"Oh," she said. She shrugged.

She meant, I think, he's grown-up and so not quite so clever as he was. And for the first time I guessed Dagger's adult wisdom comes from her being a *kid.*

That's why she's made allowances for me, too. My age.

I'm grateful.

We walked off a little way and sat down on a smoothish stone in the dark.

"Here," said Dagger.

I thought she was going to stab me after all. Then I saw it was her other dagger she'd taken out, the one she'd given me as a wedding gift. It had been really shined up, and it still was.

"Wanted you to have that." she said. "I gave it to you before, so it's still yours."

"Oh, Dagger—thanks!"

"I'd have brought your horse, your Sirree. But someone would have seen and stopped me. Anyhow, I don't think Sirree'd want to go in that Star contraption."

"No."

I held the dagger Dagger had given me. Weapons don't often appeal to me. But this one—was like a slice of old friendship, high-polished. I felt I'd never let it go.

"Listen, Claidi-baa," said Dagger. "If you ever *need* a horse—try the towns northeast. You get good horses there. Some of the Hulta ones come from there, when we need new stock."

"Uh—thanks, Dagger."

"And," she said casually, kicking her legs on the side of the stone, "you might just find him, there."

"Do you mean Argul?"

"Yep. Could be. Hulta trade there a bit. We're going west right now. But he might have gone that way. East, north. There's a place. It's called Panther's Halt." I waited, speechless. "Y'see, his mum had a house there."

"Zeera," I breathed.

Zeera, Argul's mother, who had once been Ustareth, the mother of Venn.

They hate the Tower City. They don't know that *she* originally came from there. That lovely Zeera, who they liked such a lot, was a woman born in the Wolf Tower.

And now really wasn't the time to tell Dagger.

"So you think Argul might have gone northeast to—Panther's Halt. Was he—" I faltered. I said, in a whisper, "*How* was he?"

"Sore," she said. "What do you think?"

"But to stop being leader—"

"Yes," she said. "That was bad. 'Specially since you say everything was a put-up job."

"Oh, Dagger, thank God you believe me."

"Well, you're not always so bright, but you're not a hundred percent *crazy.*"

I hugged her. She let me a moment. Then pulled away. She picked up her own knife from where she had left it on the ground. "Well, I guess it's so long for now."

We shook hands.

As I walked back to the Star, I heard a faint music from the Hulta camp. A dance, drums and pipes and clapping. Maybe to show the Star they weren't afraid of it, were carefree, being so tough and well able to fight. Or to show me once and forever that now I was an outsider of the Hulta Family.

I knew, didn't I, that something was wrong, all the time I was getting here. I don't know how I knew.

But now I shall find Argul. I shall convince Argul. One day, I'll bring him back to them and make them see the truth.

Do you believe me? I mean it. Stay with me, please, my unknown friend that I talk to, that perhaps one day will read these, my *real* diaries, and trust me not to be lying. Stay with me.

I ran up the ramp of the Star.

"Yinyay! Can we find a town called Panther's Halt?"

DOWN TO EARTH

Five days now, gliding *so slowly* through the sky, heading northeast.

Lots of water below, lakes, I think, and rivers, then marshland, very green. Then—another of those awful deserts. From up here, like a cement floor littered with grey rubble, but the larger mounds must be hills, mountains perhaps.

Once, we were a bit lower and herds of things were running, disturbed maybe by the Star. But I couldn't make out what they were.

The sun came up to the right and sank on the left. Now it rises more in front of us as the Star veers east.

No doubt about this ship being able to locate Panther's Halt, It can find almost anywhere, virtually anything.

I did ask if it could simply trace—Argul. Apparently not, unless he wore a Tag the ship was set to recognize. (Like the Tag the Wolf Tower had someone put in my first diary, unknown to me, by which they traced me to the pool and were able to nab me.)

So I'm glad the Star can't find him without some gadget or by skillful guesswork. It means some things can be concealed from the frightening frightful science-magic of the Towers, and people like Ironel Novendot, and Ustareth-Zeera.

(All those years with the Hulta, when U-Zeeera used her abilities only to help them. And lied, or hid the astonishing other things she could do—

make jungles, breed monsters, make a doll that was her own double—was she really by then tired of her science, as Venn said he thought she was?)

A large flock of big, black, croaking birds flew by earlier. They're ravens. I've seen birds like these in Peshamba, and here and there.

Yinyay says these ones come from the north.

There was a Raven Tower once, in the City, but apparently, in the historic wars between the Towers (Wolf Tower, Boar Tower, Tiger Tower), the Raven Tower was destroyed.

Might as well stop writing.

Nothing much to say.

All I can think of, all I want to write is—What am I going to say to him when we meet? How can I prove to him I didn't do what he thinks? Is he going to believe me? Or—is he going to act the same as Blurn?

It was late morning when it happened. I was sitting in the main area, looking at some more pictures of people from the Towers and aristocratic Houses, etc., having nothing better to do. This time the pictures showed in a little panel in one of the metal desks.

Suddenly I lost the picture, which had been of a tall man, with what looked like a rhinoceros on a leash. Then the lights bloomed all over the desk, and the other desks; very decorative it was.

"Oh, look, Yinyay."

I don't think I was all that startled. I mean, the whole of the Star is a mystery to me. Should have realized anything like this could only mean trouble.

Yinyay swayed from desk to desk. Then she activated her hatch and abruptly slid down through the floor to the even-stranger areas in the lower part of the ship, where no one else is allowed.

Presently she came up again and went into one of the cupboards in the second room.

By then, all the viewing window-walls had cleared. We'd decided to blank them out earlier, because the east-rising sun was so bright. Now, staring out, I saw that we were much lower. Lower than we'd been at any time, except when we landed for the Hulta.

And then I saw we *were* landing.

Which was peculiar, because this didn't seem to be the most absolutely best place for it.

We were over another forest of some kind, thick and tangled. And now the upper branches were brushing against the ship. And now they were *thrashing* the window-walls, and showers of leaves and pine-needles were spraying up. Hundreds of birds erupted all around us!

I yelled and threw myself flat. And the next thing was a series of crucial shudders and thumps, a sound like a piece of the Star being *ripped* right *off*—a seething in of shadow and darkness—and then a horrible bumping crunch of impact.

I was sliding, and then I hit something and stopped. What I'd hit was Yinyay.

"Are you all right, Yinyay?"

"I am of course quite fine. You are fine too, except for a bruise on your left elbow and one on your right elbow—"

"Ow. Yes, I know about the elbow bruises—"

"And left knee."

"Wooa*ouch*."

"That is the worst one."

"Yes, Yinyay, thanks, I *know*."

She slithered silkily over me and went to inspect the desks and things.

"The ship has lost power. The magnets have failed. This never occurred before," said Yinyay, sounding sad.

I stood up. "How long," all jollily confident, "will it take to put right?" I asked.

Yinyay came out of a cupboard and offered me some cream for the bruises. I rubbed it in, still confident. She was so faultlessly clever, she had even been able to work out where I'd been bruised before *I* did.

But Yinyay said, "Princess Ustareth's ship never fails. I have therefore no knowledge of what must be done to repair it."

"But—but you—but—"

"To alter things, of course," went on Yinyay, calmly, nearly wistfully, "to adapt. But a failure is never possible. I have no thought process to remedy such an event."

Great.

We sat there. Well, I sat there on the floor, and Yinyay coiled around a bench, and we gazed at each other, I and this amazing mechanized being. Both of us now entirely (as Ro would have said) up a cuckoo tree.

A while later, some lunch zoomed out of the slot in the wall.

So that still worked.

I nibbled the nut-cheese bread toast and drank the iced tea. I had to admit, though I hadn't the heart to say it, the tea was a little warm and the toast rather cold. So, even here the Star wasn't working quite as it had. No doubt the food supplies would also soon break down.

Without saying anything to Yinyay, I went to the bathroom and ran some water. It seemed all right. But then a small lizard splashed out of the tap.

"Oh."

Yinyay arrived around me, gathered the lizard gently in her hair, and deposited it outside the ship.

With the doorway open, I looked into the forest.

Shafts of noon light pierced through the trees. They were high bluish pines and wide coppery beeches, and straddled moss banks and dells. A pleasant scene. It was quiet now but for birds, singing on and on to get over the shock of a Star (us) crashing among them.

Was it worth asking Yinyay *why* the Star's powers had failed? Probably not.

"Is there anything that can be done?" I now unconfidently asked.

"No," said Yinyay.

I noticed then the final and most worrying—I mean *terrifying* thing—Yinyay seemed to be—well she *was*—sort of shrinking.

It had happened very suddenly. But so had the crash.

"Yinyay—you, um—what are you doing?"

"I regret, Claidi, I am automatically being shut down."

"Which means?"

"My power has always been connected to the ship's power. For now, I shall rest in the storage section, where I shall learn what may be done. This may take years, or longer. And since the storage section is a very small section—" her voice too was getting littler and littler—"I too must become very small. It will be interesting," she added, obviously cheered by the notion, "to learn so much of the ship. While in this tinier form, I shall have the ability to move through the inside of the walls—"

"Yinyay, you said years—"

"Almost certainly much longer."

"Can't you—"

"I am so sorry, Claidi. Perhaps there are other possibilities. . . . But it will have to be good-bye for now. It has been"—a teeny little squeak: "So nice knowing you."

She was little as a worm, smaller even than the lizard that, twenty minutes ago, she had competently raised and deposited outside.

Then a weeny slot opened in the floor. And with a bye-bye flick of her itty tail—she was gone.

Oh hell.

After about an hour, I went and changed my clothes. In the Star, Yinyay had seen to it I had dresses to wear, but also there were still the clothes

I'd worn going through the jungle with Venn, a tunic and trousers and high boots. I added the coat.

Through the belt I put the dagger Dagger had given back to me.

I also packed my bag with my most important stuff, and a sandwich, and a bottle of the tea—I didn't trust the tap water anymore, and I didn't (ridiculously) know how to get more food before the dinner hour.

I tied my hair back.

Outside, the forest looked suspiciously adorable.

Cute little brownish squirrels were playing through the trees, and the birds sang and sang. But I thought: Claidi, you know this doesn't mean much. Around the next artistic bush may lurk some hulking THING. This is what my utterly silly life has taught me so far.

I've never before *traveled* alone.

Now I have to.

Hope Yinyay is all right.

I might even have stayed until tomorrow. It was not knowing how to close the door-opening for the night that decided me.

(In a way I feel disloyal to Yinyay, too. But what else can I do?)

At least I have a direction to take. East now, that's the way I have to go. (I think.) The afternoon is young, the sun smiles through the forest, which, compared to a jungle, is easy.

Come on then. Put this new book into bag with first book. Sling bag over shoulder and secure buckle. Down ramp and into forest and off we go. Not once looking back.

FOREST WITH PANTHER

As I'd assumed, the walking part was easy. The hardest pieces of terrain were where I had to pick over large, old tree roots, step through a shallow stream or two, and climb a small hill.

The wildlife was nice, and also nonbig. Squirrels: a couple of little red catlike things with striped tails, playing up a beech tree; birds; a beast with bristles, snuffling about in some ancient leaves—I think that was a small porcupine. Mice.

I actually enjoyed walking. Sitting in the Star day after day had made me a bit rusty. Soon I felt good.

I kept thinking, I could really enjoy all this, under other circumstances.

And then thinking, Just be careful. Watch out.

Water wasn't, so far, a problem—there were lots of streams, and I saw animals drinking from them, so they were nonpoisonous. Of course, I didn't have any food beyond one sandwich. But maybe I'd find recognizable berries or fruit or salads—the Hulta had taught me quite a lot about food-things that grow wild. But also again, I'm fairly used to going without food, where I have to. The cruelty of the House, where a frequent punishment was loss of meals, had taught me *that.*

The worst thing, obviously, was not knowing how far off was this town called Panther's Halt. And what the rest of the walk was going to be like. I mean, this forest was fine, but the countryside might well change. Also, the *name* of the place now bothered me rather.

I'd recalled something Ro and Mehmed had once talked about. A forest "over north" with *panthers.* And—trees that leaned down and grabbed people, wound them up in something (?), and then slowly digested them, over months—!

Unfortunately I began to think more and more about this.

By now I'd walked for hours, with one rest. The light was deepening, thickening, and slanting in sidelong behind me, making rich golden ponds on the narrow earth path. In other words, it was getting near sunfall, and so nighttime. And even the kindest woods can alter after dark.

Don't get feeble, Claidi. You can make a fire; you know how to do that now; the Hulta taught you. And we'll sit by the fire and drink the tea and eat half the sandwich, and then maybe sleep. And besides, it won't *be* dark for at least another couple of hours. . . .

Just then, I came out through a wall of birches and conifers and saw that the forest was coming to an end.

The unnerving thing was, it really did just—end. A few more tall old trees, heavy with sun-struck foliage—and then this wide gap of only sky.

I marched forward, through the trees. And stopped. I had to. The land I was on had itself come to a stop. It was a cliff's edge. No way down, at least for me. The rock, though still green with shrubs and plants, seemed to drop more or less sheer to a plain far, far below. Yes, I know I tend to exaggerate, but it looked at least two hundred feet down.

(I've noticed, I think more in feet and yards now, more than I did before I was with Venn at the Rise. (Even being with Hrald and Yazkool, the two who kidnapped me—then vanished so weirdly—even with them I think I started to.) In the House I didn't bother much with those sort of measurements. With the Hulta, I picked up their way of saying man-heights (about six feet). Oh well. At least I used man-heights when I was shouting at Blurn.)

To get back to the point.

The cliff dropped down and down as I stood there, and my heart and stomach and spirits did the same. Down and down.

The land below looked empty and bare—but that wasn't my immediate concern.

What now?

Well, there was only one course. I'd have to pick along the side of the cliff, follow the forest edges along, until I came to a part where I could descend. I'm not going to try bravely to climb down. I'd make a mess of it and fall.

Anyway, I started to walk along the cliff top, going with the forest. I kept roughly about *one man-height* length from the edge, except where I had to cross back in a bit, around trees. I was wise to do that, because here and there, the cliff had crumbled. In one place a massive oak hung out across the gulf, some of its roots showing where the rock had given way.

The sky meanwhile melted from blue to violet.

The light of day soaked into the forest behind me. When I looked back, it was one moment all gilded red and jade-gold, and then it turned black, then ashen—then the light was gone. The forest became formless and dark.

That huge sky, hanging in a luminous sheet out there, will also go black soon. I can already see a few stars.

I've sat down and written this, and now I can hardly see what I'm writing in the light of the fire I made.

It's night.

Already I've heard weird sounds from the forest. I expect it's only owls or something.

Time to throw another branch on the fire. Or would it be better to get up a tree? Safer, that is.

Really it wasn't confidence or courage that made me fall asleep. I was tired. The dying of the firelight woke me, as I'd hoped it would, so I could build the protective blaze up again.

As I leaned over to push in more dry twigs, I saw the panther, sitting across the fire, looking at me.

My heart did what it does at such times. Stopped, then jumped with a jolt that shook me. I never find that very helpful.

Perhaps I made sound. A sort of stifled squawk, most likely.

The panther twitched its ears.

It was very black, its pelt like costly velvet. Its eyes were a silvery moon-yellow, but emerald where the fire caught in them.

How do I know how to identify a panther? I've seen pictures. Even on the Star I had looked at the picture of a panther in an interested way, because of the name of the town.

I now remembered the knife Dagger gave me. I eased it from the loop in my belt.

I thought, I can't kill a panther. I don't *want* to. And anyway, I've never learned to fight—

Then, the panther *spoke* to me.

Right, I've gone mad. No, it's a dream. It's a dream *and* I've gone mad.

The panther said, "Get up, follow. Come on, I will not wait."

Well, it was a dream, so why not?

Anyway, was I going to make a scene and *annoy* it?

I stood up.

The panther said, "Bring your luggage."

My—? Oh, it meant my bag. How thoughtful of it to remind me.

"Kick dirt over your fire." said the panther, evidently very responsible. "You will not be returning."

"Er—why not?" I nervously asked.

"I am to show you." said the panther, "the way down to the valley."

It had a cool, bored voice. Yes, it sounded bored. This was a nuisance for it, having to leave its normal panther-type activities, and come and help me down the cliff since I was too duppish to have figured out a way for myself.

I kicked leaf-mold and dirt over the fire.

Apparently not adequately, because the panther now stalked up—I shrank—and paw-brushed more stuff over it.

The moon was up, another panther eye in the sky.

"Ah—thanks."

"Follow me now," said the panther.

I can remember things in books about talking animals. They were always funny, or wise. This one just went on sounding matter-of-fact and *bored.*

It walked ahead of me, swinging its lean hindquarters, the velvet bell-rope of tail flicking from side to side.

"Mind the roots," it presently said, so I minded them. Felt I had to thank it again.

But when I stubbed my toe anyway, I thought, No, I'm not dreaming. This is real.

Next there were some very tall trees, and the panther walked in between, and when I did too, there was a hump of rock coming out of the cliff, a kind of chimneylike structure. In the side of it, a hole, or opening.

"There," said the panther.

"Yes?"

The panther shut its eyes. It looked—exasperated.

"Inside the rock is an entrance to caves that run through the cliff. Follow the slope downward, taking no side turnings. This will bring you to the valley floor."

"Right."

"Do not," said the panther, eyeing me sternly, "wait until daybreak. For then the bats return."

"I don't mind bats," I wildly confessed.

"However, they may not care for *you.*"

"Ah yes, I see. Of course."

The panther gave me one long stare, then turned.

"Wait—" I heard myself (disbelieving I did) call.

"What do you want?"

"Look, I apologize for asking—but—how is it you can talk?"

"I might," said the panther, "ask you the same."

Shattered, I stood there gawking. Then I said, "Look—no, people do talk, But animals—don't."

"How do you know?"

"I don't *know* but—oh come on. Do they?"

"Generally, they do not."

"Then why is it—?" I began.

The panther turned again. It walked back toward me, and I wished I'd kept quiet.

It came so close, I felt the living heat of it, the muscular terrible strength. Its head was level with my ribs, but it was overall very much bigger than me, and heavy—yet *light,* sprung steel with a coat of plush. It smelled of night and darkness, and its breath stank of raw meat—the last thing it had killed and eaten.

"Claidi, who must always ask questions," said the panther.

"You know my name."

"You ask too much, but now is the time for action, not words."

My legs felt watery. On the other hand, my mouth was too dry to speak.

It gave me, the great black doglike cat, one last look of lingering disdain. And then it leapt around and bounded into the forest.

I tottered into the rock chimney. I leaned on the wall.

Then, by some trick of the outside moonlight, I glimpsed the curve of the wall, and a sloping stony track angling down.

I wandered onto it, started to descend. All the questions I hadn't asked were beating around and around in my head.

I realized a bit late why I could see my way. Clusters of fireflies were there, hanging like necklaces of topaz and green beryl, or dancing over pockets of water.

The ancient sinews of the stone arched overhead. Twisted trunks of stone strained up to hold them.

Everything reeked of the absent bats. And here and there the odd grape-bunch of bats was still hung up, having overslept or something.

Once one bat, a pale one, an albino, flew right at me. And as I ducked I thought, *What is it going to say?*

But the bat didn't speak, except maybe in battish, so luckily I hadn't a clue about it.

I was still so stunned that finally I sat down on the rim of a largish pool, where the dancing fireflies reflected like candles.

Some things have happened to me since I left the House. The Waste outside, I was always told, was full of bizarre and horrifying creatures. Though the House lied a lot, certain parts of the Waste—the world—are exactly what I was told they would be.

But no one warned me about talking panthers.

What can you do with something so curious and unsettling? Just shove it to the back of your mind, and carry on.

I'd filled the by-then empty tea-bottle with water in the forest; there'd been a spring near my fire, with a squirrel drinking in the dusk. When I at last got out of the caves, I tried a sip. It tasted rather bitter, but all right. In fact it was.

The exit from the cliff was another cave, very wide and high, a great arch which showed plainly from inside, because by then it was getting on for dawn.

Apart from falling asleep again briefly by the pool, I had, it seemed, walked all night.

The bats were streaming home to bed as I moved out of the last cave. They passed over me, a chattering, soft yet spiky wind of shadows.

It was a cold morning.

It was dim; I still couldn't see much. But from above, the valley-plain had looked uninviting.

Wait for the sun. It should come up—over there.

By the cave-mouth I sat and dozed.

When I woke again, the sun was up, shining in my face.

The valley was what it had looked like. Arid slopes and hummocks, with sparse, dun-colored grass. One or two wan and spindly trees. Stones, boulders. No water I could see.

This muddled on to the horizon, and on the horizon there was nothing new.

Lovely.

All this to do on a small bottle of water, half a sandwich, three or four hours sleep.

Too bad. Ahead (somewhere) lay the town. With Zeera's house. And

Argul. He would be there. He must be there. Or if not—someone who would know something.

In those books I read, a talking animal that guided you always did so for a good reason.

I allowed myself one chomp of the half-sandwich, and reduced it to a quarter-sandwich. Then I strode off east, toward the sun.

THE TENT

Anyway, less than ten minutes later, I found a ROAD.

There was no doubt. It was even *paved*, if not very well. Along the sides grew a few more of the poor old trees. Coming around the slight upslope, I'd mistaken it at first for some natural gully. Fortunately went down and looked.

It wobbled off northeast, but soon there was a big rough-cut stone that read (in my own language, which I must *not* forget is also the language of the Towers), *Panther's Halt—Keep Right On.*

Also I hadn't been on it more than half an hour before some carts came bumbling along out of the wasteland and got onto the road about thirty yards ahead of me.

So far as I could see, there were three carts, all drawn by what looked like goats.

To begin with I was glad they were ahead, and I lagged back. In my experience, it isn't always sensible to trust one's fellow travelers.

Then I thought maybe they were all right, and might know something, so I quickened my pace.

As I got closer, I could see they were glancing back at me, even the goats were glancing back, but they made no effort to slow down.

There were three men and three women, and three goats. In the drab landscape they all wore very gaudy clothing, of reds and oranges, while the goats were black and white, or would have been, because somehow somebody had dyed their white parts, so the goats were black and puce, or black and aquamarine blue.

"Fine morning," I said, trying to sound and appear both harmless and well-armed, smashing good company and nobody's fool. Thinking about it, I suppose all the things I *totally* never am.

The carters looked me over, still not hesitating. One of the men said something, and it was in some other language. So I had to shrug and look ever so sorry—yet not concerned. (And also as if I might secretly understand—in case they were plotting something.) (I mean, *what,* for heaven's sake? Dying me blue and puce, perhaps. Well, you never know.)

Then one of the women leaned from her cart and said a couple of things in the other language. And then: "You go Panther's Halt, you do?"

"Yes," I exclaimed, all plots flung to the winds.

And I thought perhaps she would ask me to sit in the cart. But no such luck.

"You want goat?"

"A goat? Oh, no, thanks."

"Glamorous and work-good goat. See! In bestest color."

"No, thanks, really."

One of the men chipped in quickly, "We change the color if you want."

"No—no."

"Any color—merf, cashrob, coppice—ranaky, we do *ranaky* for you. Even horns we do!"

Why is it I *never* meet anyone normal?

Is it *me?*

"No goat," I said firmly. "*Thank* you."

At which they all, goats included, turned from me and refused to speak to me again during the rest of the trek to Panther's Halt. At least the *goats* didn't try any sales patter. After the panther, I'd half expected them to.

Not long after this episode, we went up quite a steep small hill, and from the top I could see, some way off, something blooming there on the dullness of the plain. It looked absurdly like a great, deep-pink flower.

"What is that?" I asked the goat-people.

But they wouldn't talk to me, so I had to wait to find out.

I don't think Argul ever was here before, or perhaps he was. . . . But Dagger wasn't, surely, or she'd have told me about this unusual—to me—town, Panther's Halt. Or are there lots of other towns just like it?

Panther's Halt is all under one vast *Tent.*

And not just any enormously vast tent, either. It is made of some special weatherproofed material and is raised at its top at least twenty feet higher than the roof of the tallest house on the tallest hill up there, inside the town. Standing in the streets of the Halt, you look up and see these higher streets and buildings tapering up into the cyclamen-pink dome of the Tent. It's like being under an always-blushing dawn.

There are millions of tiny holes made in the material, secured by thin rings of some metal which, it seems, can't rust. (?) Through these ringed holes faint musical whinings of breezes blow, and the very occasional single spot of rain. But as a rule, the Tent keeps off all weather, including the searing midday sun, which otherwise burns and drains the valley.

Inside the Tent, trees grow on the streets. They're still pastel but quite luxuriant.

At night, lamps will apparently come on, far up in the canopy of the Tent. So that even at night, the blush-dawn effect will continue.

These lamps never have to be lit or put out. At night they light, at sunrise they darken. They have a soft clear radiance, which doesn't flicker. Familiar? They're exactly like the lamps at the Rise. *Ustareth's* lights.

Is that really so surprising?

She has this house here, Dagger said.

Did Ustareth-Zeera therefore arange the lights and the town's Tent?

Around the edges of the town, just outside the Tent, are canals, into which any moisture or rain, which collects on the Tent-top, is eventually dislodged.

After heavy storms, or when there is a buildup of water on the Tent-top, there is a Rope-Shaking Brigade, who go outside and shake the ropes fixed between the ground and the upper Tent, and so knock off the water. The Brigade is highly respected. They wear a uniform—black, with Tent-pink epaulets and buttons, and black-lacquered helmets to protect them when they shake the water down to the canals.

The canals are additionally full of ducks. The ducks, plus thousands of other birds, come in and out of the town by means of folded-back openings kept wide by day. Lots of birds perch along a sort of scaffolding which in places upholds the Tent from inside.

I have a language problem here.

Despite the stone on the road, not many people speak mine. They do speak a bit of Hulta, which I've learned rather haphazardly. (I know a lot of Hulta swearing, and affection-words, and even whole songs, and lots of whole sentences—but, well, I was only really starting to get properly to grips with it when—when I was taken away.)

But it's not too bad. Just—oh, completely frustrating. I simply haven't been able to ask about Argul, because I haven't the words. Not even about U-Z's house, which is almost certainly where he is staying, if he is here.

I've been wandering the streets all day, too tired now to feel anything but violently alert and awake, too hungry to want to eat. But I'm thirsty.

They have these fountains here. They are on almost every street, and in the big square, where there is a market, there are four. The sparkling water gushes over them, and on each, in several different languages—including mine—are these big black words: DO NOT DRINK.

At first I thought it was just nastiness. Then I realized the water may look all right, but it's probably *not* drinkable, poisonous even. (I am sitting by a fountain now, writing this, and it's driving me nuts.)

I'm thinking of going out again to the canals for a drink. Full of ducks and duck feathers, not to mention little parcels of ducky doo.

Of course, I have no money. And they use money here. Also barter—but I have nothing I can afford to let go. I'm walking around with a diamond ring and an embroidered Hulta wedding dress in my bag, and I have a honed blade through my belt. But these are the most precious things in my life.

I've done this all wrong.

Without any difficulty, I'd say, Yinyay could have found me some money notes, or something marketable, before she shrank. Didn't think to ask. Or even search.

How typical.

Serves me right then.

Oh, there goes another goat. Black and pea-green. Very tasteful.

(Those goat people must have brought them to sell them, and when I came belting after them, thought I wanted to buy one quickly. So they weren't as dotty as I reckoned. Though they *were* rude.)

And *another* goat—black and pink, like the Rope-Shakers. (An old man told me about the Rope-Shakers, in halting Hulta, after some of the Brigade swaggered by. A passing girl also told me about the lamps, seeing me staring up at them in the Tent top. Possibly they just have these sightseer sentences ready-prepared in many languages.)

There are no horses for sale in the market.

When I said (in Hulta), "Horses?" to someone, just to see, this person laughed. I *think* he replied, *sold out.*

No panthers either. Not that I've noticed.

I *am* tired. I'd like to lie down and sleep somewhere quiet. And I'm thirsty enough to drink a bath full of pooey duck-water. And really I'm starving.

This room's all right. The woman warned me I'd be woken by the noise of the morning market starting under my window. But I didn't wake. I must have slept from late afternoon yesterday until the same today.

I feel much better. I can think more clearly. Which is a shame, in a way, because now I can really worry.

And the worst thing of all? In order to get this room in this inn, and a meal and so on—I sold my wedding dress. Do you think I'm beneath contempt? I feel very, very bad about it.

What happened was, I was sitting by that fountain, when this man came up. He looked rather like the goat-people in dress, but then he thrust his face into mine and squinted at me with his narrow little eyes.

"What you selling?"

"I beg your pardon?"

"What you selling? Great strong girl like you—" somehow he made this sound insulting, as if I were extremely tall and beefily heavy and loud—"come on, come on. I'll hire you."

"For what?" I said.

I felt threatened, and although there were plenty of people about, I didn't know whether they'd care if I got attacked.

"Well," said the repulsive man, "you can clean up. Do the washing. Cook the supper. How's that?"

"No, thank you ever so much."

But he leered, He reminded me of certain servants, and even the occasional royal person at the House, who I'd always tried to keep well clear of.

"Come on," he said. "You might get to like me."

"You're very nice. But I'm waiting for someone."

Then he swelled like a toad, got even fatter and uglier, and I put my unskilled hand on the dagger in my belt. And then someone else leaned over *him,* and dragged him bodily away, as if he were a bag of rubbish, and just sort of threw him casually down several feet off.

"Leave the lady alone," said the new someone.

I thought there might be a fight. But instead the first man was groveling there on the ground. "Sorry, sorry," he was mumbling, "didn't know she was with you—"

The newcomer said, "She's not." Then he turned to me and gave me a jaunty salute.

He was tall, thin, and dry for the other one's oily, stout shortness. Not young, or old. A black stubble of hair crowned his head. He wore creaky black leather.

"Are you here on business, madam?" he politely asked.

I got up. He *towered* over me. But he spoke my language (so had the other one, alas) so I said, "No, I'm here looking for someone."

"And who is that?"

"Well—" cautious now, I added, "for their house, really."

"A house." He gave me a dry thin smile. His skin looked like that paper you can sand things down with. "I regret, I'm a stranger here myself."

And then he *bowed* and walked off. Couldn't help noticing, people got out of his way.

To my dismay the other one came gobbling back at once. But he only wanted to say, "Sorry, dear. Sorry. Didn't know, miss, you knew Jelly."

Then he too hurried off.

Jelly.

At Peshamba I saw *jellies* served for the children. They'd been set in exotic molds and had come out in the shapes of rabbits and lions and stars and suns, and all in jewel-like colors. Happy party food.

Jelly???

Still, it had been lucky he was there.

I decided then I'd better get sorted out, before anything else happened. And I went straight over to a booth that was selling clothes, some of which were clearly secondhand.

Without letting myself think, I produced the embroidered wedding dress. "What will you give me for this?" I didn't know if they understood—they seemed to understand what I was trying to do at least. "It's a family heirloom. Hardly worn. I know it's stained. That's from a long sea voyage, therefore interesting. The embroidery is Hulta."

They gave me coins and rushed my WD away behind the booth, so I was fairly sure I'd been done.

I've felt horrible about it ever since, even dreamed about it, I think, during the deep sleep in this inn-room.

But I still have the diamond ring. I'm not confident enough to wear it after the thing with the rings, at the Rise. I don't know what powers it has—and they're erratic. But I would *never* sell it. Even though, before she gave it to Argul, it was *hers*. Ustareth-Zeera.

Now I'm up, washed (even hair), have had some breakfast-lunch. I'm going to find that house today.

Wonder how Yinyay is managing in the storage of the Star—learning things, did she say? I wonder too how Venn is, all across the ocean. And Jotto and Treacle and Grem.

And Argul. How and where are you?

Really, I think I was just certain by now I wasn't going to find Argul at Panther's Halt. That the best I could hope for was a clue.

Why was this? I'd suspected I would *feel* something electric in the air of the Tent town, if he had been here too. Then—I *had* felt that, sort of—but didn't trust what I felt.

The already-late day got later as I trudged around the streets. They were paved, but hilly. And also the paving was fairly cracked and rather unsafe. Yesterday I hadn't seen the lights come on; I'd been asleep. But now, as the daylight through the under-Tent began to fade, suddenly the lamps opened their cool eyes, and everything went pinker than ever.

The birds were flying in to their scaffolding roosts, tweeting and trilling. No doubt the lights also help keep them warm during the cold nights. Trails of birds arrowed and darted under the pink dome "sky." Droppings fell like white streamers, and people dashed to gather them in little pots(??).

Between dodging droppings, I was trying to get a look at all the bigger houses on hill tops. Wouldn't *her* house be one of these? A commanding view of the town, and so on. Then again, she might have wanted a concealed house, tucked away in a big garden of thick bushy trees.

I had just reached the wall of such a garden. A wide gate stood open, and down a long coiling path I could now see another sort of light among the shrubbery. Paper lanterns, rose, crimson, blue. There was the sound of merrymaking and clink of glasses and jugs.

"Why, hallo again," said a dry voice behind me. "What a coincidence. Are you too going to the goat-wedding?"

I jumped around—hadn't heard a step or anything—and there he was. Jelly.

"The—what did you say?"

"Goat-wedding. Shall we?" He bowed, as he had before. Something about the bow—it's what they do for royalty in the Houses and the Towers.

Had he followed me?

Was I only being oversensitive?

But he'd put his hand courteously under my elbow, and we were walking into the garden. As if on a long-arranged outing. "Let me introduce myself," he said. "I am Jelly."

"Hi." (His hand was icy. I was glad when he removed it.)

"And you?"

"Oh." Efficient as ever, I hadn't thought beforehand I might not want to give my name to everyone. So I hadn't prepared a fake name, and for a moment I dithered.

"If I am being too forward, there's no need to say, naturally," he assisted me, sounding now indescribably threatening and sinister.

An idea surfaced. Chancy—but let me see how he took it.

"Of course I can tell you my name. It's Ustareth," I announced.

And he stopped dead. His long thin face stared down at me, all chin, and even the *chin* looked *interested.*

"Uss-taar-eth," he intoned. His pouchy eyes glittered. "What a fascinating name."

"Thank you so much," I gushed.

"A City name, I think," he said. "The City on the River, surely. From a Tower?"

"Wouldn't know," I said. "My mum thought it up."

"Your mother *thought it up?"*

"Oh, they all used to laugh in my village," I rambled on, unwisely warming to my game. "Bat's Junction Village. You know it? No? I thought everyone had heard of Bat's Junction. Anyway, they used to tease me rotten."

"How trying," he said.

He seemed to like this too, and that chilled me down. Games—he liked games—the Towers like games. The Wolf Tower.

He is from the Wolf Tower? From *Ironel—*

"*Your* name is so much more interesting," I twittered. *"Jelly— "*

"Oh let's not talk about me."

We were in among the paper lanterns now, and the noisy crowd was falling back from us, cheery faces going all tense as they registered *him.*

"I believe you said you were looking for someone's house?" he now asked me.

"Did I?"

"I'm sure you did."

"Oh yes, that's right. The house of my mother's cousin—"

"And who is that?"

Hell, another name to think up on the spur of the moment.

"Pattoo," I uncleverly blurted, picking the name of a friend from my slave-maid days.

"All this is most interesting." said Jelly. He strolled beside me. "I wonder if," he said, "on your travels about the town, and in the house of your mother's cousin Pattoo—if you have come across a young woman by the name—" he paused. An abrupt shouting and music burst all around.

For a moment I had the feeling he had seen something that had startled him, broken off to check this something out—but then I realized.

He was playing.

He's standing there, and he's going to say *Claidi.* Or Claidis or Claidissa. Those name changes the Wolf Tower gave me.

Cat and mouse. And I'm the mouse.

I waited, gaping at the crowd all breaking apart in a dancing procession, with high-held torches and bottles and garlands of gold tinsel flowers.

Waited, not really seeing anything, *waited* to hear him speak that name—

Only he didn't.

I couldn't bear another second. I turned to confront him, this—Jelly—

He was gone.

Vanished. He'd just slid away among the shadows of the garden as if on wheels.

Idiotically I looked back at the festivity.

And here came the bride.

She was a goat.

I frowned, but no, she was. How then did I know her to be the bride? Easy. She wore my own Hulta wedding dress.

The evil Jelly was gone, and now the crowd was pushing into and around me, so I gave up and was also carried along through the garden. And so I was next able to watch the wedding. If the bride was a surprise, the groom was more of a surprise.

Like before, a chatty old woman soon came up and started to tell me what went on, in my own language, more or less. Is it worth recording? Yes, I suppose it is.

The goat in (my) wedding dress, was one of the black and green ones. They "married" her to a panther. This was lighter in color than the one that had spoken to me in the forest. You could, in the light, see the paw-print pattern in his coat.

"Have no feary," said the old woman. "The panther do no harm to the goat. We train they panthers here to live with goats as family. And they goat-people train their goaties same. See now, they making the friends."

This was a fact? The goat and the panther were standing and leaning on each other, all relaxed. Now and then the panther rubbed its head, like a big cat, on the goat. The goat was so calm, it was grazing the grass.

"In us valleys," said the old woman, "they panther do be guardy goaties herds. None so safe as they."

(I'm only jealous. I wish I could speak another language even as well as she was speaking mine.) (Then again, though, she wasn't really.)

Desperate, I rounded on her.

"A woman called Zeera," I hissed, "or Ustareth—her house—do you know where it is?"

She giggled at me. "Juppa yipto?"

"You don't really speak my language at all, "I accused. "It's just this sightseer stuff you've learned by heart, isn't it?"

She beamed. She inquired, helpfully, "You like a goat?"

As I hurried away from her, I saw, across the red flap of the torches, lit as I had so often seen him, by fire, Argul, standing on the slope above.

LIGHT OR DARK?

Had he seen *me?*

I didn't think so. He was looking down at the bridal procession which was now swirling around again, weaving about every tree—

Had he seen the *dress* on the goat? The dress that had been going to be mine on the day I should have married *him?*

I remember saying, when I first met Argul—I was afraid of him. He was just so absolute. So *entire,* complete.

And now, as the bouncing crowd pushed me back and forth, staring up at him on the lawn above, again I was afraid.

I'd forgotten what he truly looks like.

Under the shift of firelight, his dark skin one instant like bronze, and then like gold. His black hair that hangs to his waist. His face—his face.

Another panther, with two or three goats—bridesgoats and Best Panther, perhaps—thumped into me. I was toppled back good-naturedly against a tree by the crowd.

Then the crowd was past, rioting off through the garden toward the town, and I got my bearings—but I'd looked away one whole thin-as-a-splinter second, And in that second, Argul had moved.

I was in time to catch the flare of his brown cloak, crack of one golden inch of tassel-fringe, as he strode away into the trees above.

All the time I'd spent asking myself: When I find him, how am I going to approach him, what am I going to say to him?—Of course I was simply pelting up the garden, and now I was yelling his name.

But there was still a lot of noise, not least from the wedding orchestra of squeaky trumpets and throaty drums.

He hadn't heard me, couldn't have.

I ran.

On the upper lawn, the trees divided to form an avenue. Again, I was just in time to see him striding along it.

Rushing through the avenue. He is around the next turn before I get there. I mustn't lose him. *Mustn't.*

At the turn, there is a hill. Argul is striding up the hill. How far ahead of me? Quite a lot. I stop and try yelling his name again.

But the night seems full of distant calls and songs. To him, so far ahead of me now, my cry will sound only like one more of these.

Argul, wait. Please wait. Stop for something—spot an interesting rare type of owl perched on a tree or a pole above—catch your cloak on a briar—hesitate because some memory has come into your mind—some memory of me—

No good. I start running again.

He is at the top of the hill—for a moment in silhouette against the bright-lit Tent dome. Look around, Argul, look back—here I am—

He doesn't. He's going on over the hill, down the hill.

Running uphill isn't my favorite mode of travel. Have a stitch. No breath to shout. Long knotty grass. Now I've stumbled, tripped. More or less fall over, scramble up, tear on, ignoring another prize-winning knee-bruise to add to my knee-and-elbow bruise collection—

As I splurled over the hilltop, I had this nightmare feeling he would simply have disappeared. And he had. He had.

I dropped on the slightly less bruised knee.

Try not to go mad. Think. What is down there? See, it's obvious. A paved path goes down to those houses over there, and it's quite well lit from the Tent lights, though they seem a little dimmer here. If he were walking on the path, I'd still see him.

But first there is that single building, tucked in among those cypress trees. Darker there. It must be—*that* is the house, and he has gone into it.

And exactly then, a lamp burns up yellow in one window which seems caught in the boughs of a cypress tree.

I leapt to my feet—

"Felt like a bit of a run, did you?"

—and nearly plummeted right off the hill.

Now I was so unnerved, frenzied, no pretense seemed worth the effort. I whirled on him.

It *was* Jelly.

"Are you following me?"

"Am I? Hmn."

"Get lost," I barked.

"Tut tut. But where are you sprinting to in such a hurry? Tell me, madam, have you ever run professionally? My word, swift as a gazelle."

"What's a gaz—*look*, Jelly, what do you want?"

"Ah. So many things. A little cottage by a trout pool. A reasonable wine-cellar—"

"Who do you think I am?" I challenged.

"You told me," he said. "Ustareth."

"You say you're a stranger here," I said, "but they all seemed to know you."

"Word gets around."

"Which word?"

"My name. Jelly," he said, modestly.

I wasn't going to go down to the cypress house until Jelly was gone. Right now, I didn't dare even look at the house except quickly, once. The light still burned. As if to be my beacon.

"Wolf Tower," I said to Jelly. "Yes?"

"Ah?" asked Jelly, rolling innocent pouchy razor-sharp eyes.

No one else was around. The garden—park, really—was deserted here. And the Tent lights, as I said, were not so bright from this point.

If it came to it, I didn't think I could get the better of this man with a dagger.

How to get rid of him?

Now he bent down and down to me. (He must be nearly seven and a half feet tall.)

"Tell me, madam, you *are* the Lady Claidis Star, aren't you?"

"Who?"

"Claidis Star, Who goes more often by the pet name of Claidissa. Or even . . . Claidi."

"My name's Ust—"

"Good night," said Jelly.

I stood there, mouth open. There he went, off back down the hill, the way we had both come. (His walk, seen from a distance, is extraordinary.

At every step he bends at the knees, and yet he covers vast amounts of ground on his enormous feet, like a sort of power-driven spider.)

I descended the other slope, very slowly and carefully now, keeping clear of trees, looking back again and again. I anticipated every moment he'd rearrive: "Oh, before I go—"

But he didn't.

Below, I hung around for ages. No one about. Yet I had this awful sense that Jelly, if he meant to, could still creep up on me, unseen, unheard.

Roosting birds stirred nearby, had a little singsong, and went back to sleep.

I crept among the cypress trees.

Somehow this was like her other house (Ustareth's) on the lake, when I was with Venn.

And the light above me, that was like that other time with Venn, under that room of his in the gardens of the Rise, looking up at his lighted window in the dark, lost and friendless, knowing him to be my enemy.

Argul isn't my enemy. But—he thinks I am his.

It took a while for me to get my courage together and knock on the carved door under the arch.

I kept thinking it *would* have been far simpler to have galloped up to him screaming.

Obviously I hadn't knocked loudly enough. There was no answer.

So I beat with both fists, boldly. The night seemed to shake, and oddly, nearby, one of those duller lights overhead went out, as if I'd damaged it by making a row.

It was black now, or seemed to be, in the cypress grove.

Still no one answered.

Then I knocked and called. Then I went and stood under the lighted window. And after all that, I yelled again!

The lamp was behind a filmy curtain. I couldn't see what was in the room.

Perhaps he'd left the lamp, forgotten. Gone to another room.

I walked around the house, here and there having to go up steps or crawl over low walls with extra thorns. I shouted and called, using his name. I even threw a couple of small stones to rattle the glass window panes.

Some while after, I sat under a bush.

Then I tried to *break* into the house.

But I'm useless at that sort of thing, and nothing would give; the only windows I could reach were locked. Didn't want to smash them, I mean, Hi, Argul, here is the vile horror you think ran off with another man without even telling you, and now I'm back, and I've just broken your window, too.

I did climb up a tree. After all, it was a shame not to add cuts and grazes to the bruises and thorn-scratches, I tried to crane over and bang on the lighted window. Couldn't *reach*.

I did a bit more calling and shouting, and right then, a band of six or seven young men came along the path toward the hill and waved up at me delightedly. "Look, lads, it's a foreign female mad person!"

Colossal laughter and congratulations to me. (Please note, the words were carefully spoken in *my* language.)

When they had at last gone on again, I did think at least their noise must have woken Argul—but it hadn't.

Then I thought, He isn't sleeping. He has either seen or heard me. He knows it's me, out here. And out here is where he means me to remain.

Later, much later, a panther and goat trotted by together under my cypress tree. Friends for life.

Argul, if a panther and a goat can be friends—surely you could at least listen to me, hear me out.

But in my head, I heard a voice that answered, He is doing to you what he thinks you did to him. Misled and made a fool of him. Used and lied to him. Left him out in the cold.

If he could unbelievably abandon the Hulta because of what he thought I'd done, then what do *I* matter to him now?

He must hate and loathe me.

By the yellow glow of the lamp (*his* lamp), I've written this.

Another overhead light has gone out. They must be faulty here. Is there any connection between this and Ustareth's Starship developing a fault and crash-landing?

Shall I tear a page out of this book and write him a letter? Saying what?

Maybe it's all I can do. But it's harder to see to write, even his lamp is burning low. I'll have to wait until daybreak. I might as well stay up in this tree. It may be safer up here. If only from Jelly.

Morning. The overhead lights all went out in one blink, and a grey predawn turned the Tent top amethyst.

In this eerie dusk, I rubbed my cricked neck and almost fell out of the tree.

Below me, a young man was there at the front of the house. He led a horse, saddled up and ready for riding. A brown, satiny horse, strong as a tiger—

The door opened. Argul came out into the cold first light that smelled of cypresses, birds, and Tent.

If they spoke, I didn't hear the words. He just walked over to the horse and mounted up, swinging into the saddle as if weightless, the way I'd seen him do so many times now my heart seemed to dissolve. There was a carrying bag, too, fixed on behind the saddle.

I'd only been building up my breath and throat. Now I shrieked at him.

The *other* man's head shot up all right; he nearly sprang out of his skin. But Argul didn't even look my way.

Though I heard him speak. To the man.

"Noisy birds you get here."

"Yeah—" said the other, stunned.

Argul touched the horse lightly. He was riding away. Then he was racing away.

I fell down the tree.

Trying to run after Argul, my knees gave.

"Morning," said the young man as I landed at his feet. "Legs not so strong as your lungs, eh?"

I realized he was speaking in Hulta.

Hulta phrases spun in my head.

"Argul—where's he going?"

"You know Argul?"

I nodded vigorously until my head seemed about to fly off.

"Shame he didn't realize it was you," said the young man. "He's off north. Over the burning Fiery Hills."

"Horse—" I burbled, in Hulta. Of all Hulta words, that word is anyway the first anyone ever learns.

"Yes, Argul's is a great horse."

"No—no—me—I want—horse—"

"Can't have it, luv," said the young man. "It's *Argul's* horse."

Shall I just kill him?

No. Keep trying.

(*He* saw me. *He* knew me. He doesn't *want* me, I don't care. Until I have convinced him of the truth—then I can allow him only to decide. It may still go against me. I'll worry then. Die, then.)

"For me—a—a *new* horse."

Had I said *new?* Thinking back, I think I said a *fat* horse. In Hulta, the words are similar.

But at last this pest got my drift.

"Oh, you won't get a horse now. Sold out last cow-day." (I *think* he said *cow*-day.) "Tell you what, though, my dad can probably fix you up with a riding animal—not a horse, but something."

"Anything." What else could I say? (Only actually, I may have said, not anything, but any *gherkin*.)

ACROSS THE FIRE HILLS BY GRAFFAPIN

This creature is *not* a horse. But the burning Fiery Hills *do* burn. They flame. Yet, to be fair, they are not on fire, as such. They look spectacular, particularly after sunset.

The graffapin doesn't look spectacular. It looks peculiar.

It's like a horse slightly. That is, the back is broad enough and the legs muscular enough so you can ride it. No real tail. The neck goes straight up—and up. I measured the neck, and it's the length of my arm from shoulder to wrist. Then comes the head, which isn't horselike either. More sheeplike. Big dark eyes, with *lashes.* Two upstanding ears. All of it covered with dripping long blond fur—or pelt—or fleece—or hair.

It smells insistently of damp hay, despite the grooming it had at Panther's Halt.

"Does it have a name?" I'd uneasily asked.

"Graff," said "Dad"—that was all the name *he* had, that I heard.

Graff cost very little, or rather, the coins I'd been given for my WD (now fashionable goat-wear) were worth more than I'd thought (so they hadn't ripped me off).

Supplies were thrown in, plus some food for the graffapin called Graff.

I don't even know if it's a girl or a boy—and apparently that's quite hard to discover.

It mutters to itself as we trot along, low gurgles and snuffles. But it goes fast when you say *Yof-yof*.

They warned me about the Hills.

Oh, ever so funny, silly foreign woman who looks upset when they tell her the hills are on fire all the time.

I didn't see them until two days' ride from the Tent and Panther's Halt. Graff was galloping, because although I'd been told by "Dad" that Argul would take the only decent road which I "couldn't miss," I was petrified of missing both road and Argul.

So then, it was getting on for sunset, and I thought these upper slopes were just catching the westering sun. Couldn't quite see how, as they faced me, therefore south.

As the light ebbed, the hills got brighter. Then I had to admit what "Dad" and his son had told me was presumably a fact.

It was night by the time Graff and I rode up to them. And sure enough, there was the road, another badly paved mess but still just about intact. On either side, fluttering and flickering, and lighting the lower sky like copper, the flames flashed and rippled.

They are red, with roots of saffron and fierce blue. No smoke rises—a giveaway.

"Dad" had said it was a "chemical reaction" and wouldn't hurt. Not fire at all, said Dad, proud of his superior knowledge and living in such a pride-worthy, eccentric area.

I wondered if the graffapin would take fright, throw me and bundle off. It just ambled up onto the road and trotted along, its fur-drippery shining as if it had on an expensive fringed tablecloth.

I stared.

Finally we made camp on the road, which is broad. I didn't light a fire, as the chemical fire gives off some warmth and is very bright.

As I was eating my supper, Graff managed to get out of his/her tether—he/she is very good at that, something to do with the long, twisting neck—and wandered off among the fires, puffing and admiring them, like a lady in a flower garden.

Despite appearances, Graff did not catch alight. Nor I, when I went after and hauled he/she/it back out.

But there is no sign of Argul.

Six days and nights now, since I left PH.

I said to Dad and son, what lay over the Fire Hills? And they pulled a face—they both pulled the same face at the same time. Anything beyond the Halt doesn't matter and/or is bad?

"But where is Argul going?"

"North."

"What is in the north?"

After some thought, Dad said, "It's bloody cold."

Startling wildness of fire today, flaring up and up.

No animals or birds, except once, large black birds went over—ravens?

Still no Argul.

Am I on the wrong road? Are there two—three others—or has he just gone elsewhere—even asked or paid Dad and son to lie to me?

Please don't let that be so.

This morning, eighth day, I was high up. I saw Argul ahead.

My wonder and relief were slightly spoiled by *also* seeing another rider behind me. From the unbelievable look of him, it is *Jelly.*

That night I found a cave and went and sat in it, with Graff tied up very securely to a rock inside. If I went to sleep, I didn't want Jelly happening along and surprising me again. He had seemed quite a way behind me—but with Jelly, who could be sure?

He didn't come by. Or if he did, nothing woke me. (I had tied some of Graff's spare tether across the cave entrance, so anyone trying to get in would get tangled up with Graff and cause some noise.)

Graff, though, is such a peaceful beast. He—maybe he is a he—was just quietly singing to himself when I got up. I put on his nose-bag for him, and he sang his uncomplaining way through breakfast.

"Yof-yof!"

Off we briskly went.

I felt I must try to reach Argul now. Catch up with him. Yesterday, up ahead on the next piece of the hills, he had seemed to be traveling steadily but not fast.

One thing about a graffapin, or this one, it can really run, and *keep* running. Finally I had to say *Frum-froff*—the command to slow him down, because I'd realized he'd been haring along for about fifty minutes at around eighty miles an hour.

He didn't seem out of breath. Just started to gubble and snuffle to himself again, which, when going flat out, he hadn't.

No sign of Jelly today, but the lay of the land has no doubt just hidden him. He could be anywhere. Even riding *beside* me over there, somewhere, concealed by the high hill-shoulder and the fires.

And I haven't caught up to Argul. Or seen him again.

The road is worse. Whole bits missing.

Passed a fire-fountain, a cascade splashing over from some tall rocks, green-shot red.

"Are you still singing, Graff? You're a good boy."

Of course, I've begun to ask myself, did *she* (Ustareth) breed these animals, these graffapins, one more experiment, some unthinkable cross between—what? A horse, just maybe, and a sheep . . . ?(!)

And yes, I have thought about the panther I met in the forest, the talking one. I recall the people around the Rise, girls with flowers growing alive in their hair, and the woman who had two voices, one human, and the other all different birds' songs going at once.

A talking beast. Ustareth (Zeera): could she have managed that?

Sunset, and there's no handy hiding place tonight, no caves. The fires light everything up, including me.

I had a rest and a walk up and down, and some of the boring journey food. Now I'm going to mount Graff and go on, sleep in the saddle if necessary, use the night to travel. Perhaps I can catch up with Argul that way.

Jelly is on a horse. I assume it's the one he rode on into PH, as PH was "sold out." I had a chance to admire Jelly's horse, since they came galloping up to me in the black and moonless depth of the night.

"As we're both going the same way," said Jelly, friendly, "I thought we might as well travel together. What do you say?"

What I said was a Hulta swear-word used, even by Badger, Ro, and Mehm, only now and then. A curse you really do save for best (or worst).

Then I yowled *Yof-yofff* . . . and off we yoffed. Heaven bless lovely Graff, who inside two minutes had outraced the horse—already tired from racing after me—and kept on going.

"Good Graff—wonderful *handsome* Graff!"

Everything whizzed by in a whirlwind of fires and stars and fluttering graff-fluff.

We were speeding uphill, up and up, and I had a vague idea this might be unwise, we might hit the sky—or just plunge over some steep place at the top—when the hill flattened out and everything went jet black.

"Frum-froffy-frum—oh, whoah!"

Graff careened to a halt, and I nearly came off.

What had happened?

Something totally normal, so *naturally* utterly unlooked-for. We'd reached the end of the fires.

In front, the plateau ran away to the dark sky. And everywhere else the land poured over into the shadow of an ordinary night.

For a few minutes I sat there, getting my bearings, getting used to the dark. And I hoped Jelly too would come thundering up here and get thrown.

And then I saw there was one fire left, a small one, over there under that tumble of stones. Some outpost of the bigger fires? It looked like a campfire. . . .

Had I—was it—

I clicked my teeth at Graff, who trotted on. Time had stopped. And in the timelessness we reached the stones and came around them.

The fire was straightforward fire-color and set inside a ring of smaller stones. Nothing was roasting over it, spitting and smelling appetizing. I'd have expected there would be. Like me, he must already have eaten.

The brown horse was grazing the unburning turf. Argul sat against the wall of stones.

The fire caught in his eyes. Was it only that which made them so hard and brilliant, like black windowpanes, *closed?*

I dismounted, and he sat, watching me.

No pretense now. And no greeting.

"Argul?"

I stood in front of him, across the fire.

Soon he looked away with a terrible little smile. (Venn disturbed me so, resembling Argul so much. And now, the other way—Argul—is so like *Venn.*)

"Claidi." Said Argul, complete with a period.

In the tone he used, the voice he used, my name became a smear of dirt upon a distant path, long, long, ago.

"I know what you think."

"I'm sure you do. Even you, Claidi, aren't so dumb you wouldn't know that."

We had always been insulting to each other. Part of our play. Never *never* meant. Love and respect. Not anymore.

"Argul," I took a step forward, not realizing I had, and he said, "Stay that side of the fire. Maybe a shock to you, I don't want you near me."

"Right. Look, here I am. But will you let me tell you—" I wavered, had thought he would interrupt—"what really happened? It's not what you think."

"Suppose I don't care."

"If you knew the truth—"

Was this, after all, the hardest thing I'd ever faced? Dealing with enemies is bad enough, but an enemy who was a friend, someone I'd loved, still loved—

"Argul, I *have* to explain."

And then, right then, Jelly rode up. Having not been thrown at all—or made any noise I heard.

I only knew because Argul glanced up from that deep other place he was gazing down into because he didn't want to look at me. His eyes fixed beyond me, and he got to his feet.

"Mate of yours?" he asked softly.

"If he's about eight feet tall with black stubble hair, riding a vicious—looking blackish horse—no."

"My lord, my lady," called Jelly, bowing in the saddle, "what a stroke of good fortune."

Argul came past and around me. His cloak brushed over my arm. I shivered.

Jelly sat there, smiling his dry split of a smile.

"Why have you been following me?" I demanded.

"Because I hadn't yet caught up with you," outlined Jelly, with intelligent reasonableness.

"You know what I mean. You're from the Tower, aren't you? Who sent you? How did you trace me? There's no Tag on me now, none in my book—was *it Ironel Novendot?*"

Jelly was busy looking at Argul. Jelly's narrow eyes were knife-edged slits. He was concentrating.

Argul said, "I don't think she wants your company."

"I don't," I agreed.

Jelly widened his pouchy eyes to glinting slots.

Just then, I noticed he had a rifle slung over his shoulder. And Argul—didn't have one.

"This is the famous Argul, is it," said Jelly. "Leader of the Bandit Hulta Horse-People. Most pleased to meet you, my lord."

Argul said nothing.

Jelly, to my added horror, swung crankily off his horse.

"I have," said Jelly, looking now over at me, "something for you."

"What?"

"I've been looking for the right moment to give it to you."

"What?"

"This does not seem, much, the right moment."

Argul said, "Get back on your horse and go."

(Jelly, at eight feet, was taller than Argul.)

"That would be easier, wouldn't it?" nodded Jelly.

"But then. Know why they call me Jelly?" he asked me casually, looking at me past Argul now. (No one eagerly asked Why? Why?) Jelly said,

"You were correct. Wolf Tower. The Wolf Tower molded me *like* a jelly, into the form and type I now am. I am a jelly of the Wolf Tower, and I am all *set*."

Was this amusing, absurd, or ultra ghastly? Before I could decide, Argul took two strides. It happened so fast. Argul's fist crashed up into Jelly's middle, and Jelly made a noise and tilted. Then Argul's second fist hit Jelly square on the jaw, just like in a book.

Jelly spun, turned around as if about to march away, and fell splat, flat on his face. Didn't stir.

"Oh," I said, with my usual display of flawless wit. Felt slightly sick, actually.

"Get on that thing you're riding," said Argul. He was already in the saddle.

I ran to Graff, scrambled aboard.

As we tore off along the plateau, over its crest and down the other side in darkness, I cried out inside myself—*We're together now*—

But some minutes further on, when the pace slowed, Argul, riding at my side, said this:

"You can talk to me later, if you must. I don't want to hear it; it won't change anything. For now, shut up and listen. I'm going into the North. I'll take you to the town there. Then you are on your own. That's it. And Claidi . . ."

"Yes," I whispered.

"If you start yattering, or if you put one finger on me, you're on your own here and now. Keep your distance. And keep quiet until I tell you."

He is no longer like himself, at least with me. He sounds now like Venn at his worst, or like—Nemian. He sounds like the *others,* the *Wolf Tower* (He has their blood. I never remember—he too—*he*—is Ironel's grandson.) Have *I* done this to him—made him into a monster, at least in my company? Yes, it's me. My fault.

WINTER

Once there used to be seasons. They were called, I think, spring, summer, fall-of-leaf, and winter. As the desert areas grew and the weather altered and became erratic, seasons more or less ended, as such. Sunny days can be followed by gales, and frosts by months of scorchers. Leaves are always falling off and at the same time new ones growing, fruits and blossoms can appear together, or else trees may stay bare for years. (Or else do things like sprouting froth.)

In the North, however, winter *is.* As you get near, they call it that. They even say, "Are you going on right to Winter, then? Then you'll need to buy this fur-lined jacket," etc.

After we came down that night from the hills, we kept on riding. The sun was already paler, and it was as cold by day as the nights had been, beyond the hill fires.

Bumpy ground, boulders, and ragged pines. Ravens flew over. I didn't pay much attention. Being so careful, as I was, to keep my distance and not speak.

Argul rode always a little ahead of me.

We came to a village inside an untidy wood fence. I thought, *He's going to leave me here.*

He didn't. When I asked, "Is this where—?" he said, "I'm taking you on to the town."

"Thank you. Can we talk then?"

"I've said yes."

We stayed in the village overnight. There was a kind of big room, divided by a leather curtain. I slept on the "Women's Side" and thought he would be on the "Men's Side"—but he wouldn't even do that; he went off to sleep in some other house. (The houses had pointed roofs, and the people had pointed, fed-up faces. Cold. Oh yes, cold in every way, weather and heart.)

No sign of Jelly. That was good. (I have to confess I've felt anxious about him—was he all right? I am nuts.)

Wrote up some of diary. Such a habit, now. Do it even when I don't want to, like now.

Would it be any use asking him to read this diary—as opposed to the fake one *they* gave him? Venn did that and proved to himself I was all right. But Argul—this *new* Argul . . . I can't really ask him anything, suggest anything. If he even lets me speak when we reach this town, then he won't *hear* what I say.

I could be making it all up. That's what he still thinks.

How can he think this of me?

Was I really always so terminally silly and underhandedly filthy? If so, why did he ever like me?

I go over and over what I will say to him when I *am* permitted to speak.

Then I get so nervous.

Then I want to slap him.

I want to *bite* him, I'm so furious about this *INJUSTICE.*

And then—despair.

Why *should* he believe me? Would I, if I were him? If he had just left me, and I was told he'd gone to be with the one he really loved, and I read that too in his own handwriting. And then he swanned back months after, chirpy, and said, "All a mistake. Heigh-ho, I was kidnapped. But here I am now. Of course you want me back."

Yes. I'd have believed him.

Even if I hadn't—could I have let him go if there was a chance he might want me still? I'd have given it one more try.

Maybe I'd have been a fool, but there. He and I were meant to be together. He knew that before I did. The glasslike science-charm he wore around his neck, that Ustareth-Zeera left him, showed him that—I was the one.

And now I can't even say to him, Pass the salt.

I can't even touch his hand by accident—which nearly happened the other morning when we were picking through some fur jackets and mantles, in some other run-down village. Our hands almost brushed each other, and he shot his hand away, as if I would *burn*.

He bought me the jacket, though. And this mantle, lined with thick white fur, and the long leather gloves. (Nothing for him. His warmer stuff must still be packed.)

"Thank you for the winter clothes, Argul."

"All right."

". . . I haven't any money—you do know?"

"I know you are useless, Claidi."

"But—"

"Leave it."

He won't take any responsibility for me. Won't even let me freeze. I have to be safe and sound so he can desert me in this town we're approaching.

Isn't he cold yet?

He's still just in everyday wear, and I'm already well into the jacket.

This last place we've stopped, where we arrived today, (always spending most of the time apart—weirdly like when I was with Nemian on our journey to the Tower) is built up through rocks and caves, like a honeycomb. Not a sweet one though. It's the most depressing dump. Dark and cold, lit by very smelly fat-candles. Everyone sneezing and moaning, arguing, miserable, nasty.

This hostel-house is for "Unwed Maidens." Argul must have been pleased.

I've been more or less alone all day. I've sat writing by the guttering light, and outside, through a crack in the stone, which has no glass, not even a shutter, the drizzly lemon sun crawls from right to left over the smoky sky.

The girl with the slop-pail—yes, no bathrooms, either—just came coughing by, wiping her nose on her long hair. (Unfortunately, they all speak my language.)

"Off up north? Off to Winter, are you?"

"That's right."

"Be cold up there."

"So I've heard."

"This is boiling hot compared to Winter. Going to Ice-Fair?"

Am I?

"I don't know."

"Mind ice don't give way and drop you in the river. Be a deada in seven seconds from the cold of the water." And at last, I heard someone happy here, for off she went in merry peals of laughter at this enchanting thought.

"Wouldn't catch *me* there," boasted she.

After she went, I mooched through the caves to the stables where the graffapin is being not-very-well looked after. Gave him some food and groomed him. Cried on his neck. Mopped him up and regroomed that bit. He put up with all this, singing to himself No glimpse of Argul's horse.

Of course, maybe Argul's gone.

At least still no Jelly. *Molded* by the Wolf Tower.

We all have been, in an awful way.

Did he really have something to give me? What? A bullet from the rifle probably.

Tonight Argul and I ate together in a big cave-kitchen. What with everyone else sneezing and grumbling so loudly, kicking each other, and flicking greasy food about, we couldn't have said much. Which was good, as we didn't say much. He didn't eat either, now I think of it.

Coming out, I stood back to let him go ahead through the door, and he did the same for me, and for a fraction of an instant, through trying so hard *not* to touch, his arm flinched against mine. His felt like stone.

"How long to the town now?" I asked. Trying to sound adult, sensible.

"Tomorrow. The next day."

"So soon."

He was gone.

But he hasn't been eating. Now I think, I've only seen him play with food. Is he still so angry and unhappy that he can't eat? And does that mean there *is* a chance—because if he still feels all that, he must care?

We have reached a river, and a shambles called Ice-Walk.

Even the way I feel now, I have to try to describe this, because it is absolutely strange.

We came uphill, and then the land swept over. From high up where we were, you see—The North. There it is.

The North is divided off by the straightest line of water, this river, which looks as though someone drew it there with a ruler.

A wide river too, a mile or so across, but from up here one could see the further banks. They were marble white. With snow. Only this marble snow, then, stretching away and away, featureless, a desert of white.

And onto it, constantly, a shimmering mist of new whiteness coming down, as new snow nearly endlessly fell.

The sky the far side of the river is purple—as dark almost as night.

But halfway over the river it's mauve, fading back to grey-white on this side.

Halfway over the river, too, the ice starts to form. From the high ground it looked like great dulled silver plates. These fused together as they neared the other side. Wedged up through the ice were *crags* of ice, very tall; they must be tall as hills? And curiously shaped, like complicated buildings with balconies and archways, spires, turrets—

The crags are overall white too, but in places an amazing transparent peacock blue *gleams* out, or luminous green. Shafts of daylight seem trapped inside the ice-crags, shining as the sky doesn't. But all the time, the light shifts, changes, and the colors, too.

Little lights sparkle down on the ice as well. What could they be? Oh, it's this Fair the girl told me about.

He was already riding off along the track, toward the uninviting mess I've since learned is called Ice-Walk Town. It lies along the near side of the river.

And so this is where he is going to allow me to speak to him, and then leave me forever.

"There's a Fair on the ice," he said.

"I know. Yes. Are you—"

No answer.

The unadorable town looked like lumps of bricks to me. Extra-dirty smokes rose, clotting the whitish rain-not-quite-ready-to-be-snow.

The inn-room was empty, but for us. Everyone was always out at the Fair on the ice, said the inn-woman.

A fire groaned away on the hearth, warming the chimney and cheering the room only with smoke.

"Argul, please can we find somewhere more private?"

No answer.

He had sat down on a bench against the wall, stretched out his long legs. His eyes were fixed on that other place he looks at, in order to avoid seeing me.

"All right then. I've waited," I said, "I've had enough. Can I tell you now what happened? Yes?"

No answer.

I went and sat across the sort-of-table from him. (It was a plank on three stones.)

"I'll take it silence means yes, then."

Trembling. Panic and anger.

But I couldn't go on with this any longer.

So, I spoke.

Thinking back, I think I was pretty clear in what I said. After all, I'd said it to him in my head so often, gone over and over it, in proper order, leaving nothing out yet not exaggerating too much, I thought, or wandering off the point. . . . No, I think I did it well, putting my case. Explaining all that had happened. Why I left, where I'd been, how I got back.

Some of it does sound—how could it not?—incredible.

How long did I talk? Too long? My throat was hoarse when I finished—but that could have been the fire-smoke. (Once the woman came in and plunked a jug of something to drink between us, and lurched out again. Neither he nor I touched it.)

In the end, I'd said everything I could. I had told the truth. I said, "And, as always, I love you." And then I sat there.

He hadn't moved. Didn't look at me. Didn't even become fidgety, didn't sigh or turn to me, swear, or even say, "Claidi—now I see I had it all wrong—" None of that.

And now, too, he did nothing either, and the minutes stretched, became centuries.

I could hear a clock ticking over the fire. It didn't really tell the time, having only the minute hand left, but that went around and around.

Outside the window, was it darker?

"Are you going to say anything, Argul?"

He wasn't.

He just sat there.

The fire lit his eyes and gilded his hair.

"Argul?"

I put out my hand and set it on his arm. He didn't move. His arm felt like steel. He didn't even trouble to shake me off.

I removed my hand from his arm and rose.

Humiliating tears were on my face.

"Then Argul, you can go and put out your light—go and *fry.* If you're so stupid—so damned stupid—then what's the use?" My voice was shrill, then too deep. "That's it. You're an okk, blind and an okk, Where *I* went wrong was thinking you were all right."

And I raised the jug of whatever it was, and I slung the contents all over him. And then I ran.

I don't remember where I ran, saw nothing. The town might have been invisible, and the people didn't exist. I was all alone. I never even felt the cold.

* * *

It was getting on to evening when I came back out of the nowhere I'd run off into.

I managed to find my way here to the inn. Had to, because my stuff is here. No doubt I should have been surprised no one had stolen it, but he must have paid, because my bag was up in a room on the second wonky floor.

Wind gusts blow, and the room swings one way, then another. It's like being on the sea-ship again, the ship he doesn't believe I ever *was* on.

He wasn't here when I got back. I knew he wouldn't be. Now I hurt so much I can't feel it, just numb.

Impossible. I shall never see Argul again.

The most stupid thing of all, I keep thinking how I threw the rotten beer, or whatever it was, over his hair and clothes. He *deserved* it. But I feel so bad about it, even now. His lovely hair, the cloak that wasn't warm enough. It's making me cry.

WINTER RAVEN

When someone knocked on the door of the seasick room, I ran to open it. I knew it wouldn't be Argul. But even so—

Flung open door.

Door hit wall and nearly fell off.

Outside—

As I had known, *not* Argul.

Face striped with tears, I drew the dagger from my belt. *"What do you want?"*

She just stood there.

Cool, she asked, "A little politeness?"

"Prance off."

"My," she said. "I've dropped by at a bad time, I can see."

I hated her at once. And that gave me back some energy, if not much sense.

"Look, if you want the bathroom, it's along the hall."

"Do I seem to need a bathroom?"

"Then *what?*"

"You," she said. "I'm calling on *you.* You're not a *bathroom,* are you? You do look rather *damp*."

Sarcastic horror.

"This is sharp," I said, of the dagger.

"So," said she, "am I."

She is.

Whatever I think of her, she is, she is.

Let me describe her, as I saw her there.

A young woman, my age, I thought, about my height, too, really, though she seemed taller.

She had very white skin, but a sort of *dark* whiteness. Eyes ink-black. Her very thick silky hair was chopped short just under her ears, and so black it looked like liquid. Strings of white beads looped in this hair, some ending in small gold disks. She had a necklace of heavier gold disks, set with round, polished pieces of amber. Her longish belted coat was black. Her boots were dyed strawberry red and had *silver bells* on them.

The two most astonishing things were (1) her cloak—a great swagger of a cloak that seemed sewn, on the outer side, with hundreds of black, black feathers, and (2) her good looks. She is beautiful. That's the only word.

Now she took a turn on the narrow landing in front of me. Showing herself off? Letting me know what I had to deal with? (She sounded, from all the jewelry, bells, beads, like a Hulta horse.)

"Coming down, then?" she said. "Claidi?"

"You know my name."

"I do."

"How?"

"We'll come to that later."

"No, you'll tell me now."

"Wrong."

Fortunately I didn't try to attack her. Instinctively I knew she would be able to disarm me and probably snap my wrist at the same time. Which I now think is definitely true. She's been trained to fight?

But I said, "Don't tell me, you're from the Wolf Tower too?"

"Me?" She gave a snarl of laughter. "Most people, I'd make them sorry they said that. But you—well, you've been having a funny time of it, haven't you, lately? What with unkind old Argul and all."

I swallowed. Then I slammed the door in her face.

Of course she flung it wide open again, and this time it did come off its hinges.

She strode into the room.

"Look, Claidi, name for name. How's that? I am called," she paused, understandably dramatic, "Winter Raven."

"That's quaint."

"*Thank* you. I think it's a good name, Meanwhile," she said, "my men are downstairs, And we have a friend of yours, all tied up."

"Argul—"

"Come off it. That man called Jelly."

"You have Je—"

"Jelly. Tied up in a bow."

In a kind of trance I picked up my bag—I was still wearing my coat—and followed her down the earthquake-y stairs.

It was true.

The first thing I saw, in the inn's mostly empty main room, was Jelly, curled into a really uncomfortable position, his knees up to his chin, and his hands behind his back, and all of him ringed by thick ropes.

He could just turn his head, which he did, and gave me his same old crease of smile. Despite the swollen bruise of Argul's punch, and how he was now placed, Jelly looked as he always had—awful. But unbothered.

There were also six men standing around the hearth, drinking from mugs. They wore black, like the girl, but on the back of each cloak had been outlined in gold the shape of a bird with curved beak and outspread wings. Ravens?

Winter Raven. *Raven.* Something crackled through my mind.

"This is Jelly, right?" asked Winter Raven, of me.

"Yes."

"We were pretty sure, but he wouldn't say. Despite what Ngarbo promised to do to him—" an approving nod at one of the six around the fireplace. "We don't usually cross to this side of the river," she added. "But under the circumstances we've had to. So. Your graff's ready outside. Shall we go?"

"Wait."

"What?" Impatient, she waited.

"Who are you?"

"You don't know? Thought you read about the Towers and all that junk, when you were at the Rise."

I said, "Raven Tower."

"Hey! *Claidi!* Wow."

"The Raven Tower was destroyed in the ancient wars between the Towers, in the City. That is what I read. Pig Tower and Tiger Tower and Wolf Tower survived. Raven Tower didn't."

"As you see."

The inn-woman came in right then, and Winter Raven strode over to her and handed her a great wodge of those bluey-green money notes. The woman stood speechless with glee, and somehow everyone else, including me, walked out, with tied-up Jelly carried along in the middle.

There was a boat to take us the first mile over the river, to where the ice starts.

Outside the inn, Winter's "men" had loaded Jelly in a sort of box on runners and attached it to his own horse, which also had a big bundle strapped on its back. That seemed rather unfair on the horse. As for Jelly, he was then dragged through the streets of Ice-Walk. People pointed at him in the box and made fun. No one tried to intervene.

I had already assumed I was a prisoner, as he was, though not tied up.

The others walked. I led Graff. As usual, he sang away to himself, snuffling peacefully. At one point *she* turned to me and said, "Don't you just love them, graffs; they're so easygoing."

"Divine."

She flashed me a look of scorn. "You know," she said, "when I think about it, I could really *kill* you."

"I thought you were probably going to anyway," I sulkily rejoined.

The boat waited by the quay. We got on, with Graff, and the horse pulling Jelly.

The boat was a sort of ferry. Lots of other passengers.

She walked off through the crowd and left me, obviously thinking I wouldn't simply jump off into the freezing water—where, according to that cave-girl, I'd be a "deada" in seven seconds. Perhaps I should jump? I couldn't face it. Oddly, I now found myself standing next to Jelly in his box.

As we were poled over the black varnished water, in under the canopy of purple sky, Jelly spoke.

"They've strung you along since Panther's Halt. Did you know?"

I didn't reply.

"Mmn," said Jelly. "I should have given you what I had for you, before. Can't reach it now."

My face was so cold it was best not to try to move my lips.

Jelly said, thoughtfully, "You don't know, do you? Shall I put you out of your misery? I must admit, it even had me—well, puzzled—until I came right up to you, on that hill."

Are my lashes freezing? Concentrate on lashes freezing.

"Argul," said Jelly, regretfully, "*wasn't* Argul."

"Oh, who *was* he then?" I screeched, scattering all the ice off my face.

"No one. You should have figured it out. Didn't you have experience with those sorts of things? At Peshamba. Later at the Rise, in the jungle."

Now all of me seemed scattered. I fell apart.

I found myself leaning over him, gripping him by the collar. The bruise on his chin had gotten worse. Now he was all bruise. *"What?"*

"A mechanical doll," said Jelly. "Like the completely realistic Ustareth-doll which Ustareth left for Venn."

"* * * ?? !! . . . ?"

"Yes, madam. The ones who can make them, can make them *most* convincing. Have you forgotten—even Venn was fooled by the one he thought was his own mother? These dolls can even keep up a conversation, up to a point, providing it isn't too complicated. They can react and say the right things. And they can learn whole paragraphs to spout at you. Why do you think it kept telling you not to get close or touch it? It hadn't any warmth. Made of metal with padding over, and stuff that looks like skin. If you'd only rushed up and kissed it—" he shook his head.

I let go his collar.

He said, "See this bruise it gave me? I don't usually get done over like that. But it moved faster than a real man could. And, well, a steel fist. Lucky I did manage to dodge a bit, or it could have been worse. It was trained to do that, too—thump almost anyone who got in the way. It was your guide and guard."

Did I trust Jelly? *Jelly*—Believe him—?

Yes, oh yes.

"Why?" I asked. I added pathetically, "Why, Jelly?"

"To get you along here. It was meant to get you all the way over the river, judging from what this lot have been saying, all the way to a town on the other side. Not just to Ice-Walk. The cold, no doubt, affected its mechanisms. It broke down. So this Raven crowd, who've been watching it—and you—had to come over instead and fetch you."

"How—watching me?"

"Spies. Even some way through the doll . . . until it stopped working."

That scene, which I would never—never will—forget. The way he sat across the inn table and never spoke. And even when I threw the beer over him—had he stirred? No. I'd thought it was his utter disgust at me, his self-control. But it had been because he was a *doll.* He hadn't been *Argul at all*—

"Jelly—"

"Mmmmm."

"Jelly—"

"—"

"They can *make* things like that? I thought only Ustareth could do that. I mean, that *real.*"

"Seems not. See that bundle on my horse? That's where it is now.

"—the doll."

"The doll."

I stared at the horse. Then back at him.

"Why do they want me so much?"

"I have a suspicion."

"Will you share it?"

Who is my true enemy—this Wolf Tower man, or *her,* Winter Raven, and *hers.* All of them, no doubt.

But Argul. It wasn't Argul—who hated me and wouldn't hear me. Not him. Not.

"This is getting a bit chatty, isn't it?"

Ngarbo, the black Raven, was standing over us, smiling crushingly.

Jelly's mouth closed up like something sewn together. He wouldn't speak in front of them.

He's brave, though he's horrible.

And Ngarbo may be handsome, but he's one of *her* people. None of them are worth anything. Even *she* isn't.

Why does she say she wants to kill me? What have *I* done to her?

The nose of the ferryboat grated into the ice.

More madness. She and I went off across the solid ice, to see the Ice-Fair (her idea, of course), and like friends, arm-in-arm, because she *took* my arm. Ngarbo, knives and rifle, swaggered behind.

"I ought to stop hating you, Claidi," she said.

"Please do. Then can I go?"

"Ha ha."

Would *not* ask her why she hates me. The Wolf Tower? My run-in with the Tower Law—how could it be that? I *destroyed* the Law—or tried to. Do these Ravens *like* the Law? They seem not to like the Wolf Tower itself.

The fair idled around the ice-crags which gleamed. They're called icebergs (she said). They never melt entirely, but sometimes a crack thunderingly appears. Slabs of ice that weigh a ton crash off and thump onto the people below. All good sport, it seems.

Torches burn on the poles, and braziers stand around *flaming* on the ice. It's so thick, only the slightest moisture forms around these.

Skaters, like at Peshamba, sailed by.

Winter Raven bought some hot roasted nuts in a cloth. She offered one to me. "No thanks."

What does she think I am?

Stalls on the ice sell everything. Marvelous colors. Another time, it might have been very fascinating . . . the silks and furs, the books with gold lettering on their covers, some in letters that look like curls or other strange shapes. The different foods—I'm hungry but will *not* say so. The jugglers and other performers. A bears' dinner party—I think they were bears, very big and well-groomed and hairy. A man sawing—I almost yelled—a girl in two pieces—in *half* they called it. How? As each "half" emerged from behind the screen, the girl had become *two* identical girls.

None of this was like the dreary shore with the town of Ice-Walk.

My life, too, has been cut in two pieces, and changed. Despite all misgiving and fright, I was almost happy. It wasn't, wasn't Argul.

But then . . . where is he? While I am here, *captured* again.

"Oh, look," said Winter R, sounding like an excited kid, "a fortune-telling bird!"

Up we skidded over the ice, bell-tinkling from her boots.

I looked at her in the torchlight. One minute she was like some haughty commander. Then like a child of five—

The bird sat on its perch. It was large, with sunset feathers and a long straight bill.

Winter Raven held out a coin. But the man seemed to know who she was and waved the coin aside. "Honor, lady. Good health to your Tower!"

The bird shuffled along its perch, jumped down, and landed in a big dish of sand. There it walked about, then dived its beak in, and came up with something, which it presented to WR.

Grinning—she even looks beautiful when she grins—she unwrapped the sparkly paper.

She read out, *very* seriously, *"Today is a day for making new friends."*

Oh yeah?

The man was bending over the bird's claw marks in the sand, as it hopped back to its perch.

"But also, lady, beware. An enemy—" He looked genuinely uneasy for her.

"Oh, that," she said. She gazed at me. "Is that you, Claidissa?"

I turned away, and the bird whistled mockingly.

"Your men have pulled Jelly out of the box," I said flatly. "They're rolling him along the ice." This made me feel very uncomfortable. I added, "I don't think they'd have got the better of him in the first place, if he hadn't already been hit and knocked out and bruised." She only glanced. "Rolling him along? Hit and bruised? Good," she said. "Wolf Tower scum."

Then she dragged me sliding off.

Her men did everything she told them to, even to loading Jelly back in the box again, but not until one of them had kicked him.

When this happened, I went over and slapped the man's face. He looked surprised and raised his fist—and *she* shouted, and he put the fist down.

"What's it to you?" said her man, who I'd heard her call Vilk, to me. "Fancy him, do you? Eh, grandpa, lady *fancies* you."

Jelly (who wasn't *that* old) looked rather ill, but blank. As if none of us were there. His skin, under this dusk-day sky, also seemed darker, sort of blue, and his scalp-stubble was growing through fast. His feet are so big. He's disgusting—but, well, what harm has he done me really? He may even have helped.

"I only thought," I said, "kicking him like that, you might have hurt your poor leg, Vilk."

"*Come on*," said she.

We walked through the rest of the Ice-Fair, as if it were invisible.

The further shore was steep. The Raven men helped the horse pull Jelly. She and I helped the graffapin. He kept sliding and sitting down. We had to be careful, though *Graff* didn't seem upset.

"The snow-road up there is better," she said. "He'll be all right on that, won't you, boy? What's his name?"

"Graff."

"That's what they're *all* called. Couldn't you even *name* him?"

This was beneath me. (He had *come* with that name.) I ignored it.

We arrived on the far shore. Now we were across the river, in the North. In the winter-white snowland.

Right then, the snow didn't fall, but the sky must be full of it, ceaselessly making it.

There was no landscape. It was a forever of white, which even in the gloom shone like the moon does.

But the road was there at once, and you couldn't miss it. Though nothing else stood out on the landscape, the entrance to the road did. It was marked by two enormous stone beasts. A hundred feet tall? They were shaped almost like square, four-legged tables, with long necks that rose and rose. White stones, splotched with a sort of pinkish stone in patches.

"Giraffes," she said to me. "The town's full of live ones. Long-haired, of course, for the cold. Your Graff is part giraffe. He's going to love it there. Cheer up, Claid. You'll like it too."

"You think so."

"I haven't been fair to you, have I? Mother'd go on at me."

I tried to picture Winter with a mother, going on, telling her off.

"She's a lady of the Raven Tower," I said.

"*The* lady of the Raven Tower."

"Right."

Winter looked at me long and hard.

"You really haven't worked it out, have you?"

"I'm very slow."

"That's fine," she said. "It's been good, paying you back."

"Paying me back for what?"

"But not fair," she infuriatingly went on, "no, I haven't been fair. Look, there are the zleys."

I looked where she pointed, and at the zleys. Four high-fronted vehicles, carved, painted rich reds and magentas, and gilded, strung with bells like her boots. They have runners, which glide over hard-packed snow, as if on a road. Each zley was drawn by a team of three cream-white panthers.

"She bred the panthers," said WR.

"Who?"

"My mother. She's really a genius. Bred the graffapins too."

"And she can also make extremely lifelike dolls, real enough to be taken for human beings—is that her as well, this genius?"

Offhand, "Oh, yes." As if she'd known even very slow Claidi would work it out in the end.

But this had begun to sound like Ustareth-Zeera. Yet I know she is dead. Who then, is *this* one, this Raven woman, who makes clockwork people—or however she does it?

"*Who* is your mother?"

"Thought you'd never ask. You'll *know* the name." Something crossed her face—anger, a jeer. Then, almost preparing me—pity. "My mother is Twilight Star."

As they were pulling the wrapped bundle off Jelly's horse and into one of the zleys, I walked over and lifted the cloth away. There he was. There *it* was. I'd told myself I must get a look at the doll, to make sure. I'd been dreading it rather. Now—I just looked.

Argul lay there. Only not Argul. Lifeless, solid metal, clockwork . . . It no longer even looked like him, somehow. Oh, when it had been with me, it had been made to seem to breathe, to blink, to *think.* But—how could I ever have thought, even for one second, this was *Argul?* You see what you expect. Get what you look for. I'd been thinking he would behave as Blurn had done. And they had made him behave exactly like that. But oh, again, *how* had I been fooled?

I tapped its chest. Hard, metal, un-human—

My legs nearly gave way.

It was Ngarbo, moving in as if to catch me when I swooned, who brought me around. I straightened up and glared.

"Why don't you undo that man, I mean Jelly. At least don't keep him all folded up like a sandwich. There are six of you after all. Or maybe you're still too scared of him?"

"What," said he, all charm, "the Wolf Tower bod? We've already loosed him. Can't have him getting uncomfy. Not yet, anyway."

They had undone the ropes. Even tucked him in the zley under a fur. But Vilk and Vilk's gun were Jelly's seat-mates.

The men took three zleys. Winter was driving this zley with me. She rapped her command into the dark air. Part of the snow leapt forward—the panthers. We were off.

CHYLOMBA

Shall I describe this room first, or the town? Or the zley ride? That might have been glorious, under other circumstances.

The icy, lemonade-y speed-wind, rushing spangle-sprays of snow, runners going *zzsrrrh,* and all the jingling bells.

Graff trotted fast behind, steady on the solid, frozen snow. The horse had no trouble either, particularly without Jelly or the doll-thing. Sometimes the Raven men sang or shouted. And Winter Raven joined in the song. (Her voice, of course, is very good.)

Only Jelly and I kept quiet. A lot to think about, Jelly and me. I *wish* I didn't feel so much abrupt kinship with him. He too is my enemy. But we are now both prisoners of the Raven Tower. Even if—even if Twilight Star is my mother.

Everything has seemed to link to Twilight, in a way. Or does so now. If—I am her daughter, then Winter is my—sister. We're not much alike. I've never been sure that what Jizania said about my parents was true. Am I now really going to learn? If so—*when?*

The town is called Chylomba.

It's encircled by walls, which, where the snow is melted off them, burn with color. The whole town does that. Even when the sky fills with night—which anyway eerily reflects back the snow and the lamps, and goes a kind of metallic tangerine. Lamps light everywhere. The streets, the town hills, and the builidngs. But these lamps are also colored, like cats' eyes or gems.

Snow never stays anywhere for long, except on the roads, where gangs come by to pack it down hard. Even if snow covers the buildings, it melts off soon, due to a form of under-brick heating. (So the old servant says.)

Chylomba looks, from up here, like a toy. Lots of colored towers, and also all these little terraced hills, on which little pavilions or small towerlets perch, and they are the most colorful of all. From my high windows, I can see several of these hills. One is mauve. By which I mean every terrace, and its crowning pavilion too, is a mauve shade. Then there is one that is all a sparkly crimson. Over there, facing the sunrise, if ever the sun comes out, one hill blazes gold—I do mean gold, not yellow. No, the primrose yellow hill is over *there,* more southward. . . .

All this, with the snowed-white straight streets and squares cutting through, makes the town, more than a toy, look like a board game.

I don't like that. For if the buildings and hills, streets and squares of Chylomba are the board of a game—whose game? And *who* are the game-pieces, the counters, or whatever?

High up, birds wheel. Actual ravens, I suppose. But if so, their way of flying is odd, and also they look too big.

This *room* is very big. Always warm.

Everything velvets and assorted furs. So many furs I was relieved when the old servant told me most of these are false fur, man-made, as they do it at Peshamba.

The ceiling is painted like a summer sky. With, naturally, a flock of ravens painted in.

The day sky is seldom blue outside, over Chylomba. Now and then a break comes in the cloud. It never lasts. Frequently snow falls, thin, like a mist. Once, muffle-thick.

"Is there ever a thaw?"

"No," said the kind old servant. "*This* is a warm season."

I watch the buildings go white, then all the color melt back through.

Always, day and night, lots of coming and going. Along the streets, zleys rush, drawn by panther-teams. Riders trot along, some on horses, or on graffs.

The *giraffes* pass too, like stately towers on table legs. They have long, grey-white fur, mottled almost with the markings of leopards. No one rides them; they just seem to roam at will. Once I did see one relight a lamp that had gone out, using a sort of wand lifted in its mouth. A giraffe-accompanying crowd applauded and then fed it things.

I've been here, in the Guest House, since yesterday. Nothing has happened, except down in the streets.

At first it was nice to wallow in a hot bath, to find clean, glamorous clothes that fit, hung ready in a cupboard.

The old man, or a girl, take my requests for food and bring me anything I ask for, even though I've tried to ask for things they *couldn't* bring.

"Where do you grow *pineapples* in this snow?"

"The hothouses," said the kind old man.

I'd heard his name. It had sounded familiar. Perhaps it's like the name of someone I've known. What was it? I'm afraid I've forgotten.

I'm not quite a prisoner. I can leave my room and trail about through the Guest House (now and then meeting other "guests," who all seem either in a Chylomba-type hurry, or as dazed as I feel).

Am I a "guest"? The town is also, they say, free to me. I can go where I want, I've been told. (Graff is ready in the stable. Or they can provide a zley.)

Yesterday, on arrival, I asked about the two relevant matters, but only once. I asked Ngarbo.

"Where are you taking that man Jelly?"

"To be questioned."

"Oh," I'd shaken inside, wished I hadn't asked. "Questioning" may mean all sorts of cruelties. I did say, "I know he's from the Wolf Tower, but I don't think he knows much, really." Though even I didn't believe that.

Loftily, Ngarbo said, "Leave it to us, lady." Patronizing twerp.

We were by then standing on the steps of the Guest House, in the new-falling snow. Despite everything, I'd dozed off in the zley and woken up coming in at the town gate, guarded by guards in black and gold, under a weird snow-light sky. Next moment it seemed the zley stopped. She, Winter Raven, sprang down and was gone, tossing the panther-reins to a groom in passing. Not a word to me. She'd probably said enough.

In the lamplit snow and muddle of moving figures, I lost her at once.

Stuck-up Ngarbo then took charge of me. He took me to the Guest House. We were on the steps when I asked my two questions. (Which I'd have asked WR if she had stayed.)

The second was, "When am I to meet Twilight Star?"

As I might have guessed, he just looked at me and raised his eyebrows.

"Are you meeting Lady Twilight?" he drawled.

"Yes." What other outcome could I expect? "So, tonight?" I said. "Tomorrow?"

But Ngarbo only said, "Search me."

I hadn't been able to see what happened with Jelly, if they mistreated him again while dragging him off somewhere.

Before I could think of anything else to demand (uselessly) of Ngarbo, an old man undid the Guest House door.

"Tower guest," said slap-deserving Ngarbo. He didn't give the servant my name. He told me the servant's name—no wonder I don't remember.

I don't want to ask the servant what he's called.

I've been a servant myself—I was the lowest sort, a maid. And it seems so ignorantly insulting, immediately to have forgotten his name.

This is the END!!! (Which I thought had already happened.) (Several times.)

I stamped back to this posh room and *threw* things and shouted, just like some spoiled brat—Jade Leaf at the House, for example—

Now I'm sitting here, and in a minute one of them is going to come and knock, ever so courteous and flirty, on the door. "Oh, Claidissa, are you ready yet?"

And I have to go out with them, pretend to be—well, not pleased—but pleased-in-spite-of-myself In order to find out what is going on. If that's even possible. Which I doubt.

Because this is all a game. All of it. That becomes more and more obvious. I am angry. So very—

Sorry! I apologize. I mean, I know you're perhaps used to me by now, but you don't know, do you, what has happened?

Right, I'll tell you.

This being my second day here, and nothing having changed, no one arrived to speak to me or summon me—I thought I'd have to make a move.

I keep thinking how I was stuck at the Rise. I have a kind of sore place in my mind where I recall Dagger saying to me that night I found the Hulta, "It doesn't sound like you—didn't you try to get away or *do* anything?"

It's as if I have to keep on an extra amount now, to shut up her voice in my head. I keep wondering if I've gone soft, or sloppy. I mean, should I have tried to run away yesterday?—or at least tried to get to see this woman Twilight, who may—or may not—be my—

My mother.

Anyway.

Today was getting on for sunset. The purple cloud had cleared a lot westward, and a flaming band of apricot sky appeared, where the sun was thinking of sinking.

I went out through the very straight corridors here, which snap one into another, all alike, with endless doors and silk hangings. Then down a straight wide stair.

Below was a long room I hadn't seen before. Its walls were hung with what looked like carpet. Two posts at the stair's bottom had ebony ravens carved on them. There were carvings of ravens everywhere else too, and even painted portraits of ravens. Flying, sitting, doing clever things—like holding little flags in one claw, or, in one case, riding on a large rabbit. Under these pictures were brass plates. They said things like, "Ninth Raven Imperial: Jorthrust." "Twenty-second Arch Raven: Squawky." "Lady Maysel's Raven: Parrotine Inkblot."

Bemused, I was reading these, when I heard a door open behind me.

I turned around quickly. It was a man. He and I let out a yell.

Then, he yelled over his shoulder. "Hey, man. Come and see what's in here!"

Then the other one stepped through.

Framed in carpet and ravens, there they stood, gazing at me.

Hrald and Yazkool. My first abductors.

"What are you doing here?" I tried not to scream at them.

"Might say the same," droned Yazkool.

They looked sick-makingly elegant. Spotless finery, all in icy whites. Even their hair—Hrald's tinted greenish pale and Yazkool's palest blue. I just knew they had matched themselves in color to the Cold North. A fashion in Chylomba?

I'd last seen them at the Rise. Then they'd vanished suddenly from a terrace, leaving their breakfast, broken plates, and toppled chairs. And later Venn told me how he thought they must have been grabbed by some sort of gigantic preying swooping bird. Venn's favorite servant, Heepo, had vanished like that too, he said, when Venn was about seven. One second there—then a flick of shadow, and gone.

But H and Y are so unreasonable. It had always been hopeless trying to find out anything at all useful from them.

So now I tried to look casual. Thought I succeeded.

"Well, it's fascinating to meet you both again."

"Likewise," said Hrald.

"Speak for yourself," said Yaz.

"Ssh," said Hrald loudly, "look how hard she's trying to be cool."

"Bird that carried you off not eat you then?" I asked. "Didn't think you were tasty enough? Might give its kids food poisoning?"

"Bird!" They both howled. They both went into fits of laughter, holding each other up. "Bird—*bird*—she thinks it was a bird—well, she *would* think that—wouldn't *you* have thought that, Yaz?"

"Oh yes, Hrald, I would—"

They fell into chairs by the raven-carved hearth.

Don't say anything, just wait.

But they went on and on laughing.

Finally Hrald surfaced. He stood up again.

"How do you find it here, Claidissa? They treat their compulsory guests well, don't they? Every luxury. I've even taken up the mandolin again."

"I'm so glad," I said.

He waved me into a chair, wouldn't sit down again till I had, though Yaz sprawled there.

Hrald took out a tobacco beetle from a beetle-box. Yaz produced a long blue tobacco pipe. Clouds of fragrant smoke coiled around the ravens.

"Oh yes, no expense spared," said Hrald.

They rightly thought I too was a "compulsory guest."

"Have you seen the town?" asked Hrald.

He was always deadly keen on travel and sightseeing. I said, "Not yet."

"Let's go out then. They do a splendid meal at the Raven Tea-House. And there're the Winter Gardens—and all the Hills."

"Primrose Hill," put in Yaz, "Red Hill—"

"How can you resist?" said Hrald.

How could I?

So I said I'd go and put on my coat and gloves.

"Oh, and maybe not those clothes—a *dress?*" asked Hrald, not wanting to be publicly embarrassed by me.

I'd realized why they have, as I do, the run of the town. No one can escape here. Chylomba has those watcher things, those machines that watch—I've seen them on the upper parts of buildings. Also, the walls of Chylomba are high and the gates guarded. Outside, the snow.

Upstairs I changed. Sweetly put on a dress for them. Brushed my hair, powdered my face, and did my eyes.

Then I went mad and flung things at the wall—cushions, some crockery. The crockery didn't break. It wasn't even satisfying. (Though I'm glad in a way; it wasn't the cup and saucer's fault.)

Ah—there's the knock.

"Be right out!" I twinkle.

AN EVENING WITH ENEMIES

The man with red hair pointed at the orchestra. Seven trumpeters stood up and played a fanfare. The vast roomful of people rose to their feet, clapping, cheering, raising glasses and cups. All those smiling, glad faces.

We, all three of us, looked around to see who had come in.

It was us.

"Too kind—oh, well, too, too . . . No, no, really—"

Hrald and Yaz bowing and preening.

I was too startled to do anything much. *Why* was the whole of Raven Tea-House making such a fuss????

We were led by a smart servant woman up to a high platform at the Tea-House's center.

Here we were placed at a table with red plush cloth and flowers in a vase so tall they went up six feet taller than we did when seated.

"What are the flowers?" I confusedly asked.

"Orchids," replied the woman.

"They're good . . ."

"Some shall be sent at once to your room."

"No—er—it's all right—"

She'd gone.

Hrald and Yaz looked properly impressed.

"We've never had treatment like this before," said Hrald. "It must be because of you, Claidissa."

The fanfare was still ringing in my ears.

Everyone in the Tea-House had settled down, gone back to their food and drink and friends. But now and then, someone would catch my eye, raise a glass again. To me.

Me?

Why?

What did we eat?

H and Y had some roast thing, a hippotamus it looked like (hope it wasn't) from the size, as it rested by the table on a dish *longer* than the table. I had—what did I have? Tomatoes on toast, I think.

Yaz became very loving to me, in an untrustworthy way. Hrald seemed actually in awe, kept saying, "Shut up, Yaz. Can't you see she really is important here?" But Yaz only said, "Give us a kissy, Claidissy-wissy."

They drank a lot of wine.

Then the orchestra came up on the platform with us and played a song just for me. It was in some language I didn't understand, though everyone else seemed to. I was so self-conscious I poured tea in my glass of wine.

Then, to my utter disbelieving *horror,* everyone in the Tea-House started doing it. Tea into wine, or wine into tea. Servants were rushing everywhere with extra bottles and teapots.

"A new fashion," warbled Hrald. He did it, too.

Only Yaz wouldn't.

I began to prefer Yaz.

"Perhaps we could go on somewhere," I said, as they began to tire of the roast, and the chocolate thing they'd had after (which was nearly as big as the roast, or had been before they ate most of it.)

"Yes, up the Lavender Hill," said Yaz. "Romantic place. Might even be a moon tonight." He smiled grimly.

Hrald, the sightseer, said, "The terraces of Lavender Hill are laid with amethysts and planted with lavender trees."

"Or the Gold Hill," said Yaz, "pure gold hardened by silver. A *long hard drop to the ground*."

Someone else was walking over.

What *now?*

"Oh, Ngarbo!" yodeled H and Y in happy voices, "Come and have some of this chocolate-cream giraffe." (It wasn't, was it?)

Ngarbo flung himself marvelously into a seat, which started to look more attractive itself, simply because he was in it. He wore his splendid Raven uniform, black and gold. His face, though, was rather spoiled by a nastily-split lip and half-closed right eye.

"Is it war?" said Yaz. "Has Ironel sent Wolf Troops to rescue us and take us back?"

"Why would she want you back?" asked Ngarbo. He shot a (half) look at me. Then back at Y and H. "There's been some trouble though."

"Nothing to do with us," said Hrald. "We try to be good."

"No, it's *her* friend, Jelly," said Ngarbo. He helped himself to wine, as a servant quickly carved him a great slice of the roast, with vegetables.

"Jelly isn't," I said, "any friend of—"

"Escaped," said Ngarbo. Then forked food into his damaged mouth with care.

I am of course mental.

When I heard him say Jelly had escaped, it was as if I lit up inside. *Jelly.* He is yukkily terrifying and evil. And from the Wolf Tower.

But the way they had treated him—

"Was this," I mildly asked, "before or *after* you, um, *questioned* him?"

" 'Fore," said Ngarbo. "We were taking him to Raven Tower, and the umblosh" (some new rude word?) "suddenly got free of his bonds, thumped Vilk out cold, bashed Beaky on the nose—it's an easy target with Beaky—and smashed me, as you see. Then he was off and away. We fired," he added. "Missed."

"Oh *dear*," I said.

"Madam wasn't pleased," said Ngarbo, gloomy.

"That's the fair Lady Winter, is it?" asked Hrald.

"Yeah, she didn't like it. Nor the lady Princess Twilight."

At her name—Twilight's name—I got hiccups.

Oh, wonderful, Claidi. Up on a high platform in front of three hundred people, after a fanfare and so on, and hiccuping.

Surprising me, Ngarbo leaned over and slapped me on the back, which stopped it.

"He's one brave bod," said Ngarbo, "that Jelly. And clever. I'll give him that."

"Where is he now?" I wondered.

"Up in the mountains, no doubt," said Ngarbo. "We were on the mountain road when he got loose, going to the Tower. Search parties are still combing the snow."

"What does umblosh mean?"

Ngarbo thought. "Prisoner," he replied.

About twenty other people, complete strangers, went with us, H and Y and N and I, around Chylomba.

We went up Lavender Hill, where the lavender grows in warmed tubs among the amethysts. And also up Red Hill (rubies, garnets), Copper Hill (copper), and Primrose Hill—which is topazes and primroses. Are all these precious stones real? They look as if they are. In the end, you just get used to it, treading over slabs and pebbles that are jewels.

The Winter Gardens are at the top of Silver Hill (silver). Our twenty-four footsteps clanked and clanged on the steps.

By then the moon had risen in a half-clear sky.

The Gardens are partly heated and partly not. The snow lies on the ground, thick and white, and some of the trees are hung in snow like lacy blossoms. Other trees, evergreens, yew, eucalyptus, are cut in globes, arches, fountains, or animal shapes such as bears. And, big shock, ravens. There are holly trees loaded with scarlet berries. A heated fountain plays, a jet of liquid silver—like the Hill—but the edges of the pool are frozen, silver that has set.

There are ice statues, too, that look like tall people of milky glass.

The crowd that had followed us (me?) wandered about. Everyone pointed at the moon, which, like the sun, in the North isn't often seen. It too was an ice sculpture.

"So, it wasn't a giant bird that carried you off at the Rise, Yaz?" I asked.

"No, it was—" Yaz smiled, "a *raven*."

"A monster raven?" I probed.

"No. Just a raven. Really two ravens. Another two got Hrald. At breakfast, you see. And then—up and away."

We were sitting in a warm arbor. Hrald and Ngarbo had gone off like old friends. But none of us are friends, are we? Enemies, old enemies.

Yaz seemed more relaxed. I let him put his arm about me and tried to get some sense from him.

"So—ravens carried you off, these two—four—and brought you both here."

"We stopped a couple of places on the way. But about right, Claidissa-kissa."

He kissed me, but I managed to move, and he kissed the side of the arbor instead.

"Oops," said Yaz, not really put out; well, it was quite a nice arbor.

"Are you the only ones?" I said.

"For you? Of course I'm the only one."

"Yes, Yaz. But I meant are you and Hrald the only ones to have been carried off—by *ravens*—and brought *here?*"

"Nah," said Yaz. "You know," he added, "*I* play the harp."

"Do you? How sensational. Could you have seen an old servant man who was also carried off? And were these ravens a little bit not usual? . . . His head leaned over on mine. He had fallen asleep.

I eased away and left him lying on the arbor cushions.

Outside, a white-haired girl came up.

"Would you sign this?"

"What is it?"

"The hem of my dress. I'll keep it to honor."

"Honor what?"

"You!" she enthused.

"Er. Sorry, I don't think so."

Somehow I didn't dare ask *why* I was so important.

Ngarbo and Hrald were peering over into a silver tank full of colored fish. Then I saw they weren't fish, but butterflies—

"Are they in *water?*"

"No. It's a picture."

"But it moves."

"True," said Hrald.

"Hrald," I said, "tell me about kidnapping me, then double-crossing the Wolf Tower and taking me to the Rise."

"Oh shush," said Hrald. "I don't want to think about the Wolf Tower."

"You used to LOVE the Wolf Tower."

"I've developed."

Ngarbo said, "Lady Claidis, just a word." He drew me aside.

We stood under a black palm tree whose bark was encased in silver, and from whose fronds hung icicles. Somehow it was growing, it was strong. The moon sailed over and put on a cloak of cloud.

Moon in a cloud.

I thought of that song at Peshamba. I thought of Argul for a second that seemed to last a month.

Ngarbo said, "Tomorrow, she wants to see you at the Tower. We'll need to start early, it's a longish journey by road."

"Who?" I said.

"Lady Raven, Princess Twilight Star."

My head went around. I said, "All right. I'll be ready."

"The road's good. Would you prefer a zley, chariot, or carriage?"

"My graff."

"I'll see it's arranged."

He's much more respectful now. More friendly too. (These friendly *enemies*.)

Someone else came up for me to sign something, his cuff. I wouldn't.

Ngarbo grinned. "They'll get used to it."

"Ngarbo, why are they behaving like this?"

With the unclosed eye he looked me up and down. "You don't know."

"I always ask to be told things I already *know*."

"Better wait and have the lady tell you."

"*You* tell me."

"Better not."

She is my mother. It must be that. I'm the long-lost royalty, refound.

I don't know what I think of that. Not much. And yet—

"Actually, I'd like to go back to the Guest House."

"Sure," he said.

Ngarbo walked me down the terraces. We were silent. The sky was closing over like his eye that Jelly had battered.

Was Jelly out there in the winter waste? What chance did he have?

On the street, a servant bowed me into a zley, this one horse-drawn. Ngarbo nodded and walked off in another direction.

On the pretty buildings, the mechanical watchers turn, *watching*.

EXCITEMENT BY WINDOW

My room had been filled with orchids like rainbows, spotted, flounced, and filled. The scent nearly knocked me out.

As I was carrying some into the corridor, the old servant man came up with some hot chocolate for me.

"I didn't ask for—"

"Help you sleep," he said.

"You are very kind."

"I like to be kind," he said quietly. He looked at me. He has such—a *face.* Not wise, or cunning, but not foolish, or even innocent. A face that has seen and known many things but keeps inside only the memories it likes. Like being kind, and liking to be?

I sipped the drink. "Thanks anyway," I said. "Really."

With the door shut, the room smelled like the inside of a perfume bottle. Despite the cold, I opened the largest window a crack.

Now I'm in the comfortable bed. The steady light will fade and go out when I lie down. Tomorrow I shall meet her. Twilight. And then maybe all this tangle can be sorted out.

I dreamed about Argul. He was galloping on a chestnut horse, then a black horse, then a white horse—over the snow, along the road toward Chylomba's gate.

I was up in the air, looking down. Wanting him to get here but unable to do a thing.

And somehow, though the ever-altering horse raced on and on, it never reached the town.

Awake now. But I must sleep. I need to be alert tomorrow.

Well, I couldn't sleep again, despite the hot chocolate. The orchids still in the room were giving me a headache. I started to think, were they somehow drugged by someone—anyone of my new, and old, unfriends, who might prefer me not to be very well tomorrow?

Just as I'd decided to get up and put them all outside the door, I heard this awful soft scrabbling sound.

It was exactly the type of sound that belongs in a nightmare—or a ghost story.

Whispery, scratchy—creeping near.

Was it in the room?

I sat up slowly, when I would much rather have crawled right down inside the bedcovers. The light came on.

Then I realized the grisly noise was *outside.*

Something was scratching its way over the roof or walls of the building. Probably nothing, only a—surprise, surprise—raven. A real one. Or some other creature, a pet got out of a window—

Then I recalled my own window, which I'd left ajar.

I had an immediate idea that something *not* a pet, but unusual and dangerous and possibly supernatural, was clawing its way up the wall, aiming for my room, and look, there was my now bright-lit, open window, all ready *to let it in*—

Would it be more sensible to sprint for the window and slam it shut?—or for the door, which looked much nearer—

I made the wrong decision, it goes without saying.

Leaping from the bed, I sprang downward, caught my foot in my nightgown, and plunged headfirst among the orchids. There was quite a row as vases spun in every direction—nothing breaking, only going *bang-boingg* as they rolled into other things. Since I was now lying on the carpet, the light again went out.

The thick rug, and even the orchids, had broken my fall, and I didn't have time to worry about a new bruise collection, because right then I heard the window swing wide.

I vaulted up and around—the light exploded back on—and I screamed at the top of my voice.

The *thing* in the window, now stepping through into my room, held up a shapeless wodge that might once have been a hand. Out of the shapeless *bulb* of head, a voice said sorrowfully, "Please shut up."

I started a second scream—which stopped in a croak.

"Yes," said the sorrowful ghost-monster. "Thank you."

". . . Jelly?"

He sighed.

My eyes were better used to the light now, and I could finally see that what was there was not a demon or ghost, but a tall man, his hands and face wrapped in bandages, leaving just slits for eyes and mouth—

"Jelly—what did they *do* to you—?"

"Never mind," he said, quite crisply now.

"They said they *missed* with the guns—"

"Yes, they *can't* shoot," he said. Smug?

Right then, perfect timing, someone thundered on my door.

"Jelly—hide—get under the bed. I'll get rid of them."

As he crawled from view, I lugged the covers across, then pelted to the door, trying to find excuses as I went for the din I'd made—sleepwalking? A *very* bad dream—

Outside stood two ladies in beribboned wrappers and hair-curlers.

"This is too much," said one.

"Far too much. Even if you are who you are."

"Who am I?" I blurted.

They blew down their noses like annoyed horses going *ptusk!*

"Sorry. I'm sorry."

"You had a tantrum earlier," they said, more or less as one. "Throwing things and screaming. We guest-prisoners do get upset. We understand. And that one was before dinner. But now it's long after midnight."

"Yes, I see. I should have thought. No tantrums after midnight."

"Do your screaming by day," said the more curled lady. "Perhaps you'd care to join us when *we* do it. Poppy," she nudged the other lady, "has even found some *breakable* plates. And she's an excellent screamer. My knack is tearing pillows with my teeth."

"Oh—excellent."

They were chummy now, smiling at the thought of the jolly plate-throwing, pillow-ripping Tantrum Party we were going to have.

"Nighty-night!"

We waved goodbye around the door. I shut it and went back to Jelly.

As he crawled out, I felt new alarm at his bandages.

"Are you all right?"

"Obviously not. However, let's get on."

I sat down, and he sat down on the next chair. He handed me several folded papers.

"What is this?"

"A letter."

Well, I could see that really. It was even sealed. White wax, with the shape of a bird in it.

"Who is it from?"

"Suddenly you can't read?"

"I can *read.* My own language, anyway."

"Then read it. It's in your—this—language."

"Whose seal is it in the wax? A bird—a raven?"

"Vulture."

Still I sat there.

Jelly said, sounding grumpy, "Before she married Khiur of the Wolf Tower, she was from the Vulture Tower. Ironel."

Somehow I often forget about the Vulture Tower.

Trying to forget about Ironel, perhaps.

He has brought me a long, long letter from Ironel. Venn's grandmother, and Nemian's. (Argul's, too.)

The woman who was Wolf's Paw, giver of the Law.

"You're sure this is for me?"

"Yes."

"Is it poisoned?"

"I hope not. It's been in my pocket for months."

"What does it say?"

"Claidi— " Exasperated, he had called me by the only name I think of as mine.

It made me act. I tore the letter open.

It's *very* long. I read it all, somehow, in silence. Then again.

After that I got up and walked up and down.

Then I read the letter again.

He remarked, "The more you read it, the more it will say the same things."

"Why didn't you give me this before?" I said.

He didn't say, *I've been trying for the past hour.*

"The time was never right. You were often spied on."

"Now it is?"

"Now it's the only time left I can."

"You know what it says?"

"Maybe."

"How *dare* you know! Did she tell you—did you read it—?"

I was being very unreasonable. "I'm being unreasonable. Would you like something? A cup of tea—food—?"

"Eating through this bandage will be rather messy, don't you think?"

He wasn't talking to me as he had. Probably we've gotten past all that. I'm past everything now.

I read the letter again.

My dear Claidissa, it began, *I hope this finds you well—*

Of all the—

I mean.

Rather than copy it all out here, I'll just put down the "facts" (?) as Ironel gives them to me, all in her handwriting, formal yet as curly as the hair of Poppy and her friend. And also decorated in phrases such as, "Your time among us, which was of such flowerlike interest to us both."

Flowerlike *interest*—I'd been tricked, lied to, imprisoned.

Like now.

The Wolf Tower had made me follow Nemian to their Tower. The Raven Tower has made me follow Argul—who *wasn't* Argul, but a doll—to theirs.

What Ironel says is this:

First she reminds me of her family tree, her marriage and the results, which are here as I copied them into my other book, but with the other information I've gained since.

Basically Ironel had two daughters.

One (Alabaster) married a prince of the Wolf Tower and had a son, who was Nemian.

Ironel's other daughter was, of course, Ustareth. Ustareth was married to a prince of the Vulture Tower. He had that foul name, Narsident. Their son is Venn—that is, Prince Venarion, born at the Rise.

After Ustareth left the Rise—and Venn—she called herself Zeera, met Argul's father—and their son, of course, is Argul.

Ironel tells me *all* this, including about Argul. So she knows Argul is her grandson too!

"He helped you to leave the City and the Wolf Tower," she says. "A valiant and practical young man. As I would expect, seeing he is my daughter's other son." *Typical.* Even Argul is only any good because he is related to *her.*

But then comes the rest.

According to Ironel, she is not the one who sent the balloons after me, to capture me and take me back to the City for punishment. (She just vaguely says that others in the Wolf Tower, more Lawfully minded and unkind than she, wanted that.) Ironel says that, when she found out what was planned, *she* hired Hrald and Yazkool, paid them to reabduct me. Then whisk me over to the Rise and to Venn, where I'd be safe.

Can this be true?

She did it—to protect me? Why? Oh, she gives a reason. I am, she says, Twilight's daughter. And Ustareth and Twilight, when at last they met, were dear friends. They had for so long admired each other for their individual rebellions against the Tower Law, and the House Rules. After meeting, they thought up some scheme or plan. . . .

What plan? Ironel goes vague again. She grandly says it's to do with Family, and the Future.

But anyway, getting me locked in the City cellars for fifty years wouldn't be part of U and T's plan at *all.* So she, Ironel, had me rescued.

During the kidnap, I recall Hrald and Yaz being nasty about Ironel. I thought they were trying to see if the others would agree and help double-cross her. But now I think they were just trying to see how far the others would take her side.

Ironel says she has learned since (how?) that I've left the Rise, come back, and got myself involved in searching for Argul at a town called Halted Panther. (Am childishly glad she at least has the towns name wrong.) But obviously she sent the letter and Jelly after me there.

Then she says this.

"I fear, by traveling further north, you are going in quite the wrong direction. Argul, after leaving his people, has made his way back to our City. To the Wolf Tower. He came straight to me. If you value him, then you must add this extra gold to his crown. He came disguised, evaded all attention, misled my slaves, and found me alone. He then declared that he was only too aware the Wolf Tower must have taken you. Even the faked diary had not fooled him for an instant. He had simply pretended to believe in your faithlessness in order not to involve his people in the plot, and so keep them safe from us. (His people are these horse-riders—Hultarr, are they called? Ustareth was always irritatingly untalkative about them, with me.)

"Argul, then, came to me on his own. He said he would buy you back from us with Hultarr wealth, which I gather is considerable. Or we might have him in your place, if we let you free at once. I replied that now, surely, we had both you and he trapped in the Tower, our prisoners. He said we might *try* to take him prisoner, if we wished. He would enjoy the exercise of killing every one of us."

She sounds proud of him. It—the letter—sounds *real.* I can just hear him, wonderfully bluffing like that.

Then she adds, all casual, she knew by then he was Ustareth's son. Again how? Had Ustareth told her all those years ago—but when? (She says Ustareth mentioned the Hulta . . . ?) (Let's face it, the Towers seem always to know almost everything.)

Of course, being U's son, and more important, Ironel's grandson, he's matchless.

She is not going to have him harmed.

I want to believe all this. Believe that he believed in me.

Ironel continues that now Argul is living in the Wolf Tower with her (bet he *loves* that) and knows he is a prince.

If so, why didn't he send me his own letter, with hers?

Did she "forget" to put his letter in?

"The man by whom I send my letter," she says, "may also be trusted to give you word from Argul."

And why hadn't Argul come *with* Jelly—or *instead* of Jelly?

I look at what she says about that. It's too dangerous to allow Argul into the North. (After he got into the Wolf Tower??) Since I, that is me, have gone unwisely rushing off in the wrong direction, fooled by the rumor that Argul put about that he would be going that way. (Which he did to protect the Hulta, throw the Wolf Tower off his track.) But it seems the North is a Bad Idea.

"The North is Raven country. The Raven Tower is strong. Though they would be your friends, I am not sure of them in the case of my grandson."

So there we are. She wouldn't risk Argul, and he did what she said. And—the Raven Tower are my friends, are they? Is this because of Twilight?

I don't trust Ironel. I never have.

But Argul seems to have done.

Then there's Jelly. Can't trust Jelly, can I? Even with this message from Argul.

Disturbingly, she ends her letter with this:

"Claidissa, when you entered the Tower that day, boldly wearing before me Ustareth's own diamond ring, which of course my grandson, Argul, had given you, I knew it at once, even in its Hultar setting. So you see, Claidissa Star, I could have crushed you then, if I had wished to. But no, I let you break the Law in pieces. I let you escape. Think of that, when you are deciding whether or not I may now be believed."

Her name is signed all coils and flourishes.

She then adds this.

"*Argul*—such a barbaric name. I must advise him to choose another. Something more civilized."

That is so—*like* her. So—*true.*

SAYING GOOD-BYE

No time . . . The sky was getting lighter between the roofs of Chylomba. A couple of those huge birds I'm always seeing here were soaring over. What on earth were they? I stood glaring out.

"Go on then, Jelly. What message did Argul send me?"

Jelly made a slight noise, a cough or a grunt. But I didn't care anymore about his injuries.

"Said he hoped he would see you soon."

"Why didn't he come *with* you? *Is* he a prisoner of theirs—of the Wolf Tower's?"

"No," said Jelly.

I turned and glared at *him.* What a sight. Like this, though, he doesn't seem so overwhelming. Even his feet seem to have shrunk. Slumping in his bandages, pathetic.

"If it were you, Jelly, would you trust Ironel?"

"Who else is there?"

"Quite."

I don't feel relieved or even very upset. Mostly furious.

"It's getting light. You'd better go," I said.

"Not going to hide me, then?"

"Look, Jelly, I don't know what's going to happen to *me* today. Ironel says the Raven Tower is my friend—because Twilight is there and she's my mother, presumably. But then there's Winter Raven, and she can't stand me. So you'll probably be better off getting out. Can you find a horse?"

"Mmmn," said Jelly.

He got up.

Stooping—he must be *badly* hurt?—he made me feel guilty after all.

"I'll go the way I came," he said.

"Oh, look—have some breakfast first, or a new bandage or something—"

He swung out of the window. *Is* he hurt? Could he move like that, so agile, if he were?

"So long, Claidi-baa!" he rasped, as he slid away down the roof, dislodging quite a lot of snow. Slipping over an edge—he just dropped into the dawn below. I suppose he's all right? Didn't hear a crash or anything.

Claidi-baa—how does he know to call me that? (Argul has talked to him.) How *dare* he call me that? (How dare Argul *tell* him—)

No time either for sleep.

I got ready, putting on another of the showy dresses from the cupboard. I walked up and down before the cupboard mirror. Am *I* a princess?

My bag was packed, and I put in the letter. Then, I took out the ring, the diamond. Ironel had known it, had she? I slid it onto my finger. It felt right, as it always had.

Full light arrived, as much as you get here on a normal day, when the old man knocked on my door.

He brought me tea and some hot bread. About the only things I could face.

"Thank you for all your kindness," I said. "It *has* helped."

He smiled.

I said, "Look, I'm sorry—that man, the Raven Guard who brought me to the Guest House. He said your name but I didn't catch it. What are you called?" Somehow, it didn't matter now, asking.

Nor did he look fed up. I'd known he wouldn't. He said, "I'm Hedee Poran."

"And—I'm Claidi."

"Yes, I know. Lady Claidis Star."

"Well . . . If I'm ever back this way, I'll drop in if I may."

He said, gently, "It would be a pleasure, madam."

"Claidi, please."

"Claidi, then."

He went out, and I was glad I'd asked his name. I might never see him again.

Five minutes after, a brisk Raven-Guard-knock announced Ngarbo, and Vilk (unfortunately), looking brushed and polished. Even Ngarbo's swollen eye had opened up a lot.

"Are you ready, lady?"

We went downstairs. I said to Ngarbo, "That servant man is first-class. He must be ninety? Should he be working so hard at his age?"

"He likes the work; he's said so. Chose it. Caring for the guests. Some of them even call him by a nickname, they're so fond of him."

We went around a corridor-corner. Vilk said, "Old fool. Brought here by mistake is how I heard it."

Turning another corner, there was Poppy, her curlers under an ice-green butterfly of veil. She fluttered at N, but also at repulsive V. Then pattered up to embrace me.

"Buck up, lady," said Vilk, to her or me, "we haven't got all year."

Poppy was offended.

"I was only saying farewell, noble Raven."

"You've said it now. Three or four times you've said it."

Poppy said, "Now I'm upset. Oh, other noble Raven," looking piteously at Ngarbo, "would you be so kind as to tell Heepo I've been upset. He'll bring me a cordial."

"That's it, *Heepo,*" said Vilk. "Old stick from that jungle place oversea."

"No, a *cordial*," bleated Poppy.

We were walking on, Ngarbo promising to tell Heepo on the way out, and I was breathing so fast I thought I'd burst.

"Heepo," I finally managed. "His name's Hedee Poran."

"Nickname. He was once servant to a prince, some kid, couldn't or wouldn't say the whole name. It got shortened to Heepo."

Dear old Heepo—Venn had said that. For Heepo had been Venn's servant, carried off, as Hrald and Yaz had been—but years before them. Fifteen years or more.

"I must say good-bye to Heepo," I declared.

"Now, *she's* doing it," growled Vilk. "He's only a damned servant. Forget it. We're already late."

I stopped.

When they too stopped and looked at me, I thought of the incredible Old Lady at the House, Jizania, supposedly my gran, if Twilight is my mum. I put on an air of royalty as I had put on this dress.

I stared at Vilk.

"You know who I am, now."

"No—" he started.

"Be quiet," I said. "Twilight Star shall be told how you behave toward her favored guests."

Ngarbo was solemn. Too solemn?

Vilk looked nasty, but Vilk always looks nasty.

They took me to the room with all the raven carvings and paintings. They waited in the doorway, while one of the girls fetched Hedee Poran.

He made no comment, the old man, as I drew him aside under a very big picture of a raven balancing an orange, labeled, "Two-hundred-and-first Flight: Yak, Balancer of Oranges."

"I'm sorry, I don't want to shock you, Hedee—but you were with Venn—"

"Venn . . . ?"

"Prince Venarion Yllar Kaslem-Idoros."

His face paled, but he was steady as he said, "Yes, indeed."

"I was with him not long ago. He's always remembered you—always worried about how you were carried off—from a high balcony, wasn't it?"

"Ah," he said, "yes."

"Hedee—how *were you carried off?*"

"Lords of the Raven Tower," he began. He stopped. Ngarbo and Vilk were abruptly approaching. Powerful I might turn out to be, but right now there were limits.

"I apologize, lady, but—" Ngarbo said.

"Put a lid on it," said Vilk.

Heepo looked me deep in the eyes and said only three more words.

"They can fly."

No one moved. In the silence, I heard myself say, swift and light, "Oh, Heepo, what a relief. I was so bothered they'd be stuck up there, on the roof."

A juicy pause.

"Eh?" said charming Vilk.

"Those poor ravens on the roof outside my window upstairs," I warbled. Inside I had turned to liquid ice. "I thought they were flightless and stuck. But Heepo says it's all right; he knows them and they *can* fly."

Heepo bowed.

"Mad old fool," grumbled Vilk. N and V looked at each other. N shrugged.

We walked through other corridors I didn't see, and out into the freezing appalling world of Chylomba and the Raven Tower, where—they *can fly.*

Oh yes, it all made an awful sense. How else had it been possible to take three grown men from the Rise, grasp them and lift them and spirit them away too fast for anyone to see where they had gone? Even Hrald and Yazkool laughing about ravens—birds—hysterically. They wouldn't have laughed much at the time.

And that odd remark of Ngarbo's about our journey today being longish, slow by *road*. What other way could we go? Over the hills? In the snow, that wouldn't be faster. So what other method was there? Only one. The air. I think I'd vaguely wondered if they had balloons.

Those figures I've seen in the sky—too big, always too big for birds—

Graff was waiting, groomed and saddled, on the street. There were to be ten outriders, seven on horses, and three on other graffs, these grey ones. Men with faces muffled against the cold, black furs and gold trim. All the horses and the graffs, including Graff, had been given plumes.

It *was* cold. So cold.

Somewhere a dog barked, coldly.

I am going to the Raven Tower. To these people who have captured me and are maybe going to tell me they are my friends, and I belong to them. And they may be lying. And they can fly.

THE TOWER

Raven Road goes over the Ups.

They call the country this because of the hills, up and down and up. The road cuts through sometimes, but often follows the curves of the hills, which are short and rounded, taking, each one, about ten minutes to ascend, five to go down.

Pines and firs like dark arrowheads stuck in the snow.

Beyond, above gradually the mountains appear from the thin, snowy mist. They seem at first to be adrift in the sky. Islands, cake-iced with white. They are hugely high.

I wonder if Hrald has made this journey, nudging Yaz, "Look at *that*—what a view!"

Don't think so, somehow. Not many "guests" get brought all the way to the Raven Tower.

Lucky Claidi.

She is there.

Venn would understand this, I think, the feeling I have now, iron cold on cold iron in my stomach. When we went to the house on the lake to see his mother, Ustareth. Only she was a doll.

But Twilight isn't a doll. Why am I so sure? *Argul* was a doll. (And the real Argul is in the Wolf Tower, being a prince with his grandma. How do I believe *that?*)

There is so little I can believe, I have let go. I'm just adrift, as the mountains seem to be, though not attached, as they are, to the earth, or to anything.

I've written this at a stop. They put up a silk tent, lit braziers, brought me a hot drink, and hothouse grapes. (Graff liked the grapes.)

"Only two or three more hours," says Ngarbo, encouraging.

"Oh, be gone in a blink," I say.

I don't dare say anything like, "We should have *flown* up, shouldn't we." I am afraid of the whole idea.

Most of the outriders sit huddled, broodingly, in twos or threes, or apart. I've brought them out when they had better things to do? Shame.

Anyhow, soon

I'll

see

my mother?

If you are still reading, hold a kind thought in your mind for me. Please. I'm alone, and I feel as small as anyone could, under those mountains, under this tumble of shadowy sky.

The Raven Tower rises suddenly out of the hills, among the lower spires of the mountains.

The Tower is enormous.

I remember the Wolf Tower as big and dark, but the Raven Tower is high as sky and black as coal.

The top of it hasn't got a statue, like the Wolf Tower. No, the top of the Raven Tower is itself shaped and carved like the head of a raven. Beaked, scored by feathers, glistening and black, with just a cap of snow. Seen from the Road, the head is turned. It seems to look sidelong at you, as a bird would. And where the eye would be, there *is* an eye—a great high window, fire red.

"Impressive yes?" asks Ngarbo, riding at my side.

He is stuck-up over the Tower.

"Very nice."

"Oh, girl, come on."

Ngarbo was probably right. (?) But I'm not going to be friendly. Not now.

I leaned forward to pat Graff.

Graff was my *only* friend at that point. Dear old Graff, wuffling and burbling away to himself, singing in the silver air, with snowflakes melting on his lashes.

"You're just cold," said Ngarbo, making excuses for my loutishness in not praising the Tower. What did he expect!

But then, I didn't know what any of them really knew about me, or anything.

We rode on up the Road, up the Ups.

The snow was coming down more heavily now. The horses and graffs were trotting quickly.

An arch appeared, a hole in the hills, under the Raven. As we jounced nearer, I saw torches burning there. Then, I saw they weren't torches but more of the hard, still science-magical light.

How did they defend the Tower, out here in the snow-waste? There were no guards I could see.

As we got close, the dark arch undid itself Doors swung back to reveal a tunnel. Very uninviting it looked. No one stood in the way. We rode through, and in.

"Who's that, on the end?" Ngarbo asked, craning back, as we clattered into the tunnel and the snow-Road changed to metal. The hard lights lit the way.

"Not an idea," said the other man, not Vilk, riding the other side of me. "He didn't sit with anyone at lunch. Looks like he's got in an argument now."

"Must be Eggblat," said Ngarbo, "He's always in a fight."

"No, Eggblat's off on his vacation."

I lost interest as they bickered over the last rider of the escort. What did I care?

Then there was a racket.

The metal-faced tunnel roared and rang, and even Graff was shaking his furry head.

Ngarbo and the other man went galloping back down the tunnel. From the lit dimness behind, men shouted and cursed, and then there was the sound of a shot.

Suddenly a rider, another Raven, I thought, muffled up and black-cloaked, on a black horse, rushed past me and on up the tunnel.

All the others then also came plunging up the tunnel after him. I pulled on Graff's reins, and we just got to the tunnel-side out of the way in time.

Then we sat there.

We had been almost trampled by our escort, and left behind.

"This is lovely," I said to Graff, "isn't it."

I thought of turning around and batting off down the tunnel again, out of the doors—if they hadn't shut, or would open, off over the snowy Ups to somewhere or other. To freedom.

But right then Vilk rode back down the tunnel to me.

"Come on, it's safe now."

"Is it really."

"We got the rotten nerbish." *(What is that?)* "Well, he surrendered to us."

"Did he really."

"Thought we'd seen the last of *him*. Must be potty. What's he up to? Gets away—then comes *back* with us?"

"Who?" I asked.

I already knew.

"That Wolf Tower stinker *you* like. What's-his-name."

"Jelly," I answered.

It's carved up through a tall hill or small mountain, the Tower.

When you come out into what they called Hall One, everything is massive but rough-hewn, the inside of a vast towering cave. But it's warm, and not only from the two great fireplaces, alight at either end. There are hot-water pipes working. It's quite up-to-date.

In fact, of course, it's more than that.

I'd expected lifts, but no. Under the heavy banners, (showing ravens in gold on black, black on red, purple on gold) a stair piles up. It looked like metal.

"Hold onto the rail, please, lady," said one of my guards.

So I did. Just as well.

I gazed down queasily.

"The stair is moving?"

"Sure is."

This reminded me of the Rise, sections of building, stairways particularly, always diving about. But the moving stair of the RT isn't like that. It does it to be helpful.

And how had they made it move?

"That knob down there."

Why should I worry about this stair? They can *fly* upstairs if they want—or some of them undoubtedly can.

At the top, where the stair came to a standstill and we got off, was Hall Two.

Here I was asked to wait.

I sat in a chair, staring around at the soaring stone walls, not seeing much.

Most of the escort left me. (Lots of flaring cloaks. Cries of "By the Raven!" which I think I've heard them do before, but here it sounds sort of religious.) Ngarbo and Vilk had already gone, to deal with Jelly again, I imagined.

Jelly was certainly mad. But I hadn't room to think about him right now.

Then, through a high door, came drifting a maid of some very well-dressed sort. What I recall is that her hair had been dyed in stripes of black and lilac.

"Lady Raven will see you now, in the Raven Chamber."

I got up. How, I'm not sure, as I seemed to have no body.

I followed the maid across Hall Two, out of an arch and along some passages. Then there was an everyday stair, which we climbed. At the top was a door made out of complicated colored glass in patterns. It glimmered from some soft clear lights on the other side.

The maid opened the door, stood back.

I was to go in.

For a second, I couldn't move. Then I just walked through, the most ordinary thing to do. But this was the answer to my life I was walking into. The *reason* for my being alive, perhaps, and for much of what has happened to me. And I thought *wait*—but it was already too late for that. Because there were only two human figures in the Raven Chamber. I didn't need anyone to tell me who they were.

MY MOTHER

Two people—and about fifty ravens. The two women grew up like long-stemmed plants from a black grass that waddled and croaked, and now and then flapped up in the air and sailed over the room. Ravens perched in the raven-carved rafters, too. One swung back and forth, enjoying itself, on an ornamental lamp.

She had one on her shoulder. I mean, Winter Raven. She was dressed in a long, narrow white dress. The raven stood on her amber necklace, pecking the beads—silver today—in her hair.

The other woman was older.

How old was she? Old enough . . . to be my mother.

She had dark skin. Her hair was like honey, and her eyes like paler honey. (There was a little dusting of grey in her hair.) She was slightly heavy in build, graceful.

She wore a plain black velvet dress, and around her neck was a ring of gold from which hung a turquoise so finely cut and burnished, the dark of her skin showed through it.

She's beautiful.

She's Twilight Star.

"I am Twilight Star," she said. "My daughter you've met." She had an accent. What was it? Oh—I thought—it's the accent of the House, the Towers—which somehow I no longer have. I must have the Hulta accent now. I'd never noticed. "And you," she said, quietly, "I must call—Claidi."

"Thank you," I heard myself say, in my Hulta accent.

"Will you sit down?"

I sat.

It would be simple to detest her for being so *un*tense and in control. But *I* didn't sound too bad. Was it costing her as much as it cost me, to keep calm?

Winter *wasn't* calm. She was snarling at me, sizzling. (My sister?)

A couple more maids had appeared. I was being offered a tray with glasses of this and that—including a glass of hot tea—which is what I took, mostly because the glass hadn't cracked from the heat. (As I took the glass, I saw Twilight's gaze flick over my hands. Was she looking at the diamond ring?)

"A long journey from the town, I'm afraid," said Twilight Star.

"Yes," I said.

"I hope you're not too tired to talk."

"No."

Winter had taken a glass of something bright blue, which she drained in a gulp. As she turned and stalked away over the chamber, her shoulder-raven flared its wings.

"You don't mind birds, I hope?" asked polite Twilight.

"No." I drew in a breath. "What I mind—"

"Is being kept waiting for an answer?"

"Wouldn't you, madam?"

Couldn't call her anything else, could I?

She too had sat down by now, in a chair under a lamp. As the turquoise pendant swung, she touched it to make it still. She seemed one of those people whose every gesture counts.

A carved raven on a beam flew up. It was real.

Everything is like that. What seems fake is real, and what seems real—is a *lie.*

So, watch it, Claidi. Watch out.

"Why am I here?" I asked. "I mean, why did you try so hard to get me here? The Argul-doll and everything."

"Yes, we did try hard, didn't we? I'm sorry for that, the deception. But we wanted to see you. It was important."

"Why?"

"You saw how they treated you in Chylomba," she said.

"Which bit?"

"When they cheered and drank your health, and asked you to sign their clothes—and you—Claidi—being you, refused."

"Why would they *want* me to sign their clothes?"

"There's so much to tell you," she said.

"We'd better make a start then."

Suddenly she smiled. She said to me, "You are *exactly* the way everyone describes you."

"Oh, *smashing.* Everyone?"

"Mother," said Winter, from across the room, "you can see what she's like. Do you want *me* to tell her the facts?"

"No, thank you, dear."

"Then perhaps you ought to *do* it. You want that too, don't you, *Claid?* You want to know?"

I didn't even glance at her. I kept my eyes fixed on Twilight.

Twilight said, to Winter, "Darling, try to be patient with me. Or I'll have to ask you to wait outside."

"I *won't* go!"

"Then please . . ." Twilight folded her hands. "I'd prefer—Claidi—to tell you everything in some sort of order. So, I have to begin at the House in the desert waste."

"The House and Garden?" I asked. (*My* beginning.)

"Yes. But then, it begins before that even. When the Towers were at war, and the first Raven Tower was destroyed."

Her voice was smooth.

I felt I must sit and listen carefully.

Then, Winter Raven was laughing in harsh long shouts.

Twilight glanced at her.

Winter said, "Just look at her, mother. Like a baby waiting for a story. Hey, *Claidis-Claidissa*—how *old* are you, Claid? Three, or four? Thought you were my age, *Claid.*"

"My name," I said, "is not *Claid.* Or Claidis. Or Claidissa. My name is *Claidi*."

Twilight's voice, no longer so smooth, like a knife's edge, cut through. "No, I'm afraid it isn't."

I turned, staring at her.

"Oh, I am *sorry*," she said. "But why go on pretending? Your name isn't any of those. Certainly not Claidis, nor the pet name, Claidissa. Those are the names of my daughter. She, the angry girl there, who calls herself Winter, is my only child. And Claidis—even Claidissa or Claidi—is not your name, never yours—but hers."

Now I know it all. I feel I have been *stuffed* with it like a cushion. Then sewn together around it. This knowledge. The Truth.

I sit here, stupid as a cushion. I can think of nothing, except what I've just been told.

All this way, for *this.*

I can't remember many of Twilight's actual words. Can't remember what Winter—no, what Claidi/s/ssa did. But I can remember the "story" Twilight told me. Let me write it down then. In case I ever forget and start to think I'm Claidi, ever again.

Long ago, in that ugly City on Wide River, the five Towers fought, made it up, quarreled and fought again. Pig Tower with Wolf Tower, Wolf Tower with Tiger Tower, and Vulture Tower and Raven Tower. In the end Wolf Tower won all the wars. Became Top Dog—Top Wolf.

Every Tower had taken a beating, lost men and women, lost land and property, been damaged. But the Raven Tower was totally destroyed. And most of the people left alive from the Raven Tower—they were made into slaves.

Worse than just having to be slaves in the City, plenty of them were sent to other places far away. There were lots of towns or settlements that had a link with the Towers. One of these was the House in the Garden. Years passed. I don't know how many—hundreds?

Jizania was from the Tiger Tower, but she married a prince of the House, Wasliwa Star. Finally they had a daughter, who they called Twilight.

Twilight grew up in the House, a princess, living a life of pleasures and riches. The one thing that got on her nerves was the endless Ritual, the Rules of the House. So she ignored them wherever she could. Especially she ignored the one about making friends with a slave.

Twilight's friend was the slave Fengrey Raven. He was descended from several generations of captives from the Raven Tower. He liked Twilight, too.

By the time they were twelve, they were inseparable. When they were sixteen, Twilight told the House that Fengrey was no longer a slave, but her steward. This caused an uproar. But Jizania was powerful, and so was Wasliwa, so Twilight got her way.

Fengrey and Twilight fell for each other. She said to me she thought they'd been in love since they were children. But when they were eighteen, she told the House they were going to marry.

The House refused.

Even Jizania couldn't change that one, and Wasliwa, by then, had died.

So Twilight and Fengrey lived as husband and wife, made no secret of it, in fact showed off, in front of all the House.

At first it was a scandal. No one would speak to them. Twilight laughed, didn't care. Then the House decided to pretend nothing unusual was happening after all, and made out Fengrey was only Twilight's steward still.

This went on for quite some time. Until Twilight found she was going to have a child.

Nobody in the House was allowed to have a child without permission. (!) I knew that. Slaves and servants who broke this rule were exiled at once to the Waste. Aristocrats were usually treated more sympathetically.

But Twilight's baby's father was a slave. Worse, a Raven slave.

The House exiled Twilight and Fengrey to the Waste.

When I was at the House, we—the servants—were told the Waste was hell-on-earth. Nothing and no one could survive in it. But in Twilight's time—and even in mine, perhaps—the royalty knew the waste wasn't all like that.

So Twilight and Fengrey got ready to leave.

Then the House inflicted the real punishment for their disobedience.

They were told they might not go until after Twilight's baby was born. Then, when they did go, they must leave the baby behind, to serve the House, a slave or servant, in Fengrey's place.

Probably for the first time in her life, Twilight had been out-thought, and was truly scared. As for Fengrey, he went crazy. *He* had had to grow up in this House of enemies. Now they would do it to his child!

Both Twilight and Fengrey were kept prisoner. Then Twilight's baby was born.

Twilight said her mother, Jizania, thought of the solution to the problem, and managed it.

At about the same time Twilight gave birth, so did one of the slave-women of the House.

Slaves counted for nothing. Only Fengrey ever had, because Twilight loved and valued him. So it was easy for Jizania to take the slave's newborn child away from her and give it to Twilight.

Jizania said, "Make out this slave baby is yours. Beg them to let you keep it. They'll force it from your arms. Meanwhile I will hide your real child, and see it comes to you in secret, and leaves the House with you. They can keep the slave-brat instead."

That's what Jizania said. That's what happened.

Twilight and Fengrey got away, with their own real daughter hidden in a basket of clothes and jewelry.

And the slave's child? Well, it was only a slave—the sort that wasn't fallen royalty from a Tower. Just a slave.

You could say it was even fortunate, because rather than being a slave, it was given to Princess Shimra, who had been Twilight's friend. And Shimra gave it to her own daughter, the unspeakable Jade Leaf, as a maid. And—that child, that slave-child—that was me.

My mother. That was my mother. My mother was an unknown slave.

Oh, I *asked* Twilight, Who *was* she? What was her *name?*

Twilight—I do remember her words on this—said, "I'm sorry. I don't know. She was a slave, you see."

Which means—she was *nothing.*

Nameless. My mother, the slave. Nothing.

I think back—how can I help it?—the times I saw slaves—dragging the princess about in chariots, being slapped, whipped, pushed around. Saw them sleeping in rooms like holes, in the House, in actual holes in the rotting tunnels under the Garden. Have I ever looked into my mother's face—and not known her? And did she know *me?*

I always said, I was no better than a slave there. I was right.

As for my father, well, obviously, absolutely no one could know who *he* had been.

Are they alive—or dead?

I've been asking that question since I was tiny and first heard my parents had been exiled, as I thought.

Twilight said to me, "Probably dead, by now. A slave—unless cared for—seldom has a long life."

After that, she was telling me how some of the other Raven Tower people had meanwhile gotten away and set up a new Tower in the North—or resettled an old Tower. I don't know. Who cares?

I'm a slave. I'm not interested in royalty.

But anyway, this Tower was here. And Twilight and Fengrey came here, and later, after Ustareth visited them, scientific wonders took place, and they lived happily ever after, Twilight and Fengrey Raven and their daughter, Claidis (nickname Claidissa—or Winter).

Then, there in the Raven Chamber, I heard Twilight and her daughter having this exchange.

Winter: "I think we might let Claid keep the name, don't you?"

Twilight: "Claidis is *your* name, Claidis."

Winter: "I don't *want* that name, I've told you, now she's been using it all these years. She's messed everything *else* up for me. At least let me keep the name that *I* gave me.

Twilight: "Winter is a false name, my dear. Your name is Claidis."

All this, as I sat there, broken open down the middle, stuffed with horror, and sewn up again.

I got to my feet in the end.

"I'd like to be alone," I said.

Oh my. Claidi-who-isn't, the slave's brat—I sounded like a royal woman. A queen.

I was—dismissing—*them.*

Twilight didn't react. She said, "Of course. But there is still a lot to tell you."

"I've heard enough."

"Another time, then. The girl will show you to your apartment.

But Winter stood there in my path.

"Aah, you feel sorry for yourself, don't you, *Claid?* You little *word-I-can't-even-think-how-to-spell.*"

"Get out," I said softly, "of my way."

The raven on her shoulder lifted its wings in alarm.

No, I'm no longer a slave.

Whatever the hell I am, I am *Me.*

Twilight said something to her as well. I didn't hear it. But I walked by, through the hopping, flapping ravens. As I reached the door, one of the low-flying ones gloriously relieved itself all over my shoes.

Wonder why that doesn't happen in there more often? Some other scientific trick, no doubt.

A striped servant brought me to this room.

What shall I call myself now? I too don't know whether I want that name anymore. *Claidi.* It was hers, but I had to have it.

It's obvious to me Ironel never knew—still doesn't—that I wasn't Twilight's daughter. That promise Ironel had gotten under the Law from Jizania, to send Jizania's own grandchild to take Ironel's place as Law-Giver—how Jizania must have enjoyed that. Sending *me.* Slave-princess Claidi.

Someone brought me some dainty food, hours ago. It sits there, as I do.

Now they're knocking on the door again.

Let them.

This room is big. A big window shows the darkening mountains. Night's coming.

Still knocking on the door. I've called out, "Go away."

But now I think, it's some servant, some slave. My own kind. So I'm not going to be sullen and rude. I shall go and *ask* them to leave me alone. And if that causes trouble, make sure it falls on me, not them.

It wasn't a slave. It was her again. Twilight. She was alone.

"I understand this must be painful for you. But I have to finish what must be said."

As the dark comes, the lamps in here *fade up* into light. Nothing sudden. It's lovely. I hate it.

"And of course—*Claidi*—what can I say—you must keep your name."

"*Thank* you."

"It *is* your name, also. Forgive me. And forgive my daughter. She's very angry with you."

"Yes, terrible for her."

"Let me tell you everything. You may then understand."

"Madam," I said, "all I want is to get out of this tronking okk's grulp of a Tower."

Look at her. Oh, I'd have loved to have a mother like this. What is Fengrey like? Great, I expect. Plus the wonderful Jizania as granny.

No, I wouldn't want them. They too play with people, use us, move us about in this game the Towers like so much.

But she had sat down. As I stood, my back to her, looking from the window at the vastness of view, she's told me "Everything."

Here goes.

Ustareth, after she left the Rise, and had met Argul's father, made contact with Twilight, here. It was Ustareth who, with her magical (scientific) brilliance, altered the shoddy old Raven Tower to what it is now. Or rather, she gave Twilight the means to do it.

Twilight also made Chylomba, or had it made by machines. (And yes, the jewels on all those Hills are real ones, dug out of mountain mines, also by machines.)

Twilight speaks of Ustareth with loving regret. They didn't meet often. But they did think up this plan—a Dream, Twilight called it.

"The evil bullying of the Wolf Tower," said Twilight, "and of the Law. The Law, where it exists, is almost like a living thing. It rules over anyone who will allow it. Ustareth and I—we believed so strongly that no one should live that way."

And their idea to solve this?

"Ustareth said she and I were powerful. Not only in what we could do. In our hearts and minds. I don't mean cleverness. I mean strength of character, willpower—whatever names one gives it."

Ustareth had said that she and Twilight were superior in this way. They had fought the Law and won. But their children would be even better. "This can happen," Twilight assured me, earnestly.

So that meant Ustareth's son, Venarion (Venn)—even though his father wasn't so good. And her second favorite son, Argul, whose Hulta father Ustareth had loved.

"Ustareth's plan," said Twilight, "was that my daughter should, when grown up, marry one of her sons. Both boys were older than my Clai—" she had the grace to hesitate, "my own girl," she went on.

Twilight explained that Winter (what else can *I* call her?) grew up knowing that she would one day be married either to the amazing Argul, or to almost as amazing Venn.

"But then, in due course," said Twilight, "*you* met Argul. And then again, when Ironel sent you away to the Rise, you met Venarion."

By now I'd turned around from the window, I admit, and was goggling at her.

"First," said Twilight, gently, "you were using my daughter's name. Then Argul became yours. Then, so far as I can judge, Venarion, too. She's a proud, fine girl, who wanted to marry a man her equal. Are you surprised my daughter wants to kill you?"

"How do you know all this?" I said. "I mean Argul and me—Venn and me—" Of all the hundred questions, this one, *How do you know?* always seems to rear its head.

"My dear," said Twilight, "Ustareth's science left us all a great many means of knowing a very great deal."

"Ustareth," I said, "also left Argul a charm—a *scientific* charm—which would show him the woman who would be right for him."

"I know," said Twilight. "It was meant to show him, er, Claidi, that my *daughter* was *right* for him. Do you see? *My* daughter."

"What?"

"Am I only being a foolish mother, when I say I think he might have liked my daughter considerably, if he hadn't met you?"

"Are you telling me—" I stopped. "Are you saying the charm is *also* a LIE? That it somehow showed Argul *I* was the one for him because—only because—I'd ended up living your daughter's life—and with my—that—name—Claidi—Claidis—Is *that it?*"

"It isn't so simple."

"Nothing is. Answer me!"

"In a way."

I dropped in a chair. From far off, I heard her say, "And Venarion, of course, was meant to leave the Rise years ago and come here in the Starship. But he never did. He hasn't, alas, the guts Argul has, has he, Venarion? That wretched Narsident—what Venarion might have been, with *another* father."

Can you follow this? I can't. Or, I can, but don't want to.

Then she said this.

"In a way, I do think of you, too, as nearly my daughter—Claidi. The ones who are valuable, the ones who rebel—who have stamina, cheek, courage, imagination—passion. Like Argul. Like *You.* Oh, my dear, in the end it doesn't matter to us that you're slave-born. You have passed all the tests. You have the magic spark. Look what you've done! Smashed the City Law—dared the Star-ship—and even after we forced the Star to come down, to test you further—"

"*You* forced—the Star—*down*—"

"Don't fret, you were wonderful. On you journeyed. Then came the panther that talked. Another doll of ours, one of our very best—do you remember, it even smelled as if it had been eating meat? It guided you. You showed no fear. You followed your instructions. And then when you found Argul, as you thought, you would not be put off. *Wouldn't* give up."

"Suppose I had?" I gasped.

"Then," she said. She smiled a dark little smile. "You'd have been worthless."

"Thanks."

"But you see, at last we have too-near-perfect pairings. You, with Argul. My own—er, Winter—with Venarion. Argul is superior and will make up for any weakness of yours. My daughter is superior and will do the same with Venarion. Two glorious chances."

"For what?"

"Ustareth and I were exceptional women, in our day. As our own mothers have been, the Old Ladies Jizania and Ironel. You and my daughter, Venarion and Argul, are also exceptional. From such a line—your children—what will they be?"

I stared at her. "Our *children*."

"Think. The Wolf Tower is our enemy, we are united in that. But some of us too have Wolf Tower blood. Even Argul has it." Speechless, I watched her glowing there. "Do you know about wolf packs, the real wolves? Only the best among them may become leader—the king or the queen. Only these royal animals are allowed to mate."

"You're saying that if Argul and I have a child—"

"The Future," she said. She was radiant as the lamps. "The Future must shine. You are a heroine, Claidi, and Argul is a hero. Think what your *child* would be,"

"Give us a chance," I said wearily. "We haven't even met for about a year."

"My dear, you wondered why they applauded you in Chylomba. This is why. You will one day be the mother of a very great woman—"

"Or *man*—"

She ignored me. "You will be the mother," she decided, "of a Queen of the Wolves."

After she swept out—and she did sweep, like a *broom*—I sat there. Now I couldn't think at all.

Then, in the end, I looked up.

In the icy dark of the star-pinned window, a man was standing, on the windowsill *outside*—about a hundred feet up from the ground.

"WE"

Jelly . . . !"

I was rushing to the window to try to open it and get him in before he plummeted down the Tower—and not knowing *how* the window opened—when it opened.

Jelly sprang through into the room.

The window shut.

I thought, insanely, He's shorter. Taller than me, but not so tall as he was—not seven feet tall—his skin is darker—much—he's *tanned* in the snow—? Why is he striding right at me?

Jelly caught me in his arms without a word.

As his mouth met mine I stopped flailing.

His mouth on mine, I knew who he was.

Into my ear he whispered, "Keep your eyes shut. Say *Darling*—"

"Darling—"

"Now listen. I know they have science here and can watch and see a lot. In this room too. Hear us as well, maybe. But hopefully not this, me whispering in your ear. Say *Darling*—"

"Darling— "

"So I can't tell you much now. If I put you off when you ask a question—will you trust me?"

"Darling—"

"Good. The thing is, agree with me, but make it convincing."

"Er—*what* darling?"

"Make it look as if I talk you around. Do you agree? If you agree, say my name."

"Argul," I said.

"Best bird," he breathed.

He let me go.

There he was. And there Jelly wasn't. "Jelly" had been only Argul's disguise.

"Claidi," he said.

"I—I'm not sure I can be called Claidi, anymore."

"Claidi-baa-baa then," he said, "a sheep in wolf's clothing."

I started to giggle. Started to cry. Got myself in order. Unmistakable. No doll, but flesh and blood, and alive. Argul. *Here.*

In fact, I think he *has* grown taller. He's eighteen—nineteen now? I suppose maybe he has. His hair is growing through quickly.

The chemical thing he now tells me he took (more of Ustareth's sorcery) to make his tea-dark skin so pale and rough, and which also made him lose weight, is wearing off. The built-up long false chin he wore broke when the doll-Argul punched him. The swollen bruise replaced it. But chin and bruise have now vanished, along with all the bandages which were also a disguise. And he's removed the pouches from around his eyes.

The boots with extra inches on the soles—half a hand's height, he says—these made him so much taller and his feet look colossally big. They're also gone. They made him walk oddly, so he exaggerated that. He had known the Towers would be watching. There could be spies . . . everywhere.

"Your hand was so cold that time at Panther's Halt."

"I was scared frozen," he says.

"Of the spies?"

"You," he says. "I know you're trouble."

He's telling me quite a lot, though. So these things must now be safe for the Raven Tower to know we know.

Are they listening? Watching? As I stare and stare at him, my one true love. NO ONE will ever make me think only some gadget brought me to be with him.

He's been so close to me all this while.

"I had to disguise myself, Claidi. Even from you. I didn't want to involve you too soon. I didn't know who was a spy, *darling*," he adds, to remind me we still don't know who our friends are but must make out we think we're safe here, "These Raven people," he adds, *looking* at me, "*darling,* they're to be trusted."

"Are they?"

It was easy to sound unsure.

"Oh, they're fine," he says. "Would I lie?"

"Well," I overact, "if *you* say so—"

"Well done," he says.

"But," even now I have to ask, "why that name—*Jelly*—that thing about being molded and set by the Wolf Tower—you said you were a Wolf Tower man!"

"I am," he says. "If Ustareth was my mother."

"How did you—" can I ask this? "—how did you learn?"

"Ironel told me," he firmly says. He looks sternly down his nose, the way I remember.

"But Argul—" I suddenly stammer—"Twilight Star—she wants to breed us—like graffs—like vrabburrs—"

"*Darling.* Come on. *Not* like that. Ironel explained to me about Twilight and Ustareth's Dream-plan. You just don't understand yet."

Pretend, he is saying. I choke. I say, humble, "No?" Feeling *them* listen.

"Raven Tower is clever. They have plans, but they're good plans. After all—you don't mind being with me?"

"Put like that . . . when *you* say it—" I gooily add, "it sounds heavenly."

He is holding my hands in his. He looks at them and says, "You weren't wearing the ring I gave you. Now you are."

I thought of Blurn, accusing me of not wearing Argul's ring. "I was just—"

Argul says, "Darling, please *keep* wearing it."

Before I can make a decision if that is to do with the Towers, or that, well, he wants me to wear the ring—*again* someone knocks.

Probably just as well. My acting was getting superuseless.

But yes, they must have listened. Known he was here and who he is, at last.

The door flies wide.

All of them were now with us.

Ngarbo and five other men escorted them, very brave and ready. Twilight was first, with Winter walking right behind her. Then a man.

Argul bowed. "My Lady Princess Twilight Star! Lord Fengrey Raven!"

Fengrey? Since Argul seemed to know everything, I assumed it must be.

Fengrey Raven was stocky and muscular, with lion-colored skin, and black hair in a long tail high on his head. A terrific face, slanting eyes which were green—He looked quite serious, and nodded, as Twilight smiled, all charm.

But Winter pounced into the room.

"And *I* am?"

She'd always thought she would get to marry Argul.

Argul looked at her. "Um? Sorry . . ." ever so confused.

"Madam," said Ngarbo, "that isn't the prisoner, Jelly. Or, it was. He's altered."

"He was in disguise," said Twilight, "weren't you? How intelligent. We heard of this alarming Jelly—none of us knew it to be you. I am impressed, Argul. But not surprised."

"Argul? Be careful, lady," said Ngarbo. "He gets violent, this Argul."

"Only when escaping *you*," commented Argul.

Ngarbo scowled, touching his cut lip. "Right. How did you manage *this* time? That prison window was a mile high."

"I'm fair at climbing," said Argul, modest.

"You're a *mountain-deer* at climbing, *and* in the town. I—"

Winter broke in. "You fooled them, *Argul.* You even fooled me. Jelly. Quite a victory. So sorry about tying you up. I'm *Claidi,* by the way."

"Really?" Argul, polite.

"He seems to know about all that," said Twilight.

I looked at Fengrey. He hadn't spoken.

Then he did.

"You must dine with us, tonight."

His voice, and what he said, were dull. He sounded much older than he looked. Old and worn-out and—uninterested.

Well, those two, T and W, must be rather exhausting.

Winter crossed the room. She looked up at Argul. "Yes, you're spectacular," she said. "But I shall prefer Venarion."

Argul gave a yack of laughter. Stopped it and bowed again.

I never saw him bow—as himself—till today. Hulta don't. Or have I just forgotten?

If I didn't know, hadn't held him in my arms—would I wonder now if this is yet another doll—another trick—?

Can I trust—him?

Yes.

He trusted me. Not once has he said, Did you want Nemian?

Winter somehow was ruling the scene.

She stood between us, Argul and me.

"Has she told you all her adventures, *your* Claidi here?" inquired Winter Raven.

"Ironel told me," said Argul.

"Oh? About the Rise and all that too? About Prince Venarion—*she* calls him Venn, of course. She knows him well."

A wave of fire went through me. I felt myself go red. This is just wonderful—out of the soup-pan into the stew-pot.

"I heard about Venarion," said Argul. He didn't seem uneasy, angry. But maybe, if he has heard about Venn—maybe he *is* uneasy and angry and only hiding it from them, or from me—or—

Winter put her arm through Argul's. She took a step, meaning them to go on a walk, I suppose, around the large room arm-in-arm. But Argul didn't move when she did, and so *she* nearly fell over. Covered it well, beaming up at him.

"If you get tired of her," said Winter, "I'm sure there are lots of Raven girls who would like to spend time with you. Not me, obviously, I'm spoken for. By Venn. Venn can be very possessive—did you find that, Claid?"

In the doorway, Ngarbo and the other guards were blank. Twilight was smiling and smiling, enjoying this—probably still testing us all, to see how we matched up. (But they all do this, Tower people.)

Fengrey yawned.

I said, "It's such a shame no one ever told Venn that you were waiting here for him, Lady Winter, so loyally. I'm sure he'd have rushed to find the Star-ship and been over the sea to you like a shot."

"Yes," she said. "But *you* were supposed to be me. Enough to put anyone off me, if it was *you.*"

Catty and underhanded.

But she had left Argul; she was standing with me now.

"Shall I tell her?" she asked herself. She considered. She said, "Remember that letter Venarion was sent, a flying letter, he called it. It said what a nuisance you were, Claidi, how you'd caused problems everywhere. Then insisted on being sent to him, and he shouldn't believe anything you said, you were a practiced liar. It quite put him off you, didn't it, for a while?"

I stared at her.

"When I found out," said Winter, suddenly low and fierce, "that old Ironel, the interfering old bag, had sent you to him—*him*, Venarion—*my* Venarion—well." Her voice loosened and was playful again. "I naughtily sent him that letter. I signed it 'We'—do you recall? That sounded just like an upper authority of the Towers. *We.* We—was me, Claidi, and it serves you right."

How odd. Her tone all light and spiteful and satisfied. Her eyes full of tears.

She's been hurt. Really hurt. By the Towers—Wolf, Raven, whoever. Hurt like all of us.

I looked down. When I looked up again, her eyes were dry. She was dancing off to flirt with Ngarbo, who seemed pleased, the total dope.

Twilight was leading Argul away too, and he was letting her.

I had to trust him.

Agree to things.

Fengrey looked back at me and nodded, stifling another yawn. "Until dinner, madam."

"Oh, whatever shall I wear?" I dimly tweeted, feeling completely shattered. (She—had been—*"We."*)

"Better to think," said Fengrey bleakly, "of your wedding gown.

Did I say shattered? *Now* I was shattered.

I must have looked about sixteen question-marks at him, My mouth, naturally, fell open.

"You're to be married to Argul; I gather it should have happened before, but the Wolf Tower intervened. Now Twilight would like you wed as soon as possible. In the next couple of days."

"I see."

"Good evening," said Fengrey. Off he stalked, his embroidered coat and hair-tail swinging. (So I thought of the talking doll-panther in the forest and abruptly suspected it had had Fengrey's bored voice!)

Writing this now, I wonder if *they* will try to read my diary. Why not? They pry into everything else. So, it stays with me at all times, both books. They usually do anyway. And when I sleep, I shall tie them to me, around my waist. That'll be *really* comfortable.

THE OVER-MARRIAGE

All that was yesterday. This morning they brought my wedding dress. It reminds me most of the clothes I had to wear in the Wolf Tower.

Very stiff, the skirt so narrow I can hardly take a step, with a pattern like layers of silver feathers. A huge fanned-out collar sewn with pearls. There's also a headdress of lots of little glass drops. And—glass shoes. Well, they look like glass. I can see my feet through them, carefully tended, each with a flower drawn on, and my toenails painted silver.

I've only seen Argul when other people were there. Like at dinner last night, in what they call Hall Three.

Elaborate dishes of food, every mouthful tasting of something different (and odd). A huge fireplace shaped like an open mouth, with fangs. (Yuk.)

House ravens did tricks. Feathers in everything.

There was some dancing, too. Argul and I danced now and then—they asked/told us to. But they were always those dances where every other step you change partners. . . . We only ever seemed to get to dance that kind.

Winter only danced when it was a one-to-one dance, and then she danced with everybody, *except* Argul. She even got her father to dance with her. After that Fengrey went off with most of the older men, to play cards in another room.

Argul *seemed* completely at ease. Not ecstatic exactly, but—content. But Argul is a master of disguise of every sort.

I kept quiet. Seemed the best idea.

Only once, when we had half a second alone by a window, I said, "Can't we get out of here? I mean, get away?"

"There's a good reason to stay."

"Which is?"

But Twilight had by then sailed up, smiling her smile, wanting us to meet and "spend a moment" with some important Old Ladies of the Raven Tower.

I kept thinking, he had escaped them several times, run rings around them. He'd come into the Tower to be with me, protect me as best he could. But was I now holding us both back? After all, unlike him, I didn't think I'd be much use at climbing up and down the Tower.

They let us (told us to) kiss good night on a staircase (nonmoving) watched by about ninety people, who *clapped* and cried "By the Raven!" (Double yuk.)

But under the noise, I said to him quickly, "Are we trapped?"

"No," he said. Then, *"Darling"*—our warning code word now—"*Darling,* you said you'd trust me."

So "*Darling,* I do," I gooed.

I couldn't sleep. I kept wondering if Argul would suddenly appear again at the window somehow. But obviously he wouldn't risk the climb now, and he is watched. Why must we *stay?*

The wedding dress and shoes—all fit perfectly. To them, getting that sort of thing right is simple.

One extra thought. *Me* getting something right. I asked for some thread, ripped up a petticoat, and sewed a pocket in the lining of the dress, down by the hem, for both these books to go in when I wear it. And if they "watched" that, let them.

Apparently it's tomorrow. The wedding.

An unappetizing man, called the Wedding Controller, came and lectured me on how I must behave during the Ceremony.

I never thought I would ever dread marrying Argul.

Now I do.

The marriage is in Hall Four.

But—Hall Four is *very* special.

Hall Four—is in the sky.

I should have been prepared for anything. I thought I was.

Once the maids had gotten me ready, I was escorted up to a terrace high up around the side of the Tower. (We went by moving stair.)

I thought this terrace was Hall Four, and was very put off, because it was in the open air. But crowds of people were there, all massively overdressed. Little trays of sweets and beetles and other muck were going around. It wasn't snowing, but freezing cold under the grim damson sky.

I couldn't see Argul.

Craning about, I tried to. I thought frankly he'd spot me first, as of all the overdressed herd I *was* probably the worst. I stood there, in the slim-line, overwide-collared dress and hair-thing—like some sort of sparkly Peshamban toffee-apple.

"It's thought unlucky," said Twilight, abruptly beside me, "for the groom to greet the bride before the wedding."

"That's why he's hiding from me?"

"Yes. You must hide from him, too."

"Quite a challenge, in this outfit."

She looked *lovingly* at me. Even my sarcasm was being measured and approved.

All this time, because of what Argul had said to me, I'd been trying to be adorable with Twilight. But whenever I met her—my skin crawled.

She looked glorious. What else? Her dress was scaled crocodile green.

"I haven't been able to prepare you for the ceremony," she said. "I think the Wedding Controller gave you some instruction?"

"Yes, thanks."

I thought of the stick he'd kept slapping repeatedly on his boot, instead, I felt, of where he'd like to slap it—on my hands. But the wedding was simple enough. Just another case of doing as I was told.

Among the Hulta, one of the Old Men would have married Argul to me, and an Old Woman would have married me to Argul.

Here it was apparently to be Lord Fengrey who would marry us, at the altar of the Tower god.

That had sort of surprised me. In the House, and in the Wolf Tower, there had been no gods, and seldom mention, that I ever heard, of God. (In the House, never even that.)

The way the Controller spoke of this god, though, it/he/she didn't seem to amount to much—just some ritual object. (Although they seem to swear by it.)

I hoped they'd do the marriage soon. Wanted it over.

But I knew really, being a Tower, the marriage would be extreme in every way. Should I have guessed how extreme?

Some servants came marching along the shivering terrace, bearing what I thought was another, very big, tray.

I didn't ask what it was, but what it turned out to be was something that they had to put down in front of me, and onto which I had to step. So, on I got.

And I didn't say to her, either, Why am I standing on a great big tray? No doubt some other ritual, which the Wedding Controller had forgotten to tell me about.

Then something strange. There were now four Raven Guards standing, two either side of the tray. They were attaching themselves to the tray, by shoulder-harnesses, and long chains that went through the sides of it.

Ngarbo was there, and as the chains pulled taut, he said, "Please grasp two of the chains, lady, and hold very tight."

I had time to think, That sounds like the moving stair again; they must be going to pick me up and carry me—

When—

Now I was a silver toffee-apple with her mouth hanging wide open in disbelief. But it was handy to have my mouth open, because in a minute I was going to want to scream my head off.

One by one, then in groups, in clusters, the people on the terrace—were *rising up into the air.*

They rose with the ease of blown soap bubbles. Weightless, smooth.

Some of them were even laughing and talking on together. So I almost thought—Do they know what's *happened* to them?

And then—oh—we—*we* were going up too.

The four guards were lifting upward. The tray lifted quite steadily and effortlessly between them. Not even really a jolt.

I saw the terrace leave their feet. Their feet leave the terrace. The terrace sank away and away and *away.*

We were in midair.

All around us, relaxed people, rising through the sky, still having idiot conversations, of which I heard snatches, "Oh, I *do* like your sash." "Have you *seen* Maysel's *hair?*" "Oh confound it, look, I dropped my glass."

They can fly. Somehow I had thought it would be like birds. . . . Why would it? They don't have wings.

No, they "fly" merely by *rising off the ground,* going up and up—and since I can't, they have to carry me, on a tray—

Where is Argul? On another tray? Did he *know* about this—if he did, why didn't he warn me—

In the crowd, the rising flying crowd—I still couldn't see him. And now low clouds were swirling around us, like fog.

I'd been in the Star and seen clouds wrap around the ship. But *in* the Star. Safe inside.

"It's all right, lady," said Ngarbo. "We won't drop you."

Was it mockery—or a thoughtful reassurance?

It can't have taken long. A few minutes. I'll never forget it. That rising, clutching two of the chains, seeing these overdressed, chattery people floating up with me, through a fog of cloud, their crystal goblets and jewels glinting. And every so often, the colossal walls of the mountains glimpsing through all around, so huge and far off and *near* all at once—

I thought I'd be sick.

Was looking around and down at who I thought I'd like best, of the ones rising up below me, to be sick *on*—when Ngarbo said, "See, we're there."

No longer rising, they were all taking weird swimming *steps* forward—walking now, in the sky. Something loomed, warmer, bright—we *were* there.

The tray grounded. Ngarbo took my arm to stop me falling flat on my face. My chest felt tight. I was dizzy.

Someone else had my other arm.

"That was a rotten trick—she didn't tell you about that, did she? My mother can be a real so-and-so."

Blearily I turned and saw my arch-enemy, Winter Raven, was helping hold me up. She wore gold striped with black—and looked like a wasp.

I shook her off. Stood straight.

"No, I think she did somehow forget to mention it."

"It's these," said WR. She pointed at her amber necklace. "And her turquoise. We all have jewelry that can do it. Lift us up, get us down. They have magnets in them."

That was like the Star. Yinyay had said—the ship's magnets reacted to gravity, absorbing and canceling it to let the Star rise, gradually reintroducing it to let the Star land.

Why was WR being friendly and sympathetic? Some new plot—

I turned. Argul was there.

Even in a state, I saw he looked amazing. All in scarlet and gold, his still-short hair gleaming black silk, his skin tea-dark again. But he was strained, his eyes wide on me.

"Are you all right, Claidi?"

"Are you?"

"That was either meant," he said, "to be a brilliant thrill for us—or a big smack in the gob."

She spoke, "Smack in the gob."

"Well, you'd know," he said.

"All right," she said, "I am *sorry* about the other day. But look—I'd have at least *told* you about this beforehand. I don't like the games they play either, you know. My mother, my father—when he can be bothered. They mess me about, too. I've had seventeen years of it."

Green crocodile Twilight was there.

"Now you *can* be together, my dears," she said to Argul and me. "It's quite all right."

"No one told them about the flight up" said Winter.

"Really? I'm sure someone was meant to . . ."

I saw Argul give her his first unliking look. She raised her brows.

Up here—for the first time, standing beside him, I looked around. I mean, where on earth—where *off* earth—were we?

We'd come in through an arch, very tall and wide. There was a floor of tiles, dark and gleaming. If it hadn't been for the shine of the lamps and candles on their stands, the shine of them in the glass walls of the great chamber—I might have thought we were just balanced on one more tray, up in the air.

The high ceiling was glass too, but mirror. Everything and everyone was reflected up there. Staring up, I looked into my own far-off upturned face.

At the other end of the long room, a great fountain. Even I could see it wasn't water. Out the spouts in the beaks of white stone birds, from the held-high trumpets of white stone people, gushed gushes of something tinted every color in the world.

"Air fountains," said Winter Raven. "It's necessary. The air's thin up here, you see." (I was relieved I hadn't just been panting from being cowardly.)

I thought, Hrald would *love* this.

I thought, How does this glass room stay put? Like the Star-ship, maybe. More magnets, of course.

I've never understood about those magnets. And I wasn't going to ask now.

Argul was there, and I could feel the warmth and strength of him, and when he took my hand, it *was* him. Not any trick—

Only, there had been so many tricks. Even he—had tricked me, misled me. He'd had to, he'd said. To fool the ones who *watched.*

Even so.

I hadn't known him—at Panther's Halt, the Hills, Ice-Walk, Chylomba—all that time I'd ridden after Argul, only it hadn't been him but a mechanical doll. And meanwhile he, disguised as Jelly, had ridden after *me.*

Now musicians were starting to play a stately tune. The crowd drew aside, leaving an open lane. At the top of this lane of people, exactly in front of the gushing air fountain, I now saw what must be the altar. It was a stone thing with a black stone raven. Lord Fengrey was there. Looking bored but resigned.

The Wedding Controller appeared.

"Now then," he clucked, tapping his posh stick on his boot.

So. Argul and I must walk up the aisle, between the staring people of the Raven Tower. Up the aisle of the room in the sky. And when we came to the stone altar, Lord Fengrey would marry us. (If he hadn't nodded off from uninterest.)

We walked, in time to the slow music, as the Wedding Controller had just told us we should. Twilight and Winter walked behind us, but not very close.

Argul spoke to me, under the music.

"This is it, Claidi."

"Yes."

"I don't mean this tronk of a marriage. I mean, Claidi, you are really going to have to trust me—Claidi—listen, whatever I tell you to do, *do* it. Will you?"

"Yes, Argul."

"You don't know what I'm going to ask, Claidi."

"No. Something—difficult."

"See that bird thing on the altar?"

"Their Raven god—is it—?"

"In a way. When we get there, put your hand out, the hand with your diamond ring I gave you. Don't let them stop you. Right?"

"My hand with the diamond . . ."

"Touch the raven."

"Why?"

"Claidi, though I love the way you always ask questions at the wrong moment, now is the wrong moment plus."

"But—"

"Touch the raven. It may spit or something. Don't worry."

"Spit—is it alive?"

"Claidi—no, it's not alive. Just touch it."

"Yes, Argul."

"Do you want them to marry us?" he abruptly added.

It was a long way to the altar. The music we must keep time to made the walk very slow. It helped muffle what we said.

People were laughing on both sides, or laughing *at* us.

I could smell the strange acid smell of the air fountain.

"Don't you want to marry me anymore, Argul? I—I thought you still did."

"I don't want *this* load of morbofs to do it. God, Claidi. They overdo everything. Their rituals, their *games*—their clothes, We wouldn't be married, we'd be—"

"Over-married."

"Right. Claidi-baa-baa, we'll marry, but somewhere else."

I could see Fengrey so clearly now, standing there, piled with robes, at the altar. This bored, overdressed man—I didn't want him to have anything to do with us. And T and W lurking at our shoulders. And—breeding us, as Ustareth bred her peculiar animals. Let's face it, as Venn had almost said—Ustareth bred *herself* too, to see what she would get. (1) Venn—not good enough. (2) Argul—a success!

"When you've touched the stone raven," said Argul, "I want you to do just one more thing."

"Yes, Argul?"

"Jump over the fountain."

"—Argul? It's about ten man-heights high, isn't it?"

Suddenly this explosion of women in frothy dresses boiled out of the crowd, singing and chucking flowers, and we were surrounded.

"Darling," growled Argul violently.

So I knew I mustn't ask another thing.

OUT OF THE CAGE

We had reached the altar.

The music ended. The crowd went quiet. I could hear only the gush of the fountain, and the spat-spat of flames in the real lamps.

I turned and looked up at him. And in that second he drew a knife that maybe they—and certainly I—didn't know he had in his wedding finery.

Fengrey's noble mindless face—swelled as if about to pop.

I reached forward and gripped the head of the raven statue on the altar. I used both hands, in case.

A spray of sparks!

I staggered back, wondering if I was on fire or had been struck by lightning.

"*Jump,* Claidi!" Argul shouted.

I think I knew. It wasn't only that I trusted him. Perhaps I didn't trust him, not even Argul, right then.

But the diamond ring, which had seemed to have such odd powers at the Rise—the diamond was blazing heatless blinding white—a firework.

So—I jumped. Right for the top of the fountain, sixty feet up in the ceiling.

Then *I* was in the ceiling. I was up there, by the mirror—I shrieked as I saw my own reflection rush toward me—a screaming young woman in a silver dress and too many pearls—and just as I thought I'd strike her head-on, smash her and die—the whole roof opened like the petals of an obliging rose—

And *then* I was arrowing on into the plum-black cloud—and then Argul grabbed me.

"It's all right. Down now—we're too high."

"But Argul—you're flying too—"

"You bet."

I found we were quite still. Hanging there in midair, midcloud.

Ridiculous to the last, I noticed I'd split the skirt of the silver dress.

"How have we stopped?" I asked.

"You meant to stop, and so did I. That stops us. But we should get down lower. This air's too thin."

"What do I—"

"Tell it *down,* or *think* down. Either."

Yes, The ring reacted to thought, didn't it. Oh . . .

We dropped, quite quickly but not frighteningly so, and the cloud dissolved.

It was—too mad—too *dream*like to be scary now. Although—I must be scared.

"Argul, how can *you* fly?"

"Later, Claidi-baari."

He veered away, and I found I was veering with him.

Incredible—

We whizzed through a gulley between two towering crags that gleamed in their armor of snow. Behind, over there, that white-capped dark thing *far down* was the *head* of the Raven Tower. (Up against the cloud, I couldn't see the glassy bubble of Hall Four.)

Now Argul was landing like a splendid scarlet eagle on a ledge. So—I landed there too. Faultlessly. Then I sat down with a bump. (If I fell right off, it wouldn't matter, would it?)

"We haven't long," he said. "Look."

I peered back into reeling distance. A flight of bats was circling out against the snows.

"They're coming after us."

"What else? Most of the Tower Guard can fly, and all the nobles. Let's make this fast."

We dashed up again. Into the air. I thought what good targets we'd present. I in the flashy silver and he in the red. Could they shoot—as it were—on the wing?

I thought—But we are *flying.*

How? Why? What is going on?

We went so fast now. Too fast to think. I simply did what I'd seen him do. Where he dipped, looped, I did. The freezing wind hissed in our faces. My headdress finally came undone and blew away behind me.

It wasn't like that tray with chains—I could even look down—as if I'd done this before . . . or as if the ring knew and had told me—

But when I turned I saw *them,* those dark shapes—they no longer looked like birds or bats—they were *running* through the air.

It isn't flying. I too was doing this running thing, like Argul. We were leaping on and on, upright, not lying flat on the air, and holding our arms in to our bodies.

We raced around a tall white spire that looked almost like a terrible face. Spinning in, I came up on another ledge and this time didn't sit down. Argul landed beside me.

"The ring," I said.

"It does what it's supposed to," he said.

We were both gasping from the scanty high mountain air, the cold and rush, the escape. I said, "If we keep running, they may keep on chasing. They may catch us. This ring—I think maybe, though I can't know—I think it can protect us. What I'm saying is, it has more powers than flight. What do you think?"

He looked at me. He smiled. He said—*he* said—"I'm in your hands."

The flank of the mountain still hid our pursuers. Yet I could feel them getting near.

At the Rise, the diamond had done the wildest things, not all helpful. And then in the end it hadn't worked at all. But as I looked at it now, it glowed up like an icy sun, answering my unspoken thought. Whatever the ring had been before, now it was itself. And *mine.*

In case I made a mistake, I said the words aloud. "The ones chasing us, don't let them take us. Even if they get within arm's length—keep them off. Please."

The ring flared a beam of white fire.

Will it work?

It had to.

And—it did.

As we stood there, crammed in against the wide of the mountain, out of the bottomless snow-corridors of the upper air came sky-running the Guards of the Raven Tower.

They burst around the mountain, circled in space a moment, calling to each other.

I saw Vilk, and another one I recognized, seven more, then Ngarbo. None of them looked anymore like anyone I'd ever known or would ever want to. Their faces were hard and changed. But they glared—*right at us.*

Now they'll fire. Can the ring deflect bullets?

They didn't fire.

It was Vilk who dived over to the shelf of rock where we stood. As he clutched our bit of mountain with one hand, his eyes met mine—looked *through* mine.

He cursed and dropped away. "Only a damned shadow."

And so I knew.

Invisible. We were invisible.

"Come on, Vilk!" Ngarbo shouted. "Why are you wasting time?"

Vilk veered off.

They stormed by, and after them swirled another ten, twenty men, all looking around, looking right through us. Furious not to find us, angry ravens against the grey-white crags. Then only small as birds again, bats, flies, Blind—to us. They were gone. Silence closed behind them.

There was a cave we'd found. We were sitting in it. I'd tried the ring, and the ring had made a neat bright fire for us with one mild wink.

Perhaps oddest of all, I was already used to the ring, to asking it to do things—astonishing things—and having them done.

"You say please and thank you every time," said Argul.

"I prefer to."

"You have a good heart," he said. And I thought of Venn's grating comments on my thanking of doll-servants and Yinyay in the Star.

We were warm in the cave, but outside darkness was falling. Then it got light again—white thick snow was coming down.

Argul had brought some food for us. He had known we'd be leaving the Tower. (I, of course, had only sensibly brought these books. Oh, and Dagger's dagger.)

Once, we heard more of *them* go by outside. Or the first lot coming back to double-check. Our fire shone in the cave-opening, and they didn't see it. I don't know how the ring does this. The main thing is, it does.

We sat on his marriage cloak.

"I suppose the ring can't summon some pillows?" asked Argul.

"It might—but they'd have to come from somewhere, wouldn't they, and pillows flying in the air might be a giveaway—"

"True. This rock is nice and soft, after all."

He put his arm around me. He said, "I can try to answer all your million questions now, Claidi."

But somehow, we waited a while for the questions.

They are so arrogant, the people of the Towers. Wolf, Tiger, Vulture, Pig, Raven. The Houses too, with their names like Sea-View and Holly Trees.

The women are the worst, the ones I've met. The Old Ladies, like Ironel and Jizania. And the princess-ladies like Twilight Star, who I'm so glad *isn't* my mother.

But it's science-magic and power that makes them so deadly.

Am I now going to turn into someone like that?

I must watch myself, every inch of the way. But he's there too. Argul. To anchor me to the earth. To give me wings of the heart.

The answers to the other questions? I'm going to write them out. Hope I don't miss anything. You've been very patient.

THE RINGS

I thought it was best to write about them first.

Argul, who told me all this, knows everything *he* does because Ironel told him everything *she* knew. Which was quite a lot. But I'll come to that in a minute.

Ustareth-Zeera made two or three rings, all with great powers. Later she was able to put these powers, or some of them, into other sorts of jewelry as well—necklaces, pendants, and so on.

Her main reason was selfish, She *liked* to experiment—I think we all know *that* by now. But she was also a genius.

She left her *topaz* ring at the Rise for two reasons: (1) For Venn, if he could be bothered to look for it, but (2) because it had more or less stopped working. It was an early model. And its power ran out—rather the way a candle will burn down.

Meanwhile she'd made the diamond ring, and this she took with her. Among all the other things it could do, the diamond had—as we've seen—the power to give its wearer flight—by which I mean she can defy gravity, traveling at any preferred height and speed.

That was how she got through the jungle, got across the sea. Under those circumstances she hadn't needed her Star-ship. So she left that for Venn too—again, if he had the brains and spirit—or rashness—to search it out.

Maybe even then she did hope he'd follow her one day. Maybe she was sorry to leave him, only two years old, there in the Rise, with just an Ustareth look-alike doll to be his unloving mother. Until it too broke down.

When Ustareth got with the Hulta and became Zeera, she wanted to be sure her diamond ring was safe from anyone else. So she had it reset in Hulta gold. *That* lessened its powers, or fully shut them off from anyone but her. Which was why, when she died, no one ever thought the diamond was anything more than a beautiful ring. And when Argul gave it to me and I wore it all the time, nothing weird at all happened. (Or if it did, I didn't connect it up.)

Even when I was kidnapped, the ring did nothing. Its power was locked up by the setting, and I had no way to let it out—even if I'd known what it was.

Then though, when I was at the Rise, even when I was on my way there in the jungles she made, the ring sort of began to wake up.

Locked in the cage of its setting, it couldn't work properly, or do anything I really needed.

But all those mechanisms of hers at the Rise set it off all over the place.

In the library, though, the ring *was* able to do things like opening a door, or making the library machines bring me a book. I think her power was very strong in that room. Or, maybe, the ring was just beginning to get used to *me*.

Later in the jungle, when I was with Venn, the topaz didn't work—it had given one slight show of power, rather as a candle might flare up just before it goes out. After that it was spent. The diamond didn't seem to do anything either. When we were attacked by vrabburrs—but then, they were attacking Venn, not me, and I didn't know what I could do—and anyway, we were rescued.

When I came back, I took off the diamond. I didn't trust it. Perhaps if I'd kept it on, tried to—well, talk to it, practice with it—it might have gotten stronger. Or not.

What it really needed was a powerful direct charge from another of Ustareth's machines designed to do exactly that. Something that would get it to work, despite the Hulta setting, full-strength again.

The Raven "god" of the Raven Tower did that. That is where all of them recharge their power-jewelry, if they think it's getting weak. It isn't a god. It's a—well, a sort of—what? All I can think of is, if the fire gets low, you throw on another log. The raven-god is like throwing another log into the fire.

Only, Argul says, now the fire will last in the ring. Last forever. At least, so long as I keep wearing it. It was her *own* ring, you see. The best she ever made.

He'd been told by Ironel the recharging raven was here. Which was why he wanted us to get to the Tower, and stay in the Tower until we found it, or they showed it to us. Argul didn't know, Ironel hadn't, where they kept the wretched thing. Of course they'd put it out of harm's way, up in the air!

Eventually they might, Argul said, have given me the power of the ring—if I was a good girl and showed I was repulsively loyal to them. After all, I was against the Wolf Tower, and Raven Tower is Wolf Tower's number-one enemy.

(Does it go to show that, by trying to be against one bad thing, you can end up as disgusting yourself?)

"Why," I said, "did they ever risk letting us into Hall Four, where the raven was?"

Argul shrugged. "The interesting thing, to me anyway, is that Zeera—Ustareth—my mother, left the ring for my wife. She told me, when I was a child. She said, when I found the woman I wanted, this was the ring she must have."

"Your wife was meant to be Twilight's daughter, Winter," I muttered, scowling.

"Whoever it was, Claidi, that power was meant for her, not me."

But Ustareth-Zeera had left something for Argul, too.

I think I've covered the rings, so I'll say about *that* now.

THE SCIENTIFIC CHARM

When we first met, Argul and I, he looked at a glassy object hung on a string around his neck. Later he'd told me it was a kind of scientific charm his mother gave him, to show him if the woman he wanted was right for him, and he for her. (And, as I learned in the RT, that should have been Winter Raven he was gazing at right then.)

Which I shall ignore. For he and I—are meant to be together.

"Ironel," he now said, "took this out of some box and gave it to me. It somehow sticks to the glassy stuff."

He had taken off the charm by then, there in the cave. Handed it to me. In the center of the glassy bulb was now a dark blue gem. A sapphire, I think. When I touched it, it didn't move.

"*Ironel* gave you this?"

"It's the missing piece—only I never knew anything *was* missing."

Ustareth had left the sapphire with her mother, Ironel, to give to Argul if—brace yourself—he ever had the brains and the spirit—and sheer rash craziness?—to wander into the Wolf Tower.

"Another endurance and brains test," I said.

"Seems so. I passed, anyway. Ironel gave me the jewel, told me to attach it. Then told me what it could do."

"Is it the same as the diamond?"

"No. I said, the main power was for whomever I wanted to marry. For you. This has more limited powers. Like most of the jewels in the Raven Tower. But it did let me fly and open a few windows."

"So that's how—"

How he got away from the Raven Guards—twice. Climbed up a wall of the Guest House, up the Raven Tower itself. He didn't climb. He *flew.*

When they shoved him into a tray to go up to Hall Four, he acted as appalled as I was. As in everything else, he'd never let *them* know a thing, until it was too late for them.

But this explains more than that. It explains how he got to Panther's Halt in time to meet me—he bought his horse *there,* because after that he didn't want any spies to notice what he could really do.

And how he kept sneaking up on me, unseen, unheard—to fool them, but it freaked me out too. Of course, when he was unwatched, he'd risk a short flight for speed. (Disguised as Jelly, they would only watch him at first when he was with me.)

"I wasn't that good at it," he said, "a couple of times I sailed off the ground. When I saw you."

I gawked. "That's why you seemed seven feet tall. But the jewels are easy—they just do what you say—even what you *think* to them."

"Yours does," he said. "Yours is special. Or Claidi, just possibly, *you're* special."

I sat and frowned.

He said, "I don't know. But it seems to me, it's the person involved as much as the jewel. The Raven Tower think that, you know, girl. Why they want you."

When I didn't reply, he didn't go on.

And I think I won't, here.

I did say, "These spies everywhere. You mean men from the Towers."

"I mean almost anything, Claidi. Like the doll-man who looked rather like me—"

"He was your double—"

"Oh come on—"

I said firmly, "You mean there were more of those?"

"There might have been. Ironel said that Ustareth had a scientific formula for making them with likenesses like that. So any man, woman, or child—even an animal—might have been something working for the Raven Tower."

I thought. I said, "Even ravens?"

"Why not. The northlands are full of them. Not all real birds? If you don't know—how *can* you know?"

Spies . . . ravens that aren't ravens. People who aren't—people.

I was afraid of the Wolf Tower once. But this Raven Tower—

At least, because of the diamond, now they can't see or hear or find us. But how far does their filthy controlling web extend? I have so many memories of looking up into some sky—and seeing huge circling black birds. . . .

Let me put down the last of the answers, all I have.

IRONEL/USTARETH-ZEERA/TWILIGHT

Whether it was fair to expect him to, or not, Argul *had* gotten to meet Ironel. (He almost met her before. Perhaps she'd been hoping he would, that time he got me away from the Wolf Tower City.)

I think Ironel is just one of those women who like men better than other females. Nemian she seemed to like. Argul she seems to have liked a lot. Her own daughters—well, she never mentioned them to me. Ustareth, at least, I think Ironel respected. But mainly, Ironel likes playing games.

Argul says, once he'd gotten into the Wolf Tower, she whisked them away upriver, to some out-City estate of hers. A looming house of pale grey walls, leaning right over a lake—as if, he said, it wanted to throw up in it.

Here it was she told him all his own history, and everything she knows about Ustareth, and the Rise. And me. Then she gave him the sapphire and told him about that.

"I felt sorry for her. I knew she was dangerous, Claidi. But what has she got? Nothing. Ustareth made her those false teeth—the pearl ones she can't eat anything with." Argul looked into the fire. "She wears them because they were Ustareth's present. But are they a present—or an unkind joke?"

"Both?"

"Yeah."

Ironel hadn't helped Ustareth during Ustareth's unpleasant marriage to Narsident. When Ustareth was sent off to create the jungles at the Rise, mother and daughter hadn't even written. And they can send flying letters out of machines in walls, so distance was hardly a problem.

Then, when U came back, got with the Hulta and became Zeera, had Argul—then she started to visit people.

"Ironel?" I asked.

"Ironel, and Twilight Star whom she admired for her rebellion over Fengrey."

"Didn't the Hulta notice—was Ustareth often away?"

"Never for long," said Argul. "She used to go off sometimes, she said to get herbs, find minerals. Never more than a day and a night. But she could do it, Claidi. She could cross a whole country in a few hours. She could fly. None of us ever knew that."

We sat and thought of this. Ustareth-Zeera whirling along the sky, to the Wolf Tower, the Raven Tower. Friend to both?

"I know about the plan to breed Top Child, preferably a daughter," said Argul. "A ruling female, like in a wolf pack."

"Men and women are equal," I said. "Wolves have kings, too. Why this *thing* about women?"

"Perhaps my mother," he paused, "didn't agree with you about the equal part."

Ust—Zeera—she *was* Argul's mother.

He had never said all that much about her. He didn't now. But he kept looking away. Into the fire, the shadows. At the thick curtain of white snow falling outside, as if the sky could never make enough.

Ustareth told Ironel all her plan, and Ironel was all for it. But Ustareth didn't trust Ironel entirely. She never revealed to Ironel that Twilight's true daughter, so much part of the plan, wasn't the girl left behind in the House.

Ironel knows plenty. (The Wolf Tower has its own machines and tricks.

More than I'd ever come across.) But in some areas she's been fooled as thoroughly as I have.

Twilight and Ustareth kept Twilight's secret. After all, they didn't mean T's real daughter to end up Wolf's Paw. No. She had to be free to marry one of Ustareth's sons, and so produce a Wolf Queen.

"You've wrecked their plans," said Argul.

"I hope so. Unless—"

He said, "If and when, Claidi, no child of ours is going to have to put up with *that*."

"They went to so much trouble, though, to try to put you off me. Snatching me away, giving you a fake diary to convince you I was—scum—"

"It's possible," he now said, "that Ironel was behind that part. She may have thought you'd be more suitably *mated* to Venarion—what do you call him—Venn. That was naturally before she *met* me," he added, not at all modestly, grinning.

Who can be quite sure of anything the Towers do? Only sure it's a game, and how they like to play—

Look at how the Ravens had snatched Hedee Poran, and later Yaz and Hrald—why? To find out about the Rise, I think, and how Ustareth's jungles were doing, even how Venn was. H and Y were doubtless able to tell a lot about me, as well. But also—what a *game.*

Argul said, "The joke is, marrying me, because I'm Ustareth's son, makes you Tower blood. Though to Ironel you're Tower blood already—she thinks you're Twilight's girl. While to Twilight you're just another First-Class Rebel she wants for her cause."

"Yes."

"Did you find, the Hulta didn't say much to you—about Ust—about Zeera?"

"No, they didn't. I thought because I was an outsider."

"The Hulta loved her. Put her on a pedestal. And they were afraid of her. And was I? I don't know. She could be wonderful. She knew the name of every plant and animal and planet. She could crack shells and tiny creatures, a million years old, out of the rocks. She could heal almost any illness. Except her own. No, she wasn't perfect."

"Argul . . ."

"It's all right. I thought so much of her. Still think like that. But she was wrapped up in what she wanted to do. She was a kind of glamorous stranger. After all, she's played her game with me too. Even after she died—she's still been playing with us. All these tests she left—telling one person this part of the puzzle, that person another part—letting—*making* us run around to find things, find each other—and if we didn't, like poor damn Venn—we'd miss them and miss out altogether."

We watched the fire, shadows, snow.

"The Hulta made me leader very young; I was fifteen," he said. "Guess why? Not because I was the leader's son, or fantastically worthy. Because she was my mother. That was her power, even after she was dead."

After a long while, I said, "You do believe Venn wasn't so important to me? That Nemian wasn't ever, really."

"It wouldn't even matter," he said quietly. "I'm yours. You're mine. Whatever we did, that can't change."

"Yes." I sighed.

And what *else* matters, I thought, but that?

The ring makes as much light as I want, so I can see to write. (I can't sleep. So I've sat here writing. Argul *is* asleep. He looks very young. Older too. Strange.)

One major thing I must note here. Despite the stuff I'd heard from Yaz and Hrald about Wolf Tower Law starting up again in the City, Argul says he saw absolutely no sign of it. And when he mentioned the Law to Ironel, she'd leered and said, "The Law is in the wastepaper bin of life." (!)

Right after I wrote that, this ring mended my skirt, which I tore kicking off into flight. I was looking at the tear, wishing I could sew it or something. And there was this sort of tugging, and the ring pulled my hand down over the tear. Which—did itself up. Miraculous. Only thing is, once I fly off in the morning, it'll probably rip again.

If I've wrecked their plans—how is it I have the power ring like a reward?

I'm so confused when I try to think it out. I mean, is it just that Ustareth thought whoever got this ring would do what *she* wanted? Ustareth is dead.

I keep thinking, though, about Twilight, all alive. What is *she* doing? Plotting? Ironel was so leery of Twilight and the RT, she didn't tell me half the truth in her letter, in case they saw it. She lied about Argul, too, to keep him out of their clutches until he was ready for them.

Tomorrow, he and I can fly-sky-run away. But are we then going to be on the run for the rest of our lives?

"Argul, I'm going back to the Tower."

"You're—*where?*"

"The Raven Tower. I don't need you to come with me."

"Wait a minute—"

"I'd rather you didn't. It's—I'd rather handle this alone."

"Claidi— "

"*Argul.* Nothing can happen to me. Remember the ring?"

We stood in the cave mouth. The snow had stopped falling. Snow had become instead the whole world under the black granite sky.

"Look, Claidi—"

"Once before, at the Wolf Tower, you trusted me to do something alone. Please, do that again now. I *did* succeed."

"All right then." He let me go.

"Will you be safe?" I then asked. "I mean, without the ring—"

"Yes, Claidi. I'll just about be able to manage."

I turned. Glancing down the precipice, I gulped. Idiot. You can fly.

I flew.

A HUMAN FACE

And then there was a dawn. . . . It was as if never before had the sun come up, and now it did.

Strands of lavender cloud drift away—the dark has parted like an opened door.

The wide sky is rose-peach and glassy lemon-gold—and every mountain, every one of the little, down-there humps of the Ups, stroked over with this eatable light.

Oh, what it is to fly! Running through the air. Better, so much better even than riding in the Star with Yinyay—I heard myself laughing from sheer joy.

Then, high above, I spotted a tiny dark blot that didn't move. Thought it a cloud, realized it wasn't. It was Hall Four, its dark tiled floor barely showing in the sky.

And below—the Raven Tower.

A white raven now. The snow had completely covered it, at last, and frozen solid.

I swooped lower. The ring does everything the moment I think of it.

The Tower might have been deserted. Not a lamp, not a single visible sentry. None of the narrow windows showed up through the icy crust of snow. But then, circling the head of the raven, I found that one great red window I'd seen before from the Road, burning like a ruby.

I knew it was *her* window. Who else, but one of those four fearful women (Jizania, Ironel, Ustareth, Twilight) would make for herself a window like that?

The thing with the ring—perhaps the strangest thing of all—is how I'm *used* to it, what it can do. (It had even made me warm, as I felt the snow-chill outside the cave.)

I remember when Argul first gave it to me, and I said, "It feels like it's part of my hand." Its power, now it works, is like that too. Why? I don't know. It's as if Ustareth made it for me. In a way she did—After all, her second son and I were made for each other. By something. By God? If it isn't too cheeky to say it.

Anyway, as I landed on the outer sill, I knew even Argul's charm with the sapphire could open windows. And besides, the ceiling of Hall Four had opened for my ring. So this fire-ruby window would open too.

And it did.

The chamber inside was all smoky twilight colors; it was the lamps and fire that made it glow red.

She hadn't been asleep. She was sitting in a tall chair, and when I jumped down into the room, she got to her feet. She looked—terrified.

Then she controlled that and was all smiles, all Twilight-Star-smiles.

"Good morning, Claidi—I'm so glad to see you."

My landing had knocked snow off the sill onto her carpet. She glanced at that and gave a little wry frown, sort of, Oh, dear, such a welcome guest, mustn't mention her clumsiness.

"I've come to tell you something," I said.

"My dear, of course. Please do sit."

"It won't take long. By the way, don't bother calling your guards—I imagine your turquoise can do that; it's quite strong, isn't it?"

Her face, empty now. "Yes," she said.

"But you know, I think I'm stronger."

I looked in her eyes. Even now, it wasn't that easy.

"Ustareth's diamond," she said. "Yes, her ring is very powerful. How lucky that he knew, and that now it works for you. What are you going to do, kill me?"

That shocked me. That she'd think it, say it. But they *would* think like that, Tower people.

"No, thanks. This is just a warning."

"I see."

"Do you? I hope you do." I could hear myself. I've heard myself sound like that before, now and then. I hope it's not me, merely an act I can put on. I said, impatient with myself, "If it was so dodgy, me being near the raven in Hall Four, you shouldn't have gotten us to marry there."

She looked affronted. She said, "Marriages always take place in Hall Four. It would be unthinkable anywhere else. A tradition of the Tower."

"A tradition?" I said. "You mean a *rule?*" She didn't like my saying that. "Look, Twilight Star," I went on, "I don't belong to you, nor does Argul. We won't ever do what you want or be what you'd like—or follow any of your *rules.* But if you leave us alone from now on, we'll give no grief to you."

"What a Hulta phrase!" she cried, *so* amused.

"They say something like it in Peshamba, too. And Ustareth was responsible for Peshamba, wasn't she? So it's also an *Ustareth* phrase."

"Very well. You've put me in my place."

"Stay there then. Stay in your *place*."

"As *you* did, Claidi?"

She'd caught me off guard after all. I blinked at her, and in that moment—

I saw a white spinning shoot away from her. It came off the turquoise hanging at her throat. Right for me. And the air blazed up as if it caught on fire.

And then all the fragments of burnt air fell down like black petals. I watched them. I hadn't felt a thing but silly surprise. The ring—had protected me, saved my life, I truly believe. If I hadn't had the ring, I too might have fallen everywhere, in fine black petals.

"You should be careful with that," I said, "it could go off and hurt someone."

But I was shaking.

I could see that she was, too. Her honey-dark skin was sickly. Her eyes drooped.

"I was unwise," she said. "But at least, now I see what I'd be up against. Excuse me, Claidi. I won't try again."

"No, don't ever try again. That's all I came to say. Keep away from me and mine."

Then she did the final most disgusting thing of all, worse than merely trying to scorch me to cinders. She dropped on her knees in front of me, the way some people do before their God or gods.

"Oh—you *are* She," she said. "You—it's *you*—only second generation—*You* are the Wolf Queen, the daughter of power who is *power.* You. And we didn't even *make* you. You're a common *slave*—"

"Yup," I said, "that's me. A common slave. So long." I rose up lazily and rested in the air. Her wet carpet now had a large burn in it. Serves her right, the cow.

The window, which had shut, opened again to let me out.

I sailed around the side of it. The air was icy, and I needed that to steady me, so the ring let me stay cold.

But as I floated past the raven's white head, I reached the beak. Up there was Winter Raven.

She looked over at me.

"Hey, Claidi. Been giving mother some more trouble?"

"A social call," I said.

I could see she had been playing on the beak, to which she had flown, stamping patterns of footprints in the softer snow.

"Don't rush off," she said, "without saying goodbye."

She wore her feather cloak. She looked forlorn, like a beautiful old child that can't remember properly how to be childish.

I found myself sitting on the raven's beak. She sat beside me. We dangled our legs over the vast gulf beneath, knowing that neither of us need ever fear to fall.

Does she realize her mother is a monster, who a short while ago, tried to kill me? Probably. Does she then think I've killed Twilight? To Winter, all that would be normal? Normal, after all, is only what you're used to.

"She's all right," I said.

"Mother? Oh, yes." Silence. "You're soft," she said. Then, "I'll look after your graff. He's nice. They always are. I might mate him to *my* graff." I must have pulled a face. She said, "He won't *mind,* Claidi."

"No, I suppose not."

"And—Argul's horse—I'll take care of that, too."

From the corner of my eye—she's blushing? *Winter?*

"Winter, look—Ustareth used this ring to cross the sea. Would your necklace be strong enough to let you do that?"

She stared at me.

I said, "You know how to find Venn. You sent him a letter there. So, couldn't you just go and *meet* him? He *is* gorgeous," I added temptingly, and generously. "Why don't you talk to Heepo—Hedee Poran, at the Guest House. He knew Venn when Venn was a child. He could fill you in a bit on the situation. I don't see that she—your mother—will stop you. She *wants* you to team up with Venn. Only, I think you have to do it *your* way, not hers."

Winter said nothing, only looked away suddenly. We both did.

We stared down and down into the gulf that had no fear for either of us. No, it was just life—our futures—that were scary.

"Claidi," she said, "I said I was sorry about the way I went on. And that letter, full of lies. Well, there's something else."

My heart sank and my stomach rose, They collided with a bang somewhere around my waist. "Really?" I idly asked.

"She—mother—wanted me to Tag your diary-book. So if you went off any time, they could keep track of you."

"Right."

"The Wolf Tower did it, didn't they, put a Tag in your diary. That yukko Nemian, or someone."

"Yes."

"Look, let's get this straight. I'm not afraid of my mother. She wouldn't hurt *me.* But—I've gotten used to obeying her, and it takes a lot to say No."

"Right."

"I don't think, now that your ring works for you, Tagging the diary would matter anyhow—the ring would just conceal you—perhaps let you know to look for the Tag. But Claidi. I would like you to know. I *didn't* do it anyway."

"No?"

"No."

"Was that only because you couldn't get *near* my book?"

She smirked. "I *knew* you'd say that. No, Claidi, I got near it."

I thought how I'd kept both books close, even before I'd really become supercareful. Slept on the bag they were in, finally tied them to me.

"How?"

"Not saying. I have to keep a few secrets. You know about everything else about me. But get the ring to check the diaries. You'll find I didn't Tag either book. *But* I left you proof I'd gotten at them. I wanted you to know I behaved with—honor."

I stood up. "What's the proof then?"

She told me.

I said, "If that's true, then that means you read my diary."

She, too, rose. She confronted me. "No, it does not. My amber necklace can do stuff too. It *scanned* your diary, looking for a suitable name, and then—well, what I said. *I* haven't read a word. I swear, by the Raven in Hall Four."

"*That* isn't a god."

"By Venn then," she said flamboyantly. "By gorgeous Prince Venarion Yllar Kaslem-Idoros, whom I'm going to meet across the sea."

Will you? I thought. *Will* you go? Just—*do it.*

We shook hands, slipped, fell off the beak, and floundered apart, skywalking and laughing.

As I turned to go, she was performing somersaults in the air, in the first blue of that clear morning. And I'd ripped my skirt again.

The ring guided me back to the cave. I didn't have to think about that, so I thought about what Winter had said.

Argul was waiting, sitting against the cave-wall, with a new fire that wasn't visible from outside. I told him what had happened. His face—anger, then laughter. I'll never get used to him. Never want to. Even when we have been years together, I know I will often look at him and start with startled delight.

He said some Raven Guards had gone by, still searching for us, but not very thoroughly. Hadn't even bothered to come near the cave.

I took the diaries out then, from the sewn-in piece under the marriage dress. I opened the first book with care, as if it was too hot. Sat staring.

"It's true, what she said?" he asked. "She got hold of them?"

"It's true."

My horse with the Hulta, this was what Winter had found, or the necklace had. My horse called Sirree. Later, after I was kidnapped, I mentioned Sirree now and then. Someone—Winter—has changed the spelling of Sirree's name to Si*r*ee—one R. Very skillfully, so it really looks as if that is the way I have spelled it. Only I wouldn't have.

Did she really do all that and not read it—even the parts about Venn? About Venn and me?

I'll never know.

I'm rather jealous anyway. How unreasonable. Can't help it. But I've thought, Venn only really got interested in me for the most obvious reason. I was the first and only woman he'd seen apart from his mother, and Treacle—who was such a wild thing anyway. So, he sort of fell for me. And I felt keen on him—because he was so like Argul.

But when Venn sees *her*—Winter—*if* she goes there—well. She's stunning. He won't stand a chance. Oh, Venn.

I hope Winter isn't going to turn out like Twilight. Maybe if Winter can only get a life of her own—she won't.

Argul said, "Your hands are like ice."

And right then, as he was warming my hands, this little white thing blew in over the ledge of the cave.

"What's *that?*"

We bent toward it. A small snow-object—no, it was a weeny little *snake.* It gazed up with gentle eyes. And shook its silvery hair.

"Yinyay . . . How—"

"I was called," said Yinyay, her voice rather larger than her size, "by the ring."

"But Venn got you to wipe out all knowledge of Ustareth—"

"The ring," she said, "is still the ring."

"But you're so—little—all this way—from the forest where the Star came down—"

"That presented no difficulty," she said, "once I had learned enough." And then she grew bigger, in a lovely rippling surge, and stood there on her tail, gazing at us kindly, exactly as I remembered.

"So—the Star-ship's repaired?"

"The ship no longer works," said Yinyay. "But that is unimportant. Since the ring has now connected to me, I am not as I was."

"How *are* you?"

"Now," said Yinyay, "I am the ship."

And she showed us.

Argul and I stood there. For the first time ever, I saw his mouth drop open, as mine is always doing.

For Yinyay, gliding from the cave, balanced there in the blue void between the mountains, began again to grow. And—G—R—O—W—

Up and up went Yinyay. As this happened, her snakelike body straightened out. The white crags reflected on her own polished whiteness. She was tall, and wide. The height of several mansions piled one on another (as they say). Broad as any palace. Straight as a pale sword, but with her excellent metallic face and flowing tinsel hair still there, at the very top.

"That," said Argul, "is a Tower."

It was true. She was. A *Tower*—in the air.

Her mild voice came to us, only humanly loud, but carrying, and melodious as a song.

"I am quite ready now, to receive you, and take you where you wish. Or I can become small again. As small as you find useful. Small enough to fit in a pocket."

For now, we've kept Yinyay as a Tower. She's magnificent. She has magnets, naturally, to deal with gravity. She has seven stories, lifts, windows that clear or close over, machines that make food and drink. Bathrooms. Furniture. A library—! Plants . . . All sorts of things. Everything. As she flew us away, whirling in a protective globe of force, visible—but entirely beyond any attack—we explored our new domain.

Below, the glaciers of the Northern mountains melted away.

* * *

I suppose we really are safe now. As safe as you can be, if you're alive in this world.

We've talked about what we may do. Of course there are the Hulta to consider, though Argul has said to me, "I can't really go back, Claidi. It's Hulta law. Once a leader lets go the leadership, that's it." *"Law!"* I shouted. But he only shook his head. I don't know how this will work out, then.

He did it for me, left them. And Blurn would be a great leader, no matter what Blurn said; otherwise, as Argul told me, the choice would have been impossible.

But he gave up his title, his people, his power—for me.

As Yinyay flies now, this circling Tower, the night has come. We're on the third floor. Soft lamplight and armchairs. Argul is sitting reading a book from Yinyay's library. It's in a language I certainly don't know, all marks like arrows, and squares—

Argul seems at home. None of this, after the first seconds, has thrown him. But he's seen more of the world than I. And well, he's Argul.

I've been writing this up.

What do you think?

Is it going to be all right?

There is a chance the Hulta might, somehow, join us, or we join them, or . . .

But this—is a Tower.

I looked up then and said that to him, to Argul.

He said, "Ustareth" (he never now calls her Zeera) "made this setup. Your Yinyay blossoming into *this,* when the ring started to work again. Ustareth still *thought* in Towers."

"Then this *is* a Tower."

"The other Towers have animal emblems," he said, "Wolves, Ravens—but the top of this Tower has a human face."

A human face. A Human Tower?

We'll marry in Peshamba. Under the CLOCK. They do weddings there. Neither of us will have a single friend to celebrate with us, not a single family member. His mother and father are dead. Mine are—unknown forever.

Perhaps, though, there is now some way I could rescue some of the girls I knew from the House—Daisy and Pattoo—Dengwi—and Blurn *might* just come to the wedding. And Dagger. I might even get to see Sirree, with two R's, again.

I'll stop writing now. There are so many blank pages left at the end of this book. It worries me a little. Will I still write to you, my friend I'll never meet, in the future? Or will I ever know you, or your name—your names?

Maybe not. But you know *me,* better than most.

What do you say—was Twilight right? Am I this dire thing, the "Wolf Queen?" No, you know I'm not. It's what Argul said: Claidi—a Sheep in Wolf's Clothing.

That's me.

Tanith Lee is an award-winning fantasy writer here and in the United Kingdom. She did not learn to read until she was almost eight years old—and at nine, she began writing. Since then, she has written thirteen children's books, forty-two adult novels, almost two hundred stories, four radio plays, and more. She has won the World Fantasy Award twice and the August Derleth Award, and has been nominated for the Nebula. She lives on the southeast coast of England with her husband John Kaiine.

Visit her Web site at **www.tanithlee.com**